THE REGRET

DAN MALAKIN

Print ISBN 978-1-912986-67-5

For Delia

SPEAR PHISHING

W ant to know how to break into someone's life?

Send them an e-mail supposedly from their bank, or Amazon, or eBay. Same logo, same corporate talk, some lines of scaremongering spiel. *We have detected a problem with your account.* If they're dumb enough to click on the link, they'll go to a web page hosted on your server, where an authentic-looking form will capture their login details.

That kind of phishing attack, it's like a net. Throw it far and wide, and hope you reel in someone stupid. But if you want to target one person — let's call her Rachel — and if she's savvy enough to swim around the net, then the attack can be fired.

It's called Spear Phishing.

This is how it's done.

Get to know everything about Rachel's life. The shifts she works as a nurse at St Pancras Hospital. The relationship she has with her three-year-old daughter. Use that to plan for when Rachel will be so busy she'll miss a cleverly worded, smartly disguised e-mail that'll convince her to download a piece of spyware to her phone to capture her passwords. Facebook, Instagram, Snapchat: these are the digital doors and windows to our private lives, and people are sloppy with the locks. Despite who may be lurking outside.

This e-mail can't be some syntactically tortured spam, like a plea for airfare from a disgraced Congolese prince – soon as he lands, he'll pay you back from the millions locked in his offshore account, promise. The mail needs to be important, requiring immediate attention.

It's about getting her to click on the link.

Easiest way to make an e-mail look authentic? Add more mails to the bottom, so the one they receive looks like part of a chain. People scroll down, glance at the history, and believe it's real.

It will be the same for Rachel as for the others.

Think of it as a kind of seduction.

PART ONE

CHAPTER ONE

Rachel

No matter how organised she tried to be, preparing her uniform the night before, laying out Lily's clothes, something always made them late. Her nurse's fob watch vanished or her daughter refused to brush her teeth. The half hour to get dressed, scrubbed, and out the door, inevitably disappeared.

That morning, they were falling at the final hurdle – shoes. Lily wanted to put them on herself. That was fine until she got to the buckle, where she had to slip a slender leather tongue through a delicate frame, and impale the tiny hole in it with a flimsy prong. No chance. The sun would grow to engulf them all in a fiery inferno before that ever happened.

'Please, honey,' Rachel said, kneeling in front of her. 'Let Mummy.'

Lily twisted her body away, cheeks bunched in concentration, and lifted her heel to her eye to get a better look at what she was doing wrong.

Rachel looked out of the window at the grey skies and sighed. Another grimy morning, the rooftops of the Victorian terraces stretching down the street slicked with autumn rain; the summer had disappeared way too soon. London always looked so concrete under grey skies. Sometimes the gloom seemed to seep into her soul, especially the way she was feeling today. It didn't help that Konrad had got in late last night, crashing around downstairs, waking her up. It took her ages to get back to sleep. She didn't mind him coming back to hers after a night out, it made more sense than him trekking to his parents' in High Barnet, but the least he could do was be quiet when he got home.

Then again, he'd been acting strange all week – ever since he'd turned up with those bruises covering his cheek. At the time he said that Pete, his best mate and partner in their office relocating business, had accidentally caught his face closing the van door, but that didn't explain how he'd been since then. Ignoring her calls during the day, and moody when she did see him. Drinking a lot too, like the other night when he finished a four-pack of beer in front of the telly without even saying a word to her. It was so different from his usual easy-going nature.

'Sweetheart,' Rachel said, trying to grapple the shoe from Lily's hands. 'We're going to be *late*.'

She pulled away. 'No, Mummy! I do it.'

'If you don't give me that right now, then I'll tell Daddy no cartoons after school.'

Who knew bribery would be such a big part of parenting? It was a wonder that all children didn't grow up to be corrupt politicians.

Rachel felt her phone vibrate in her pocket. She rocked back, got it out and saw she had an e-mail. Probably just some mailing list, but it could be her dad about picking Lily up later; she was staying at his that night. When his phone ran out of credit, he sent her e-mails from the computer in the public library.

It was from work, the payroll department. The subject said: *Bank check urgent.* She opened the message.

Hi Rachel, there was an issue with the payroll software overnight, and some people's bank details may be out of date. Please can you check the attached file to confirm yours are correct, and let me know.

It's kind of urgent. Sorry!

Thanks, Ian

She didn't have time for this, but if there was a problem, she needed to know. They lived month to month on her wages, so by now, on payday, her current account was down to single digits. She scrolled through the mail and saw it was the last of a chain, with lots of important people copied in on the previous ones, even the chairman of Camden and Islington NHS Trust.

The attachment was called *Rachel Stone details.pdf.* She tapped on it and waited for the file to download. Nothing happened. She pressed it again and again, but still nothing. Stupid phone. It was a white Samsung S4 Mini with a cracked screen and a broken headphone port, donated by Mark, Lily's dad, after Rachel's had fallen in the bath while lifting her daughter out. Another of its "features" was its tendency to turn off at the *most* annoying moments, such as right now.

Rachel scowled at the blank screen. Great, typical. She'd have to call HR from the hospital. *Sorry, Doris, can you hang on for your analgesic. I'm just on hold listening to the same piece of smooth jazz for the thousandth time!*

Konrad's voice startled her. 'Morning, beautiful.'

He was leaning against the doorway, still in his going out clothes, his cream Diesel T-shirt crumpled beneath his charcoal overcoat. Cute with his bed hair, Rachel almost forgave him for having woken her up. And if that had been the only thing, she probably would have done, but this wasn't an isolated incident. How he was acting couldn't go on.

'Are you annoyed with me?' he asked.

'Whatever gave you that idea?'

He tried for a smile. 'Your face?'

'You don't remember coming in and crashing round downstairs? I don't know what's going on with you, but–'

'I'm sorry, Rach,' he said, dropping into a crouch beside her. 'I'm *really* sorry.'

She recoiled from the smell of alcohol clinging to his skin. 'I bet the sofa stinks of booze now as well.'

'I've been a bit stressed, that's all. With work and stuff. Last night I had to blow off some steam. But I promise, I swear, if I get that hammered again, I'll head back to Barnet. I won't come here and wake you up.'

She wanted to believe him, but the way his eyes darted one way then the other when he spoke, like he was checking no-one was behind him, made her think he was lying. Was it something to do with her? She'd been stressing about it all week, but couldn't think what she'd done wrong. The last eleven months with him had been like something from a romance, the way their lives had clicked, albeit a slightly boring one where the two leads went to work every day then snuggled on the sofa in the evening to watch *Love Island*. Amazingly, the feelings were just as they'd been described – the jump in her chest when he came to her mind, how she couldn't wait to see him in the evening so they could share funny stories about their day, the sense that she'd maybe found *the one,* long after giving up the idea that such a thing was any more real than the tooth fairy. She didn't want to lose that.

Rachel squeezed her forehead, the start of a migraine pulsing in her temples, and glanced at Lily. Still struggling with her buckle. As she would be until the end of days.

'*Fine,*' Rachel said. 'Let's leave it. Just don't be late tonight, okay?'

'Six thirty, on the dot.'

As they embraced, she felt the tension seep from her stomach. They pulled apart and she saw him wince in pain, his hand going to his forearm.

'What's wrong?'

'I banged it yesterday at work, that's all.'

'Let me see.'

He pulled his arm to his chest, eyes wide, looking – what? Scared?

'I've really got to go,' he said.

Rachel looked at the faded yellow bruises on his cheek, creeping out the top of his stubble. 'I want to see your arm, Konrad.'

'Okay,' he said. 'But don't freak out.'

CHAPTER TWO

Burns

'What do mean, a *game?*'

They were in the bathroom, Konrad sitting on the edge of the tub while she hunted in the cupboard under the sink for the Dettol and cotton pads.

'Drinking game,' he replied. '*Way* too much vodka. Someone suggested we try to see who could stand the most pain... I know, I know, it's stupid. You don't have to tell me!'

She uncapped the antiseptic and tipped it on the pad, the medicinal smell calming her, making her feel more in control. When she first saw the wounds – three raw crimson circles, each the size of a ten pence piece, crusted round the edges, and spotted with black in the middle – she thought they were bullet holes. She even flipped his arm, expecting exit wounds, but the underside was clear. Then she realised – they were *cigar burns*. Someone had *stubbed cigars* out on his arm.

He winced as she dabbed at the pus collecting in the crevices of the scabs. The shiny pink skin edging the worst of the wounds was concerning; he'd need to monitor that, maybe get antibiotics if it got any worse. She knew how quickly sepsis could spread, even when you were as young and healthy as him.

'So who were you out with?' she asked. 'When you decided to use each other as ashtrays?'

He shrugged and looked to the side. 'You know, the lads.'

'Pete there?'

Another pause, a frown. 'It wasn't Pete's fault.'

'Oh, *right*. Now I get it.'

'Rach, come on.'

There was no love lost between her and Konrad's best mate. How could there be? There was never any love to begin with. The first time they met he looked her up and down, and sneered, 'So you're the bird who stole my wingman.'

From that day he'd treated her with disdain. She was an irritation, a distraction, the Yoko to his Beatles, if the Beatles spent their time sleazing up to girls at clubs instead of writing albums. In fact, never had that description *sleaze* been more appropriate for someone than for Pete, with his sad man bun and tribal tattoos and his misplaced delusion that every woman gushed like a raincloud in his presence. He even called her toots. *Toots!* To her face. That was what she and Lily called farts.

'If this is what happens when you hang out with Pete,' Rachel said, 'then maybe you shouldn't.'

'I told you, it wasn't—'

'I'm telling *you*.' She felt tears rising up and held them back. No way did she have time to do her make-up again. 'You can't bring... trouble into my house. Not with Lily here. I don't want to lose you—'

'You won't, you won't! It'll never happen again, I promise.' He took her hands. 'Please, Rachel. You and Lily mean the world to me. All I want is for the three of us to be together.'

She fixed on his pale green eyes. Before the last week, he'd never been anything less than a perfect boyfriend. So as much as she still didn't think he was telling her the *whole* truth, if that was what he said happened, and if the previous night was the last time he did anything like that, didn't he deserve the benefit of the doubt?

'This is it, Konrad,' she said. 'No more.'

They went to kiss, but before their lips could touch, Lily shrieked. Rachel ran to the bedroom to find her pouting at the shoe, defeated. She knelt and fitted it on Lily's foot, catching the time on the lock screen of her restarted phone. Seven thirty-eight. If they hurried, they'd make it to nursery on time. Scooping up her daughter, she sent a smile of gratitude to the heavens.

Perhaps today will be a good day after all, she thought, unaware that nothing would be further from the truth.

CHAPTER THREE

E-mail

Rachel worked at St Pancras Hospital, on the Oakwood ward, caring for eighteen beds of pleasant patients, many of whom remembered a time before the NHS, and appreciated how much effort the nurses put in to looking after them. Senior health care hadn't been her first choice; part of her reason for becoming a nurse was to give something back, after the time she'd spent in hospital as a teenager.

When she first qualified, she took a job at The Northside Centre in Wood Green, a place devoted to adolescent mental health. But the hours, the stress – the kids there were needy, damaged, tormented – along with looking after Lily, as well as her gran when she got sick, was too much. So Rachel took the position at St Pancras.

Life on the geriatric ward, however, was no easy ride. That morning was worse than most as they had two new admissions, including a sweet old gent whose entire left side had frozen after a stroke. It was half eleven before she even had time to catch her breath. She needed to call HR to confirm her bank details before they went to lunch.

She hurried into the break room. First things first – more coffee! The kettle was still hot, so she grabbed an *I Heart NHS* mug from the drying rack, heaped it with instant, filled it half with boiling water and topped it up with cold from the tap. She paused, the cup to her lips, her stomach spasming with hunger. Last night she'd managed one mouthful of pasta, giving up after the food sat in her stomach as solid and full of mass as stone, and she didn't even attempt breakfast this morning. Better have something now, as she might not get another break until the end of the day. She hunted in the cupboard under the sink for her sachets of vanilla Ensure, a sickly sweet high-calorie powder she could always somehow force down, no matter how stressed, and poured one into her coffee. *Calories are calories. Don't make it a big deal.*

First, check her bank details in the e-mail. Maybe there was nothing to even worry about. She finished half her drink, got her phone and opened Gmail, but found she was logged out. Why did this always happen when she was in a hurry?

'Give me strength,' she muttered, typing in her password. God knows when she'd be able to afford a decent new handset, so until then she had to try to be grateful for this piece of junk.

Her inbox opened, and she scrolled up and down, looking for the e-mail, but couldn't find it. It had come this morning, before she left, she was sure of it, but it wasn't there. She must have deleted it by accident. She checked the Bin folder. Empty.

She froze, staring at the screen, feeling like there'd been a silent earthquake. Like the world had suddenly tipped.

E-mails didn't just disappear.

It couldn't be–

The break door beeped and Spence danced in, dressed in his pale-blue tunic, a faint bassline seeping out the red Beats covering his ears. When he saw Rachel, he did a double take and pulled off his headphones.

'That's it,' he said. 'I'm buying the boat.'

That was their running joke, concocted over too many rum

punches at last year's Christmas party. If life got too much, they'd buy a boat and cruise the world, despite neither of them having the nautical knowledge to navigate their way out of a bathtub.

Rachel swilled the rest of her coffee, getting a mouthful of vanilla sludge. 'I look that bad?'

'Caribbean, Cuba, then a few days in Miami to finish off.'

'I'm already finished off,' she said, offering a wan smile.

Spence shoved his headphones in his Adidas satchel bag. 'Konrad?'

'It's fine. He... Nothing. He got in a bit late. Woke me up.'

'And I'm the queen of King's Cross.'

Rachel clicked on the kettle. 'Drink, your majesty?'

'You want to cancel the *soirée* tonight?' He hung his satchel on a hook by the door.

'My dad's babysitting. I'm having a late one.'

'Bed for nine?'

'Ha flippin' ha.'

Although Spence had only been on the ward a year, replacing Rowena after she went to live in Australia, it felt like they were old friends. They just got each other. Rachel didn't make friends easily with men; even with Mark, who she trusted as much as anyone, she used to worry that he secretly wanted more, and would turn on her if he didn't get it. With Spence, that would never be an issue. Short and finely muscled, his bleached hair waxed into textured spikes — in gay terms, a classic *twink* — it didn't matter he was far from her type. He wasn't going to flirt with her when they were drunk, or come onto her in the taxi home. Without the twitchy frisson of sexual tension, what they had felt genuine.

'You get the e-mail?' Rachel asked, as Spence dropped a peppermint tea bag in his mug.

He nodded for the kettle. 'What e-mail?'

'From payroll.'

'What did it say?'

'I had to check my bank details, but the attachment wouldn't download. Now I can't find the mail...'

Spence sipped his tea, burning his top lip and rubbing it with his tongue. 'I'm sure it's nothing important.'

'What if there's a problem with my wages?'

'It'll be fine.'

'But what if–'

'Let's get down from the ledge, eh?' He steadied her agitated hands. 'Besides, I didn't get the e-mail. So it's just you who's screwed.'

'Thanks. You're a good friend.'

She couldn't help but return his smile. His perpetual optimism, the way he could stop her negative spirals before they dragged her down, was what she loved most about his company. Not just her, but everyone. If she was the better nurse, at least technically, he was the more popular among the patients, able to charm a *good morning* out of even the grumpy ones, and beneficiary of by far the most thank you cards on the ward.

'Give them a call,' he said. 'I'm sure it's nothing.'

She found the number on the Trust's website, and called. 'It's the helpdesk line,' she moaned. 'On payday. I'm going to be here until next week.' She glanced at the wall clock. It was already quarter to twelve. 'I'd better get back. I've been off the ward fifteen minutes. It'll be mayhem out there. Grannies gone wild.'

'Carry on up the Catheter,' Spence said, grinning. 'Stay on. I'll start early.'

'But your tea.'

'Too hot. I'll come back for it when you're done.'

'I'll make it up to you!' she called, as the door closed behind him.

She gave it another ten minutes, then hung up and headed back to the ward. But no matter how many times she told herself to stop stressing, that if there was a real problem with her bank details, then HR would get in touch again, and at the worst she could borrow from Mark until her wages came through, she couldn't relax.

E-mails didn't just disappear.

The last time that kind of thing happened, it was during the worst eighteen months of her life. She thought back to that time, nearly ten years ago, and the same fear shook her spine.

Something was going on. She could feel it.

CHAPTER FOUR

Snap

After work, Rachel hurried to get the bus. The 91 was waiting at the stop with three people left to board. She sprinted to it, swinging inside a moment after the last person got on, slamming her debit card on the reader and saying a breathless thanks to the driver. He dragged the wheel right without looking at her. *Ah, London. City of a thousand scowls.*

She stayed downstairs, dumping herself on the raised section at the back, and got out an Innocent berry protein smoothie. A couple of exploratory sips went down okay, so she took half the bottle in one. She couldn't let her hunger get to that again, where it felt like her stomach was wringing itself out, although it had helped to distract her mind from all the stress the day had heaped on her. At least she'd been paid − she'd checked her account online − so she could stop fretting about that. The HR department had probably recalled the e-mail, which explained why it had disappeared.

So that only left Konrad to worry about. Despite telling herself to forget it, that she'd accepted his explanation, she still didn't buy it. Sure, some of the blokes he hung out with, Pete in particular, were a monobrow away from being Neanderthal, but she couldn't see them sitting round stubbing cigars out on each other.

What was really going on? Not just last night, but how he'd been acting all week. Did he want her to break up with him? Was he one of those men too chicken to dump you, so behaved in such a way that you did the dirty work for them? Twenty-six years of scrabbling through life, searching for nuggets of happiness, and she was finally settled in a relationship, her head together, or as much as it ever could be, and it felt like it was slipping away! It was so disappointing. Not just for her, but Lily as well. Her daughter had become attached to him, and he was great with her too, happy to play tea parties, or read the same *Elmer the Elephant* book on repeat, or to crawl with her on his back, whooping and kicking her heels into his side. What other thirty-year-old bloke would not only accept her daughter, but welcome her into his life? Plus, he was hot. Protein-shake muscles and sighing green eyes and cheekbones you could rest your teacup on. No matter how many times he called her beautiful, she still sometimes wondered what he saw in her, a stressed skint single mother. She imagined her profile popping up on Tinder, her eyes stained black from never having enough sleep. *Swipe left! LEFT!*

Mark, Lily's father, was already convinced Konrad was trouble. *Dodgy as a .biz website,* were his exact words. At the time, she'd dismissed it – boys like Konrad, confident, handsome, good at sports, probably tormented geeks like Mark in school – but what if he was right after all?

She got out her phone and opened Instagram. Konrad didn't use social media much, but his mates did, and she wanted to see if she could spot him in any of their photos from last night.

She froze, goosebumps prickling over her neck.

That was weird. Just as with her Gmail account earlier that day, she was logged out. She went back to her home page and checked Facebook, then Snapchat. Same for both of them.

Stay calm. Don't panic.

She logged into each of them and scanned up and down her timelines, in her messages, her heart pounding in her throat.

Nothing.

She breathed out. See? All that had happened was her barely working phone had glitched and reset itself.

No more sinister than that.

Except, she couldn't shake that same unbalanced feeling as before. Like the world was being slowly pulled from under her feet.

Rachel got off the bus at the gym. She hurried through the reception and past the step machines looking onto the road, wondering not for the first time about those who had the confidence to use them in full view of passers-by. Showing your gurning exercise face to the world was never a good idea, in her opinion.

She rushed into the changing room, pleased that she'd put on her active vest and gym shorts under her uniform before leaving work, so all she had to do was slip off her nurse's dress. Even though she was as comfortable with her body as she ever had been, she hated getting changed in public, the way everyone flicked their eyes around, comparing, judging. It made her want to shrink into herself and disappear.

Her height, that had always been the problem – at five eleven, she could step over most railings, or comfortably wear men's trousers, or maybe both at the same time – and there wasn't anything you could do about that. No diets, no pills, no operation to lop off a couple of inches. For as long as she was alive, she was stuck with looming over people, stuck with feeling cumbersome and big-fingered when shaking hands. It was a world away from what she'd always wanted to be, what Becca and the other popular girls at school had been: pretty and petite.

In fact, where was Becca? She was supposed to be meeting her here after work. Rachel glanced at the wall clock and saw it was twenty to six. Why was her life always ten minutes behind? There was no time to wait for her, not if she was going to get to Mark's to pick up Lily for half past. Maybe it was for the best. Becca was a pain at the gym anyway, preferring to chat and ogle guys than exercise.

Rachel headed to the weights room, hoisted the ten-kilo bar from the second bottom rung of the stack and turned to find a space on the mats. When she saw who was there, she let out a groan.

Konrad's mate Pete, by the pull-up station, in a low-hanging Raiders vest, surrounded by his usual crew of hooting show-offs. Sure, they had fit bodies, but they were always so loud and obnoxious, and she was too tired and frazzled to deal with them.

They didn't usually come in until after six. *Why do they have to be here early tonight?*

Thankfully, they were crowded round Pete's phone and hadn't noticed her. Hoping they wouldn't recognise her from behind – her threshold for their "bantz" was low – she carried the barbell backwards to the mats. She turned her head to check if they'd seen her, just as Pete glanced up. Warily, she raised the end of the barbell to him, a gesture she hoped said, *Hi, but in the nicest way possible, leave me alone.*

Pete slapped his hand over his mouth. His eyes zigzagged and he drove his elbow into the ribs of the pumped-up stocky one who always pretended she wasn't there. When he saw her, his face dropped open.

What was the matter with them? She felt like she was standing there with one of her boobs hanging out. The rest spotted her. They gawped at each other, then collapsed in breathless laughter, clawing at one another's shoulders to stay upright.

Rachel's cheeks flushed, her mouth went dry. *Idiots.* She couldn't use the barbell now, squatting in front of them. She dragged it back to the stand, her arms shaking as she spilled it onto the hooks. *Bastards. Bastards, bastards. Just piss off!*

She went to use the lat pulldown machine. They carried on snickering behind her back. Did she have a wedgie or something?

Children. She set the weight to twenty kilos, two heavier than normal, and grabbed the bars.

'Don't worry 'bout no photo,' called Pete. 'I prefer the real thing.'

A sick feeling spread through her so fast it felt as though it were being pumped out by her heart.

Photo? What photo?

She shook her head. *Ignore them.*

She lowered the bar, lifting the weights, and clanged them down. *Stupid Becca, she should be here.* They'd never do this if there were two of them.

'Rach? Hey Rach?'

She dragged the bar again, holding it behind her head. *Please. Go away.*

'Check your Snap. Sent you a reply.'

More laughter. High fives like fireworks. Her phone vibrated on her arm – she kept it strapped there in the gym. She focused on the weights. Pull, hold, drop. Pull–

'*Fuckin' prick tease.*'

She let go of the bar. Metal slammed metal. She launched off the bench and crossed the rubber floor. 'What did you say?'

Pete widened his stance and lifted his chin.

She stopped, unsure. She wanted to back away, but he couldn't talk to her like that; she was Konrad's girlfriend. He needed to show her some respect.

'Check your Snap, *Rach.*'

Still staring at him – she wasn't going to give him the satisfaction of looking away – she removed her phone from the Velcro pouch on her bicep. She saw the notification for a new Snapchat message, and tapped on it. At first she couldn't understand what she was seeing. The base of a weird brown tree, surrounded by thick black grass. But the angle was strange, the lighting fractured, and it was blurry. Then she got it; blood rushed to her face; she gasped and fumbled her phone, dropping it to the floor.

It was his *dick*.

Pete grabbed his crotch and shook it. 'See it for real any time.'

The sounds of the gym – clanking weights, spinning wheels, grunts and coughs and pounding feet – became muffled as though she'd been pulled underwater. She felt herself flushing, tears building in the back of her throat, and had the horrible feeling that she might actually start crying in front of those *utter shitheads*.

Her phone had spun under the shoulder press. She half crawled, half stumbled towards it. She got on her knees and reached under the machine, cheek pressed to the cold metal frame, her fingers finding the corner of the case, but pushing it further away. Meanwhile they laughed and wolf whistled, and called out, 'While you're down there, love!'

Why would he send her that? *Why?*

CHAPTER FIVE

Photo

Rachel pushed into the changing room, shouldered her way to her locker, knowing it was rude, but she had to get out of there. What kind of person *does* that? She cringed at the memory of herself scrabbling under the machine to get her phone, prickling again as she recalled them laughing at her. Was it something to do with last night, with what happened to Konrad? Should she be happy Pete didn't lunge at her with a lit cigar?

Outside, the evening air was fresh and sharp, and cleared her head. She started for the top of the road, phone to her ear, calling Konrad. It went to voicemail. He'd be on the tube, heading to hers. She wanted to leave a calm message, explaining what had happened, how upset it had made her, but it quickly became a garbled, sweary rant about how that *prick* obviously hated her, had always hated her, and how could he stay friends with someone like that? And yes, as much as her heart ached even thinking about them breaking up – it was either that *sleaze*, or her.

Check your Snap. Sent you a reply.

What did Pete mean by that?

She opened Snapchat. A message had been sent from her account, less than ten minutes ago. Not only to Pete, but to Becca,

and Spence too. It contained no words, no message. Just one thing –
a photo.

The photo.

The one from ten years ago.

The one that had brought *him* into her life.

She turned the phone around in her hand, as though it were a
puzzle box she'd just been handed. What the fuck? What the *actual*
fuck? She went back to the app, checked what time the chat was
sent. Ten minutes ago.

When she was inside the gym!

How was that...? But before she could even complete the
thought, she knew how. And who. It had his fingerprints all over it.
He used to love messing with her head, making the people around
her think she was losing her mind.

He was back.

Alan Griffin was back.

She'd managed to convince herself that when he got out of prison
he'd be too busy trying to rebuild his own life to come after her
again, but maybe she'd been wrong. Maybe he'd risk going back
inside, for revenge.

Stop. Take a moment to think. If it was really Alan Griffin, how did
he get her password? Was he somehow watching her when she
logged in on the bus? How was that possible? And even if it was
possible, it meant he'd have her Facebook and Instagram passwords
too. *So why not do more?* Why not take over her accounts, lock her
out of them, and pretend to be her. Just like he used to do.

She scrolled up and down her timelines again, looking for
anything suspicious. She wasn't a huge poster on social media, more
a watcher, a liker, someone to weigh in with an encouraging remark
only if ten other people had replied first. After what he did to her
last time, she preferred to keep a low profile.

Nothing.

She forced herself to take a deep breath. Think rationally. Wasn't it more *likely* that Pete had found that photo of her on the Internet – she knew there were plenty of copies of it floating around, many with her name in the title – and done what? Sent it to himself from her Snapchat account, just so he could reply with his stupid self-portrait and get a laugh from all his mates?

Was that such a ridiculous idea? As well as being in business with Konrad, didn't Pete also run a stall in Old Street station that unlocked mobile phones? So without doubt, he'd be able to hack into her account, or find someone who could. And he was at the gym early, when he knew she'd be there...

What if it wasn't a joke? What if it was part of a plan to break her and Konrad up? To convince her boyfriend that she'd been coming onto his mates so–

Her phone came to life in her hand. Becca calling on video, through WhatsApp.

Oh *shit*. She'd been sent the photo as well. Rachel rubbed her eyes, knowing exactly what Becca would be thinking.

She accepted the call and went on the defensive. 'Listen, I didn't send...' but her words were drowned out by the sound of chatter and clinking cocktail glasses. Judging from the slightly pixelated screen, Becca was at some swanky city bar, the kind of place with loud men in pinstripe suits and cocaine residue on the toilet paper dispensers, and fifty different types of gin that no-one ever ordered. Where was she getting the money to go to these kinds of places, now she wasn't working? Becca was leaning into the screen, looking dressed for a night out, her sparkly eyes screwed up as if she couldn't believe what she was seeing, ranting something that couldn't be heard over the din.

Rachel shook her head and pressed her finger in her ear, feeling like an escaped mental patient as she half mouthed, half shouted, 'I can't hear you!', with a whole bus stop of people twenty metres away pretending not to look at her. The wind picked up and she shivered, wishing she'd changed into her clothes.

The noise of the bar went quiet as Becca pushed into a corridor. '... mean seriously, Rach. What's with all the *drama?*'

Great, she was drunk as well. This wasn't going to be easy. They'd known each other for twenty-two years, had been friends from the first day at primary school, and that photo, the one sent to Becca, was one of the more toxic relics of their past.

'Please, listen to me,' Rachel said. 'I didn't–'

'You trying to make me feel bad because I didn't come to the gym?'

'I swear I didn't send you that.'

'It came from your Snap account!'

'I've been hacked.'

'It's been ten years, Rach. Can't you let it go already?'

Rachel wanted to crush the phone in frustration. *See how easy it is for him to mess with your head, even now.* 'Listen to me. No – listen. I didn't send you that. I think... I think something bad is happening. I'm worried that...' She didn't even want to finish off the thought.

Becca would know what she was implying but, either from meanness or stubbornness, didn't take the bait and instead waved her away, the tips of her manicure catching the light. 'Whatever. Are we still doing yours tonight?'

It was supposed to be just a chilled evening, a nice way to start her birthday weekend. Becca and Spence coming round, some canapés, a few glasses of fizz, but already it was ruined. By the time she got home, Konrad would be there, and they'd have to get into what happened at the gym. He was going to have to make some tough decisions. If he couldn't, then she doubted she'd be doing much celebrating – and however annoying Becca was being, Rachel might still need a friend.

'Just come over,' Rachel said. 'Bring drink.'

CHAPTER SIX

Scam

This scam's particularly good.

Call someone. Say you're ringing from Microsoft. An urgent warning has appeared on your system about an IP address registered at their home.

An IP address, you tell them, is the computer's location on the network.

If they start to reply, *But wouldn't my IP address be dynamically assigned whenever I connect...?* Hang up. Don't wait for them to finish. They know too much to fall for it.

Most people don't know an IP address from an artichoke. If you tell them an IP address is what the cool kids call where they take a shit, they'll believe you. Nine times out of ten, they suck in air, mutter, *Oh no*, and ask what the warning's about.

'First,' you reply, 'I need to do a security check. Can I confirm this is Mr Willing Victim, of ten Foolhardy Lane?'

Of course it's him. You got his name and address from an online phone directory. But the fact you have his details gives you credibility. It gets you through his first defence.

Go on to explain the Poseidon virus has been detected on their computer. It mines your old web history and extracts your bank details. We need to act fast to catch it.

What happens if they go, *Whaaaa?*

Hang up.

If they go, *Hold on a minute, that sounds like a load of bu−*

Hang up.

Most times, they say, 'Tell me what I need to do.'

Explain they need to go to Microsoft's website and run a program to scan and clear the virus. Give the website www.microsoft.virus-scan.com.

If they say, *Hold on, that doesn't sound like it's part of Microsoft's website.*

That's right. Hang. Up.

Most times, they go to that page. It has the same pale blue and white colour scheme as Microsoft's website, the same icons and fonts. Always, it's about the detail.

There's some blurb about Poseidon. *Click here to run virus scan.*

Say: 'I hope we got it in time.'

They click, a progress bar appears, it seems to be working − then their screen freezes.

Put some hurry in your voice as you say, 'Let me contact the tech team. They will call you right back. Don't switch it off. It won't come back on.'

If they restarted their computer, it would be fine. Unfrozen and working as before.

Guess how many restart it?

Leave it twenty minutes. Time for them to search for details of Poseidon on their smartphone, a search that will lead to the fake websites you've created for the virus, including a link to Microsoft's supposed virus scan. Then call them up. Say Eddie in Customer Support passed their details your way, and you can help.

But first, you say, I need to take the advanced technical support charge. Eighty-nine ninety-nine please. We take cards.

They always object, but that's fine. The thrust and parry is half the fun.

If they say they're not paying, you say fine, you'll have to take it into a shop. You have your original copy of Windows, right?

If they say they'll call back to complain, give some made up name and extension for reference. But be warned, our lines are red-hot containing the spread of the virus. It could be days before you get through.

Say: 'Listen. I'm just a techie. You don't want to fix this, no problem.' Then start saying goodbye.

Not everyone pays, but it's not about the money. If it were about the money, it would be easy to hack into their bank account.

The second best part is the moment before they pay, when they apologise for getting annoyed with you.

Say, magnanimously: 'That's okay. You're not the worst I've had today.'

Laughs all round.

Ha ha ha.

Now give me the card details.

Tell them to wait one minute and put them on hold for ten. Say you've sent a fix through the network, so when their computer restarts, the virus will be eradicated. They switch it off and on and – surprise, surprise – their computer is fine.

We got it! You're all clear!

The best part?

When they thank you for being scammed.

CHAPTER SEVEN

Mark

R achel stopped outside Mark's apartment block, panting hard, having sprinted from the gym, as though she could somehow outrun her thoughts. But despite the burn in her lungs, the molten pain in her thighs, they'd continued to swarm: Konrad's injuries, Pete's dick pic, *the photo* reappearing after all these years, bringing with it the feelings of shame and terror that she long ago thought she'd left behind.

She typed Mark's apartment number into the silver keypad and tapped her foot while she waited for him to buzz her in. He lived in one of the glassy new high-rises beside Archway tube station, a young professional ghetto that emptied its entire population onto the train every morning. Sometimes, when she dropped Lily off, she looked at the women striding to work from the building, those sleek slick packages in pencil skirts and chiffon scarfs, compared them to her bedraggled self – dress skewed, hair barely trapped in the only saggy band she could find that morning – and felt such a pang of jealousy that she had to hurry away, her head down, as though she were a lower-class wench trespassing on a lord's grounds.

Living there was like being in a hotel, down to the daily cleaning service, which suited Mark as it meant fewer distractions from his passion: computers. He worked with them, he played with them, he slept with at least one laptop in his bed, she was sure. In every room lay machines in various stages of autopsy. Circuit boards, metal carcasses, and disembodied DVD drives with wires streaming out the back covered the surfaces. Although, after Rachel found a screw in Lily's mouth, he became fastidious about keeping chokeables safely stowed.

The door buzzed and she pushed into the airy reception, her trainers squeaking on the marble floor. Grab Lily and go, that was the plan. Get back home before Konrad so she could compose herself before he arrived. Her mind felt like a deck of cards after a particularly malicious round of fifty-two card pick up. How was she going to explain that photo being sent to Pete from her Snap account? How was she going to explain that photo at all? Tell him about Griffin? What if they broke up and he told other people? If the police found out what she did, then even after all this time, she could still go to prison.

What would happen to Lily then?

Rachel's muscles still fizzed with unspent adrenaline, so she darted for the stairs, taking them two at a time. At Mark's floor, she padded down the carpeted corridor, steadying her breath. Her body was in full-flight mode, which he would spot a mile away, and she couldn't face one of his tender but annoying probes about her mental state. He only meant well, and she'd be just the same with him if he seemed stressed, but there was a time and a place for therapy, and here and now was not them.

Mark pulled open the door before she could knock. 'Hey Rach!'

Rachel had her "in a hurry" spiel all ready to go, but when she saw him, she was momentarily too stunned to talk. Instead she looked him up and down and checked the apartment number.

'Very funny,' he said. 'Why don't you come in before you start mocking me?'

'That's okay. I can do it just fine from the corridor.'

When did he make *that* decision? The greasy unruly upside-down bird's nest that had been perched on his head for as long as she'd known him had been replaced by a stylish haircut – shaved around the sides, short on top, and casually ruffled at the front. It actually suited his slender cheeks. Stick him in Hackney with a vintage denim jacket, a pocket square, and some big-framed plastic glasses, and the hipster chicks would flock to him.

'They finally declare your scalp a biohazard site?' Rachel asked.

Mark patted his hair, as though to reassure himself of its continued existence. 'I thought you'd be pleased. You've been on at me for years to get it cut. Anyway...' He gave her the eyes. 'You run over then?'

She pushed past him into the hallway and shucked off her rucksack. Stupid. Should have got changed in the corridor.

'Don't start,' she said.

'Why didn't you get changed after the gym?'

'I didn't run here.'

'So why not get changed?'

Rachel motioned for him to step back. She wasn't obsessive about exercise, not how she used to be, although that didn't stop Mark from declaring the fact that she squeezed a visit to the gym into most days *symptomatic of unresolved issues.* Maybe he had a point, but you'd have to be a rock in the desert to reach your late twenties and not have a *few* things unresolved. And was it so bad if the issues lent a little bit to keeping her fit and healthy? She knew what was going on – there was no escaping her past. But also, there was no point living in it. She was far from that now, and had no intention of returning.

'I left in a hurry,' she said. 'I was going to be late.'

'You're five minutes early.' Mark tapped his bottom lip. 'That's good for you. *Suspiciously* good.'

'Stop giving me the fourth degree.'

'Fourth degree? I thought it was the third degree. What's with the other degree?'

'I'm not in the mood.'

'Lighten up, Rach. I'm messing with you. Same as you did with me two minutes ago.' She allowed him to half lead, half drag her down the hallway. 'But I know you're lying about running here.'

The reception room was stylishly decorated with recessed spotlights and soft cappuccino walls, which made the tech scattered around the place all the more incongruous. A stack of flattish rectangular machines, like electronic paving slabs, stood on the dining table, wired up and flashing in a hundred places at once.

Rachel nodded to it. 'Sending news to the mothership?'

'Routers. Network stuff.'

She made a sound that implied what he'd said made sense, then asked, 'How's Lil?'

Their daughter was stretched out on the L-shaped sofa, transfixed on Peppa Pig on the flat-screen television mounted on the wall. Having Lily when she was just twenty-three hadn't been part of any life plan, but the doctors had made it clear: after what she'd put her body through, her fertility was wrecked. She had a year, two at most, to conceive.

The disease had stolen so much from her life, and the thought it would take the chance for her to be a mother, for her to finally have someone love her the way she deserved to be loved, had been too much for her to bear. Yes, it was a lot to take on when she was single and starting her career as a nurse, but in so many other ways, the timing felt right. She had built up her weight and was maintaining it at a healthy level; her gran was still with her, and was overjoyed to share the responsibility of raising a child; their local NHS trust even provided IVF funding for single women, especially those with her medical history. The main problem was finding the father. She loathed the idea of a random donor, some bloke she didn't know, who could even be one of the men involved in what had happened.

At the time, Mark was the only man she was close enough to ask, but she knew how he felt about children. Which made it all the more surprising when he'd said, 'I'll do it. I'll be the donor.'

Wiping her tears, she'd replied, 'You'd do that?'

'As long as you don't mind it being smarter than you.'

She'd thrown her arms round him. 'Thank you! *Thank you!*'

'One thing,' he'd told her. 'It's *your* kid. I don't want to be a dad, not now, maybe not ever. And I definitely do not want to watch it eat, or wipe poo off its bum. Yuck!'

Hadn't that changed. Within the first week of his daughter's life, Mark was besotted. After a month he moved house to be closer to them. He was such a good father to Lily, always calm and measured, even when she threw a strop, which, as a temperamental three-nager, happened on most days.

'Okay, angel,' Rachel said. 'Home time.'

'You want something to eat?' As Mark asked that, she got a deep gravy scent of roast chicken that sent her stomach into convulsions of hunger. 'It's nearly ready.'

'Saving myself for canapés.'

He gave her a suspicious look and went *Hmmmmm*.

'Here's a question, though,' she said, as she pulled the sleeves out of Lily's jacket. 'If you wanted to get into someone's Snapchat account, how would you do it?'

Mark's frown deepened. 'What's happened? Has someone—?'

'Not me, Spence. Someone logged into his Snap and sent out rude pictures.'

'What's going on, Rach?'

'I just told you.'

'Are you—?'

'Do you know or not?'

'Jesus, Rachel. What's with you? You're so... irritable.'

She shook out her shoulders. 'Sorry. Rough day. So?'

Mark tipped his head from side to side. The new haircut really suited him, enhancing the shape of his face. But... why hadn't he spoken to her about it? This was the kind of thing he would debate endlessly, his wanting to attract women on one side verses his natural apathy towards anything remotely stylish on the other. She'd tell him how much a cool cut like that would cost, and he'd reply, *Fifty pounds! For a blimmin' haircut!*

And yet here he was, already coiffed.

His lips lifted into a crafty smile. 'What *I'd* do is phish him with an e-mail. Get him to click on a link, download some spyware onto his phone. Make him enter his passwords again.' He shrugged. 'Or something like that.'

The payroll e-mail. The link to download her bank details.

That's how it had been done.

But by who?

She tried to keep the shock off her face. 'So what should he...? How can he get rid...?'

'Meh, easy,' Mark replied, flicking his hand. 'Tell him to change his passwords – *not* on the same device. Then rebuild his phone, and try not to be such a noob next time.'

Damn. She'd already changed her passwords once, but on her phone, shivering outside the gym after she'd hung up from Becca.

'Thanks, I'll tell him,' Rachel said, then shook Lily's jacket at her. 'Okay, missy. Let's saddle up.'

'Before you go,' Mark said. 'Can we have a word?'

She followed him into the hallway. 'Listen, Mark. I know what—'

'Have something,' he said, nodding at the kitchen.

'I've got friends—'

'You know what I'm saying.'

'I'm *fine*, Mark. I promise.'

'Not what I asked.'

She started back to Lily. 'I don't have time—'

'That's crap, and you know it.'

'I told you—'

'I can tell by your aura.'

'My *aura?*' Rachel poked her head in the lounge. Lily, thankfully, was still engrossed with Peppa and her pals. 'One meditation course and you're Ravi bloody Shankar.'

'You're moody, you're paranoid, you're running *after* the gym. Talk to me, Rach.'

She squeezed her eyes. It felt like she could sleep for a week. Should she tell him about what happened at the gym? If Griffin was behind the photo, Mark would want to know. But what if she was wrong about that? Back when they used to talk about Griffin a lot, Mark had been certain that there was no way for him to trace what they did back to them – and if he didn't have revenge as a motive, then why come after her again, all these years later?

Besides, she knew how Mark's mind worked. He'd look at the evidence, run it through statistical analysis, and conclude: a. Konrad knew her Snapchat password; and b. he'd found the photo of her on the Internet, and not only forwarded it to his mates as a laugh, but scored extra bro points by sending it from her Snap account.

That's what blokes like him do, he'd say.

'I'm just a bit tired,' she said.

'I know when you're tired.'

'Give it a rest, okay?'

'It's Konrad, isn't it. What's he done?'

'All because you don't have a relationship, it doesn't mean you have to keep shitting on mine.'

Mark pulled his chin back. The pains of his non-existent love life were well known to both of them – they'd talked long into the night about his fear of ending up alone. That kind of thinking had, in part, led to his illness.

'I'm sorry,' Rachel said, taking his hand. 'I didn't...' He was looking at her curiously, his mouth bunched to the side, like he was weighing up whether to let her in on a secret. 'What? What is it?'

He shook his head. 'Nothing. It doesn't matter.'

She didn't have time for this. 'Home, *now*,' she said, striding away from him.

Lily slid off the sofa with a disappointed huff. Mark dropped to her level, kissed her cheek, and asked her to wait by the front door.

'What now?' Rachel sighed.

Mark waited for Lily to leave the room. 'Sort this out. I can support you, I'm always here. But it's got to come from you.'

'I'm telling you–'

'No. I'm telling you.'

She opened her mouth to speak, but the ferocity of his stare shut her up.

'Think of Lily.'

'What's that supposed to mean?'

'It means I'd do anything to protect my daughter. Just remember that.'

CHAPTER EIGHT

Release

Rachel bustled Lily through the front door, then raced to her laptop, open on the coffee table in the living room. 'Five minutes' play time,' she said, logging in.

Why hadn't Konrad returned her call? As she changed her passwords again, she imagined Pete accosting him off the tube, thrusting his phone in his face – she saw in Snapchat that he'd taken a screenshot of the photo – and saying that she came onto him at the gym. *So I replied with a picture of my dick,* he'd say. *You know, as a laugh.* She imagined Konrad looking heartbroken, but still nodding in agreement as Pete told him he was better off without her. That bloody photo! Hadn't it caused enough damage in her life?

When she'd finished, she hurried Lily up the stairs. 'Quick shower,' Rachel said. 'Granddad's coming soon.'

While Lily shuffled out of her jeans, Rachel stuffed an overnight bag. Toothbrush, mummy and baby teddies, clean clothes for the morning, and a couple of Elmer books, though she was certain her dad would ignore them in favour of watching television.

The splash of the water muted as Lily got in the shower. Rachel poked her head round the door, and despite how stressed she was feeling, couldn't help returning her daughter's smile as she stamped gleefully in the tub. 'Remember to wash, sweetness,' she said. 'Use soap.'

Five minutes later, Lily was wrapped in a towel in her mother's arms. Rachel cradled her, nuzzling her cheek and singing *You Are My Sunshine,* happy for this lovely moment in what, so far, had been a ridiculously horrible day.

One that, she was certain, was going to get worse before it got better.

It was nearly seven, and there was no sign of Konrad.

Rachel was tipping a box of Iceland Italian Platter canapés on an oven tray when the front door opened. She raced through to the living room, but it was just her dad. He shuffled inside, meekly looking round, like he was unsure whether it was the right house, only smiling when he saw Lily rushing towards him.

Until her gran got sick with ovarian cancer, Rachel hadn't seen her dad since she was eight. Since he chose drinking himself into an actual gutter over raising his daughter. Being with him always made her feel like she'd taken a swig of spoiled milk. The complexion of his wide-lined face made her think of mincemeat left out of the fridge, and since getting sober he'd ballooned to the point where his gut pushed against his T-shirt like he was well into a second trimester. With his height and his vanishing hairline, he looked like a giant thumb. She put up with him, she tolerated him – she appreciated how hard he'd worked to get sober, *eventually* – and he did help out a lot with Lily. But that didn't mean she had to like him.

'Her bag's there,' she said. She crouched by Lily and pushed out her cheek. 'See you in the morning, angel.'

'Let's go, Granddad,' Lily said, pulling him towards the door.

Rachel watched her go. Such a cruel irony that the more a child was loved, the less they seemed to need you. The world was full of sad kids pining for runaway dads, for the attention of absent-minded mums, but make sure they know you are always there and they can't even be bothered to give you a kiss goodbye.

'Hold on a second, lovely,' her dad said. He pressed his chest and took a moment, as if the very act of talking left him breathless. How could he let himself get so huge? 'You mind if we have a chat?'

She could tell by the maudlin expression on his face that he meant *that* kind of chat. A support group deep and meaningful – of a sort they were both used to – and she didn't have the head for that. She'd seen that look once before, when they did step nine together, his *making amends*, although how a grovelling apology could give back fifteen years of blaming herself for being so unlovable that her own father felt compelled to leave was still a mystery to her. Since accepting his "apology" they'd only communicated on a surface level. *Hi, how are you, what fine/miserable weather we're having?* What else was there to add? *And by the way, you leaving when I was a child set off the chain of events that crippled me emotionally for my whole life. So, thanks for that, Dad!*

Besides, she just needed a bit of space to think. Konrad was an hour late. She saw in WhatsApp he'd last been online at five thirty-two, but since then, nothing. Every time she rang it went to voicemail. Even if Pete had showed him the photo, you'd think Konrad would at least want to hear her side. After everything he'd promised that morning, how could he do this to her again?

She began clearing the coffee table. 'Sorry, Dad. I'm a little busy. I've got–'

'It's just I've had the little one a few times this week, and–'

'I thought you liked having her stay.'

He twisted the zipper of his denim jacket, looking down. 'I do, I do. It's just...'

She felt the blood rising to her face. 'If it's an inconvenience, I can ask any of the other mums next time.'

That wasn't quite true. There was maybe one she could beg, but seeing as her little Chloe was out of bed eight times a night with sleep regression, it probably wouldn't be the best idea, not least because she'd have to return the favour and risk the whole house being up until dawn. But he didn't need to know that.

'That's not what I mean,' he said. 'Look, don't take this the wrong way—'

'Don't say it then.'

'Please, Rachel. I have to. I watched your mum push everyone away—'

'*Stop*. I don't want to hear it.'

The last thing she needed was him badmouthing her mum, not after everything he'd put her through.

'If you can't come here and keep your mouth shut about Mum,' she said, 'then maybe you shouldn't come here at all.'

'You don't look *well*, is what I'm saying.'

'This coming from you?'

'This isn't about me.'

'Just leave me alone, Dad.'

'I'm not going anywhere. Not anymore.'

'Yes you are,' she said, moving towards him, hands out, as though she were ushering sheep through an open gate. 'Healthy food, please. Beans on toast or something. Not crisps.'

'But—'

'Bye, Dad,' she said, and closed the door. That kind of concern she could take from Mark, but not from him. She let her father be a part of Lily's life. That didn't mean she wanted him as part of her own.

Rachel found her phone and opened WhatsApp. Konrad *still* wasn't online. She looked back at the messages he'd sent that afternoon, one saying, *Can't wait to see you tonight, tomorrow night, and every night x*. After that had come a picture of Prince Harry – Konrad had been teasing her ever since she said she found him surprisingly handsome. They were supposed to be going to Madame Tussauds that Sunday for her birthday, followed by as much ice cream as her daughter could cram in her three-year-old stomach at the huge Baskin-Robbins on Baker Street, and it'd been a running joke for weeks that he'd catch her sneaking a kiss on his royal waxwork. The two blue ticks next to her dashed off reply – *I'd rather have you than all the ginger princes in the world!* *X* – showed he'd read her message.

What if Pete was involved in a sinister Facebook group that got kicks out of degrading innocent women? She was sure one of his mates was taking a video when she was scrabbling for her phone. What if this was part of their stupid macho games? Konrad had lost some bet and was being forced to watch her humiliation as punishment? Worse, what if he *was* behind it? What if he had two sides, one the fun sweet bloke she loved spending time with, the other a psycho who liked to stub cigars on his arm and humiliate his girlfriend?

No. No way. He might carry himself like a bit of a lad, and he might hang around with some people she couldn't stand, but even this last week he'd never been cruel, or mean.

What if it was nothing to do with Konrad or his mates?

Could Alan Griffin have set it up? Could he have been spying on her, getting to know her boyfriend, his mates, and sent that photo to Pete, knowing he'd tell Konrad afterward?

Could he be out of prison and trying to destroy her life again?

Pulse fluttering, she sat in front of the laptop. When Alan Griffin was first arrested, checking the forums for updates became Rachel's obsession. The one with the biggest community, the most up-to-date information, used to be www.paedo-hunter.net. When the front page loaded and she saw the camouflage colour scheme, an involuntary smile pricked up her lips. She typed in her username and password, worried her login wouldn't work anymore. She was thrilled when it did.

If information about his release would be anywhere, it'd be here.

At the time, his case attracted a lot of attention. A haul that size was big news. Not just the images of children, although there were over five million of those, but links to live-stream rapes in the dark web, screen prints of attempts to groom on chatrooms, and Word documents filled with grizzly stories about torturing and dismembering teenage girls. Way more shocking than what she thought they'd find. The prosecution questioned his sanity, and he'd ended up in Broadmoor. A twelve-year sentence, with the option of permanent incarceration if deemed necessary to protect the public.

That meant he had another four years before his release, at the very least.

Didn't it?

The website was as busy as ever, the top bar showing five hundred and thirty-eight registered members, with twenty-six active. It was a community of victims, their families, ex-policemen, concerned citizens. They swapped entrapment methods, uploaded videos of perverts presented with printouts of their filthy chats, and posted updates from the sex register.

In the search bar, Rachel typed *Alan Griffin*. A topic with his name came back. Her finger trembled on the touchpad. *Please let him still be inside.* She clicked on the link, went to the last page, and scrolled down.

The latest update was a few days ago, from someone called *Guardian Angel*.

Released from Broadmoor on 27 September.
Location unknown.

CHAPTER NINE

DOxed

Rachel stared at the laptop screen. She felt the anxiety growing in the back of her throat, and then passing slowly down, like she'd swallowed too much in one go and could only wait in discomfort for it to clear.

He was out.

Alan Griffin was out of prison.

Why wasn't she more prepared? She forced herself to focus. There'd be plenty of time for endless self-recrimination later. She ran into the kitchen, pulling out the drawers under the kettle, hunting through the coupons and bills and loose change to find a ball of old Blu-Tack. She went from room to room, checking the windows were locked, then closing the curtains and sticking the corners to the sills, getting agitated as the fabric kept coming away, in a state of near panic by the time she finished the curtain in the living room.

Alan Griffin. Alan *bloody* Griffin. He'd been out of prison for *two weeks* already. Her hand quivered as she rubbed her face. And she had so much more to lose now.

Lily.

He'd know about her daughter.

Rachel went through to the kitchen, turned on the tap and splashed her face, hoping the shock of the cold water would clear her mind. All because Griffin was out of prison, it didn't mean what happened at the gym was because of him – if Mark was right about that payroll e-mail, then he definitely would have had access to all her social media accounts. *So why not do more to her?*

The smell of breadcrumbs and melting cheese coming from the oven made her hunger unbearable. She yanked it open, grabbed a dishcloth and pulled out the tray. At the sight of the canapés, her throat clenched into a length of knotted rope. The mozzarella sticks looked the most cooked so she blew on one and shoved it in her mouth, wincing as the coating burnt her tongue, making her teeth chew, almost gagging on the puttyish texture, the milky taste, forcing it down with water from the tap.

That was the other thing. Her eating. What was the point of lying to herself? She was in it now – she could feel the pressure building inside, the start of an episode, like the sea contracting before a tsunami – and the sooner she faced that and addressed it, the quicker it would go away. She'd allowed it to creep up over the last week, worrying about Konrad. A few skipped lunches, some half-finished dinners, until she got to now. Nothing for dinner last night, nothing for breakfast this morning, a sachet of Ensure at lunch, and a smoothie on the bus. Two hundred calories, at most, in twenty-four hours. She probably hadn't topped a thousand in days. No wonder Mark had noticed she'd lost weight. No wonder he thought she was being irritable. When she did an internal check, she could feel the fizz of it, the fidgety manic up-all-night energy that came at the start of a starve.

Rachel fell onto a chair. She tried to keep her breathing calm, to stem the dread rising through her. She'd spiralled into it, been pulled in by its strange gravity, the black hole in her core. *Anorexia.* God, she hated the word. It sounded so dramatic, like an Egyptian queen, or a celebrity baby. Such a grandiose name for such a insidious condition.

Why did she keep doing this to herself? Over the years she'd lain on countless couches, dissecting to death her lack of self-esteem, the shame of being almost six foot of flaws when compared to the glossy miniature babes in music videos, repeating the same mantras about how, in the Instagram age, contrasting your own disappointing timeline to the beautiful galleries of others can crush you inside. One psychologist put forward that perhaps she wanted to stay a young girl forever, that starving herself was an unconscious attempt to live in a time before her dad left. Another suggested she was trying to make herself as small as possible so she wouldn't be a target for men like Griffin anymore. Yet another said she needed to stop punishing herself for her mum's death.

Rachel didn't have many memories of her mum, and could bring to mind only fragments. How her fingers were red and cold, even in summer. Or how she was always scrubbing something, the kitchen, the bathroom, the stairs down to the cellar, even the front pavement, when there was nothing left that hadn't felt the force of her brush. The scent of bleach clung to her skin like perfume. For years Rachel thought she must have been a germophobe, but now she knew her mum was doing it for the exercise, to burn the few calories she consumed.

After her dad left, her mum started getting sick all the time. Always a small woman, she shrank before Rachel's eyes. At meals she'd push her food around her plate, or sneak it out of her mouth with a napkin, or say she didn't fancy it and would make something later, although she never did. Every night she sat on the back step, mouth dour, knees pressed to her skeletal chest, looking at the sky, smoking and sighing. Within two years, she was gone. All through her teenage years, Rachel blamed herself. *She chose to die rather than be with you.*

Enough. Take a breath, calm down. The direction of those thoughts led only further into the darkness, and she couldn't let that happen. Not with everything else going on.

She forced herself to bite another mozzarella stick. She just hated it though. She hated all of it. How every time life became stressful, her body rejected food, and she had to learn how to eat all over again. How the anorexia voice grew louder and more powerful as the disease took hold, like a parasite feasting on her brain, telling her it was okay not to eat, that people could go days without food, that if she starved herself she wouldn't feel guilt, or shame, or even grief anymore, because when you were hungry enough, nothing else mattered. But what could she do? It would keep coming back and coming back until her final breath.

And why?

Because it was as part of her as the brown of her eyes, or the beating of her heart.

The doorbell rang. Was that Konrad? Had he forgotten his keys? She spat the mouthful of mozzarella into the bin, hurried through to the living room, and opened the front door.

'Hi babe!' Becca cried, grasping a bottle of M&S Finest Prosecco by the silver foil throat. 'I bought birthday fizz.'

She bustled past, dressed in going out clothes, a black camisole, gold hoop earrings, and red strappy heels that made Rachel's calves ache just to look at them.

'Konrad's not here,' Rachel said, wiping her mouth, wanting to get the crumbs off her lips.

Becca dropped onto the sofa, groaning and peeling off her heels, like she'd just stepped in from clubbing. She looked considerably drunker than on the video call, her pink lip gloss smudged, and a pale dribble, spilled wine most likely, on the front of her white jeans.

'He should have been here at half six,' Rachel said.

'Men!' Becca lifted the wine. 'Glasses?'

Rachel hovered by the armrest. Was that it? Couldn't Becca see that she needed to talk about this? 'You have to hear what happened.'

'Choppy chop, babe. Unless you want to see me drink from the bottle.'

Rachel stormed through to the kitchen. Becca could be such a *bitch* sometimes, especially when she'd been drinking, which seemed to be *all the bloody time* these days.

In fact, why was Rachel clinging to Becca? They weren't in school anymore; they didn't have to stay friends. It was always her trying to make plans, just like at the gym, which she blew off without an apology. And tonight, inviting her round, trying to keep going a friendship that she clearly didn't want. Why else would she turn up smashed?

Rachel took two wine glasses from the cupboard, then sagged against the door and rested her head against the cool wood. Why was she being so hard on her? She had a bad habit of doing that, of thinking the worst of people, as though by making herself annoyed with them she could stop what they did from hurting her. Such a stupid defence mechanism. All that happened was she ended up angry as well as sad.

How long had it been since Becca quit her job at Orchid? A couple of months, at least. They hadn't seen each other much in that time, and being honest, that was mostly down to Rachel. She'd been too wrapped up with Konrad, spending most evenings with him – and if she fancied a quick pint, that she knew wasn't going to turn into ten, then it was easier and simpler to grab one with Spence. But what if Becca wasn't so fine about quitting as she'd made out? She'd told Rachel she'd been sick of working in PR – the long hours, the hyper competitiveness, how everyone backstabbed to steal the hippest clients – but if she was really okay with it, wouldn't she be doing more with her time than getting leathered and posting duck-lipped selfies on Instagram?

Because she's not happy. She just doesn't want to admit it to you.

For as long as they'd known each other, *Rachel* had been the screw up, with the broken home, the mental health problems, the weirdo stalking her. Meanwhile, Becca grew up with two sane functioning parents, a younger brother to terrorise, even a family dog that snuffled into bed with her in the morning. She went to parties, had boyfriends, got into university and landed her dream job when she got out.

But look at them now, and hadn't their roles reversed? Rachel was the one with the boyfriend, the family, the career, while Becca was single, unemployed, getting smashed every night – and putting on weight. When she sat down, the denim strained at the top of her jeans. No doubt about it, she would be secretly fuming about that.

Rachel sighed. Really, she wasn't such a good friend herself. How could she expect Becca to fawn over her problems with Konrad now if she'd barely been there for the last few months? Whatever happened to make her leave her job, it had messed her up, and she should have been more supportive.

She carried the glasses through to the living room, where Becca was taking a pull from the bottle. She belched and looked up guiltily. 'Ooops!'

'Ladies cover their mouth,' Rachel said, falling onto the sofa beside her. She took the bottle and poured two glasses.

Becca mimed sipping tea, her face prim and her pinkie stuck out. 'There are no ladies here, my dear,' she said, in a fragile falsetto.

'That much is very clear,' Rachel replied, smiling at their old joke. 'Listen, Becca...'

'Yep?'

'About what happened with your job at Orchid–'

Becca made a noise of disgust. '*Ughhh*. So where d'you say this bloke of yours was? He bringing anyone?'

'No, it's just him. Well, it's supposed to be. And Spence.'

'Oh, so I'm the beard, am I?'

Rachel saw some of Becca's interest in the night fade from her eyes. 'I just wanted to keep it small. A few friends, you know? I don't need to be making chit-chat with people I don't know, especially after the day I've had.'

She left her sentence dangling, hoping Becca would grab the hook.

'Oh yeah, right,' she replied, massaging her temple, looking pained. 'You want the goss?'

'Sure.' Rachel, all clenched up, listened to her go on about some girl from school she didn't remember who'd been arrested for shoplifting and was undergoing therapy for chronic kleptomania.

'She's just so *thirsty* for attention,' Becca said, then looked at Rachel sideways and barked a laugh. 'Sorry! I didn't mean–'

'You still think I sent you that photo, don't you.'

'Fucking hell, Rach. Can't we just chat? I can't stand the drama.'

'It's not *drama*. It was pretty humiliating actually. You don't know what happened. That photo was sent to Pete as well. You know, Konrad's mate. From his business. And now Konrad's not here, and the night's ruined, and I think… I think…' Why was Becca looking at her like that? Rachel had been close to tears, had battled them down, but the expression on her friend's face told her the truth – she thought she was making it up.

'Do you have to do this?' Becca groaned, wafting *eau de Prosecco* into her face. 'You sent it, all right? Whether it was supposed to go just to me, or you managed to epically fail and send it your boyfriend's mate, can we cut the crap? I don't care. You've got your "problems". Big deal. What's new?'

'*Why would I do that?*'

'I don't know. Maybe you were bored.'

'That's ridiculous.'

'I don't know what goes on in your head.'

'Listen, Becca. I think… I think it might be Alan Griffin. He'd want you to think I sent it.'

'*That* bloke? The perv who used to harass you? But, I mean, it's been such a long time. Why would he come back now? You're not so, y'know… young anymore.'

'Don't you remember what he used to do to me?'

Becca squinted, not even attempting the keep the disbelief off her face. 'Just tell me one thing. When that photo was sent, you were in the gym. Right?'

'Okay...'

'And were you logged into Snap?'

She must have been. She'd put in her password on the bus and didn't have to again after that. A cold feeling crept up from the hollow of her throat. 'Well, I was–'

Becca flung out her hands – *got you now!* 'If someone else was using your Snap account, you'd have been logged out on your phone.'

'But... I don't...'

'I tried it. I logged into Snap on my tablet and checked my phone. Boom. Gone.'

'*But why would I do that?*'

'But you were logged in!'

'On my life, Becca. How could you–?'

Becca cut her off with an exasperated tut, and finished her glass. 'Who gives a shit anyway? You're a fuck up. I'm a fuck up. Let's just get drunk, eh? Might as fucking well.' She looked her in the eye and snorted out a laugh. 'You dopey cow.'

Rachel stared, cheeks flushed, mouth open. A rap on the front door broke her stupor. She went to get it.

Spence was on the doorstep, still in his nurse's tunic, smiling, but in an unusual way, like someone was standing in the shadows, a gun trained on him, telling him to look happy. The photo. Of course. He'd been sent it as well. Why those three? She didn't have many contacts in Snapchat – she mainly used it to catch up on celebrity gossip while on the loo – but why not send it to her whole address book? It didn't make sense.

'You've seen it?' she asked.

His face flitted through confusion, to suspicion, then back to a smile, although it was somehow even less certain than before. He handed her a birthday card with her name in green neon highlighter pen. 'Did... did you want a photo of me?'

'Oh, Jesus,' she said. 'Come in.'

'Spence!' Becca tilted the wine bottle towards her mouth, then jerked forward as it spilled down her front. 'Better hurry if you want fizz.'

'Only if your herpes has cleared up,' he said.

'I prefer to call it spreading the love,' she replied, and took another drink. 'Mmmm... it's so nice to feel something sparkly in your mouth. Makes the world that bit more bearable.'

'Where's your beast of a boyfriend?' Spence asked Rachel.

'Not here.'

His eyebrows rose, as a question.

Rachel blew out her cheeks. *Long story.* 'Sit down, I'll get you a glass. Unless you want to add to the backwash.' She remembered the canapés. 'You want food?'

'Missed circuits this morning.' Spence patted his flat stomach. 'So nothing for me.'

'Sling 'em this way,' Becca said.

Rachel went to the kitchen, found a clean plate in the cupboard, and slammed the door closed. Konrad wasn't coming, that much was clear. So that was it. Eleven months and it was all over. Her mind flashed with an image of him leaning in for a kiss; she felt the soft press of his lips, the heat of his breath, the touch of his fingers caressing her cheek. Goddamn it. This was so fucked up. Only last week she'd been daydreaming her reaction to him saying *I love you.* She didn't want it to be over. She didn't want any of this. She tipped the canapés onto the plate and clattered the tray beside the sink.

'Fine,' Spence said, behind her. 'I'll eat your stupid food. Just don't smash the place up.'

He had his arms out for a hug. She fell into them and started to cry.

'It's all right,' he said. 'It's okay.'

She pulled away and wiped her eyes with the heel of her hand. At least she never got round to touching up her make-up, otherwise it'd be halfway down her face. 'It's not okay.'

'I grabbed the screen.' Spence got out his phone. 'You look

great. I'm going to save it in my contacts, so whenever you call I can check you out, little miss hot stuff.'

'Can you delete that please?'

He mock-rolled his eyes. 'Uhh, if I must.'

Before he could press the little trash can icon, she pulled the phone out of his hand. Rachel looked at the picture properly, her seventeen-year-old self. Was that really taken nearly ten years ago? Lying on her side on the bed, naked except for white panties and knee socks, she was thin, but not sick thin, not yet. No thigh gap or bikini bridge or collarbones like diving boards. She was definitely more attractive than she thought at the time, before illness and pregnancy warped her body out of shape.

'I didn't send it to you,' she said.

'But it came from your Snap account.'

'Someone hacked it.'

Spence pulled an *oh wow* face. 'You're joking. Do you know who did it?'

'I think so... maybe...'

'Let me guess – a vengeful ex?'

'Not quite.'

'Don't leave me hanging!'

'It was a mistake, a stupid mistake. Just me and Becca messing about.'

Spence's eyebrows spiked.

'Nothing like that!' She paused. It wasn't a period of her life she particularly liked to talk about, but he'd seen the photo, so he might as well know the rest. Well, some of the rest. 'Have you heard of doxing?'

'Oooh, I read about that. It's when someone gets their personal details published online.'

She pinched out the photo, zooming into the pinboard above the bed. 'See that?'

'What? A letter?'

'From the hospital, a referral for low blood sugar.'

'So?'

'So it had my name and address on it.'

'But how did...? I still don't get...'

'*Fine.* I'll tell you. But *please* don't say anything to anyone.'

Taking the photo had been Becca's idea. Back in school, a group of sixth form lads, lean footballers with styled hair and cool clothes, had a Hotmail account. Saved in it were pictures of the girls they liked. Most were topless. All were provided by the girls themselves.

'It's quite an honour,' Becca said. They already had one of her. Sitting in Rachel's bedroom after school, swigging from a bottle of gin they'd nicked from her gran's kitchen cupboard, Becca was trying to convince Rachel to do the same. 'Means someone fancies you.'

'What if they show people? What if they put it online?'

'Like anyone's interested in your skinny butt among the gajillion gigabytes of porn. Come on, babe. Maxine Posen hooked up with Greg Clarkwell this way. It's how I got off with Finn Young.'

Could she do this? Rachel was sick of being sad and sexless. Sick of trailing after her best mate, wishing she had her life. She was seventeen. An exciting world of boys and parties, of fun memories that would last her a lifetime, waited for her behind an invisible wall. Could this be her wrecking ball?

Rachel sighed. Who was she kidding? There was more chance of her growing gills and starting a new life as a mermaid than there was of her sending a topless photo to the boys.

'Fine, sod them,' Becca said. 'Let me take a picture of you anyway. You're such a babe and you don't even know it. If you saw how your bod looked to other people, you wouldn't be so hung up about it.'

'If I want to see myself naked, I can look in the mirror.'

Becca drunkenly shook her head. 'Not the same. You look in a mirror, the angles are always wrong, the light's always bad.'

Heart thumping against her ribs, Rachel took two big gulps from the gin. Maybe Becca was right. Maybe with the proper lighting, lying in a sexy position, with her hair and make-up nicely done. Rachel would see something in a photo that she hadn't seen before, something to give her confidence, to propel her into a normal life. The alcohol was making her head swim. *Come on,* she thought. *You're supposed to do dumb things like this when you're a teenager.* And if she was going to do it with anyone, it would be Becca, one of the only people she felt if not comfortable without clothes in front of, then at least not *so* horribly ashamed.

Besides, if she hated it, which she surely would, then they could delete it and file the memory away to the Never Think Of This Again folder.

But if she didn't hate it...

Really, what did she have to lose?

Rachel still had her netball uniform on, and hesitated with her fingers on the hem of her red vest. 'Promise you'll delete it straight away if I tell you to?'

'On my honour,' Becca replied, giving her a hazy salute. 'Come on, Rach. Don't you want to feel good about yourself?'

Yes, she did. She took another swig from the bottle and dragged off her vest.

As expected, Rachel hated how she looked in the photo – all lumps and divots and masses of ugly pale flesh – despite Becca's protestations that the photo was *amazing, babe.*

'Why do you always have to be so blimmin' *negative*,' she said, as she e-mailed her own photo to the boys from her phone.

'Can you delete it?' Rachel asked. '*Please?*'

'It's deleted, it's deleted.' Becca turned her phone, showing the thumbnail gallery, 'Look, gone.' She took a mouthful of gin and shook her head in disgust. 'Now let's get super drunk.'

Rachel didn't drink often, spirits especially were hard on her stomach, but the evening had messed with her head and she needed to wipe it from her memory. What if she had been brave enough to send the photo to the boys? What if they'd seen her differently from how she saw herself? She took the bottle from Becca. Her brain swirled. Her pulse pounded with the lost possibilities.

Becca's phone rang. The name Finn Y appeared on the screen, along with a photo of him in some nightclub, his arm around the shoulders of another bloke Rachel didn't recognise.

'Oh my god, oh my god!' Becca yelped. 'They must have seen it.'

She took the call, pressing the phone to her ear even though he was talking loudly enough for Rachel to get the gist that he was apologising. Maybe he'd been too forward, although that didn't seem likely. After losing her virginity at fourteen in the backseat to some estate kid whose name she didn't remember, her best mate was no more averse to putting out than she was to trying magazine perfume samples.

Becca covered her mouth. Even with the bronze sheen on her cheeks, she'd gone pale. She was glancing at Rachel, nodding at something Finn was saying, looking as though she'd been given terrible news, a terminal diagnosis, the gory details of a car crash, that an asteroid was moments from slamming into North London.

'Send it to me,' Becca said, and hung up.

'What is it?' Rachel asked. 'What did he do?'

Becca logged into her Yahoo account. Her latest e-mail was a minute earlier, from Finn. Inside was a link, nothing else.

http://boards.4chan.org/b/thread/739373421

Rachel knew about 4chan. The boys loved it. Oldest forum on the web, home of the depraved. She'd browsed it once for ten minutes and discovered only racism, homophobia, the occasional funny meme, and a deep primeval despair at the entire male gender. Becca clicked on the link.

There, right there, at the top of the web page – *on the Internet* – was the photo of Rachel. The same one they took tonight. In her socks and knickers. She took a step to the side, reaching for the windowsill, the room listing. Gin burned back up her throat. She tried to hold it down.

'They post all the photos there,' Becca said. 'Mine too. The shitty, *shitty* bastards!'

'But how...' Rachel moaned. Her cheeks felt so hot she imagined them violently red. 'You said....'

'I'm sorry. I'm so sorry. I thought I was helping. I thought–'

Rachel's phone, a cheap Nokia, vibrated on the bed. The writing on the small green screen read *private number*. Somehow, she knew not to answer, as if the vibration itself were different, mocking, sinister. It stopped.

They scrolled down and found another photo, a close-up of the letter on the pinboard.

Her phone buzzed again. Rachel answered it, holding it away from her face, as though worried it might attack. '*Who is this?*'

Nothing. Then slow sarcastic laughter. Rachel flung the phone across the room. It hit the wall and dropped to the floor. The laughter, distant and tinny, carried on.

'Look at this,' Becca said, pointing to the comments.

Anon: Her name's on the letter. Any black hats out there wanna hack the hospital, get the rest of her deets?

Anon: Can't be too hard

Anon: I'm in. Man, these places have zero security

Anon: Rachel Stone. Age: 17. Address: 68 Hanley Road, London, N4 3DU. Home number 0207 489 6358, mobile 07942 451785. E-mail address: callmerach95@hotmail.com

Anon: You dumb bitch. You dumb, dumb bitch

Anon: Looks like this dumb bitch got DoXED!!

Anon: Pile in lads!

Anon: LOLZ!!!

. . .

For days, Rachel's life was hell. Her phone rang constantly, while filling with sleazy texts, until she just kept it off. Men bombarded her e-mail with pictures of their dicks. Someone found out what school she went to, hacked into it and made the photo the screensaver on every computer. They even bought domain names like stupidskinnycunt.com and dumbslutgetsdoxed.com and posted memes of the photo on it, embedding her name into the webpage metadata, so if anyone googled her, those were the sites that filled the first page.

But that wasn't the worst of it. Not by a long way.

'What's the hold up?' Becca called from the living room. 'You promised nibbles!'

'You can't leave it there!' cried Spence.

'You know everything.'

'Except why this photo's reappeared ten years later!' He jerked a thumb over his shoulder. 'Let's wait for Boozy McSelfie to pass out, then I want the rest.'

She pressed the trash key below the photo and watched it disappear. 'Thanks for not judging me, Spence. Seriously. I mean it.'

'Look, do you want me to postpone my flight tomorrow? I can−'

'No chance,' she said, carrying the tray of canapés back through. 'I want you to be happy.'

In the living room, Becca was leaning back on the sofa, chest up, phone at arm's length, pouting at the camera. 'You two! Groupie time.'

Spence took Rachel's arm and pushed out his lips. 'You heard the woman.'

'I'll pass.' She didn't need to be part of anyone's social media parade right now.

Spence crowded behind Becca as she covered all the angles with her arm. Afterward, while she looked for the best one to post on Instagram, Spence opened a bottle of red and poured two glasses.

Rachel asked him about his trip to Greece, even though they'd spoken about it daily since he'd booked the flight. Anything to stop herself from checking her phone for messages from Konrad every two minutes.

'I don't even know if Andreas is still into me,' Spence said. 'I've been messaging him all day and heard *nothing*.'

'You and me both, sister,' Rachel said, toasting him. 'He wouldn't have invited you out if he wasn't into you.'

'He invited me, I invited myself. Is there *such* a big difference?'

'Come on, Mr Positive.' She rattled his knee, although in truth she had her own doubts about the trip. Whenever Spence spoke about Andreas, whom he'd spent seven days rubbing against on an Adriatic cruise in July, everything came with a qualifier. Andreas wanted to move to London, but he might go to university in Athens to do a masters in tourism; he wanted to introduce Spence to his parents, but this trip wasn't the right time. She hated being negative in front of him, kept that side of herself in check when they hung out, well, as much as she could, so only offered support for his flying out there. With any luck, when it didn't work out he wouldn't be *too* heartbroken. If the year they'd been friends was anything to go by, when this Andreas was gone, there'd be a whole new one to follow.

'No-one is getting younger, *darling*,' Spence said. 'Especially not me.'

'More Botox?'

'Don't think my face could take it.'

'From what you've—'

'Okay. Stop. I can't talk about it anymore.'

From the sofa, Becca let out a grunting snore and lolled her head the other way. Rachel hadn't even noticed her falling asleep. Her black camisole had hitched up, showing a roll of tanned flesh going over the top of her jeans.

Spence cocked his head at her. 'Shall we call the lifeguard? Tow her back out to sea.'

Rachel slapped his arm, grinning, feeling both guilty and

sneakily pleased for enjoying the insult. She still couldn't believe Becca had accused her of sending that photo herself, like it had been some kind of guilt trip gone wrong. Is that what Becca really thought of her? That she would do something like that? Maybe it was. In which case, it went to show that sometimes what you believed someone thought of you was in fact as far from the truth as you could possibly imagine.

'Pass me that,' Spence said, nodding to her phone. Thinking he was going to take a photo of the two of them, she unlocked it and handed it over. Instead he fired a few snaps of Becca. 'Now, next time she's mean to you, you can look at those and know she's not so perfect.'

'You are terrible,' Rachel said.

'And you haven't deleted them.'

They traded devious smiles.

'I guess we'll have to be terrible together.'

The photos would be gone soon anyway. She was going to wipe her phone as soon as he and Becca left, clear whatever awful software Griffin, or whoever, had tricked her into installing.

'So,' Spence said, leaning back in his chair, swirling his wine, 'back to what you were saying in the kitchen. I want the *really* long version.'

Rachel took a sip, paused with the glass at her lips, then downed the rest. She shouldn't be drinking so much on an empty stomach, but the alcohol was relaxing her, and after everything she'd been through in the last twenty-four hours, that felt more important than stressing over a bit of a hangover. Besides, it was good to talk to someone who believed her, rather than who thought she was always looking for *drama*.

'Okay,' she said. 'Here goes.'

CHAPTER TEN

Griffin

After the doxing, unable to face school, Rachel stayed in her bedroom. Days passed curled under the duvet. Becca visited every evening to grimly relay the latest – two of the boys who'd uploaded the photos had been excluded, the rest suspended. Yes, *everyone* had seen it, but they'd finally managed to remove it as the screensaver on the school computers. With every update, the will to starve grew stronger. What was the point of eating? She'd never recover from this.

Except, it wasn't only Rachel who suffered. Her gran was nearly seventy, with arthritis in her knees and a pharmacy of heart medicines to take every day. She was a strong woman, had outlasted her husband and raised two boys, but this was a different kind of stress. The worry of watching Rachel waste away, getting sicker and more withdrawn, aged her.

That more than anything pushed Rachel back into the world. The first day at school was tough – jokes, snide remarks, girls giggling when she passed them in the corridor – but by the second day, no-one really mentioned it. She had the backing of Becca, who was popular, as were the other girls who'd been duped by the boys into sending a picture. Their photos had also been posted on 4chan, and so, knowing any of them could have been doxed, they defended Rachel.

Before this happened, she'd been doing well in class, getting two As in her mock A-level exams, Biology and Maths, and had wanted to apply to university to study nutrition. The careers counsellor had spoken to her about a bursary she might be eligible for, considering her financial situation, as long as she maintained her grades. Rachel thought if she worked hard she could catch up on what she'd missed, get back on track.

Then Alan Griffin had barged into her life.

She remembered the first time she saw him. She hadn't even been back at school a week. He'd been outside the back gates, a heavy-set middle-aged man. Dark eyes, black hair combed into a side parting, smart in a navy blue suit and buttercup yellow tie, like he was waiting for one of the teachers, maybe to go on a date.

Their eyes met as Rachel approached the gate, and his mouth spread into a smile. He waved her over. She carried on walking, throat tight, heart racing. Ten minutes after the bell, there were plenty of other kids around. She stepped up the pace, not looking back, hoping she'd been mistaken, that he'd been signalling to someone behind her.

She lived a twelve-minute walk from school. The first half was along Hornsey Road, busy as usual, the shops still open, but then to get to her road she had to cut off, weave between the back streets, cross a grassy crescent. She glanced over her shoulder and there he was, closer than she expected, sweating through his shirt.

'Rachel, wait,' he said, his voice low, like he didn't want anyone to hear.

'I don't know you.'

'Can we talk? Two minutes.'

'Go away!'

Snap decision. She sprinted for home. She'd run track for the school since she was thirteen. No way he'd catch her. She took a winding obscure way, and made it back, panting, fumbling for her keys, letting herself in and slamming the door, wishing this were an isolated incident, but knowing from the way he'd looked at her that it wasn't. Something bad had started, she'd known it in her bones. Something very bad.

Alan Griffin became a constant presence in the periphery of her life. If she stepped outside, he was there, sitting in a car across the road, or watching from beneath a tree. At the cinema with Becca, she looked around at the ticket line, and there he was, at the cashier beside her, buying a single for the same movie. She hid in the toilets until the film started, weeping and wishing he'd leave her alone, then sneaked out the fire exit.

Her weight plummeted. She was being sucked back in, the urge to lock herself away, to deprive herself, growing stronger.

Not again.

Not after she'd fought so hard to get back.

The next time she saw him loitering by the house, she stormed out. 'Go away or I'll call the police.'

He straightened the lapel of his suit. 'If you gave me a chance—'

'You sicko!'

Instead of being cowed, he seemed confused, a bit put out, like he'd fed money into a vending machine, watched his snack drop, but couldn't find it in the bottom.

'You're the one putting dirty pictures of yourself online,' he said. 'You're the one giving out your phone number and your address.'

'That wasn't me.'

'Sure looked like you.'

An elderly couple she knew were walking their Westie, and further up the street she saw a young family, the mother pushing a pram and the father pulling a young boy on a red scooter. Rachel pointed at Griffin. 'This bloke's a pervert!' she shouted to them.

'Stop it,' he said.

'He followed me home from school and... and tried to molest me!'

'Shut your mouth. I'm warning you.'

The elderly couple had stopped, watching. The father was coming quickly towards Rachel.

'He's been waiting outside my window!' Rachel shouted. 'Playing with himself!'

Griffin stared at her, his lips tight and quivering. 'You evil bitch,' he hissed. 'I'm going to *ruin your life*.'

After that, he carried on stalking her, although he only made his presence known when no-one else was around. She'd walk past a car and see him in the driver's seat, holding up a pair of binoculars so she knew he'd been watching her from afar. If she waited at a quiet bus stop in the evening, he'd step from the shadows and stare at her. Even when she was at home, he harassed her, calling the house phone continually, until her gran pulled the plug from the wall, and posting printed notes through the letterbox at night. Things like, *Every time you leave the house, I'll be waiting* or *Very soon you will be all mine*.

Worse was when he took his attacks online, hacking into her social media and changing her passwords. While she struggled to get the accounts unlocked, uploading scans of her passport and waiting days for Facebook to believe it was her, he trolled her time-line, posting as her, trying to sound like her, but mean, snarky, like she was a total bitch. From her Yahoo account, he sent e-mails to people telling them what she really thought of them, then deleted both the original mail and their response, so Rachel could never be sure what he'd said. She told people what was happening, that someone else was doing all this, but she could see not everyone believed her. Some of them thought the doxing had pushed her over the edge.

Every time she managed to get into her accounts, Griffin was back in control of them by the end of the day. Back spreading bile in her name. Back alienating her from her friends.

She compiled a journal, collected evidence, as all the stalker websites suggested, and took it to the police. The two detectives who interviewed her were sympathetic, but said there was little they could do. At the time, she didn't even know his name. And her description of him as a "middle-aged man, black hair" wasn't going to photofit its way onto Crimewatch. When she insisted the police do something, they exchanged glances and asked how she knew it was this particular man doing all this to her. Didn't she say many men were involved in her doxing? Perhaps if she avoided posting topless pictures of herself online, then this kind of thing wouldn't happen.

All they saw was a manic paranoid teenage girl, sickly thin, who'd invited this trouble into her life.

Later, after Griffin went to prison, Mark worked out how he kept getting into her accounts.

'You keep your laptop in the same place?' he asked. It was on the desk in her bedroom. When she nodded, he went to the window, where a tall tree stood outside. 'I bet...' he murmured, scanning it. 'Aha! Look at this.'

Nestled in the crook of a branch, pointing into her bedroom. A tiny black box with a lens in the middle.

'That's a camera,' Mark said. 'He watched you logging in. That's how he got your passwords.'

'So, go on,' Spence said. 'What happened to him?'

Rachel paused. Did she really want Spence knowing what she'd done to send Griffin down? What if she told him and he wanted nothing more to do with her?

She cleared her throat. 'They found all these pictures on his computer... kids.'

'He was a proper paedo!'

'Something like that.'

Spence looked at her thoughtfully. 'But if he went to prison for being a paedo, why would he be stalking you again when he's out?'

'It's too much of a coincidence, getting hacked weeks after his release.'

'I still think it's that guy in the gym, Konrad's mate. Trying to dick shame you. You should have stuck your phone in your pants. *Click!* I see your penis and raise you a pussy!'

'Yeah, great idea there. And how would I explain that to Konrad?'

Spence looked around, apologetic. 'What Konrad?'

'Don't! I'm so gutted. You can't believe how much. I... I mean that has to be it now, right? I told him this morning it's the last time, and he's done it again.' She sniffed back tears. 'He promised me he'd be here, and – and–'

'Oh, shit, I'm sorry! I was just joking around.'

'No, you're right. *What Konrad?*'

All night she'd swung between being worried about him, to being furious with him, but now she felt resigned. And sad, *so* sad. A helpless, sunk into the bones kind of sad, the kind that felt as though it may last forever.

'He might still–' Spence began, but Rachel waved his words away.

'Whatever,' she said, suddenly exhausted from the alcohol, the lack of sleep, the stress of the last day. 'It's just life, isn't it. It's not the first shitty thing to happen to me, and I'm sure it won't be the last. At least I'm not alone. I've got Lily.'

'What am I? A turkey sandwich?'

She wiped the last of her tears and smiled. 'More like a fruit tart.'

'Cheeky!'

Her dad wasn't dropping Lily off until eight tomorrow morning, and as much as Rachel loved being woken before dawn by her daughter dive-bombing her bed, a lie-in sounded like exactly what

Rachel needed to get her head straight. She yawned, stretching her arms and rolling her shoulders.

'That my cue, is it?' asked Spence.

'Sorry!'

'That's fine, I know when I'm not wanted.' He pushed off the armchair. 'Okay, I'm going to use the little boy's room. Then I'll heave-ho snore face off the sofa and we'll get going.'

'Oh, Spence?' Rachel called as he started up the stairs.

He ducked his head back under the landing. 'Yes?'

'Thanks again. You're a good friend.'

'Don't worry about it.' His smile grew broad. 'I've probably got years of nutty boyfriends ahead of me. You'll make it up.'

Rachel began clearing the coffee table and had her hands full of wine glasses and dirty napkins when she heard a scrabbling at the front door. The sound of a key searching metal. That had to be Konrad. She dumped everything and hurried to get it, her blood rushing, torn between wanting to scream at him for not showing up before, and throwing her arms around him and giving thanks that he was safe.

The door slammed open before she could get to it. Konrad staggered inside, his eyes wild and bloodshot. He looked terrible, his cheeks puffy, his bottom lip busted, his clothes damp and filthy and stretched out of shape. A rip went up the side of his overcoat, making it hang away from the back, like a wing in a crappy home-made bat costume. Seeing the fury on his face, Rachel tried to duck away, but he caught her shoulder and shoved her back on the stairs.

He loomed over her, blocking the light, his head becoming a hard silhouette. 'Why Pete? Why my best mate?'

'Konrad, listen to me, please. I didn't send that photo. My phone—'

'Fuck – *fuuuuuckkk!*' He grabbed his forehead like he was trying to rip it off. 'Don't fucking lie to me, okay? I saw it.'

'I called you! I told you what—'

'Stop lying to my face, all right? Everyone saw what you did.' Up close he smelled of vomit and vodka and mud. 'You sent Pete that Snap, then you bent over and shook your ass—'

'I dropped my phone!'

'All the guys were there, so you can keep your fucking nice-girl butter-wouldn't-fucking-melt act, because I'm done. I don't need this psycho bitch *bullshit* in my life right now.'

Enough! Whatever had happened to him, it didn't excuse him pushing her over, or refusing to hear her side. 'I'm not the one showing up with burns on my arm. Or like I've – I've just lost a fight with a fucking power shower.'

'Oh, so that's it. Some kind of revenge. Not paying you enough attention, eh? So you thought you'd humiliate—'

'Don't talk to me about humiliation! Your best mate did something *horrible* to me, and you don't care. You're not even interested in listening—'

'So everyone else is lying and—'

Spence's feet pounded down the stairs. He skirted round Rachel and pushed Konrad two-handed in the chest. 'That's it,' he said. 'You're done for the night.'

Konrad righted himself and stepped back towards him. 'You want to get involved, eh?'

'I told you, you're done.' Spence folded his arms. 'Now go home and sleep it off, or I'm calling the police.'

Rachel saw Konrad's neck tense, his mouth go hard. For an awful moment she thought he was going to hit Spence, or at least push him back – he was almost twice his size. Thankfully, his fire seemed to fade. His shoulders dropped and his breath became fast and broken. He pushed his fingers to his eyes as tears slipped down his cheeks.

He couldn't treat her like that, no matter what he thought she had done – and it made her sick to think that she was seeing a violent side to his personality that he'd kept hidden – but he looked so distraught that even through her anger, she felt the urge to hold him, to make it better.

'Konrad,' she said, reaching for him. 'Come inside. Let's sit. We–'

He flinched from her touch. 'Just piss off, okay? Pete told me not to get involved with you. He told me you were trouble, but I didn't listen to him.'

Spence turned Konrad towards the door. 'I think you'd better go.'

Konrad shrugged him off. 'Fuck you,' he said. Then to Rachel, 'And fuck you.'

He shoved the front door as he left. It bounced off the wall and came to a shuddering stop.

'Jesus Christ,' Spence said, closing it gently.

'Oh god,' Rachel moaned, and let go a sob that emptied the breath from her lungs. 'Why is this *happening*?'

CHAPTER ELEVEN

Bank

The woman's voice is helpful. People usually are.

'Hello, switchboard,' she says. 'Camden and Islington NHS Trust.'

'Ah yes, hi, hello. I wonder if you could help me. I work at the Chalkhill Clinic in Highbury, and there's some problem with my wages. Can you put me through to the payroll department, please?'

The spiel isn't necessary, but it makes you harder to refuse.

'No problem,' she says. 'I can put you through now.'

'It's not the helpline, is it? I've been on the phone with them for ages. Can you put me through to a person? *Please?*'

You can hear the uncertainty in her pause.

'Look,' you say. 'It's my anniversary on the weekend and I want to do something nice for the missus. If I don't speak to them in the next ten minutes, I'm not going to get paid until Monday. You understand, right?'

'Sure,' she says, and maybe she does. Maybe she too would like the dull flame of her life caressed for once, by the man she's lumped with at home. It's being able to pull that dumb empathy lever that makes this so easy. 'Let me look.'

Fingers tap the keys.

'I can try Zoe Roundstead,' she says. 'Her calendar says she's free.'

'Thank you so much, you're amazing.'

Click, click, connect.

'Hello, Zoe speaking.'

'Hi, Zoe! It's Ollie Cedar from HR.'

Be sure to have called the HR department beforehand to get that name, and to find out what accountancy software they use. Only the unprepared get caught.

'Hey, Ollie,' Zoe says. 'What's up?'

You've come through on an internal line, not the general help desk number, so her guard will be down.

'Got a nurse desperate to be paid. She's got a new bank account. I need to see if it's on the system. I'd check myself, but bloody Sage has locked up again. If I read her details, can you confirm what you've got?'

'I'm not sure...'

'If it doesn't go through in the next five minutes, she's going to miss the cut off. I'd get her to call you herself but she's gone to pick up her kids. I promise, it'll take two minutes.'

This is the tricky bit. The moment it stands or falls. But if you've chosen the time wisely, if you've found out on a previous call when exactly payroll is run – and know it is five minutes from now – then the odds are good. No-one wants to think they're responsible for someone being broke on the weekend, especially when kids might go without.

'Go on,' she says. 'You got a name?'

'Rachel Stone.'

'ID?'

'CIT42815. She said she...' Break from the phone, pretend to check something. 'Works in St Pancras.'

Clack, clack, keyboard.

'Found her,' Zoe says.

'Great. Sort code, I've got 33-44-55.'

'Not what I've got.'

Let out a long groan, like this really matters to you. 'Dammit. What you got?'

'23-76-12.'

'I guess that means you don't have account 23695434.'

'Nope. 74937482.'

'That's probably her old account. Looks like I'd better give the bad news. You've been a great help, Zoe.'

Use a sort code checker to find out she banks at Lloyds. You should already have an account with all the banks, and know their security questions. Have the answers ready.

Get a high-quality headset and software like Morphvox Pro to make your voice sound female. Call the bank repeatedly until you get a young girl who sounds like being bored would be too much effort. Give Rachel's sort code and account number and say you want to transfer some money. When the girl asks for your SecureID, explain you had it on a file, but your computer crashed, and you need to pay–

'Okay, okay,' the girl says, in all her eye-rolling I-don't-give-a-shit glory.

'So how…'

'I can text you a new SecureID. Name?'

'Rachel Stone.'

After the preliminaries, date of birth, home address, the girl expels a sigh and says, 'I've got a couple of security questions. That okay?'

'No problem at all.'

'Mother's maiden name?'

'Dougdale.'

'Memorable date?'

Give her the date, then say, 'My daughter's birthday.'

She says hold, and a few seconds pass. 'Your code's gone out. It'll be with you in the next hour, but most people say they get it straight away. Anythin–'

Get a smartphone. A crappy ten quid Motorola Droid from eBay will do. Update the firmware to make it into a radio; it has the hardware for it. Think of firmware as instructions that tell the hardware how to behave.

Tune it into the network provider's channel, in this case O2, and stand within range of the same cell tower as Rachel to receive the text message with the SecureID sent by the bank. This could be tricky as in London you can cross a corridor and be closer to a different mast. But you know the old saying about fortune favouring the brave?

Well, there's something fortune favours more.

The planner. The one who attends to detail.

St Pancras Hospital is in the range of a single mast.

Choose a time when she will be there, and be too busy to check her phone when a text comes in. Like the start of her shift, when she's doing her ward round, the conscientious little nursey nurse.

When the code comes in, call the bank again, ask for a money transfer, and give the requested two digits from the SecureID. Within minutes, her wages are gone.

Isn't this a lot of work for money? Wouldn't it be easier to put a scanner on an ATM, set-up a camera on the building next to it, gather PIN numbers, spin up fake cards?

That would be true if it were just about the money.

But it's much more ambitious than that.

CHAPTER TWELVE

List

When the progress bar on Rachel's phone hit a hundred, the tiny green android stopped pulsing and the screen went black. She held her breath, half expecting that to be it, the phone dead, but a moment later the Samsung logo swirled in and swirled out, and she was presented with a registration screen. She checked the time. Quarter past two. It wouldn't take long to register her phone, set the alarm, and then she could go to bed. But she knew there was no way she'd sleep.

Between the mud-thick coffee she'd made to clear her mind, the adrenaline still sparking through her limbs, and the hunger gnawing at her guts, she'd be lucky to get any shut eye tonight. Whatever. She'd get through it. Lily had been colicky as a baby, always refluxing her milk so bad it burned her throat; for the first six months, almost every night had been an endless sleepless trauma. If she could survive that, she'd make it through tomorrow. Hopefully she'd get a few hours before her dad dropped Lily back in the morning, enough to push through the day at work.

Rachel finished her coffee, getting a glob of vanilla sludge at the bottom that almost made her gag, then found her attention drifting back to her laptop. After Spence finally left – he offered to stay the night, but no way was she going to be responsible for him being tired when he flew to Greece in the morning – she'd set up in the kitchen and tried to get her thoughts in order by pouring them into a Word document.

What do I know for sure?

1. Someone is hurting Konrad. It's happened three times in the last week.

2. Someone hacked into my Snap account and sent that photo of me.

3. Konrad's shithead mate Pete replied with a picture of his dick.

4. Alan Griffin is out of prison.

Okay. So what was sending that photo designed to do? To humiliate her? To make her feel ashamed? If she was being doxed again, that would make sense, but only a few people got it, and of those Becca and Spence hardly constituted a receptive audience.

Did that mean the photo was sent for Pete?

And if that were the case, did it mean he was the one who sent it?

What if he'd googled her, stumbled across that photo, and realised he could use it to break them up? She'd been right enough about him not liking her, Konrad pretty much said as much. *He told me you were trouble.* What better way for Pete to prove that than to show Konrad evidence of her coming onto him?

As much as that sounded possible, and the fact that the photo was sent while they were both at the gym made the case even stronger, it just didn't *feel* right.

What felt right was Alan Griffin.

This was torn from his playbook. Same with the disappearing e-mail. He'd been out of prison for two weeks and this was happening. Could that really be a coincidence?

Except... if it was Griffin, why hadn't he locked her out of her accounts? Or do more than send a single photo. That same niggle as before. It didn't make sense.

She pushed off the chair and paced the kitchen. Maybe he was taking his time, getting Konrad out of the picture before he came after her. But what was his game? What did he want? To ruin her life again? To send her back to the psych ward? Get her committed once and for all? Or was it something even more devious? Like for her to go to the police, to implicate herself in his going to prison? She'd always wondered if he knew it was her who got him sent down – at the very least, she'd be high on the list of suspects – so maybe that photo was his way of telling her she was number one.

But what about Konrad's injuries? Was Griffin involved in those too? That made more sense than Pete being behind them. But even though Griffin had threatened violence in the past, he'd never actually done anything – then again, that was before he spent eight years in a maximum-security prison. And as for Konrad being so much bigger than Griffin, perhaps he had met some thugs inside. Perhaps he'd done some favours for them and this was their way of paying him back.

But if it happened that way, *why hadn't Konrad gone to the police*?

Unless they'd told him to keep his mouth shut.

Could that be what the bruises and burns were about? Him trying to protect her? That would make sense, wouldn't it? They beat him up and told him not to say anything, or else they'd come after her.

Rachel slumped against the counter. Her brain felt like it was being stirred. One thing was sure though: whoever was behind all this *had* resorted to violence. Not against her, at least not yet, but it was there, it was part of this, and she needed to be ready. She pulled open the cutlery drawer, found the super-sharp ceramic vegetable knife she'd bought from Seven Sisters market, and pressed the white blade to her fingertip, hard enough to pierce the skin.

A droplet of blood ran down and she brought the cut into her mouth, the rusty coin taste pungent on her tongue. She wasn't a frail five-stone victim anymore, with a tube in her stomach and arms so thin the nurses needed to use a child's cuffs to take her blood pressure. She went to the gym, she did weights. Over the years she'd built up to nine stone of lean muscle. Yes, she had relapses, *episodes*, whatever you had to call them, during her final nursing exams, or when her gran passed away – it was only natural to slip every now and again – but she'd never gone into the abyss, not since she was a teenager.

And she wouldn't go now.

She looked around the kitchen, at the life she'd built with her daughter. The collage of photos on the pinboard by the fridge, the peacock feathers they'd found on a day trip to Richmond Park, the tiny espresso cups with cool art deco designs they used for tea parties. Bits of tinsel from Lily's third birthday were still stuck to the wall, and old streamers, drooping with age, hung off the lights.

Whoever was doing this to her, Rachel wouldn't let them win. She held the knife out, blade pointed at the laptop. This was her house. Her home.

And she'd be damned if Alan Griffin or anyone else was going to drive her out of it.

CHAPTER THIRTEEN

Clothes

The closing of her front door woke Rachel. She'd fallen asleep in the kitchen, lying across the laptop lid. Lifting her head, her neck felt rigid as a steel beam, her skull radioactive, her mouth like it may have been used as a building-site toilet.

Had she taken something? She stumbled through her memories from before she passed out. No, she hadn't. She'd been tempted to raid her stash, but had held off, thank God. That was one slope she didn't want to slip down.

Lily ran into the kitchen and grinned at her mum. 'Can we have popcorn for breakfast?'

'Do you ever have popcorn for breakfast?' Rachel replied groggily.

Her dad came wheezing in, bringing with him an aroma of stale cigarettes and sausage rolls that made her stomach lurch. 'Hiya, love.'

'I understand you two had popcorn last night,' Rachel said, gathering Lily into a hug.

'Just a little. I had most of it.'

It was meant to be a jokey comment, but she could see from her father's crestfallen face that he'd not taken it that way. 'Don't worry about it,' she said, waving a conciliatory hand. 'And thanks again. I really appreciate you taking Lil.'

She expected her dad to go then – the final *thanks* was usually his cue to leave – but this time he loitered by the fridge. He cleared his throat and shifted his weight to the other foot. 'Listen, love. About last night...'

Oh God, not again. A full day at work on almost no sleep was bad enough, but having to start it with her dad's glum-bucket sincerity was too much. 'You'd better get on,' she said, nodding at the door. 'Don't want to be late, eh?'

'You don't remember this,' he said. 'But when you were Lily's age, I'd come home and you'd run over going, Daddy, Daddy!'

'You're right, I don't remember it.'

'I'm just saying you've got a great kid there, so don't make the same mistake as–'

'*Okay*, Dad.'

'You can talk to me, love,' he said, absently fingering the underside of his gut. 'You're... you're my daughter. I want to be here for you.'

She squeezed her forehead, hoping he'd see how bad he was making her head ache. 'You're standing right here.'

'I just–'

'Go to work, Dad. *Okay*?'

Rachel waited for him to shuffle out, for the front door to quietly click closed, then turned Lily on her lap until they were nose to nose. 'So, my little angel. How about I make us *both* some breakfast?'

'Ummm... can I have popcorn?'

She slid her daughter onto her chair. This was why she said no junk food. It was hard enough getting Lily to eat sometimes, let alone when her head had been turned by the lure of tasty snacks.

Rachel stuck on the radio, an old tunable one that had been in this kitchen when her mother was still alive, found a station that she supposed from the song playing – *How Deep is Your Love?* by the

Bee Gees – to be Magic FM, then got eggs, milk, butter, and pota-toes from the fridge. She whisked and sliced, whistling along, singing when she remembered the words, hoping that Lily would buy that this was just a normal morning, and not one where her mother's old stalker was possibly back on the scene.

Eight years had passed since Alan Griffin went to prison, and yet here she was again, feeling hunted, watched, afraid. Living with the constant creeping fear of what would happen next. That was the worst of it, the waiting. The Snapchat photo wouldn't be the end. She could *feel* it.

So what now? More than anything she wanted to skive work and lock down with Lily. But for a start they'd probably have a bank nurse filling in for Spence, and they always spent the first day on the ward wandering into the sluice room every time they needed new bed linen, and she cared too much about her patients to leave them short of experienced staff like that. Also, as it was Saturday, Lily was spending the day at Mark's apartment, with its keypad entry system and CCTV in the foyer. And seeing as he wasn't really a playground kind of dad – he preferred to build elaborate Lego kingdoms with Lily than push her on the swings – they weren't liable to go out much either. She'd probably be safer there than anywhere else.

How about the police? If she dropped Lily off early, she might have time to go there and report what happened. But what would she tell them? Some bloke she knew sent her a dick pic. She had no evidence, not even a screen grab. Even if she'd taken one, what then? They take Pete in for questioning? But if this *was* Griffin trying to break her and Konrad up, then Pete was just a patsy, there to relay to her boyfriend what his slag of a girlfriend sent him.

She felt a surge of guilt at the thought that Griffin was behind Konrad being hurt. After he'd burst in, she'd been resolved: no matter what the circumstances, he had no right to push her over, to make her feel scared. She didn't want to be involved with anyone who would do that. What would have happened if Spence hadn't been there? Would Konrad have hit her? She didn't think so, but she didn't want to wait until next time to find out.

But that morning, missing him like crazy – she couldn't just turn her feelings off – she longed to leap back a week, to the time before this whole thing began, to when they'd spend the day sending each other silly messages, and she could look forward to an evening wrapped in his arms. She, more than anyone, knew how Griffin messed with people. She kept thinking about Konrad crying by the door, sounding so heartbroken. If he'd been pushed right to the edge, and it was *her fault* that he'd got there, didn't she owe it to him to at least make one more attempt to find out the full story?

She piled scrambled eggs and home fries onto a plate, put it on the table, and whispered conspiratorially to Lily, 'We don't have to be at Daddy's for another two hours. If you can help me finish *all* of this, then perhaps we can get cosy on the sofa and watch *Frozen*.'

'I eat it all up,' Lily declared, and grabbed two fries.

Rachel forked some egg and lifted it, but her lips wouldn't open. Something wasn't right. No matter how many times she worked the pieces around in her mind, it didn't complete the puzzle.

But what was it?

What was she missing?

Mark opened the door wearing a preppy brown V-neck over a collarless white shirt, and a pair of pressed beige chinos, clothes Rachel didn't know he owned, let alone pictured him wearing. They were a world away from his standard wardrobe of contaminated tracksuit bottoms, and a T-shirt with a Star Wars pun or a coding joke she didn't understand, even after he'd explained it for the billionth time.

'Coffee?' he asked, nonchalantly stepping out of the way so they could come in.

'You look new, Daddy,' said Lily, her mouth worried.

Mark hoisted her over his shoulders and blew a raspberry on her bare ankle. 'I'll take that as a compliment.'

He actually looked good, the shirt and jumper combo suiting his narrow frame. With his new hipster hairstyle, all traces of his previous dorkiness had been erased from his appearance. It was so unexpected. In all the time Rachel had known him, he'd never once willingly gone to buy clothes. On more than one occasion she'd picked him up some boxer shorts from Primark because it was easier than trying to convince him to replace the ratty eroded underwear drying on his radiator. Yet here he was, dressed like he'd strolled out of a Top Man catalogue.

'I... I didn't want to say anything,' she said.

'Why? Do I look stupid?'

'No! You look nice. Really... nice.'

'Try saying that without your eyebrows halfway up your forehead.'

She followed him into the kitchen and leaned on the stone counter as he loaded a pod into his Nespresso machine.

'So how was the party?' he asked, getting some cups off the tree. 'Pretty wild, by the looks of you.'

'If you must know, it was a chilled night. Couple of drinks. Some canapés...'

'Ooh, I love canapés.' He placed a cup under the spout and started the machine. 'What canapés did you have?' he shouted over the sound of grinding coffee beans.

'You'd be mortified!' she shouted back. 'Iceland!'

'Oh, Rachel.'

She shrugged. The grinding stopped and steam billowed as coffee came out.

Mark looked at the machine for a few seconds, then asked, 'How's Konrad?'

'He's... fine,' she replied. She didn't like the sharp way Mark was looking at her, like he was expecting her to lie and preparing to pounce.

'Going okay is it?'

'What is this, the *third* degree?'

'It's just... you've not mentioned him for a while. A few weeks ago it was Konrad this, Konrad that. We couldn't have a conversation without you muscling him in. Now when I mention him, it's like, *Konrad who?*'

Rachel straightened the lapel of her dress. Should she tell Mark the truth about yesterday, that *her* Snap account was hacked? Oh and by the way, Alan Griffin was out of prison and may be stalking her again? Mark had a right to know, not least of all so he could be prepared in case someone tried to hurt Lily. But now that she'd opened the door to the *possibility* of hearing Konrad's side – and that was all it was, a possibility – it might be better if she held off.

Even Mark knowing what he did about Griffin, she could easily see him listen to what happened, think that Pete was behind it all, same as Spence had done, declare Konrad guilty by association, and demand that she cut all ties with him immediately. And that was before she mentioned him bursting in at the end of the night. The press of Mark's eyebrows told her that part of him was waiting to be justified for all the times he'd told her *that meathead* wasn't good enough. She couldn't face that showdown.

Rather than get him into a panic, it was probably better to wait, at least until she'd got the truth out of Konrad, or given up on him for good. She was on top of it. She'd changed her passwords, reinstalled her phone. There'd be no clicking on attachments. No-one was going to fool this old broad twice.

'Listen,' she said. 'I'm going to head off.'

'But your coffee...'

'I'll get one at work,' she said, stepping towards the hallway.

Mark moved round to block her. 'Wait, listen. We need to talk.' He looked at her expectantly, and when she didn't reply, said, 'You know what it's about.'

'We'll talk about it later, promise.'

He glanced around, making sure Lily wasn't loitering in the doorway, then leaned in. 'This is serious. *You could die.*'

'That's a little melodramatic, don't you think?'

Mark turned his head away, looking hurt. She needed to give him a break. This was their role for one another, as a confidant, a therapist, the one at the other end of the line in moments of weakness or despair. And if it were the other way round, she'd be saying the same to him; more than that, she'd be dragging him by the ear to the eating disorder clinic.

That was where they'd first met. Back then he was so awkward around girls that he conducted their conversations in a state of near panic, wincing between words like someone was probing him in the back with a cattle prod, and looking anywhere but at her. In fact, it was because of his shyness they became friends. After the doxing, she struggled to speak to boys, and their relationship helped her to trust them again. She liked to think he too benefited. He still didn't have much interest in anything not powered by microchips, but he was a lot more confident around women. In no small part that was down to her.

People often asked Rachel why she and Mark weren't together. Despite his geeky veneer, he was actually a catch. Smart, kind, funny, successful, and, if you liked the gawky type, quite cute. But she just didn't look at him that way – and she was sure he felt the same. After what they'd been through together at the clinic, the physical conditions they'd seen one another in, there was no unseeing that.

He lifted his coffee from the machine and took a tentative sip. Still not looking at her, he said, 'You know what you're doing. Ask yourself if it's worth it.'

He was right, she did know. Because the truth was, now this was happening, she needed the hunger. She needed it to cope. When the fear built up inside her, when she felt it suffocating her, the pain in her stomach was a distraction, a perverse comfort, a source of pride at her strength of will. To be starving and still deny yourself food, when it was all around you, how many people could do that? No, it wasn't great to use it that way; an episode would strip your life of everything, if you let it. But she was only a week into it – days if she counted from her last proper meal – so the anorexia voice still wasn't loud. It hadn't yet taken root in her brain.

She still had time.

'Hey,' she said, shaking his arm. 'Mark, Marky, Marky Mark – *Mr* Funky Bunch.' When things were stressful between them, that always got a grin, the hilarity being that he shared the same first name with Mark Walhberg.

He shrugged her off. 'This is the worst I've seen you for a long time.'

'I had a huge breakfast.'

'How much do you weigh?'

'You grab the scales. I'll nip out and fill my pockets with stones.'

'This isn't funny, Rach.'

'I weighed myself two days ago. Nine stone, okay? This week's been tough, but everyone has tough weeks. Even you, with your fancy new clothes.' She smiled, hoping to end the conversation. 'Let's be friends, eh? I've got to get to work, you've got to iron more trousers, and–'

'Stop with the jokes, okay?' He paused and licked his lips. 'I've been thinking that perhaps Lil can stay with me... Until you work things out.'

Rachel's face went hot, her scalp prickled. What was he saying? That Lily should move in with him? She loved that they were close, and welcomed Lily having the kind of relationship with Mark that she'd never had with her dad, but there'd never been any question of her living with him.

'Don't look so panicked!' he said. 'It was just a suggestion.'

'You're not taking my daughter from me.'

'*What?*'

'She's *my* daughter,' Rachel said.

'Actually,' he replied. 'She's my daughter too.'

CHAPTER FOURTEEN

SecureID

There'd been times during her training when she had regretted her decision to become a nurse. Studying the ten billion medical suffixes, going on student nurse placements, as well as filling in the endless personal development admin – most of it while either being pregnant with Lily, or sharing that first sleepless year with her – drove Rachel into a string of mini-relapses. But she did it. She got through it. She qualified, and Lily's teething subsided, and she was out the other side. For the first time, she felt pride at what she'd achieved. Her whole life, she'd always felt slightly ashamed, often without knowing why, so to not feel that way about something was a wonderful relief.

Her job was everything to her. No, it wasn't helping troubled teens, as she'd originally intended, but the work she did was still valuable. It was heartbreaking to see how an elderly patient's world would often be reduced to whether someone they loved bothered to show up for a visit that day, and in those times, to be the one to offer those people comfort, she knew she played an important role in the health system. In fact, the self-respect that being a nurse brought to her thought processes, which all too often seemed to revel in making everything seem as bad as possible, drove her through a day like today, when all she wanted to do was curl in a ball and wait for it to end.

Within minutes of stepping onto the ward, she was too busy to think about Konrad, that Snapchat photo, Pete's stupid penis, Alan bloody Griffin, or anything. The lady in eight was ringing the alarm every two minutes because she'd been fitted with a nasogastric tube that made her think she was suffocating, and the new stroke patient had a fall going to the toilet during the night, so needed to be helped into a wheelchair every time he wanted to void his bladder, which, judging from the amount of times he had to go, couldn't have been much bigger than a peanut. It didn't help that a problem with the scheduling system meant Spence's replacement wasn't booked to start until Monday, so she and Cina, the health care assistant, were manning the crazy house on their own.

For a few, glorious hours, Rachel had no time to think at all.

Late afternoon, however, as Rachel was finishing a round of checks, the hunger that had been benignly probing her stomach began a pain that felt much like she was being knuckled in the solar plexus. She pressed her hand to her abdomen and blew out her breath. *Jesus, what a baby. You used to be able to go days no problem without food.* She shook her head. Stupid thought – she needed to eat. She'd had nothing but black coffee all day. Not good enough. Hannah, the student nurse, kept a box of Jaffa Cakes at the back of the cupboard under the kettle. She wouldn't mind a few going to help a fellow nurse in need.

Rachel headed for the break room, getting out her phone to check the time. Almost four. Halfway through her shift, and still standing. She was about to put it away, but saw an envelope at the top of the screen. Her heart skipped – was that from Konrad? She sighed with disappointment when she opened the text. It was from the bank, saying her SecureID had been reset, and containing her new one.

She pulled up. Her *what?*

She checked the time the message was sent. Twenty past twelve. She'd only just started work when she'd received it, and was probably still on her first turn of the ward.

Maybe it was nothing, an automated message. She probably got the same one every six months and ignored it.

Could someone be trying to get into her bank account?

She pushed into the break room and called the bank, hunting in her bag while it connected, telling herself not to panic, that it was probably nothing. The electronic voice asked for her account number, but in her agitation she couldn't find her purse, so pressed zero until she found herself listening to hold music, Justin Timberlake's *Rock Your Body*. Saturday afternoon, was there a worse time to call?

What could he have done? Pretended to be her and reset her SecureID? What was it used for anyway? Phone banking? She couldn't even remember the last time she'd used that service. All she ever did was check her account and pay back friends, and you could do that through the app. Even if her SecureID had been reset, how would they get the text? Every article she read said that doing a factory restore got rid of spyware, so there was no way anyone else would be able to read it.

Rock Your Body began from the start. She was now number eight hundred and fifty-seven thousand in the queue. Whoever was doing this would know, surely, that she'd reinstalled her phone. They'd know they wouldn't be able to get the text from the bank. So was this just a charade, a ploy to scare her, to mess with her head, to let her know someone was watching? That they wouldn't leave—

An alarm sounded around the ward.

Moments later, Cina was calling her from the corridor – 'Nurse? Nurse Rachel?'

She shook her phone, willing it to connect. Two minutes, that was all she needed, to make sure everything was okay with her account. *Sorry, Agnes, if you could just hold off on your cardiac arrest for a moment more!*

Cina rushed into the break room. Rachel could tell by her look of pure terror there was no holding on for anything.

She'd have to call back later. Maybe then she'd get to talk to a real human before Justin Timberlake did her stalker's job for him, and sent her insane.

The rest of her shift was relentless. One heart attack (not Agnes), two new admissions, including a distraught old man straight out of surgery with an amputated foot who soiled the bed as soon as he lay down, and various other accidents and catastrophes later, Rachel headed out of the ward too weary to even lift her arm to wave goodbye to Bel, the night nurse.

A Sainsbury's Metro was open near the hospital. She stumbled towards it, head fuzzed from the day. The two "b"s, that's what she needed – bath and bed. She was shattered. And famished. Oh, and she still had to call the bank. *Great! Come on, Justin, get that body ready for rocking!*

The door to the supermarket swooshed open. Inside was so quiet she could hear herself groaning. She staggered down the aisle, feeling like an extra in a zombie flick, her eyes slipping off the food. Pancake mix? Nutella? No, nothing sweet. Fresh. A stir fry perhaps. That'd be quick as well. It was half eight, and she wanted to be in bed by ten. Get up early, get Lily from Mark's, lockdown at home and take stock. That was the plan.

She picked a clove of garlic, a head of broccoli, a pack of baby sweetcorn. Chicken breast cubes from the meat fridge, and further along, from the dairy section, a low-cal chocolate mousse. A proper meal. Time to get this under control.

On the way to the till, she grabbed an on-offer bottle of Shiraz, and imagined herself submerged to the neck in the tub, sipping her wine, her body relaxing in the warm water. She took her basket to the checkout instead of the self-service machine, needing to trade smiles with a human, to make small talk about how shitty it was to work on a Saturday night. *We should be at a party,* she wanted to say, and they'd both laugh. The young black girl, braids down the back of her maroon Sainsbury's vest, greeted Rachel with a pleasant smile. 'You need a bag?'

'Please,' Rachel said.

The girl put the items through the till, and filled the orange plastic bag herself. No small talk, but that was fine. The smile was nice enough.

'Ten twenty-five, please,' she said. 'Contactless?'

Rachel nodded and tapped her card onto the machine. It beeped, but no receipt chittered through the metal teeth. She tapped the card again, glancing at the girl, her smile slipping. Acid bubbled in Rachel's throat.

Oh god, oh no, oh god, oh no, oh god, oh no.

Same as before – a beep, but no receipt.

'It's a bit temperamental,' the girl said. 'Can you put in your pin, please.'

Rachel slid the card into the machine, pressed the buttons.

When the words appeared on the screen, it was no surprise.

Card Declined.

She squeezed her face. 'You idiot. *You stupid idiot.*' The checkout girl looked nervous. Rachel backed away, mumbling sorry, the girl calling for her to wait, hold on, but she couldn't wait, she had to get out of there, before she lost it on the shop floor. Someone grabbed her shoulder. She turned her head, saw the security guard, and twisted away from him. Her bag of shopping was still on the counter. 'I haven't taken anything,' she said.

He lunged at her. She jumped back, her heel catching a Walkers crisps display, sending bright red bags tumbling to the floor. She spun around, straight into the checkout girl.

Her expression somewhere between fear and apology, the girl handed back the debit card, then stepped away from the exit, leaving Rachel with nowhere else to go.

CHAPTER FIFTEEN

Stash

Rachel checked an ATM. Empty. Her wages were gone. She had no cash, couldn't book an Uber, couldn't even use her debit card on the bus. Her only choice was to run home.

She changed in a nearby pub, a rancid place called *The Free Man* with warped wood panels and a stale beer stench. The locals turned on their stools as she hurried past the bar to the toilets. Shivering in the cold cubicle, she forced on her running vest, still damp from that morning.

She set off at a sprint, only slowing when the burn in her lungs hurt too much. She swerved round the smokers clustered outside the pubs in Kentish Town, running like she was being chased, her thighs and calves close to agony.

On the other side of the Holloway Road, her right leg gave way, spasming into a cramp. She collapsed onto the pavement, rolling onto her side, kicking out, kneading the rigid muscle running down the back of her thigh, letting go a sob so ragged it must have been torn from inside her heart. Stupid, so stupid. She needed to be careful – the scars from her past starves ran deep in her muscles – and to push her body like that, having not eaten all day, was asking for trouble.

It took longer for her to make the final hundred metres than it had the previous few miles. Even when the cramp subsided, her legs felt so shredded, she couldn't walk. She edged sideways along the pavement, using shrubs and garden walls to stay on her feet, feeling light-headed, disconnected. Down to the second joint, her fingers were numb. She could tell her blood pressure had plummeted.

She fumbled the key at the door, white lights flashing in her eyes, pleading with herself to stay focused. *Don't lose it now.* She got it in on the third attempt and dragged herself up to the bathroom. She peeled off her shorts and vest and waited for the water to be scalding before stepping into the shower. *You'll get the money back. They'll see where it was sent. They'll see it was stolen.* She scrubbed her skin like she was covered in dried mud, then fell back against the tiles and wept. What if they couldn't find the money?

What if her wages were gone?

Coffee. Laptop on the kitchen table. She called the bank on speakerphone, searching for *how to hack bank accounts* as she waited for it to connect. She entered her sort code and account number when the automated voice requested them, and got through straight away. Not surprising seeing as it was after nine. So much for her early night.

She spoke to a young man who, despite the late hour, sounded helpful and interested when she explained money had been stolen. He asked for the third and sixth digit of her SecureID.

'Funny you should mention that,' she said. Leaning close to the phone, she explained about the text she received saying it had been reset, even though she hadn't requested it.

'Can I put you on hold a moment?' he asked.

'Sure,' Rachel replied, and instantly regretted it. Justin bloody Timberlake, still rocking his body. Did he ever take a break? How about laying his stupid body down and shutting the hell up. To stay sane, she focused on the laptop. The search returned a page of articles actually called *How to Hack a Bank Account*. It was *that* easy? She opened a number of the pages in their own tabs.

He came back. 'Hi, hello. I can see the SecureID request was made by phone, around midday.'

'Someone can call and do that?'

'They'd have to go through security.'

Rachel grabbed her dressing gown at the neck. She glanced at the curtains, making sure they were closed. 'I had over two thousand pounds. It's all gone.'

'A payment was made to... Konrad Nowak, at twenty-five past twelve. The entire balance.'

She took the phone off speaker. 'I didn't do that.'

'I'm not sure how—'

'Someone rang pretending to be me.'

'Please stay calm.'

'I am calm!'

'You're saying it's fraud?'

Finally, she was getting somewhere. 'Yes! Yes! It's fraud.'

'The problem is... do you know this Konrad Nowak? I can see lots of payments with that person, both to him and from him.'

They were always splitting the cost of things, with one paying the other back online.

'But not all my money,' she said.

'Still. It's....'

He let the words hang.

She was almost too afraid to ask. 'It's what?'

'Are they *all* fraudulent payments?'

'No, of course not.' She felt like she was clinging to a frayed rope that was one wrong move from snapping. 'It's just this... this one...'

His voice dropped to a whisper. 'Listen, Miss Stone. I can put this through for you, if you want, but there's a good chance the fraud department will reject it. You have made payments to this person in the past, and clearly have an existing and substantial relationship with him. It would have to be dealt with as a theft, a criminal case, and be referred to the police.' He paused, and then said, his voice sympathetic, 'Would you like me to proceed with this for you?'

She pictured a police car outside Konrad's parents' house, the officers at the front door, him being cuffed and led outside.

What if he was being set up?

She needed to call him first. If he was innocent, the money should still be in his account.

'Thanks,' she said. 'I think I'll... I'll call back later.'

But what if she was wrong? What if Konrad owed money to some bad people and he'd emptied her account to pay them back? That would certainly explain the bruises and burns.

No way. That was ridiculous. It'd mean their whole time together had been a sham. She didn't believe it. All those times they'd kissed until their lips were sore and their jaws numb, the nights they'd slept in each other's arms, you couldn't fake that.

Could you?

Rachel brought up Konrad's number and pressed dial. She clutched the phone by her ear, waiting for it to ring, thinking about how best to start – by talking about last night, trying to get the truth, or by launching straight into her missing wages?

Nothing was happening on the phone. She pulled it from her ear and checked the screen, thinking she hadn't pressed dial.

Still connecting.

That was weird. It either rang or went to his voicemail. Never this delay.

She hung up and tried again. The same thing happened – still connecting. She counted the seconds, hoping it would calm her breath, stop the dread rising through her.

One minute passed, one and a half. It was like the phone was toying with her, seeing how far it could push her before she snap–

An automated voice cut into the silence.

This number is no longer available. Please hang up.

Rachel stared at her phone as though she'd felt it twitch.

She called again.

Same wait, same message.

This was insane. Had Konrad been playing her this entire time? Her whole body was beating faster and faster, the pulse in her neck, the blood in her head. What now? Find him? Until a few weeks ago, he shared a student apartment on Caledonian Road with Pete and another bloke, a skeggy place filled with crusted Pot Noodle tubs, half smoked joints, and wet bath towels left on the floor for so long they'd developed sentient forms of fungal life. Seeing as he was spending most nights at hers, he'd given it up to save money and shifted his stuff back to his parents in High Barnet. Or at least that was what he'd told her.

What if he'd moved out because he was already in debt?

She lurched from the chair, painfully catching her hip on the kitchen table. The police, she had to report it. But how? By phone? Or would she have to go to the station too? She pictured herself in a cold interview room, trying to explain it all to a tired sceptical sergeant pissed off at pulling the night shift for the third week in a row.

What about Konrad's parents? The tube was still running. She could go there and tell them everything – the injuries, the drinking, the missing money. But High Barnet was right at the end of the Northern Line, plus another ten-minute walk. It was so cold outside, and she was beyond exhausted, that it couldn't have felt further away if it had been on the moon. She had fifty quid for emergencies in the house, so could get a taxi – but it would cost most of that, and what if she needed money tomorrow? Also, seeing the state of her, his parents might think she'd lost it and not believe a word she said.

No, it was better she stayed here, finally got some sleep, and dealt with it in the morning.

Rachel found herself heading up the stairs, and opening the airing cupboard opposite the bathroom. She unfolded a step stool, climbed on it, and felt around for a hidden shelf above the door.

She shouldn't be doing this, of course she shouldn't, but why did she have her stash if not for times like now? She'd resisted so far, but enough was enough. She wanted to sleep with an intensity close to desperation. Would it be so bad to get some rest? It was this, or spend the night spiralling down. Which would be better for her head?

She found the money box and the key tacked to the wall, and brought them both down. Sitting on the edge of the bath, she unlocked the box and sifted through the small clear bags inside, each one neatly labelled: Fentanyl, Tramadol, Xanax, Ambien, Clonazepam. She'd been collecting the pills for years, since she'd found her mum's war chest of prescription drugs after she'd passed away. Others came from her gran after she was diagnosed with cancer – she refused to take anything once she started chemo, complaining they made her too lethargic. Many had been prescribed to Rachel herself during her stay in hospital.

She tried to stick to some rules when it came to her stash. Never take a sleeping pill when she was alone in the house with Lily. Only take the opioids like OxyContin when her body hurt so bad she couldn't haul it out of bed, and not because the buzz made her feel happy and relaxed, and as though all the problems in her life had nothing to do with her.

Clonazepam, that's what she needed. Something mild to help her sleep, then work out what to do in the morning with a clear head. She took a blister strip from the bag and pressed one of the pills into her hand. It was fine for her to do this. It was only a problem if she let it become a problem.

She pushed a second pill into her palm.

Fresh start tomorrow.

CHAPTER SIXTEEN

Love

There's this story, or parable, or whatever.

A wise old man is strolling through a forest. Think hazy sunlight, birds flitting between branches, a peaceful trickle coming from a nearby stream. It's afternoon, the air fresh but warm. He comes to a clearing where a traveller is hunkered by a fire, devouring a freshly cooked chicken.

'You enjoying that chicken?' the old man asks.

'I *love* chicken!' the traveller replies, and wipes the grease from his chin.

The wise old man ponders this. 'You say you love chicken?'

'I sure do.'

'You love chicken so much,' said the old man, 'that you took this one, murdered it, burnt its remains, and now you're eating its corpse. No, my friend – you love *yourself*. You knew the chicken would taste good, so you took it. You took it because it made you happy.'

The traveller glanced at the chicken leg cooling in his hand, and his mouth tightened.

'You took it,' the wise old man said, 'because you could.'

PART TWO

CHAPTER SEVENTEEN

Regret

The first time Alan Griffin ruined Rachel's life, her weight dropped to under six stone. Two weeks after her eighteenth birthday – which she spent in bed, pretending to have the flu – she collapsed in the kitchen while making a celery dip. She came round to a headache, blood in her hair, and her grandmother on her knees, wailing. Rachel must have passed out and hit her head on the corner of the table.

'If it happens on the stairs...' her gran had said. She too had lost weight. A big woman, wide as well as tall, her cable knit jumper was as shapeless as a blanket. She moved through the house forever looking up and around, as though expecting someone to smash through the ceiling and drop on a rope. What did this man want? Why wouldn't he stop?

They agreed Rachel should go to hospital. The same day they transferred her to the eating disorder clinic, which refused to let her out. She didn't mind so much – the specialists, the therapists, the nutritionists, they were like her personal guards, protecting her from Griffin. He'd never be able to get to her in there.

Life narrowed down to food. She looked less like a human and more like a ladder, tall and jutting. The days passed in a constant state of choice – *Should I eat? Or should I not?* Most of the time, she chose the latter. It was hard to focus on anything else when you were starving. Anxiety, depression, self-loathing, they were nothing compared to it. Once you were so hungry you could feel your stomach digesting itself, it was hard to be crushed by the knowledge that this was your life, and you'd wasted it.

When she stopped eating completely, they transferred her to the psychiatric ward at Edmonton. There they pushed a tube so far up her nose that it scratched her throat, and slid grey grainy frog-spawn-smelling slush direct to her stomach. Enough to keep her alive. The few friends that still visited, pleaded with her to "come out of it", like she'd belligerently locked herself in a cupboard. They didn't realise she didn't mind being there. She'd seen the truth of the world, how it was relentless and cruel, and wanted nothing more to do with it. *This must have been how my mother felt*, she thought, lying in bed, dosed on OxyContin for the pain in her muscles, and longingly watching a tray of lasagne being slid from the oven on television, the meat sauce bubbling through the cheese crust. *No wonder she wanted out.*

Rachel's brain began to feel rubbery and unreal. She shifted into a different state of being, a fasting high, like those religious nuts in India squatting on mountaintops and surviving on wild berries. She became ethereal, pure spirit, disconnected from her body, floating above the mortals slaving below, always succumbing to their weaknesses. No self-control, any of them. Their petty fears, their petty dreams, their petty, petty lives. The world was all shimmers and illusions, but she was outside of it.

It couldn't hurt her anymore.

The flesh ebbed from her bones. Her weight dropped to five stone, terminally low. She hated the feeding tube in her nose and kept pulling it out, so they fitted a PEG tube into her stomach. Doctors warned of cardiovascular problems, kidney damage, osteoporosis, and, eventually, death.

Rachel didn't know what exactly switched in her head to make her fight back. Maybe it was group therapy with the other drastic cases in psych, the older women who'd starved themselves for twenty years. They'd been destroyed by the disease. Toothless, shrivelled, arthritic. A world from the glamorous *#thinspro* girls Rachel followed on Tumblr, the ones in crop tops and high-waisted shorts, over-sized shades propped on their fragile faces, making them look like a strange but beautiful race of human insects. That wasn't reality. *This* was reality: Rita from Enfield, one of the women from group, single, jobless, childless, and worn to the bone.

Or maybe it was the soft-touch psychological support finally having an effect. It wasn't like when her mother was young, and anorexia was barely known, let alone understood. They no longer strapped you down and sent a few hundred volts through your skull, hoping, perhaps, to zap you into wanting an extra plate of spaghetti at dinner. If that were the case, she'd have stuck her finger in a plug socket years ago. She didn't *want* to be like this. She just didn't know any other way to cope.

But what really kick-started her recovery was her friendship with Mark, and what he helped her do. They hadn't known each other long, maybe a couple of months – less with her repeated stays at psych – but friendships in the clinic developed with a speed and intensity you didn't get in the outside world, especially when they started on the back of the darkest shames and deepest secrets revealed during group therapy.

He was the one who tracked down Alan Griffin.

Now that she was in hospital, she thought that Griffin would leave her alone. Wrong. He posted updates on both her Facebook profile and the fake Twitter account he'd created in her name, things like *Still locked in the nut house where I belong*, and *I'm going to tell you the truth for once – I'm doing all this to myself.*

He also trolled her on eating disorder forums, accusing her of faking, turning the other users against her. That was how Mark had found him. He'd taken the troll's name, Scarlett Bishop, cross-referenced her posts with others on the same forum, and found another user called MsWild connecting from the same IP address. Deep web searches on those names threw up another: Betty Wild. They found that user harassing people on numerous websites, from teen hangouts, to conspiracy clubs, to a forum where people posted reviews of Michelin-star restaurants.

Mark opened a spreadsheet and checked them one by one, making notes on when the user joined, the number of posts, anything suspicious on the profile. 'You've got to be fastidious,' he said. 'Leave no digital stone unturned.'

Finally, they got a good lead – a user called B. Wild on a Googlebot cached copy of the member's page for a restricted Yuku forum, wearethebest.yuku.com.

'It's just another forum,' Rachel said.

'No stone unturned.'

'What does it matter? It's members only.'

'They're amateurs.'

Mark got the website version number, 3.3.1.2, from the login page, then loaded a website called xcor3.ws.

'Public forums like Yuku are full of holes,' he said, clicking on a link called Yuku_3.3.1.2_perl_exploit. A page of programming code that looked, to Rachel, to be entirely composed of colons, brackets and dollar signs appeared on the screen. 'This script finds holes in the Yuku software to extract the user passwords.'

He saved it as gotcha.perl, then opened a little black window and typed: gotcha.perl wearethebest.yuku.com

The script returned a list of users, each followed by a plain text password. Mark chose one and logged in.

This forum was different from the others, the chats general, about football, nights out, holidays. No trolling. Mark clicked on a page called *Ski trip pics*, and there he was, the man who'd stolen a year and a half of Rachel's life. He was sitting with two other guys outside an Alpine bar, beers on the wooden table, the slopes sun-glossed behind them.

The caption read: *Mad times in Morzine with Tommy K. and B. Wild.*

'We still don't know his name,' she said. 'Unless it's really B. Wild.'

'We're not finished yet.'

The page was filled with more pictures of the same man. Relaxing in a hot tub, holding a long fork dripping with fondue cheese, waving his ski poles into the clear blue sky. Mark saved the photos as jpegs, and loaded them into PicTriev.com. The first couple returned nothing, but the third brought up the same photo on Flickr.

The name on the Flickr profile?

Alan Griffin.

They went outside so Mark could have a cigarette in the shelter round the side of the clinic.

'We've found him,' she said, pulling her cardigan tight against the chill. 'What now? The police?'

'All we've got is him trolling you on the ana forum – that's if they even listen to us.'

Rachel rubbed her eyes. She should have known not to get excited. 'Thanks for try–'

'I *do* have one idea.'

'Go on...'

'Have you heard of the dark web?'

Rachel shrugged. 'Tell me.'

'It's a place on the World Wide Web that's lawless. There are kiddie porn websites, snuff films. You can buy drugs and guns.'

'A gun? Thanks, but I'd rather not swap the clinic for a prison cell.'

'Not *that*.' He flicked his butt into the bushes. 'I've a better idea.'

He'd seen it on an American cop show, CSI: Miami, or Criminal

Minds. Someone paid a hacker to plant paedophile pictures on this guy's computer and he went to prison. They could hire a hacker on the dark web to do the same.

A world without the spectre of Alan Griffin...

'I couldn't afford it,' she said. 'Not unless they're happy to get paid in angst and diet tips.'

Mark tapped out another cigarette. 'I've got money,' he said, cupping his mouth. The flared lighter filled his gaunt face with hollows. 'I'm a cryptocurrency king.'

'A crypto-who now?'

'I've been into Bitcoin from the start.'

She shook her head. 'Bits of coins, whole coins, I can't take your money.'

He gave her a *how droll* smirk. 'We're friends though, aren't we? We're real friends, right?'

'Yes, we're friends. That's why—'

'That's why we're doing this.'

'I'll pay you back, I promise,' Rachel said, throwing her arms around him.

He didn't seem to know what to do with his own, and held them in a wide hug around where she might be, if she were ten times the size.

With Griffin's real name and his photo, they found his LinkedIn profile. They couldn't access his personal details, like his e-mail address or phone number, but they could see he was working as a Network Engineer for Credit Suisse.

'Got you,' Mark said.

What he did next amazed her more than anything else. Pretending to be Alan Griffin, speaking with a confidence she'd never heard before in his voice, Mark rang the HR department at Credit Suisse, said he had moved house, and asked them to confirm what address they had for him on their files. And they told him! He lived at sixteen Eversdale Close in Thatcham, a town west of London.

Rachel gawped. 'You can't look someone in the eye when you're talking to them, but you can do *that*?'

'Don't need to look anyone in the eye on the phone.'

'Getting onto the dark web is easy,' Mark said. 'Download the right browser, Tor's a good one, then connect. The tricky bit is finding your way around. It's not indexed, like the surface web. You can't just search for sites. If you don't know where you're going, you're going nowhere. That's why on the seventh day, God gave us Google.'

He typed *dark web websites* into the search bar and selected a link called http://deepwebsites.org. As he scrolled through the list of addresses, Rachel found her mouth slowly winding down. The addresses were long random alpha-numeric strings, each ending with .onion. Beside each was a description of the site distilled to its, usually illegal, essence.

Drugs. PayPal passwords. Fake IDs.

'This can't be real,' she said.

'This is as real as it gets.'

She pointed to a description – *The Hitman Network*. '*This* is real?'

'Let's take a look,' he said, copying the address and pasting it into Tor.

A sleek black-and-chrome website loaded, like something for an upmarket city bar. Mark opened a profile – the avatar was a man's face in shadow, a pistol by his cheek – and read his blurb. *Let me fix your problem. I've been in business for fifteen years, and go by a number of aliases. No police record. I guarantee anonymity.* There were even ratings! He had five stars for punctuality and privacy, but four for value. Rachel fought the urge to slap the laptop shut, and instead clicked on the price list. Murder started at five thousand.

'This is insane,' she said. 'Why isn't someone closing this down?'

'The FBI will seize the site at some point, but that won't matter. Nothing's permanent like in the surface web. Addresses appear and disappear.'

The FBI! Rachel pictured a SWAT team bursting into the clinic, bagging their heads and hauling them to Guantanamo. They shouldn't be doing this – she shouldn't be dragging Mark into her mess. But what was the other option? Hide in the clinic for the rest of her life?

'Listen, Mark. Are you sure you're happy to do this?'

'We're already doing it.'

'Okay... okay. So where do we find this hacker?'

Mark went back to the listings site. 'Here's one. Darknet Hacking Services.'

He pasted the link into Tor. The returned page was blank, except for a single underlined word – a hyperlink.

Bit Chat

'What's Bit Chat?' Rachel asked.

'Take a guess.'

'A kind of chat?'

'Open-source, end-to-end encrypted.'

'Well? Can we click on it?'

'I don't know...' Mark hovered the cursor over the link. He tentatively right-clicked it, but nothing happened. 'Probably opens into a random anonymous address.' He rocked his head. 'You've got to be so careful down here... but you've got to click on something... I don't–'

Rachel stabbed the trackpad, opening the link, and shrugged. 'What's the worst that can happen?'

A Bit Chat installation program flashed on the screen. It completed in seconds, the blue progress bar at the bottom zipping to a hundred percent before they could react.

'Oh, *shit*,' Rachel said.

'That's fine, it's only Bit Chat. Loads of people use it. I use it.'

A plain chat window opened. In the People panel on the right was the name Regret beside a blank placeholder image of a head. The name flashed.

'He's typing,' Mark said.

You've already screwed up, appeared on the left side of the chat window. *Look at your webcam. Say hi.*

Mark rushed to close the lid. He paused as Regret's name flashed.

No need to do that. If I was going to wait for you to look at porn and blackmail you with the pictures of you strangling the bald guy, I wouldn't have told you about it. Would I?

Mark typed back, *I suppose not.*

I've disconnected from your webcam. Clicking on a link down here is like opening the front door to your computer, and there are some pretty scary people hanging around outside. People you don't want to invite into your life...

'I knew there was something dodgy,' Mark muttered. 'Rookie mistake.'

Now repeat after me. I promise to always cover my webcam, or even better, disconnect it when it is not in use.

Mark wrote, *We need your help.*

Repeat it first.

This was not what Rachel was expecting. Mark glanced at her, but her bemused shrug was probably of little help.

I promise to always cover my webcam, he typed. *Or disconnect it when it's not in use.*

Good. You're learning. So, you need a hacker. Here I am.

We want you to put pictures on someone's computer.

What kind of pictures?

Were they really going to do this? It was a *criminal act*. If anyone found out, they would go to prison. But she had to do something – she couldn't bear the thought of fighting through recovery with Griffin still in her life.

Rachel nodded at Mark, and he wrote, *Children.*

Nothing happened. Rachel waited, squeezing one hand with the other.

Regret's name flashed. *Lolz*

'Lolz?' she said. 'Is he messing with us?'

Mark typed, *Are you wasting our time?*

You got his deets? Name, address.

Yes.

No doubt he's running Windows. Most of the sheeple do. I can't see it being a problem...

They agreed on a fee of a thousand pounds, to be paid in Dash, an anonymous cryptocurrency. Give him three days.

Mark typed, *How do I know you won't rip us off?*

What happened to trust in this world?

I don't know you

And I don't know you...

How can I trust you?

You came to me.

Rachel looked at Mark – *well?* His face was helpless and apologetic, like they were sinking and she'd reminded him that he was the one looking after the life jackets.

She turned the keyboard towards herself. *Tell me something about yourself,* she typed.

What was she doing? What was he going to tell her? Where he lived? His bloody national insurance number? He wasn't replying. She had to write something.

Why are you called Regret?

A long pause, then his name flashed. *There's nothing worse than knowing what you had, but lost forever.*

She smiled. That could be the tagline for her life. *What if we regret doing this?*

No refunds :-)

It was this, or spending the rest of her life in fear.

His name's Alan Griffin, she wrote. *He lives...*

For the next few days, Rachel veered between excitement that this nightmare may soon be over, and fear they'd been tricked by some twelve-year-old kid in his parents' basement. At night Rachel woke to every sound, scared the police were coming to question her. Of all the things she'd put her gran through, being sent to prison would top the lot.

On the fourth day, right when she was ready to give up, Rachel went to sit in the rec room after breakfast. The news was on in the background. She caught the headline and froze – *Thatcham paedophile arrested.*

Griffin lived in Thatcham.

The newsreader explained the haul of images found on his computer was one of the largest ever found, some five million pictures. A live feed showed a man being led out of a front door, his hands cuffed behind his back, his doughy sleep-creased face swinging around in bewilderment.

It was a face she'd recognise anywhere.

As well as the images, the police found Word documents detailing the ways he'd like to torture young girls. He pleaded his innocence, but the timestamps on the pictures showed a gradual accumulation.

An online petition, signed by over a million people, demanded the strictest punishment.

Months later, on the day of his sentence, Rachel signed the forms for her release at the clinic. He got twelve years, with the possibility of indefinite incarceration if they thought he was a threat after that time.

Take that, you bastard, she thought. *Who's ruining whose life now?*

CHAPTER EIGHTEEN

Konrad

Despite the Clonazepam, Rachel couldn't sleep. Her thoughts scrabbled around her brain like desperate fingers trying to grip a glassy surface. How could she have been so stupid? Of course it was Konrad! Give him credit though, it was pretty amazing what he'd done. Genius even. Sending that photo from her Snapchat account made her look unstable – it destroyed her credibility. He could even say *she* was a stalker, that she wouldn't leave him alone. Wouldn't that be ironic? *And that's why he changed his phone number!*

All the drama – the injuries, the drinking, barging in and *pushing her down* – had been just that, a performance.

Meanwhile he'd shagged her, stolen her money, and disappeared.

Clearly, he had some kind of personality disorder. No-one normal could do this to her, not while being so charming, funny, and, well, nice. It reminded her of a twelve-year-old boy she'd met during her brief stint as a nurse at Northside, who was diagnosed as a psychopath. Everyone had thought he was a normal kid, until they'd found the abandoned air raid shelter where he stored his collection of disembowelled woodland creatures. They'd been crudely stuffed, sewn back up, and positioned in military rows, facing the opening to the shelter, like an army of the dead ready to protect their master. When asked about it, his reaction had been, *My dad used to collect stamps when he was young. What's the difference?*

Rachel had liked chatting with the boy in the canteen. He seemed to be a sweet kid, sharp, intelligent, self-aware in a way she couldn't imagine being at his age, so friendly she'd sometimes thought they must have got the diagnosis wrong. Weren't psychopaths supposed to be dead-eyed monsters? One of the resident psychiatrists had explained the opposite was true – psychopaths were often the most amiable and charismatic people you were likely to meet. But don't be fooled. It was a mask. Of course, this didn't mean they were necessarily evil, or murderous. Most wanted to have a normal life. But that was the key word: *most*.

A month after arriving at the hospital, the boy had stabbed another kid in the throat with a penknife because this other kid was sitting in his space in the TV room. He'd never even asked him to move.

It felt impossible for Konrad to be like that, for him to have fooled her for almost a year, but that was what had surely happened.

She got out of bed. Was there any more depressing a time to be alone with your thoughts? No wonder suicides spiked in the dead of night. She unfolded the step by the airing cupboard and brought down the money box. She needed to put it somewhere further away, harder to reach, less of an immediate temptation, but that was a discussion for another day. She couldn't live with her head like this. The sleeping pills hadn't worked. *Happy bloody birthday to me.*

She took an OxyContin – Lily wasn't there, so it was fine – and drifted downstairs. May as well get comfortable. Rachel flicked on the television and sifted through the usual twilight rubbish bin of repeats, terrible films, and bad sitcoms that should've been euthanised after the first season. Fortunately, Good Eats UK was showing an old episode of Bake Off. She stretched out and pulled the crochet blanket they kept on the sofa over herself. At the sight of the cakes, her stomach made a sound like a sick dog. As the pill kicked in, softening the sharp edges of her mind and sending a rush of warmth down her spine, she imagined the soft sponge in her mouth, the taste of the sweet sticky caramel on her tongue.

By seven, Rachel couldn't lie on the sofa any longer. She'd dozed for an hour, but her dreams had been fraught and frantic – lots of explaining and sorting, ending in inevitable failure – and it felt better to be up. She went to the kitchen to make a coffee. No more pills. She barely remembered the hours spent zoned out to the TV. She half filled her coffee with cold water, slugged it, prepared another and took it to the shower.

She'd decided to go first to Konrad's parents, before thinking about the police. She had no evidence he'd done anything wrong – where was the proof he'd hacked into her Snap account? Or that he got her SecureID reset and transferred her wages to himself? The last thing she wanted was a he-said she-said situation. His parents were good people, they were a respectable family; his dad was an aeronautics engineer, and his mother, aside from raising five children, painted floral watercolours which she sold through her website. If Rachel told them about Konrad stealing her money, they'd be mortified. They might even pay it back themselves.

After spending half an hour gazing blearily into her wardrobe – she settled on all black, jeans and jumper, plus sunglasses to hide her tired eyes – she headed into the dank morning and got on the Northern Line at Archway. Aside from a huddle of middle-aged ravers at the other end of the carriage, who shambled into the gloom at East Finchley, her carriage was empty.

She watched the greyness of north London chug past the window and tried not to think of the other couple of times she'd made that journey, Lily excited on Konrad's lap, to his parents for a Sunday lunch – or at least their Polish variation on it, the greens replaced with sauerkraut, and a sausage shoehorned onto the plate. She'd loved those afternoons at their house. With his four siblings, brother Noel already married with two of his own, it was always so busy.

They'd never had roast dinners when she was growing up. Her dad either ate in front of the TV or, after a row with her mum, went for junk food. The times her mum sat with her at dinner, always something like spaghetti hoops on toast, she'd push the food around her plate until Rachel finished. To go from such an austere family setting to passing platters of roast lamb and heaped bowls of buttered potatoes, while everyone talked over each other about politics, or renewable energy, or something philosophical, such as whether any of us are truly free, felt to her like someone had opened a door and said, *Here's that world everyone loves so much. Come on in, pull up a chair.* More than anything, Rachel had wanted that effortless normality for Lily.

Konrad's parents lived in a modern red-brick house with a large bay window jutting from the lounge. Rachel cut between the cars on the gravel driveway. No sign of his car. Of course not. What did she expect? She pulled off her sunglasses and rang the bell, catching the ghost of herself in the slanted glass of the bay window and wincing at the haggard woman staring back. Twenty-seven today? She'd be lucky to pass for sixty-seven.

Konrad's dad opened the door, smartly dressed in beige slacks, a white shirt, and a thick wool vest, despite it being eight thirty on a Sunday morning.

'*Czeœœ*, my dear!' he cried. He ushered her inside. 'We're not expecting you. Come in, come in.'

So his dad knew nothing – unless he was as good an actor as his son.

'Have you seen him today?' she asked, as they moved to the bottom of the stairs. Laughter came from the kitchen, the clatter of cutlery, Konrad's sisters chatting, probably leaning against the buffet bar having cereal. Rachel watched his father for his reaction, too hot in her coat, feeling the sweat collecting in her armpits and sliding down her sides.

'He's still sleeping. You hear him upstairs.'

'Okay,' she said. 'I'll wake him.'

She took the stairs slowly, wanting to retch. Her money, that was all she wanted, the rest of it, the psycho stuff, the messing with her head, he could keep.

She got to Konrad's door. His snores were loud enough to hear on the landing. How could he be asleep? Wouldn't he be prepared for her to confront him? Not, judging by the volcanic sounds coming from his room, sleeping off an epic hangover?

She opened his door and stepped inside. When was she here last – a month ago? It'd been spotless then, but now wadded clothes, protein bar wrappers, and old copies of the Metro covered the floor. The air was marinated in booze sweat. She spotted Konrad submerged in his duvet, his bare legs sticking out the end. As she approached, she saw an empty bottle of Smirnoff by his bed. *So brazen*, she thought. *Unbelievable.* She pushed his shoulder. Nothing. She shook him, harder and harder – *Wake up, you bastard, wake up, wake up, wake–*

He shot upright, jerking his head around, grabbing the duvet and backing into the corner. 'I didn't...' he muttered. 'I don't...'

'It's *me*,' Rachel said. 'Remember me.'

He squinted from the shadows – then sprang towards her. She jumped back, leaving him to swipe at mid-air. No, not swipe. He'd gone to hug her.

'Are you okay?' he asked. 'Did someone hurt you?'

'Apart from you?'

He found his jeans. She watched his abdomen divide into fillets of muscle as he shoved them on. *Get a grip, woman!*

'I want my money back,' she said.

Konrad stopped, one leg in. 'What money?'

'*My* money. The money I need to pay the bills and feed my daughter.'

'*What?*'

So this was how he was going to be, like none of it happened, she was making it all up.

'I want every penny,' she said. 'Or I swear, I'm going downstairs right now and telling your parents everything.'

He looked down and groaned. 'They'll find out soon anyway.'

'That you're a thief?'

'I did what I had to do.'

So that was it. So simple, in the end. He owed people money – and they'd been handing out regular beatings until he paid it.

'Was any of it real?' She felt tears pressing against her eyelids and tried to force them back. 'Or was I just a... a fucking *piggy bank* to break open when you needed to pay off some–'

'Rachel.'

'*What?*'

Konrad swung his legs to the floor, the bed creaking under his weight, his jeans crumpled around his ankle. He reached for her, like she'd started to glow.

'What are you talking about?' he said. 'I love you.'

'You *love* me?'

'It's not quite how I wanted to say it for the first time, but yes.'

Was he telling her the truth? Or was this one more twist from a tangled mind?

'Let me explain,' Konrad said. 'The truth this time.'

CHAPTER NINETEEN

Loan

'Pete should never have put me in charge of the accounts,' Konrad started, sadly picking at one of the black scabs on his wrist. 'I'm just not that person. I kept missing tax payments – we were fined twice last year. Anyway, last week, I got a letter from the revenue. We owed five grand, should have been paid months ago. I couldn't believe I'd messed up again! We didn't have it in the bank either. I thought Pete was going to kill me.' He caught Rachel's eye, but she looked away.

Sighing, he carried on. 'So next day, I get this e-mail, some loan company. Like a payday loan. Usually I wouldn't even open that stuff, but this time I thought, why not? We had some big invoices coming in. I could borrow the money until then. So I called them, and it seemed legit, they did credit checks on the phone, everything. They transferred the money to my account and I paid the bill. I thought, fantastic, I got out of that one.'

He bit his bottom lip to stop it quivering. If he was lying, then this was quite the performance. It hurt her to see him this upset, and she had to remind herself that only five minutes ago she'd been certain it was him. And he'd offered no new proof that it *wasn't* him, not yet.

'The whole thing was a trap,' he said. 'I'm sure of it. One of them even made a joke about the letter. And when I rang the revenue, they didn't know anything about this bill. I probably transferred the money I borrowed straight back to them! So when they came to collect it, I told them where to go.'

He tipped his head so his cheek was in the light. The faint yellow remains of his bruises stretched out of his stubble. 'That was their reply. After that they said that since I was defaulting on the payment, it was going up five hundred pounds a day!'

'Were they the ones who stubbed the cigars on you?' Rachel asked.

Konrad nodded, his hand over his eyes, like it was up on a big screen and he didn't want to look. 'By then it was eight grand. They got me again the next day, when I was leaving work to come to you. They drove me to some lake and – and I thought they were going to drown me. They pushed me in the water, held my head under. They said this was my last chance. If I didn't pay, they'd come after my family.'

'Oh my god, that's... that's awful. Why didn't you go to the police?'

'Excuse me, officer. I borrowed money off some very bad dudes, and now they want it back with interest?'

In the sickly light, a couple of flies chased one another in tight loops. Rachel didn't know what to think. If he was lying, why admit he owed money? He'd have to see that would make the raid on her own bank account more suspicious. And if he did do it, then what better way to soften her up, to make her believe him, than to say he loved her?

Until now, love had been hinted at, mentioned in passing – he'd said he loved her eyes, her smile, the way they kissed – but he'd never said he loved *her*. Maybe he'd seen her flinching at the word, which she undoubtedly did. The truth was, she'd wanted him to say it, she'd wanted to say it back, she'd imagined the moment countless times, but aside from to her daughter, Rachel had never said it to anyone. She wished she were more like other people who seemed to say 'I love you' as often as they said 'hello', but those words did not come easily to her lips. And yet here they were, being presented to her at the worst possible time.

'So, yesterday I sold my car,' he said. 'And—'

'You did *what*?'

He'd had a second-hand racing green BMW he loved so much that he'd ordered the cleaning leathers from a specialist shop in Germany.

'—My phone, my signet.' He pointed to his empty finger. 'Eighteenth birthday present from my dad. I got the rest from the family bank account. Four grand. It's supposed to be for emergencies, like if one of us gets kidnapped. No-one's noticed yet. You probably shouldn't be here when they do.'

'But why not tell me? Isn't that what you're supposed to do in a relationship? Talk to each other?'

'I didn't want you... you know, thinking badly of me. Like I was caught up in some dodgy stuff. I know Mark doesn't like me, and I didn't want to prove him right.'

'You didn't want me to think badly of you, but you still burst in drunk, late at night—'

'God, I'm sorry. I'm so sorry. I can't believe I did that. I don't even remember what I ... I mean...'

'You pushed me over. I thought you were going to hit me.'

'Oh, Rach. No, no, no. That's not me. I've been all over the place, not thinking straight.'

'Enough to believe I sent that picture of myself to Pete?'

'They left me by that lake. Soaking wet, middle of nowhere. When I finally got a signal, I got that picture of you from him – and loads of messages from the lads, taking the piss. I just lost it.'

'But you know I'd never do something like that, right?'

'Of course you wouldn't. As soon as I thought about it the next day I knew.' He rubbed his eyes again. 'I wanted to call you, but I kind of remembered I did something bad, not that I pushed you, but something... I thought you'd never want to speak to me again. But where did Pete...? I mean, how did he get...?'

'It's... complicated,' she replied. 'It's a long story. But I didn't send it to your sleazy mate, you can be sure of that.'

'I'm done with Pete – the business, everything. I still can't believe he sent you a dick pic. That's so not on.'

She frowned. 'No. It's not.'

'I'm not hanging out with him anymore. Or the rest of that lot. I just want to be with you and Lil.' Konrad was looking at her intently, like he was waiting for her to make up her mind. 'I want to get back to where we were last week, before all this. Are we...? I mean, if there's anything I can do to prove to you how much you mean to me.' He tried for a smile. 'I'll even let you go on a date with Harry.'

She ignored the joke – she wasn't there yet. 'I just need to know. Have you got my money?'

'What money?'

'Your bank account. Let me see it.'

'What? I–'

'Someone called my bank yesterday, pretending to be me,' she said, watching his reaction. 'They transferred over two thousand pounds, all my wages, to you.'

His body jolted like he'd touched a live wire. 'I thought when you said your money... I thought you meant I owed you for like, shopping. Not that I'd actually stolen...'

He sprang up and hunted through the pile of work overalls on his desk, spilling a stack of ring binders to the floor, pulling out an old MacBook Air covered in Panini football stickers. He logged into Barclays, mouth working as he remembered his details, tapping his fingers beside the trackpad while his account loaded.

Rachel's fists were bunched so hard the tops of her nails bent painfully against her palm. The shock of surprise on his face, the agitated glances he kept throwing her way as the page loaded, were making her doubt it was him. Yes, it could all be an act, but this felt like *her* Konrad, the man who surprised her on the morning of their three month-iversary with a plate of smoked salmon blinis and a bottle of white wine in bed, the man who loved to spin Lily round in the living room until they both collapsed dizzy to the floor. Not some psychopath who'd been stringing her along for the past year, waiting to cash in their relationship. The frames of the web page appeared. *Please let it be there. Please let him not be involved.*

The summary page finished loading. Rachel scanned it for his current account.

She found it at the top – it was empty.

A sick feeling swelled in her gut. A whole month's wages. Until now some part of her had assumed that wouldn't happen, that either Konrad was innocent, in which case the money would still be in his account, or he'd stolen it, so she could take it up with his parents. But if they'd *both* been scammed, then it was gone, really gone. What were they going to live on?

Konrad clicked into it. At the bottom was the transfer in from her account, and below that a transfer out, the entire balance, beside the description: *BRANCH WITHDRAWAL FINCHLEY CENT.*

'No way,' he said. 'It can't be...'

'*What?*'

'Don't you see? Someone took it out at Finchley Central. Our office is there – I go to *that bank*. They want you to think it's me.' He threw the laptop onto the bed and took Rachel's hands before she had a chance to react. 'Who's doing this to me? *Why* are they doing it? I've never done... I keep trying... but I don't *understand*.'

Rachel saw her seventeen-year-old self, reading the awful Facebook comments Alan Griffin wrote in her name. She saw him next to her at the cinema ticket counter, paying to see the same film, casual as nothing, as though she wasn't even there. She remembered how it felt to run into the toilets, sit in a cubicle with her head in her hands, and wonder if she was actually going insane. She felt again the fear and desperation that had dogged her every waking moment for a year and a half.

'You believe me, don't you?' Konrad pleaded, rubbing his thumb over the back of her fingers. 'Rachel, tell me you believe me.'

This is what he does to people.

'I believe you,' she said.

Konrad exhaled, hand to his chest, as if he'd been given the all-clear from a disease everyone assumed to be terminal. 'Someone *wants* you to think I stole it from you to pay those thugs.' He headed for the sock drawer, saw it was empty, and hunted among the mess on the floor. 'Let's go to the police.'

'But they'll think you stole it.'

'I have to prove to you I didn't.'

It was so clear – a perfect set-up. If Konrad goes to the police, they arrest him for stealing her money; he refuses to go, she thinks he took it to pay his debts.

'You can't go to the police,' she said. 'That might be what he wants you to do.'

'What?' He leaned against the wardrobe to put on his sock. 'Who?'

'Better sit for this,' she said.

She hadn't told Konrad much about her past, little more than that her mum had died when she was young. But in trying to explain about Alan Griffin, maybe because she was so hungry and tired that she couldn't keep her thoughts straight, she found herself going further and further back, until she had told him *everything*. Her eating disorder, the photo, the doxing, Griffin stalking her, then the hospital, how sick she'd been at her lowest point, only pausing when she got to the hacker. Aside from Mark, who was as guilty as her, no-one knew about Regret. Not Becca, not Spence. No-one. Even now, Rachel would be in a lot of trouble if the wrong person found out – more than likely both her and Mark would go to prison for a long time. She hoped to God she wasn't making a mistake.

Konrad listened in silence. 'Wow, okay,' he said, when she'd finished. 'There's a lot about you I don't know.'

'Now you know more than anyone.'

He rubbed under his jaw with the back of his fingers. 'Right, okay,' he said, staring straight ahead, his face caught in a frown. She didn't know if he was annoyed with her for dragging him into her drama, or simply getting his head around what she'd said. A brief smile came to his lips.

'What's funny?' she asked.

'If I knew all that, there's no way I would've thought you sent that photo to Pete. Not even if I was hammered.'

'I should have told you,' she said. 'I just... It's not something I like to talk about.'

'So you think this Griffin bloke had something to do with what happened to me? The money being stolen from my account? That e-mail from those thugs?'

'It has to be.' She rubbed her face and let out a noise that even to her sounded tired. 'It's the only explanation.'

'You want to grab a coffee? Work out what to do next?'

'I'm going to be late getting Lil.'

'We can't leave it like this.'

She checked her phone. Just before nine. 'Come on then,' she said. 'Let's find somewhere near the station.'

Konrad gave her a relieved smile. 'We can go to the – oh! Big problem.'

'*What now?*'

'Who's going to pay?'

CHAPTER TWENTY

Mum

Konrad borrowed ten pounds from his father and took Rachel to an artisan café on the high street called Bakehouse, the kind of place with chalkboard menus, industrial light fittings, and a million types of gluten-free muffin. 'He'll be as annoyed about that ten as the rest of the money,' Konrad had said, as they'd hurried through the spitting rain.

The café was busy with the Sunday brunch crowd, a melee of raucous kids and hungover parents. The smell of baking croissants wafting from the kitchen competed with drizzle damp clothes and last night's wine burps. Konrad went to order at the counter while Rachel ducked out to ring Mark. She'd missed his call on the way over.

'Sorry, sorry,' she said, sheltering in the next doorway along. 'I'm just running—'

'You do this all the time,' Mark cut in. 'You say one thing, then you change it at the last minute, and we've all got to drop everything to accommodate you.'

'That's not true.'

'I've got plans this morning.'

'I've said I'm sorry.'

'I'm not joking, Rach. I'm sick of being your skivvy.'

Where had *that* come from? Yes she was late, but it wasn't by long, and he never did anything on Sunday morning beside watch Nickelodeon and scratch himself – *and* it was her birthday! – so he didn't have to be such a dick about it, to be honest.

'Look,' she said. 'Give me an hour. I'm just–'

'No. I won't give you an hour. I told you, I've got plans. So get someone to pick up Lil, or better yet, take some responsibility for your life for once and get her yourself!'

Mark hung up before she could reply. What was that about? He'd never spoken like that to her before! Her brain raced back to yesterday morning, his apartment. What had happened? What did she do wrong? She couldn't think. Her mind was a fog. She called her dad; if he couldn't get Lily, Rachel would have to tell Konrad she'd speak to him later. Thankfully her father picked up and said he'd go round.

Back in the café, Rachel found Konrad at the end of a communal table. 'Weird sitting here without a phone,' he said.

'Like primitive times,' she replied, sliding onto the bench.

'Everything okay?'

'Mark's not happy. I had to call my dad.'

Konrad cleared his throat and looked at her imploringly. 'You do believe me, don't you, Rachel? I know how it looks, with me owing money and yours getting nicked...'

She wanted to believe him. As he told her what happened in his room, looking so sad and vulnerable, she'd been sure he was telling her the truth. But now her brain had sifted through everything he'd told her, doubts were appearing. His explanation sounded feasible, and it did fit in with the idea that Griffin was behind it all, trying to break them up. Plus his offer to go to the police pointed to his innocence... It was just, the whole thing was so *elaborate*. So clever. Like on a grand scale. Alan Griffin was many things – cruel, manipulative, devious – but this was a world away from hiding a camera in a tree to steal her passwords. Yes, if he was planning on stalking her again, he'd want to get rid of her boyfriend, and she could see how he could've got involved with gangs or something in prison, the kind of people who'd do him a favour by extorting money out of Konrad. But stealing money from bank accounts? That was serious stuff.

Something about it still felt off.

'Oh, sorry,' he said, looking away. 'I just thought...'

'It's a lot to take in, is all.'

'You kept stuff from me too.'

'I know, I know–'

'I mean, my car...'

Rachel put her hand over his. 'I'm sorry. I'm so exhausted, I've barely slept for days. I'm not thinking straight. Of course I believe you. It's him, I know it's him. He's trying to break us up.'

Konrad leaned in and took her hand in both of his own. 'But we won't let him, right?'

'The last few days have been so horrible. I feel like I'm losing it.'

'Jesus, me too. It's been... It's been brutal. But we'll beat this creep together.' His pale green eyes went suddenly bright, his smile deepening to make the little dimple in his left cheek she always loved. 'In fact, remember what we were talking about before all... you know, all this. About me moving in. Might not be such a bad idea, right? Have a bit of muscle around the place.'

The switch in his mood made her flinch. She couldn't work out if she was intuiting something wrong in his behaviour, or just feeling jumpy and paranoid, because she'd suddenly realised – *she still had no evidence that it wasn't him.* And the fact remained that her money was gone. What if Konrad had humiliated her, stolen from her, and was now not only getting her to take him back, but charming his way into living with her?

'It was just an idea,' he said, letting go of her hands.

'I've got to get through today,' she said.

'Sure.' He took a sip of his coffee and grimaced, as though it were bitter. 'Whatever you say.'

After coffee, Konrad went home, to come clean about the missing money. Rachel said she'd give him a call later on his parents' landline, and jumped on the tube. All the way back, she swung from berating herself for even thinking Konrad had done anything to harm her, to picking apart his story like a legal defence team, to resolving never to see him again, because if there was even an atom of doubt in her mind that it was him – and not just him, what about Pete? That fake tax letter to their business? He was quite involved in all this, with that and the dick pic, now she thought about it. And if *either* of them were involved, then she could never see Konrad again. She couldn't expose Lily to that risk.

Rachel wasn't thinking straight. Of course it wasn't Pete. This was the bloke who spent half the night on Konrad's birthday staggering around with his fly open because he was too drunk to button it up. A criminal mastermind he was not. And Konrad! What had he done wrong? Nothing, except been her boyfriend. Because of her, he'd been beaten, burned, drowned, and scammed out of all his things. Griffin had done this. Alan Griffin. So what if it was elaborate? He'd had eight years to plan his revenge!

When she got home, she'd call Konrad. See if he wanted to come over later. Start rebuilding their relationship.

But what if it was already ruined? What then? Could she take Lily and run away? Sell the house, start afresh? The way the area was changing, gentrification reaching even her high street, transforming caffs into cafés and corner shops into mini supermarkets, it was probably worth quite a lot.

Rowena, who worked on the ward before Spence, lived in Australia. Didn't she have a job at a private practice in Sydney? Rachel pictured herself on Bondi beach with Lily, sitting on a towel and looking at the swelling sea, the sun drying the water from their skin. Maybe they could learn to surf together? They could go out every morning, early, while it was still quiet, to lie on the boards and chat about some boy Lily fancied at school while waiting for the next wave.

As quickly as the daydream came on, it disappeared, and she was back in the clammy carriage, back to her dry throat and burning eyes and headache.

Back to being terrified of what was going to happen next.

When she got home, her dad was watching *Frozen* with Lily. Rachel breezed in, smile rigid, saying, *I'm just getting a drink* as she headed straight to the kitchen. She yanked open the cupboard under the kettle and rooted inside for her tub of Ensure. Where had she put it? She couldn't find anything in this house! It was filthy in here, that was why she couldn't think. She found the pastel green tub behind a stack of breakfast-crusted bowls on the counter, and fumbled off the lid. No clean glasses. She flipped on the tap, found a mug that wasn't too dirty, and ran it under the water, using her fingers to—

'I'm glad you're back, love.'

Rachel spun and yelped, nearly dropping the mug. 'Bloody hell, Dad,' she said, pressing a shaking hand to her chest.

He was standing by the fridge, shoulders hunched, like she was the one who'd summoned him, and he was expecting a telling off. 'I got you a card,' he said. 'Little something in there for you and Lily. It's by the telly.'

'Oh... thanks, Dad.'

She saw his eyes catch the open tub of Ensure, and his mouth tighten. 'We need to talk.'

'This isn't the right time.'

'I know I was away for a long—'

She groaned and turned back around. The tap was still running, so she filled the mug and turned it off.

'No,' he went on. 'I'm going to say this and you're going to listen.

You've got a lovely girl there. A beautiful little girl. Don't do what I did. Don't do what your mum did—'

Rachel slammed the mug down and faced him. 'I told you, I don't want you talking about Mum!'

'You know nothing about your mum.'

'I know what you did to her.'

'You were a baby.'

'I was eight when you left!'

'You only heard what she told you.'

No way. Rachel had been there, she knew what happened. She was the one who grew up with her parents! Although she could think of a few more accurate terms to describe the experience. She survived them, she suffered them, she bore the brunt of them. Not that either was cruel, more they were too caught up in their own psychodrama, with her eating and his drinking, the two of them forever shrieking and bellowing at each other, until they were both gone.

'This isn't about me, or your mum,' her dad said, wiping his brow with his sleeve, leaving a dark sweat patch on the denim. 'This is about *you*. You're shrinking in front of me. I can't just stand by while—'

'Then leave.'

'I watched your mum do it, and I won't—'

'After you left to get pissed with your mates—'

'I was on the streets. I was homeless.'

'Good! You deserve it. I hope it was cold and miserable every night.' Her heart was pounding, her body trembling. Who was he to tell her off? He had no right. None at all.

'I didn't want to leave you,' he said, his voice not much more than a whisper. 'But she wanted me out. She said it was because of the drinking, but I was never violent. I never hurt her, or you. Think about it, love. I never did anything, did I?'

'Fine, you didn't beat us up,' Rachel said.

'So why would your mum throw me out?'

'Because you were a drunk.'

'She wanted me to go so she could, you know, *end it*. That's what really happened.'

An image of her mum on the back step flashed in her mind, her thin fingers lifting a cigarette to mouth as she stared at the darkening sky. Was she expected to believe he was the victim here? 'I'm not listening to you.'

'She got rid of me, then she got rid of you—'

'No – that's not what happened. She was sick.'

It was infectious, her illness, that's why Rachel had to move in with her gran. She remembered her mum explaining, tears in her eyes, that it wouldn't be for long, a few weeks at most.

'I won't let you do the same thing to Lily,' he said.

Rachel looked at her dad, and a strange laugh escaped from her lips. Here he was, this man who she barely knew, this impostor of a father, lecturing *her* about how to be a good parent!

'Get out,' she said. 'You get out right now, or I'm going to throw you out.'

He faced her, back straight, tall enough to tower over even her. 'How many times has the little one stayed at mine the last few weeks? Four? Five? She's with Mark some nights too, right? You can't see it, but I—'

'But you nothing!' She dragged him away from the fridge. 'Get out – get out now!' She pushed him back through the living room, towards the front door. 'And don't you worry about your granddaughter staying with you anymore, because you're never going to see her again!'

CHAPTER TWENTY-ONE

Text

Rachel gnawed the back of her knuckle as she stared at Alan Griffin's face on LinkedIn. Such a nothing bloke. With his office hair and dumpy cheeks and boring eyes. The kind of man who cared more about the football results than his kids, who complained about his wife getting fat while he busted out his belt. It was the same picture as before he went to prison. But what had changed was his status.

I'm available for work after a long absence, and am open to all suggestions. Please contact me.

This was her last lead, and she was excited to see it hadn't come to a dead end like the rest. He had no other social media presence, his Twitter and Facebook accounts were gone, and no-one had posted on the paedo-hunter forum since reporting his release, but here he was, on her screen, looking for work – *after a long absence*. He made it sound like he'd been caring for a sick relative, or been on a round-the-world sabbatical. Bullshit to that. She wasn't going to let him get on with his life while he simultaneously tried to ruin hers.

But how was she going to stop him?

She realised her jaw was clenched and her finger was tapping rapidly beside the keypad, so forced herself to take a deep breath.

Tell Mark, that was the obvious thing to do, get his take on it. Except, she'd already found Griffin, he was right *here*, so what help would Mark be realistically? Especially when, as she looked at the LinkedIn page, a plan was beginning to come together in her mind. And she knew already that he would not approve.

Lily scrambled over the sofa towards her as the bombastic end-credit version of *Let it Go* began. 'Can we watch *Frozen* again?' she asked, her mouth pulled into a pleading angelic grin. At least she seemed happy. After Rachel threw her dad out, Lily had stared at her, lip trembling, and wailed, '*Where Granddad go?*' as though he'd been smacked by a bus in front of their eyes and flung over a fence.

'Why don't you do some colouring, sweetness?' Rachel replied. 'Or play with your Lego.'

'But I want to watch—'

'Okay, okay,' Rachel said, starting it again. She felt guilty enough already about Lily sitting here all afternoon, watching the same film on repeat — especially as she hadn't seen her for a whole day — but she had to do this, she had to take action. Griffin had stolen her money and tried to destroy her relationship. Enough was enough. She wasn't weak, not this time.

She wasn't going to be a victim anymore.

She went back to the LinkedIn login page and moved the cursor over the Join Now button. Could she really do this? Create a fake profile, send him a message saying she had a job, and ask him to meet for an interview? What was to stop him from turning around and leaving? Or acting as though he had no idea who she was? Maybe she could bluff, tell him she had evidence that he was stalking her again? Or she could threaten him. Say she'd write to every recruitment company in the whole country if she had to, telling them what he used to do to her. By the time she was finished, he wouldn't get a job delivering ice to the arctic!

Or what if Konrad bundles him into a car, they drive out somewhere remote, and finish this once and for all.

Was that so crazy?

. . .

At first, creating the profile was easy – she chose a name, Sophie Thomas, as generic as she could think of, and selected a stock photo of a well-groomed blonde woman in her mid-twenties, wearing a cream blouse and black blazer – but then she got onto the employment history section and stalled. What did she know about IT recruitment? Before Griffin went to prison, he worked as a software engineer, so the job would have to be like that to definitely interest him. It didn't help that sharp snippets from the row with her dad kept cutting into her thoughts. The nerve of him. Standing in *her* kitchen and giving out parental advice.

What next? Fire safety tips from an arsonist? Stock market recommendations from the bag lady pushing a shopping trolley down the Holloway Road? Rachel could parade Lily before social services in a bin bag and still be ten times the parent he ever was. Because he left, her mother died. Because he left, there was no father to protect her from men like Alan Griffin.

That was the truth.

She pushed the laptop aside. This headache was making it impossible to think. No doubt she was dehydrated. She stood to get some water from the kitchen, but straight away her head went light, her fingertips tingled, her heart flapped in her chest like a fish on the deck. She flung out her hand for balance, sure she was going to black out, but instead managed to guide herself back down onto the sofa. A sheen of cold sweat covered her skin. Just breathe, take five minutes. Not enough sleep, not enough food, too much stress – a toxic combination. At least Lily hadn't noticed her mum's distress.

Rachel went to stand again, slower this time, but a double rap on the front door made her jump to her feet. That was Konrad's knock, but he had keys. Was someone pretending to be him? Her eyes darted around, looking for a weapon. Had she put the knife back in the cutlery drawer? She got a vague mental picture of hiding it under the sofa. She dropped to a crouch and patted around her feet.

The letterbox clattered, and Konrad shouted inside. 'It's me.'

'Coming,' she replied, and hurried to open the door.

'Sorry, your keys are somewhere in the mess in my room,' he said, holding out a bunch of daffodils, tied with a silver ribbon. He was wearing a white polo neck, a skinny black blazer, and a cautious, but optimistic, smile. 'These were in the garden, and I thought, you know... Happy birthday, Rachel.'

'They're — they're lovely,' she said, taking them, still feeling shaky, not quite there.

'I'm sorry it's not a real present. I'll—'

'No, no! They're lovely. It's like something from a romance novel. A handsome man at the door, with a bunch of flowers he picked himself. I'm just... I'm feeling a bit off.'

He looked at her hard, as though trying to tell her something with his eyes, until she realised she was still standing in the doorway and hadn't invited him in.

'Sorry, sorry,' she said, but before she could step back, Lily darted in front of her and latched onto Konrad's leg.

'You come back!' she cried.

Konrad hoisted her up and, much to her delight, pretended to take bites out of her side. 'I couldn't leave before I finished my dinner!'

He came inside, Lily holding onto his neck, and offered his other arm. Rachel stepped into his embrace, melting against his firm body, closing her eyes and breathing in the marine smell of his aftershave. He exhaled like someone who'd finally made it home.

'I thought we were through,' he said, squeezing her close. 'All day yesterday, I thought that was it.'

Rachel felt the power in his arm and flashed back to him pushing her on the stairs, looming over her, face tight with rage. She twisted away from him, shaken by the thought.

Konrad's arm stayed up, as if round an invisible version of her. 'What did I–?'

'You're letting the heat out!' She sidestepped him, closed the front door, and pretended to shiver.

This needed to stop. That night had been a one off. He'd been pushed to his limit, and understandably lashed out. Saving their relationship started with forgiving him.

Lily climbed back on the sofa. 'Can we watch my film?'

Konrad's lips were pressed together but moving, as if the words inside his mouth were trying to get out. He turned his attention to Lily. 'What film's that?'

'*Frozen!*'

'*Again*,' Rachel said, raising a grin.

'That's lucky,' Konrad replied. 'Because *Frozen* is my *favourite*.'

She went to put the flowers in a vase, then they got on the sofa beneath the crochet blanket. Konrad sat in the middle, holding Rachel's hand. She asked him how it had gone with his parents.

He glanced at her sideways, and flashed a smile. 'Don't worry about it.'

A chill spread through her chest. Don't *worry* about it? He stole four thousand pounds from them, made it out to be a massive deal, and now it was nothing? She wanted to peek between the curtains, check if his car was parked outside.

'But you said–' she began.

'Can we not talk about the money? *Please?*' He nodded to the film. They were coming to Lily's favourite part, when Anna and Kristoff entered the frosted glen and met Olaf the talking snowman. 'This is the best bit.'

A moment later, Konrad turned his body to Rachel, and said quietly, 'We made a repayment plan. I told them I needed the money for the business, and they bought it.'

She returned his smile, but his explanation didn't feel right. It was too easy. He'd said it was a really big deal.

Stop it, you're being paranoid.

'Have you thought some more about what I said this morning?' he asked. 'I mean, I can't stay with my folks forever.'

What about how easily he lied to his parents? What if he was lying about forgetting his keys as well? What if he'd given them—?

He let go of her hand. 'Maybe later, eh?'

'Sorry,' she said. 'I can't think about... I just need to...'

'It's okay. Forget it.'

They watched the film in silence. Rachel focused on the screen, where the snowman was doing his song-and-dance about how great it'll be in the summer, while under the blanket she dug her fingernails into her arm. This was going wrong already. How could they work out how to get rid of Griffin if they couldn't get their relationship back on track? They needed a break from the tension, an evening off. One of the chilled comfortable nights that used to come to them as easy as taking a breath.

She knew what she had to do.

'Back in a minute,' she said, pushing off the sofa, heading for the stairs.

'Hold on,' Konrad said, rising. 'I'll come.'

'I'm going to the loo.'

'I thought we could... you know, chat.'

'We will, we will,' she said, starting up.

He slumped back, scowling. She wanted to say something to make him feel better, so he knew it was her, not him, that she was the problem. She was on edge; she needed to do something to stop that useless lump of matter in her skull from sabotaging tonight by spewing out stuff designed to make her agitated.

Upstairs, she placed the stool by the airing cupboard door, found the key and unlocked the money box. Konrad was here to help out with Lily, so it was okay to do this.

If she didn't, their relationship might not last the night.

After the film, they went through to the kitchen to start dinner. As

Rachel looked for the spaghetti in the cupboard, Konrad lifted her hair and planted a tentative kiss on her neck.

'That's nice,' she murmured, leaning into him. A warm sensation was radiating along the length of her spine, going up her neck, spreading out as it reached her skull and smothering the scared chattering, leaving only silence. It felt as though her brain had slipped into a warm bath, after a walk of many miles through the rain.

Konrad teased her earlobe with his teeth, bringing her back to now. 'I've still got a fiver from this morning. Should I nip to the offy, see if I can get a bottle?'

'A glass of wine sounds perfect.'

He turned her to face him, and brought her close. 'It's good to see you smile. I've missed it.'

When their lips touched, an electric spark raced down the back of her legs, giving her a pleasant shudder. 'Hurry back,' she murmured.

See? Things were already better. She should *definitely* do this more often, like how about every day? Lesson learned – just relax. Wasn't that what Mark was always saying? Or was that accept? *Relax, accept, what's the difference?* They both sounded good to her.

'I want Konrad come back this time,' Lily said, her expression so cutely annoyed, like she was the parent, that Rachel went over and kissed her on the cheek. Lily brushed her off. 'You promise Konrad come back.'

'I promise, my sweet.' Rachel cracked spaghetti into boiling water, and opened a jar of sauce. This was the way to be. Calm, composed. She stirred the pasta and hummed, something classical, maybe *Swan Lake*, she wasn't sure. Her eyes slipped closed, and she found herself swaying. Worry about the money tomorrow. Worry about Alan Griffin tomorrow. For now, just let–

A hand slid onto her hip. 'I got red,' Konrad whispered. She didn't even hear him come back. He kissed her, tenderly, from behind her ear to the top of her collarbone, as they rocked their hips in time.

The surface of the sauce popped and spat on the back of her wrist. Rachel yelped and shook it in the air. That was a shame, she'd had a nice buzz going on, gently drifting. Konrad moved away and opened the cutlery drawer, looking for the corkscrew. *Back to the real world.*

Rachel served Lily her pasta first on her pink plate, then filled bowls for herself and Konrad. As she sat, she caught her breath. She hadn't been paying attention and had given herself the same amount of food as him. Just the thought of eating all that clammed her up.

He glanced up at her. 'You okay?'

'Of course,' she replied, squeezing her face into a smile.

He stared at her, brow furrowed, like he was studying her face for a memory test. She cleared her throat and picked up her fork. *Don't get paranoid again.* She twirled spaghetti until Konrad started his meal. Her heart picked up speed, and the good feeling that only moments earlier had felt so firm inside her, evaporated like mist. When was the last time she ate something solid? Days ago.

She lifted her fork and steadied her breath. *You've got this,* she told herself. *Only last week you were eating full meals.* She checked the table one last time then put the food in her mouth – but straight away it was too much, her teeth refused to chew, her throat closed up. She couldn't breathe. She turned away, pressing a shaking finger to her lips, forcing her jaw to grind the pasta as she reached for the wine. She sluiced it down with half the glass before her gag reflex could force it back out, covering up her discomfort by coughing and banging her chest with her fist.

'Water?' Konrad asked, already half out of his chair.

'I'm fine, I'm fine,' she said, waving him down. 'Wrong pipe.'

She grabbed the salt and a twirl of paper towels from the counter. Not the right food, nothing more than that. Later on, when Lily was in bed, Rachel would have a glass of milk. Maybe mix more Ensure.

She sat down, gave her plate a cursory sprinkle of salt, loaded her fork and checked the table. Lily was busy picking individual strands and laying them flat beside her plate; Konrad was stealing glances at her, a look of amusement on his face. Rachel held the paper towels under the table, her head going hazy, and thought of her mother on the back step. *Oh, Mum.*

In a single smooth motion, she lifted her fork, filled her mouth, and with the other hand brought up the towels, to wipe her lips, and spat it out. Hand back down, twist the paper. She'd eat later, when no-one was watching.

'Lovely dinner,' Konrad said.

Rachel twirled her fork again, and smiled. '*Perfect.*'

Lily in bed, they settled on the sofa to watch television. Konrad sat upright against the arm, and Rachel was propped against him, her head resting on his chest.

'Top up?' Konrad asked, showing her the wine.

'I'm good.' She'd already had way too much. Two big glasses, along with how many Oxys? She couldn't remember. At least two. And another when Lily went to bed? She vaguely recollected pilfering the money box... Whatever. Nothing mattered but right now. The last few days seemed far away, as though they'd happened to someone else, or had come from the plot of a BBC drama she'd watched earlier in the year. *One woman driven to the edge of madness.* But not her, she was fine, everything was just fine. She pressed against Konrad and sighed.

He caressed her arm as he flicked through the Freeview channels. 'This is funny, sometimes,' he said, stopping on *You've Been Framed*, where they watched videos of brides getting their wedding train trapped in cars, grannies toppling off chairs, boys slamming baseballs into their fathers' testicles. Her eyelids dropped, and she glided along on a crest of canned laughter and pratfall sound effects. Through the soft cotton of his polo neck, Konrad's heart quickened against her cheek. She realised he was turning her towards him, and at the same time lowering his face.

They lingered with their lips touching. Slowly, he opened his mouth, and the kiss became passionate. He lowered her back on the sofa, his hand moving to her breast, his thumb tracing the outline of her nipple. She tried to stay focused, but all she could think about was the paper towel by her mouth, the wad of barely chewed pasta inside, and with it a sad feeling, like she was saying goodbye to someone she loved, and she knew it would be for a very long time. *She got rid of me, and she got—*

Konrad stopped kissing her. 'Everything okay?'

'Oh – sorry,' she said. 'It's great, it's fine.'

What had she been thinking about?

He eyed her and rubbed his mouth. 'We can stop.'

She shook her head and blinked her eyes wide, hoping that would stop her vision from splitting. 'Bit tired, that's all.'

He tipped his head towards the stairs, shrugging. She nodded, and he pulled her up from the sofa. Her legs didn't seem to be working right, like her bones had been replaced by ropes, and she struggled up the steps, missing her footing, her head swimming. The light from downstairs faded. In the darkness she became confused.

She stumbled, pitched forward, falling into a pit, but someone grabbed her round the waist. Konrad. She was with Konrad. He pushed her against the wall, his mouth roaming over her neck, his breaths short and fast, his stiff dick pressing against her waist. *Get in the mood, get in the mood.* She rubbed the front of his trousers, making him moan and grind against her. *Come on, come on. Get into it.* But her mind was slippery, her thoughts fled away. Her feet were cold. Not enough food to make heat. She should have eaten more. She'd listened to that stupid voice, lying to her. In what world was it okay for her to not eat for over a day? That'd be like an alcoholic saying, it's all right, it's only one bottle of vodka. What if she couldn't eat tomorrow? What if—

'Rach?' Konrad's voice, soft, coercing. 'Shall we take this into the bedroom?'

He didn't wait for an answer, moving her inside, almost pitch black, a tiny strip of moonlight coming from under the curtain. Too many Oxys. *Stupid, so stupid.* Just one? It was never just one. And the wine. It swirled around her stomach like acid. *Focus! Get it back. You want this.* He pushed her on the bed, their lips pressing, his tongue probing her mouth. It felt large and morose against hers. Her awareness slipped sideways. She forgot what was going on. *Konrad. It's Konrad.* His body was too heavy – she couldn't get her breath – she was spinning out.

'Slow down,' she murmured. 'I can't...'

'I tried slow, but you were falling asleep.' He shifted his weight, something clunked. 'Now I'm going to wake you up.'

The spinning was getting worse. Her fingers went numb. Her body broke into a cold sweat. What was going on? Where was she? How did she get here? Someone was on top of her, crushing her to the bed. She couldn't see in the darkness. She tried to squirm away, but she couldn't move. His hand pushed under her top. *Stop, stop.* Did she say that, or think it?

Thick fingers pulled at the top of her jeans, opening her buttons. *Stop it!* She bucked, pushed out her knees, screaming and shoving as hard as she could. He staggered back, crashed into something. She flipped over, scrabbling on the duvet, desperate to get away. *What's happening? What's–?*

The light came on.

'What the fuck, Rachel?'

She shielded her eyes from the shocking brightness. What just happened? Her mind was a blizzard. She saw Konrad by the switch, the horror on his face.

'I'm sorry,' she said. 'I – I thought...'

'What are you *doing* to me?' His voice cracked. 'I *asked* if you want to go upstairs, and you said yes. We're getting into it – then you throw me off? I don't – I don't–'

'I thought...'

'You're crazy.'

'*Don't call me that!*'

'You've lost it.'

She broke into hard sobs. 'Please, Konrad. I–'

'I'm done with you. *Done.*' He struggled to fasten his belt. 'I try to talk, you don't want to talk. I try to have sex – you make me feel like I'm *attacking* you. I've been through *hell because* of you!'

'Please, Konrad. Listen. I–'

'I'm done listening to you. You drag me into your shit. I've been drowned, beaten up. It's cost me eight grand! And instead of comforting me, you act like *I'm* the guilty one. You really think I'd, what? Steal money from your bank? How would I even do that?'

'Let's talk now.' He was still by the doorway, he hadn't left. She wanted to reach out, but didn't want to scare him away. 'I can explain. Please hear me out.'

Konrad looked at her for a long moment, then nodded slowly, as though he'd resolved some long-standing dispute with himself. 'I loved you, Rachel. I'd have done anything for you.'

She stayed on the bed, stunned, as his heavy footsteps went down the stairs. The front door quietly opened and closed. Her stupor broke, and she staggered out of the bedroom.

The air still carried the seawater scent of his aftershave. She went downstairs and turned fully around, feeling like she'd stepped into the wrong room. *What happened? What the hell just happened?*

Her mobile buzzed on the coffee table. She snatched it up – *Konrad, thank God.*

It was a text, but not from him. She didn't recognise the number.

She tapped the message to open it, and covered her mouth. The phone fell from her hand. She scrambled back, like it was counting down to explode.

The text read: YOU'RE ALL MINE NOW

CHAPTER TWENTY-TWO

Tactics

Vladislav Surkov. Russian guy, high up in the Kremlin. Pals around with Putin. Unless you're a fan of modern warfare, you won't have heard of him.

Distilled to tactics even dullards can understand – feel free to take offence – his strategy is this: instead of attacking your target from the front, the two of you duking it out, mano-a-mano, whoever's got the biggest missiles and the most disposable troops wins, you don't attack at all. You do everything *but* attack. You fund terrorism; you exacerbate regional conflicts, secretly supporting both sides; you spread lies and misinformation wherever and whenever you can. From the ensuing chaos, you take control.

The principle here is the same. Attack at random. Destabilise, weaken. Conquer.

What does she love more than anything?

Her daughter.

But the aim is to weaken, not to destroy. So leave the girl. Instead target work, her job, her role in the world as a good little nursey nurse.

Here's what you do.

Find out the software they use to store patient records. It's easy enough to do — ring the hospital, any ward, say you're calling from IT support, problems in the area, blah, blah, whatever, and ask them to read out everything on the software Help page. They'll tell you that it's called eMAR, which stands for electronic Medical Administration Records, version 2.1.8, made by a company called Principia MCP Medicines Management, which is based in Nottingham.

Next, a series of calls to Principia. The HR department to get names in the IT department, the IT department to get names in the software development team, the dev team to find out they outsource the bulk of their work to a code monkey warehouse in India run by Tata — a place probably bigger than an aircraft hangar and louder than a cloud of locusts from all the clacking keys, with rows of hunched programmers, a hundred wide, stretching into the distance.

Ring Hyderabad to get the name of someone who works on eMAR support, fire a spear phishing e-mail to Gurvinder — spoofed to look like it's from someone at Principia — and you should find yourself with a copy of the low-level design for the software.

Tomcat 8.0 as the HTTP server? The admin console is set to the default address?

You'd think companies would upgrade their infrastructure software to the latest versions, that they'd realise the vulnerabilities in the old versions are well known and easy to exploit. You'd think that, but you'd be wrong.

For software, see people — know their vulnerabilities, and exploit them.

It's as easy as breaking into the admin console, creating yourself a superuser in the central eMAR database, and changing Rachel's password.

As easy as logging into her account and going *cut, paste, edit, delete.*

Easy as calling Linda, the ward manager, with an anonymous tip off from a concerned colleague about Rachel's patient record-keeping...

CHAPTER TWENTY-THREE

Knife

The same sounds that any other night would have been nothing – a bird twittering, a wind chime two doors down, the faint fizz of energy from the lamppost outside her window – seemed as loud as gongs. Rachel had hoped that, despite everything, the Oxy throbbing in her blood might help her sleep. She could still feel it, a spacey undertone to the heavier leaden sensation of shock that had rolled across her mind, flattening her thoughts into a single and debilitating stupor. But nothing short of a general anaesthetic was going to put her away tonight. How was she going to work tomorrow if she got no sleep *again*? She could call in sick, but even thinking about sitting at home all day sent her skittering to the edge.

She drifted downstairs, filled a mug with milk – it always helped to soothe her stomach – and put it in the microwave for a minute. How was anyone supposed to be normal in this world? Physically, in the thousands of years since we lived in caves, we'd barely changed. We had the same limbs, the same ribs, the same eyes, nose, mouth. Our brains were a little bigger, but they were still the wrinkled grey synapse factories they always were. And yet, although a prehistoric human baby was probably similar to one born a minute ago, the world was completely different.

Back then, as long as you protected the front of your cave, you were safe – now you had to be prepared to defend yourself at all times, from anyone in the whole world. People you'd never meet in person could reach into your life and shake things around, just for the *lolz*. How were we supposed to adapt to that? Was it a surprise everyone was such a mess?

If it wasn't anorexia, it was depression. If it wasn't depression, it was stress. If it wasn't stress, it was anxiety, or paranoia, or a cold and terrible void where your self-esteem should have been. And the worst thing? These were the traits being passed down the family line, from mother to daughter, from father to son. Forget genes – *this* was modern evolution. The horrors of our personality going from generation to generation, as unstoppable as time, until there weren't enough psychiatrist chairs to treat them all.

The microwave pinged, but Rachel ignored it and opened the fridge. She leaned into the light, closed her eyes, and let the cold air rest on her skin. The mingling smells twisted her guts – grated cheese and leftover pasta and something citrus, the half lemon she'd squeezed over a salad days earlier. Her hunger felt as fresh as a razor slicing inside her abdomen. She took long deep breaths. To be this hungry, and resist food. How many people could do that? *How mentally strong does someone have to be to do that?*

She slammed the fridge door and took her milk through to the living room. For a while, after Konrad left, she'd entertained the possibility that he'd planned the whole thing, that she'd been the unwitting star of an elaborate masquerade. She imagined him scurrying away, sniggering as he sent that text, to meet his goon mates and sink jeroboams of champagne bought with her bloody wages, but quickly dismissed that idea. How could Konrad plan for her to get wrecked on red wine and painkillers, to the point where she hallucinated passionate fumbling into sexual assault? It was Griffin, no doubt. He probably had a camera in a tree facing her house. He saw Konrad leave, the way he stormed out, and sent that text. Griffin wanted her to rush into the streets, screaming for him to come out, so everyone would think she was losing it. Send her back to psych where she belongs!

Rachel sat on the sofa, logged into LinkedIn, and carried on building Sophie Thomas' employment history. She examined profiles of other recruitment agents, read their blog posts, looked up stuff on Google or Wikipedia. Soon she'd created what seemed to her a convincing past – two years as a junior recruiter at a consultancy called Global Enterprises, then five years as a senior recruiter at Apps IT, before joining Hays Recruitment as a business resource manager. She added in an education history, a degree in management at UCL, and joined interest groups like techUK, Recruitment Analysts, and the Independent Agency Group.

When she checked the time, it was gone two. The next day stretched ahead like a Royal Marines obstacle course – the breakfast battle, the nursery run, a full day on the ward, then getting Lily from Mark, who no doubt was still in a mood with her.

Too much, way too much.

She trudged upstairs, shoulders slumped, feeling like she was heading to the gallows. At the airing cupboard door, she unfolded the step stool. This was wrong, definitely wrong, and she didn't like it – what if there was a fire? Or someone broke in? – but she knew she was going to take something anyway, because if she didn't do something to soften her brain, she really thought it might crack.

Rachel shot up, as fast and breathless as if she'd been drowning. Where was she? On the upstairs landing? She vaguely remembered moving her bedding to outside Lily's room before whatever she'd taken – Ambien? – dragged her into sleep.

She heard a noise, soft voices, cutlery faintly clattering. *What was that? Was someone in the kitchen?* She patted around, found her phone next to her pillow, the sound going muffled when she picked it up. She unlocked the screen and saw a video of a family table, laid with a turkey and all the trimmings. Cut to the kitchen, Tom Kerridge, still in his twenty-stone days, shredding Romaine lettuce by hand into a silver bowl. She pressed the back button. YouTube. Two hours into a cookery compilation. What the literal shit. She couldn't even remember putting that on. To be so out of it that she didn't remember searching for YouTube videos while clobbered unconsciousness on sleeping pills. That could never happen again.

She remembered last night, Konrad leaving, the text from Griffin. Oh god, her wages. What was she going to *do*?

First question, Lily. She was supposed to go to nursery – should she pull her out? But she was probably safer there than anywhere, with the chain-link fence, and one-in one-out collection policy, that in the past had felt to Rachel like ridiculous overkill, but which now was a godsend. What next? The money? If she went to the police, the first thing they'd do was bring in Konrad, and there was no way she could do that to him, not after how she'd acted last night. Even thinking that her wages were gone for good made her want to weep. Mark would help them out, he'd have to. He was picking up Lily today, so she'd ask him later, when she went to get her. It was time to tell him about Griffin as well, although she might leave out the bit about trying to meet him. She wasn't sure yet. She'd see.

She flipped onto her front, wishing she could stay asleep for the whole day, pull the sheets over her head and block out the world. She slid her hand under the pillow – and yelped at a sharp pain.

She pulled her hand out, stared at the slash running over the ball of her thumb, and jammed it in her mouth. Her fingers trembled against her forehead as she probed the wound with her tongue, the metal taste of her blood tainting her saliva.

What was that? Some kind of trap?

She knocked her pillow aside and saw the ceramic vegetable knife from the kitchen, the white blade stained red. She lifted the handle like it was the tail of a dead mouse she thought might still be alive. Obviously, she'd freaked out during her Ambien haze, gone downstairs, found the knife, brought it back to bed and hid it under the pillow, all without waking up. As you do. It was a miracle she wasn't lying here with slashed wrists.

'Mummy? Why you sleeping here?'

Rachel pulled the knife under the duvet.

'I – I made a fort. Last night.'

'But you a grown-up. Grown-ups don't make forts.'

When the dirty nappy did she become so clever? What happened to being barely able to make a word without drooling? Her three-year-old daughter was outsmarting her.

In the grey light, she noticed Lily's lip quiver. 'Mummy? Are you hurt?'

She looked down. Her cut hand was out of the duvet. Blood had run down her finger and collected in her palm.

'It's nothing, angel. I just need a plaster. You get back in bed, and I'll come for a snuggle.'

Lily still looked unsure, and stayed where she was, until Rachel shooed her back in her room and closed the door. The knife. She gathered it in the duvet and flung the lot in her bedroom. Next, her cut.

As she hunted for plasters in the bathroom cabinet, she spotted the money box in the bath. It was open, the bags of medication strewn about. Some had been emptied, the blister strips from inside neatly stacked, while others had been ripped apart, like her stash had been raided by a junkie raccoon.

What had she been looking for? What had she *taken*? Best not think about it too much – she'd never know now anyway. She rushed the pills back into the box. *Sort them out later.* Better yet, bin the lot.

She got into bed with Lily and brought the duvet tighter around them, the comfort of having her warm little body beside her finally slowing her heart. If only she could stop time and live in this moment, just her daughter's morning breath, her beautiful brown eyes, her smile. She'd never want anything else.

Lily put her hands on Rachel's cheeks and, her face grave, gave her a kiss on the lips. 'That means I love you.'

'I should hope so too,' Rachel replied, kissing her back.

'You're my favourite mummy.' Lily crinkled her nose and shook her head. 'I don't like my new mummy. She looks funny.'

Rachel felt a crunch of anxiety deep in her core.

'Your new mummy?'

'It's a secret,' Lily said, working out her hand and pressing a finger to her lips. '*Shhhhh*.'

'What's a secret?'

'Daddy said not to tell.'

She pictured Mark in his new smart clothes, his preppy jumper and chinos. Was he leading a double life? Did he have a wife and kids shacked up somewhere in the suburbs? And what? *He* was behind it all? He was trying to drive her mad so he could steal Lily and add her to his other family? *Good one, brain! Outdone yourself this time.* Couldn't they have been playing families with her toys? Or maybe her daughter was making up nonsense, what with her being *three years old.*

Except... was it so impossible?

What if everything he'd ever told her was a lie?

'Come on, sweetness,' Rachel said, taking her arm, trying to keep her voice steady. 'You can tell me.'

'Let's go downstairs.'

'Just tell me, okay?'

'Off me, Mummy. You're hurting.'

Rachel's fingers sprang back. She stared at her hands in horror as Lily rolled away, off the side of the bed.

Have you finally lost it?

CHAPTER TWENTY-FOUR

eMAR

After she dropped Lily at nursery – on time, for once – she set off for work. Her shift didn't start until nine, so she ran the long way, skirting Parliament Hill, London city rising in the distance, the cold morning misting her breath, the metronome motion of her arms and legs soothing her mind. It was good to be out, the fresh air blowing away the residual grogginess from those sleeping pills. And whatever else she'd maybe taken. That had to stop.

She needed some support, but from who? Spence was in Greece. As for Becca, on top of her performance the other night, which Rachel was still fuming about, her WhatsApp message yesterday, a rather tepid *happy birthdat beeyatch :-) xxx,* showed how much she really cared. So little that she couldn't even be bothered to spellcheck birthday.

That left Mark, who she was going to tell tonight. Except... something was off with him too. The way he was with her when she rang him yesterday morning – *I'm sick of being your skivvy.* And that wasn't her being paranoid. He'd never spoken to her like that before.

I don't like my new mummy.

No, no way. She wasn't going back *there* again. That was just a silly comment, some game they must have been playing.

If she couldn't trust Mark, she couldn't trust anyone.

Maybe you can't.

Rachel rushed into the break room and glanced at the wall clock. Nearly nine. Always ten minutes behind! She didn't have time for another shower, but she had some wipes in her bag, so that would do. She dug them out along with her rolled nurse's dress, and was heading for the door when it beeped.

Linda bustled inside. The ward manager was a motherly woman in her sixties, keen on pastel cardigans and cameo brooches, who seemed to start most sentences by softly saying, *well now*. Some of the managers Rachel had worked for were ex-matrons who liked to stalk the corridors, helping with admissions or a dressing if it was busy. Not Linda. Although trained as a nurse, she'd spent more than twenty years in admin. Unless Rachel popped into her office to chat about a change to her schedule, or a problem with a patient, once a week at most, she didn't see her.

'Hi Lin...' Rachel began, but the sorry-for-the-bad news set of her eyes – it was one of the first things you learned as a nurse – shut her up. A shiver went down her back. 'What's happened?'

'Well now,' Linda said. She tried to smile reassuringly, but the effect was dampened by the dismay in her voice. 'Can you come to my office, please? Once you're dressed.'

Five minutes later, Rachel was in her uniform and meekly entering Linda's narrow air-freshened office. How was it possible for her heart to beat like this and not burst through her ribs? It was going so hard she could feel the vibrations in her tongue. Something had happened – but what? The photo? Had Griffin distributed it round the NHS? Did Linda think she'd brought the ward into disrepute?

'Take a seat, please,' she said.

Rachel sat stiffly in the plastic chair while Linda laboured over logging into the eMAR software, using only two fingers. She was one of those women who kept the same healthy snacks on her desk for years, a box of Ryvita thins, an opened packet of pumpkin seeds, but the amounts in the packaging never went down. They were probably only there to be stared at glumly once all the Maltesers were gone.

'Well now,' Linda said, turning the monitor so they could both see the screen.

Rachel leaned in, but all she saw was the eMAR dashboard – buttons to add new records, to edit existing records, to run a report. She felt her shoulders relax. Maybe this was nothing to do with her. Maybe the student nurse wasn't updating her patient records properly, and Linda wanted Rachel to keep a closer eye. It could even be about the software itself; in the six months they'd been using it, it was already more despised than a Clinical Commissioning Group. The fields were forever freezing, and occasionally a record deleted when you saved it. Not great when a patient may be taking ten types of medication over a day.

'We've found an issue with your records,' Linda went on. 'Some of them are... incorrect.'

Rachel's pulse kicked up again. Once or twice, when she'd been in a massive rush to get away, Bel or Spence had filled them in for her, but that was so rare as to be inconsequential. And besides, they were as conscientious as she.

'Let me show you,' Linda said, opening a slim brown patient file beside the keyboard. She copied the name into the search field, double-checking the page on every letter.

'It's the software,' Rachel said, as the search ran. 'Everyone hates it. It keeps freezing. Sometimes–'

'*Please*,' Linda said in a harsh tone Rachel had never heard from her before. 'You'll have a chance to respond in a moment.'

Chance to respond? What was going on? The page loaded. She scanned the screen. Everything looked okay; the medication fields were filled with sufficient details. 'I still—'

Linda held up the folder. 'They don't correlate.'

A wave of dizziness slammed into her. 'What – what do mean?'

'The medication details are not the same between *here* and *here*. And this isn't the only example. On some days there are no records entered for your shift at all! Don't you realise how vital good record-keeping is to patient care? Don't you understand you could kill—'

'No. No, no, no – wait.' Rachel thrust out her hands, waving them as though trying to stop a car reversing over her. 'I'm being stalked by someone, by a man. He's trying to ruin my life.'

Linda frowned at her for a long second, then said, carefully, 'While I appreciate you may be having personal problems, nurse, you must ensure that they do not affect the quality and standard of your care.'

Rachel sat back, feeling her cheeks go red. 'It's not... I don't...'

'If you are not emotionally fit to be on the ward, then you need to make that clear. There are processes in place to assist with your mental well-being, and I can certainly put you in touch with the correct resources, if you require. But I cannot allow you to put the health of our patients at risk in this manner. So while I'm sympathetic to—'

'No, you don't understand. *He* did this. He got into the software and did all of this.'

'So you're saying that someone broke into the NHS computer systems, and tampered with patient records?'

'Yes. That's what happened. He did it so... so you'd think I was... incompetent.'

Rachel could tell by the tight-lipped way Linda was looking at her that the question had been rhetorical, that she'd only posed it to highlight how ridiculous it sounded.

Not her job, *please* not her job. First her relationship and now this. Where would it end?

'Linda, listen to me,' she said. The space around her seemed to be shifting in different directions, and she was struggling to stay focused. 'My phone was hacked over the weekend. He stole money from my bank account. He knows how to do this stuff. It was him – I know it was him.' She could see Linda wanted to believe her, but she could also hear how deranged she sounded. 'I've worked for you for two years. You *know* me.'

Linda looked at the folder in her hand, then back at the screen, her frown a little softer. 'Well now, I don't... I mean... Hmmm...'

'Think about it – have you ever needed to discipline me? Or have any of the patients ever complained about me?'

'No, but–'

Rachel didn't try to stop the tears spilling out. 'You've got to believe me. I love it here. I'd never do anything to jeopardise my position.'

'Have you been to the police about this man?'

'I... I haven't.'

She saw the fragment of doubt fading from the ward manager's face.

'I would have thought the police would be the first place you'd go if this was happening.'

'It's my boyfriend. He... he got in trouble–'

'Ahhh, the boyfriend. I've heard about him.'

'You've what? What have you... I mean...'

Linda straightened the cameo brooch on her cardigan. 'Please, Rachel. Can we stop this silliness now? I am well aware of your medical history.'

'My...'

'The time you spent on a psychiatric ward as a teenager. It's all recorded.'

'But–'

'Here's what I think might have happened,' Linda said. 'You are having problems with your boyfriend, and it's been very stressful for you. You've been getting tired, run down, and made a few mistakes.

You're a hard worker, I know that. You didn't want to let me down, so you carried on coming into work.'

Rachel was shaking her head. 'No, it's not like that. Please, Linda—'

'In some ways, this might be a good thing.'

'What's a good thing? I don't—'

'You'll have to go on leave while we do a full investigation.'

'*What?* No! I need to come to work. I can't sit at home doing—'

'Until we do a full invest—'

'Please, Linda. *Please.*'

Linda closed the folder. 'I'm sorry, there's nothing I can do. You'll be paid the whole time.' She nodded sympathetically to the door. 'Why don't you go home and put your feet up, eh?'

CHAPTER TWENTY-FIVE

LinkedIn

Rachel slammed open the front door and staggered inside, chest heaving, sweat dripping off her chin and leaving a trail of dark spots. She massaged the molten pain in her thighs. The thoughts the agony in her lungs had kept at bay invaded her mind. *How did he do it? How could she prove he deleted her patient records? What if she couldn't?*

She hobbled around the living room, squeezing the back of her leg, trying to soften the cramp digging into her muscles. The OxyContin called to her from the money box. Just one, to take the edge off. Lily wasn't here—

No, no, *no*.

The knife? The pills in the bath? No more. She needed to keep her head clear if she was going to think her way out of this.

As her laptop started, she checked her phone. No more texts, thank *God*. She'd expected another from the same number as last night. *Ha ha! got you fired!* But she did have new WhatsApp messages from Spence – he'd sent her a sweet one yesterday, saying happy birthday. She opened the app, and looked at his profile picture, which he'd changed to a selfie of Andreas's slender olive-skinned cheek pressed to his now-tanned one.

Rachel's smile slipped when she read his messages. Linda had contacted him, asking if he'd noticed anything strange about her behaviour of late, or seen her standard of care slipping. She'd not mentioned the missing eMAR records, but said enough to leave the impression this wasn't a trivial matter. His last message read: *Ring me! I'm freaking out!! XXX*

What she wouldn't give to hear his voice. He'd make some jokes, assure her that she was a good nurse, a good mother, that she wasn't going insane. But what if he came back early? How guilty would she feel then? No. He said ring, and he was a good enough friend to say it *and* mean it. She pressed the call icon, and waited while it rang, but he didn't pick up. Probably gone for a swim, or to sunbathe. She tapped out a quick message: *Don't freak out, I'm fine. Will try you again later. You and A look gorgeous :-) xxx*

She put her phone on the coffee table and tentatively logged into LinkedIn, expecting to see a load of gibberish from her middle-of-the-night updates, but it read okay, at least to her. Was it convincing enough to trick Griffin though? Then she realised – her profile was missing one crucial thing. Friends. Fortunately, on LinkedIn, people seemed less discriminating about who they connected with than on other social networks; she simply clicked on the connect button beside every profile in the Who You Might Know sidebar. As it was during work hours, she got a lot of accepted invitations, and soon Sophie Thomas had a hundred friends in her network.

Rachel sat back, amazed at how easy it was to spawn a bogus identity and insinuate yourself into someone's life. Once she was connected to their profile, she could see their e-mail address – often their phone number! How could everyone be so open about something so private? Despite the scare stories about scams, the government campaigns saying don't trust anyone you don't know online, people were still so unsuspecting, so *gullible*.

When her friend count hit one fifty, Rachel sent Griffin a connection request and an introductory mail. The agency she worked for, a mention of a possible job, and would he like to meet to discuss it?

As for after that, who knew? It would depend on what he replied. The idea she had was to record him admitting something criminal, like stealing her money, or getting Konrad beaten up. Something she could use to make him leave her alone.

He may hate her, he may want to ruin her life, but surely he didn't want to go back to prison.

She'd have to tell Mark about it though. Even if she and Griffin met at a public place, she couldn't take the risk. No doubt Mark would try to talk her out of it, but unless he had any smarter ideas, they were going with this.

She wasn't prepared to wait to see what Griffin would do next.

She stretched, the muscles in her back painful from bending over the screen. Then she double-checked the front door was locked and went for a shower. The heat of the water on her skin felt wonderful, but she didn't linger. She couldn't relax. The splashing sounded too much like a phone alert.

Dressed in her pyjamas, she drifted back downstairs. Whether it was sleep deprivation, or lack of food, or the unknown doses of whatever she'd taken still in her bloodstream, but she felt hallucinogenic. Walls glowed, the floor tilted. Outlines drifted from objects. She staggered to the kitchen, hand out as though it were dark.

A power nap, that's what she needed. Half an hour with her eyes closed, like she used to do when Lily was teething.

She found a mug not too crusted with old coffee, washed it, got the tub of Ensure from the cupboard, and paused. Her mind parsed and rejected the thick texture of the liquid. Why shouldn't she have what she wanted? Why feel guilty about it? Was it *so* strange that she liked feeling hungry? Some people enjoyed being choked during sex. Others worshiped *feet*. Every man and woman alive was a mental mess. Why was she always giving herself such a hard time?

Rachel found a sachet of sugar-free hot chocolate mix at the back of the coffee cupboard, and poured it into a bowl. She took it back to the living room, rolling her finger in the brown powder and putting it in her mouth, the sweet cocoa flavour spreading over her tongue.

She lay down on the sofa, pulled the blanket onto herself, and flicked on the television. Good Eats UK was still showing repeats of Bake Off, although this episode looked to be from a different series than the other night. Had she ever been this tired?

Griffin – her phone. What if he replied?

She dragged her eyes open, but it wasn't on the coffee table. Must have left it in the kitchen. Through a barricade of eyelashes, she caught the clock in the corner of the television screen. Nearly one. Plenty of time. She probably wouldn't even sleep.

CHAPTER TWENTY-SIX

Qui

Her first thought was that she was still dreaming – she'd been going from room to room in the house, her father following, mumbling something she couldn't quite hear – because the clock on the screen couldn't be right. If it was after seven then... *Oh no, Lily!*

Rachel tumbled off the sofa, the room dark, looking in the light of the television for her phone. She felt spaced out, not right. Did she take something when she got home? *Come on, get it together.* She scrabbled to her feet, hit the lights, searched the living room. Not here. She found it in the kitchen, underneath a tea towel. Three missed calls from Mark, and an irate stream of WhatsApp messages, finishing with a simple, *Thanks a bunch for ruining my night.* Of course, it was Monday. Every week he got together with the nerd collective to take part in something called a LAN party, which sounded as though it should be fun, but was in fact a stuffy room crammed with Doritos-stained manboys playing army games on their laptops.

She grabbed her coat from the hooks by the door, and caught her reflection in the oval mirror. Her face was too angular, all shadow. Mark was already on about her eating, and if he saw her like this he'd make a fuss. She raced upstairs and put on another T-shirt, a long sleeve cotton top, and a turtleneck jumper. In the bathroom, she tipped the plastic basket of make-up onto the toilet lid, digging around for foundation. A bit of colour, that was all she needed. She found some Clinique, but it separated when she rubbed it on her cheek. She checked the bottle – a year out of date. *Ugh,* she thought. *FML.* She rubbed it off with a towel, grabbed the juice glass they used to hold the toothbrushes, and slugged glass after glass of water, hoping the hydration would plump her features.

It didn't work.

When Mark yanked open his apartment door, his angry bearing softened.

'Jesus, Rach,' he said. 'Look at you.'

'Just stop it, okay?'

'What have you got on your face?'

She rubbed the residue of the foundation from her cheek. 'Nothing.'

'And you're wearing two jumpers. It's so obvious. I can see the hems.'

'It's a crime to be cold?' She zipped her coat to her throat, a dumb move for two reasons – one, it was much warmer inside, and two, he could still see all the hems at the bottom. Why hadn't she noticed the turtleneck was shorter!

'You going to let me in?' she asked.

'You *know* I look forward to Monday night.'

'I'm sorry. I'm really sorry. Can we–?'

'Let me guess? Zonked on painkillers watching Man vs. Food.'

'Jesus, Mark. Do you have to be such a *dick*?'

'*Me* a dick?'

He splayed his fingers on his chest. He had on yet another smart T-shirt, this one showing Darth Vader and a Stormtrooper making peace signs in front of the Eiffel Tower, so new the fold marks ran down both sides of his narrow torso. And what was that? A *thumb ring?* It was the same kind you found on festival trustafarians, usually before they whipped out a couple of bongos and made you wish you were somewhere else.

'Nice ring, Geldof,' she said.

He covered his hand guiltily, like it was making an obscene gesture he was powerless to stop. *'You're* the one who forgot to pick up our daughter. Heaven forbid you should take some responsibility for your life, Rach.'

This was going wrong already. She was hoping to talk to him about Alan Griffin, not bicker like irritated siblings. 'Look, I'm so–'

'Sorry,' Mark said at the same time. He gave her a conciliatory lift of the eyebrows. 'I'm worried about you, that's all.'

She followed him into the hallway. In the sudden heat of the apartment, she broke into a heavy sweat. A rich roast-tomato scented cloud wafted out of the kitchen, and she staggered to the side, as though the smell carried a right hook. Mark's Quorn chilli – her absolute favourite. His secret? Four squares of dark chocolate melted into the sauce. Some of the happiest nights of her life had been spent there, the three of them watching television and sharing a bowl of chilli nachos, doused in cheese so luminous it could pass for nuclear waste. The memory of the taste filled her mouth, along with so much saliva she thought she might gag.

Mark took her arm, as if she were an old woman who needed help across a road, and led her into the kitchen. She wanted to tell him to get off, but thought if she said something, the saliva would spill like drool.

'I thought you might like something to eat,' he said.

Rachel stared blankly at the chilli simmering in the saucepan. The smell seemed to be obstructing her synapses, rendering her mute and immobile.

He got a bowl from the shelf, and a spoon from the drawer. 'It's been cooking down for an hour, so it's ready to go.' He ladled a small portion into the bowl. 'Got that cheese you like.'

Her brain sparked again. Why was he making chilli tonight?

Mark kept to a strict dietary schedule, the same three meals on the same days, plus two allocated snacks, which he logged in a spreadsheet. Whether she was here or not to share it, Wednesday night was chilli night.

'What about your schedule?' she asked.

He stopped squeezing Easy Cheese over her bowl, leaving a worm of radioactive paste dangling from the tube. 'What?'

'Monday night, what's that? Something with beans, right?'

'Three bean salad with mint vinaigrette,' he replied, cocking his head, looking pensive, maybe, she couldn't read it. 'I thought, you know... You might be hungry.'

Something was off. She was late, she'd ruined his night, so to demonstrate his, justifiable, anger he'd made her favourite meal. 'Why don't I believe you,' she said.

'Because you're paranoid.'

'I just think it's strange—'

'You think everything's strange.'

'How you're so upset with me about your night, and yet here you are making me dinner.'

Mark put the bowl on the counter and shook his head. 'It is possible to be worried *and* annoyed, you know.'

The smell of the food was crippling. Everything she'd wanted to tell him about Griffin was disappearing into the swirling vortex of hunger. Mark was right – she was being paranoid – and if she didn't get out of here soon, she could imagine herself saying something she regretted.

'I'm getting Lily,' she said. She'd call him when she got home, when she had her thoughts in order. 'I need to get back.'

Mark moved past her, blocking the way to the lounge. 'You're not taking her.'

'You try to stop me.'

They stared each other down until Mark lifted his hands in surrender. He looked away, mouth tight, and said, 'She was *so* right about you.'

'Who was right? Lily?'

'I'm your little lapdog. *Come here, Mark. Do this, Mark. Sit like a good little boy, Mark.* You have no respect for me. Or anyone else.'

'It's not true. I—'

'Isn't it? Yesterday morning, you expected me to drop everything because you couldn't be bothered to get Lily.'

'It was my birthday! You didn't need to bite my—'

'Then you spoiled Jim's day—'

'Leave my dad out of this.'

'You've ruined my plans tonight.'

'What? Your impromptu chilli night?'

'You think I can't see you're starving yourself? And you're lying to my face! Does that sound like respect to you?'

She couldn't deal with this. Her emotions were wrung out. A thumping had started in the front of her skull, slow and debilitating. She needed a dark room with a locked door.

'Let me get Lily,' she said.

'She's not safe with you.'

Rachel felt something animal rising. 'Are you going to stop me from taking my daughter?'

'I think... I think you should go back to the clinic. Until you get your head together.'

'What about Lily? How are you going to take her to the nursery, and pick her up, and – and put her to bed every night?'

Mark cleared his throat and smoothed the front of his T-shirt. Her eyes followed that thumb ring all the way.

'Key can help out,' he said.

'Key? *Key?* What key?'

'My... My girlfriend.'

'Your *what?*'

Rachel winced at how that sounded. The *what* could have been picked out the question, *what kind of woman would go out with you?*

'Glad you're happy for me,' he said.

'I didn't mean it like that. I just—'

'Just what?'

'Doesn't matter. What kind of name is Key?'

'It's *Qui*. With a Q. She's from Vietnam. Well, originally, but she's been in London quite a few years... So it's not, like, a mail order thing. If that's what you were thinking.'

I don't like my new mummy.

Fresh sweat rolled down Rachel's neck. The thumping in her head was getting louder and faster. Mark was looking past her shoulder, as though this woman was standing there, ready to take her place.

'She's really beautiful – I mean *really*. And totally into tech.' He gave Rachel a lobotomised grin. 'I can't quite believe it.'

I think you should go back to the clinic.

'I was going to tell you,' he said. 'But I wanted to be sure.'

'And... you're sure?'

'She might be moving in.'

She's not safe with you.

It all made sense. Mark knew how to hack her phone. He knew about the photo sent from her Snap account. He got his girlfriend to call the bank, pretending to be her. He knew how to get onto the dark web, to hire thugs to take out Konrad, or hackers to break into the NHS and delete her patient records. She'd complained about the eMAR software to him plenty of times.

It was so obvious. Everything he'd been doing, sending that photo to Konrad's mates, that text after they broke up, even coming here and trying to force her to eat his chilli – knowing that she'd refuse but wanting to send her hunger wild – had been designed to bring on an episode, and send her back to the hospital. He wanted to claim Lily for himself.

He had a new girlfriend, a ready-made family. There was no need for her anymore.

'You,' Rachel murmured.

'Me what?' he replied, like he didn't know exactly what she was saying.

She shoved Mark in the chest and rushed into the lounge, tripping on a cable trailing from the stack of flashing routers on the dining table, almost falling to her knees, managing to grab the back of a chair to stay on her feet. Lily was on the sofa, colouring Queen Elsa's face in crimson, while a minor politician murdered a quickstep on *Strictly Come Dancing*.

'We're going,' Rachel said.

Lily ignored her, as if she wasn't there.

Rachel hoisted her round the middle and carried her like lumber.

'Mummy! Mummy! My book!' Lily screeched, throwing her arms up, trying to squirm away.

'Oh, so you do know who I am.'

Mark blocked the way. 'Look at what you're doing.'

'*Out of my way.*'

Lily scrabbled against Rachel's chest. 'Put me down!' She started a wail that became a shriek so loud it defied her tiny frame.

'See what you've done?' Rachel asked Mark.

His bewildered shake of the head suggested that no, he hadn't the slightest idea.

She wasn't falling for it. 'Move. *Now.*'

CHAPTER TWENTY-SEVEN

Becca

Rachel pushed Lily through the front door and upstairs for a bath, still cringing at flashes of her exchange with Mark. He was worried about her eating, so made her favourite meal – *the monster!* He was concerned about the safety of his daughter, so he suggested she stay with him – *the animal!* He had a girlfriend – *the horror!* How could Rachel think, even for a second, that he'd try to bring on an anorexic episode? They'd been through recovery together at the clinic, they'd even had their NEDA tattoos done together! He knew exactly the horror it brought to your life. And for what reason? Because he loved his daughter? Crazy!

Lily got to the fifth step and began picking at a frayed curl of carpet. Rachel tried to haul her up. But was it really all in her head? What did Mark say? *She was so right about you.* Clearly this girlfriend didn't think much of her! Was it such a stretch to believe she'd poisoned Mark's mind against her, and they'd concocted this plan together? He was so naïve with women, so easily influenced. Perhaps–

Pain flared on the back of her hand – Lily was biting her!

Rachel dragged her off by the hood of her coat. 'What's *wrong* with you?'

Lily went quiet. Her eyebrows crested in the middle, her bottom lip trembled, a reaction worse than any tantrum. Rachel pulled her close, amazed at how she could spot the crushing notes of guilt among the cacophony of her other emotions.

'I'm sorry, sweetness,' Rachel whispered in her ear. 'I'm so, so sorry. Don't bite Mummy, okay? Please don't bite Mummy again.'

Rachel carried Lily the rest of the way, rubbing her back and kissing her neck. Mark was right. This was at a new level of paranoia, even for her. As soon as their daughter was in bed, she'd gather her thoughts and send him an e-mail, explaining everything in a logical manner. Once he'd read and digested it, she'd call him. Then they could work out what to do about Griffin together.

Someone banged on the front door, rattling it in the frame. Rachel lowered Lily to the floor. That couldn't be Mark, he had keys. What if it was Griffin? Or the thugs he paid to beat up Konrad? She started Lily towards the bathroom, the only room with a lock, but then she heard Becca calling her from outside. Was she drunk again?

Rachel told Lily to stay there, raced down, and pulled open the door. Becca's usually glossy hair was tugged into a shabby ponytail, her make-up smeared on her cheek where she'd wiped away tears.

'Thank God,' Rachel said. 'I thought you were him.'

'*Him?*' Becca sneered. 'Still on that, are you?'

What did she mean, still on that? Like she'd been boring people silly with her stalker talk. And there she was thinking it bad enough her best friend didn't care enough to call, now she had to put up with her arriving unannounced, drunk again – that much was clear from the pub smell clinging to her – and having *another* go at her.

Rachel turned and saw Lily creeping down the steps. 'Upstairs, angel. It's only Auntie Becca.'

'*Only* Auntie Becca.'

An uncomfortable feeling oozed through Rachel. Griffin had got to her.

'Please, Becca,' Rachel said. 'Whatever you think I've done, it wasn't me. It was Alan Griffin.'

'The *mysterious* Mr Griffin. He harasses you for years, and then – *ta da!* He disappears.'

'I never told you what–'

'Grow up, Rach. Only children have imaginary friends.'

Upstairs, Lily was singing *Old McDonald had a Farm*, but sadly, as though she'd just seen the abattoir out back. Rachel could tell by the volume of her voice she was on the top step. Growing up, she'd sat there herself, listening to her parents argue.

'Becca, please. I need to tell–'

'You followed me around school for years,' Becca cut in. 'Always *looming* over my shoulder. Everyone said you were a fucking nut job, but I took pity on you. More fool me.'

Tears spilled from Rachel's eyes so fast it took her by surprise. 'Why – why are you saying this to me?'

Becca mockingly flapped her fingers at her chest. Two of the false nails on her left hand had come off, showing the chewed cuticle underneath. 'Look at me. I'm *such* a victim. My life is *always* horrible! You were so bloody happy when those boys put that photo of you on the Internet. Finally, you had another reason for everyone to feel sorry for you.'

'You don't really believe that.'

'Everyone forgot about your mum, so now you had some new misery.'

'I can't listen to this.'

'You're a vampire,' Becca said, lifting her arms and sucking at her front teeth. 'You drain the life from the people around you.'

'Why are you being so *mean to me?*'

Becca looked down, her mouth twitching with the effort to hold back tears. She got out her iPhone. 'You saying this had nothing to do with you?'

While she drunkenly swiped on the screen, Rachel glanced up

the stairs. Everything had gone quiet. She hoped Lily had gone to her room and wasn't listening to this in traumatised silence.

Becca held out her phone. On it was a photo of a woman messily sleeping on a sofa, her black camisole ridden up to her midriff, a muffin top spilling over her tight white jeans. It was taken from a bad angle, so that the part of her face you could see appeared to have multiple chins. Rachel gasped. It was her sofa. The person sleeping was Becca. Why would she—?

Rachel remembered. Spence had taken the photo the night the two of them came round, after Becca passed out drunk. Goosebumps prickled on Rachel's neck. Static built in her brain, growing loud and agitated. How did Becca get hold of it? The photo had been on her phone, nowhere else, until she wiped it.

Then she saw the bottom of the screen, and realised it was so much worse.

42 likes

mobscene7*How do u get a fat bird into bed? Piece of cake*
tessamilliken *You go girl, let it all hang out #effyourbeautystandards*
daboyzzzzzz*I eat da fajita AAAALLL up!!!!!!*

The photo wasn't on her phone. It was on Instagram.

Rachel snatched it from Becca, pressed the back key. *Oh no. No, no, no.* How was that possible?

The picture had been uploaded from *her* account.

'I didn't post this,' Rachel said. 'I would never—'

'You're trying to get back at me 'cos I didn't believe you about sending that photo to Konrad's mate?'

'That wasn't me!'

'Course it was.'

'You've no idea what Griffin's been doing to me. He stole my wages. He got me suspended from work. Konrad... he...' Rachel trailed off. She could see from Becca's pushed-out lips and sarcastic nods that her best friend didn't believe a word. 'Why would I make this up?'

She twisted her finger viciously by her temple. ''Cos you're messed up. 'Cos you're bored. 'Cos you love the *drama*. 'Cos you can't be happy unless other people are pitying you. Unless everyone's going, poor Rachel, better not say anything mean to her in case she starves herself again.'

Something in Rachel's head cracked; it felt like the bedrock of her sanity breaking apart. 'Stop saying that. I can't take it.'

Becca started to sob. 'Why'd you post that photo, Rachel? Why'd you want to humiliate me? You've no idea what I've been going through. Since I got fired from Orchid—'

'*Fired*? You told me you quit!'

'Why would I *quit*? It was my dream job.'

'Why didn't you tell me?'

'Embarrassed, I guess.' She squeezed the bridge of her nose and sniffed back tears. 'I totally messed up, left my computer unlocked. Someone sent an e-mail from my desk to all our clients, slagging off Melinda Rodgers, saying she was a dumb bitch who wouldn't know good PR if she woke to find it shitting in her mouth.'

Melinda Rodgers was Becca's boss and darling of the PR world, with clients as cool and prestigious as Kate Moss.

'That's awful,' Rachel said. 'You should—'

'Don't pretend you give a shit,' Becca snapped. 'If you did, you'd know I'd never quit that job.'

An e-mail sent from her work account? It couldn't have been... he would still have been in prison. But why not? Perhaps he'd paid a hacker to log into Orchid's systems?

'It was Griffin,' Rachel said. The words sounded strange as they came out of her mouth, as though they were being spoken by someone else. 'He hacked into your work. He sent—'

'Stop it!'

'I know it's him.'

'You're crazy. You're an absolute lunatic.'

'On my life. On Lily's—'

'Don't say it! Don't you *dare* swear on your daughter's life.' Becca leaned towards Rachel, her eyes red and intense. 'Remember, I checked when I got home from the gym. *You can't be logged into Snap from two places at once.* I logged in on my pad, and it threw me out on my phone.' She pulled back, nodding. 'I caught you red-handed. You're a liar. A fucked-up psycho liar.'

'It's not true,' Rachel said, reaching to her.

Becca jumped back as though Rachel was coming at her with a knife. 'Stay away from me. I mean it – stay out of my life. And take the fucking photo down. What are you waiting for? *Do it right now!*'

CHAPTER TWENTY-EIGHT

Password

The door slammed so hard, Lily's coat leapt off the hook beside it. Rachel stared at the space where Becca had been. This couldn't be happening. Any second she was going to come back, apologise for the horrible things she'd said. She'd stay while Lily went to bed, then they'd have a coffee and she'd say, *Of course I believe you about Alan Griffin. I called you a psycho to be cruel.*

Becca had always been a bit of a mean drunk, liable to lash out at any perceived slight once she was a few shooters down. And this was as bad as it got. She lived online, posting on Insta multiple times a day. She would be horrified about that photo. Where was her phone? Rachel had to take it down before—

Rhythmic thumps started above her head.

Lily!

She hurried upstairs. Her daughter was outside the bathroom, lying on her back, drumming her heels. When she saw her mother, she stopped and made a show of sighing. 'I'm *bored.*'

'Come on,' Rachel said. 'Bath time.'

Lily didn't move from the landing. 'What you and Auntie Becca talking about?'

Rachel didn't want another struggle like on the stairs, so instead she stepped over her and went into the bathroom. 'Come on, sweetness.'

'Were you fighting?'

How did Griffin do it? She hadn't reinstalled her phone until *after* Spence took the photo, so that explained how Griffin got it – he would've had access to her camera folder, at least until later that night. But she'd changed her Instagram password on her laptop, not her phone, and she hadn't logged into it since. There'd been no more dodgy e-mails. So how did he get her password? Her brain felt coated in hard, slick plastic, and her thoughts kept slipping off. She couldn't work it out.

Lily banged her heels, slower and louder than before, interspersing each thud with a call of, 'Mummy!'

Mummy – thud – Mummy – thud – Mummy – thud.

'Stop it!' Rachel cried.

Mummy – thud – Mummy – thud.

Rachel lurched out the bathroom and pulled her daughter up by the arm. 'I told you to stop that.'

'Off me!' Lily shrieked, pulling away.

'Clothes, *now*. It's bath time.'

'I want my daddy.'

'You're staying here.'

'I go bed now,' Lily said, heading to her room.

Rachel covered her face, gulping back a sob. She'd wanted so much to create only happy memories for her daughter, to give her the childhood she never had, to not let her down the way her own parents had done. But what if all this was damaging Lily already? Was she ruining her daughter's life before it had even really begun?

Rachel tried to coax Lily down for dinner, offering peanut butter on toast, Snapchat filter photos, even a whole showing of *Frozen*. Nothing worked. Her daughter stayed in the corner of her bedroom, flipping through one of her Elmer books, focusing on the colourful elephant with the intensity of a surgeon making an incision. Rachel didn't have the energy to drag her. Besides, Lily had just heard Auntie Becca call Mummy a psycho, and she was loathed to do anything more to prove her right. *One trauma at a time, please!*

'Okay, angel,' she said, kissing her on the head. 'I'm downstairs if you need me.'

At the door, she glanced round, but Lily didn't look up. *Ah well*, Rachel thought, smiling grimly to herself, *she'll be with her new family soon. She'll probably be happier there.*

She drifted into the kitchen, opened the fridge, and leaned into the shelves. The cold air prickled her skin; the smell of the food curdled in her lungs. Was that really such a joke? Say Mark and this woman had something special. Say they bought a family home, a spacious five-bed in the suburbs, with great schools and safe parks, where you could look out of a window and see something other than kids in hoodies and overflowing recycle bins. Wouldn't Lily be happier with them? Maybe with some brothers and sisters? Better that than staying with her, becoming yet another lonely anxious messed-up anorexic. Like it was some kind of *fucking family profession*. If you love someone, let them go. Isn't that what people always said?

Retching, Rachel pulled her head out of the fridge and staggered back into a chair, starving but too stressed to eat, exhausted but too scared to sleep, desperate for the day to end, but terrified of what was waiting on the other side of the dawn. And guilty too, about Lily. That was one thing about eating – the guilt sat in her chest, feasting on her heart.

The photo of Becca, it was still on Insta. What was it she said? *Looming over her shoulder.* Guess she'd been right all along, that's how everyone saw her, even her oldest friend. A freak. A giant freak. Maybe she should leave it up, out of spite. She sighed and reached for her phone – she just wasn't that person, more fool her. Perhaps the best thing would be to bludgeon all the birds with one giant stone and delete herself from social media. At least then it couldn't be used as a weapon.

She logged into the app, pleased to have set the password to something she could remember – *gotohellgriffin* – and paused. *How did he get the password?* She'd reset it on the sofa, using the laptop.

She went through to the living room. The window was behind where she'd been sitting... but she'd shut the curtains by then. No way he'd been watching her from outside.

What if it wasn't from outside?

Rachel froze. She cast her eyes around the living room, carefully, like she was trying to detect the source of a faint noise. The decor hadn't changed much since her mum had passed away. The flocked wallpaper, the blue fleur-de-lis patterned carpets, the faded mahogany corner cabinet and the TV stand with the drawer that opened half way, had been part of this house for as long as Rachel could remember. She'd never had the time or the money to change it, though she longed to freshen up the place, to have a modern easy-to-clean home that didn't sprout fresh mess whenever her back was turned.

Something else that had always been in the living room, probably for longer than she'd been alive, was a set of wall-mounted gold lamp fittings, tarnished, triangular things that went through candle bulbs so fast she'd long given up changing them when they burnt out. She was so used to seeing them on the wall, she didn't notice them. Until now.

She approached the one closest to the sofa. There was something in the fitting. She reached behind the glass, detached it. A camera, the size of a five pence piece, thick as a button battery. A cable led to a squat black device pushed into the empty light socket.

A sick feeling flowed into her blood, spreading along every vein and capillary, until it filled her.

He'd been in her house. *He'd violated her home.* No wonder he knew about Konrad as soon as it happened. No wonder he knew about that photo of Becca – he saw it being taken. She pictured

Griffin before a bank of security screens, each showing a different room, his doughy face lit up. Was he watching now, aroused at her distress? He was sicker than she thought possible.

Rachel took the camera through to the kitchen, put it in a plastic container, and hid it at the back of the cupboard. Then she searched the house, checking light fittings, doorframes, radiators, plug sockets and skirting boards. She looked inside appliances, under furniture, examined every corner, nook, cranny and alcove. The kitchen shelves covered with trinkets and nick-nacks no longer seemed so heart-warming, not when they could conceal bugging devices. She inspected everything. The only room she couldn't check was Lily's, but she'd go through that in the morning. He couldn't be so sick as to watch her sleeping daughter. *Could he?*

She realised something else – her LinkedIn trap. She'd written him the message from the same spot on the sofa. No wonder he hadn't replied. She'd been trying not to think about his lack of response, hoping, perversely, he was too caught up in terrorising her to get round to it, but now she saw the truth.

He'd watched her do it.

CHAPTER TWENTY-NINE

Address

Rachel came round to find herself lying on the sofa in the dark, staring at the TV. She sat up, wincing, hand to her head. Why did it feel like someone was kicking in the door to her brain? She looked around. And why was she *downstairs*? Had she slept? Had she taken something? She didn't think so, but she felt so groggy that she couldn't be certain. The broken pieces of yesterday were scattered across the floor of her mind and she couldn't seem to put them back together.

On the TV screen, a youngish couple, cute preppy types, had started a trial on Cake Wars, an obstacle course with a three-tier chocolate gateaux. The girl stumbled on a treadmill and got a face mask of mocha frosting. In the corner, the time said five fifty-seven. At least Lily wasn't up yet.

Coffee, stat.

Rachel hoisted herself to her feet and took a heavy step towards the kitchen.

A tapping behind her, the hollow sound of a ring on glass.

She swore and jumped back. A shadow moved across the curtain. Who the hell was that?

The letterbox rattled open. 'Rach? I can hear the telly – you up? It's bloody Baltic out here.'

What was *he* doing here? She raced to the door and pulled it open. Standing on her front step, tanned and grinning against the predawn gloom, in a collarless black leather jacket and a tight yellow T-shirt with *I'm in Mykonos, Bitch* in hot pink across the front, was Spence.

Spence peered into his coffee, the surface swirling with undissolved granules. 'This time yesterday, I was sipping a gorgeous latte with the sand between my toes and a hot guy's hand on my thigh.'

'You should have called me first,' Rachel replied.

'So you could've talked me out of it?'

'I wish you hadn't come back.'

From the living room came the discordant squeals and snorts of Peppa Pig. Lily was staying home from nursery today, and every day, until this nightmare was over.

Spence sipped his drink and scowled at it as though it had wronged him in a previous life. 'I called Linda. She told me *every-thing*. How sketchy you were acting – how you'd been *suspended*. So I booked the first flight I could, bloody Ryanair to Luton at midnight. I should never have gone to begin with. I saw how all over the place you were, but I was being selfish. I was more interested in getting my end away than in being there for a mate. And I'm sorry for that.'

Rachel squeezed her eyes, but tears slipped out anyway. She seemed to have a never-ending supply these days. 'Even Lily hates me. She told me yesterday she wanted to stay with her dad.'

Spence leaned forward to give Rachel a hug. 'We're going down to that hospital today. I'm going to tell that Linda what's what. You're a brilliant nurse. Best one I've ever worked with.'

She knew he was just being nice, but him saying that made her sob into his shoulder even harder. Why couldn't Becca be this supportive? *Because you're a vampire. You drain the life from the people around you.* She pulled away.

'What?' he asked. 'What happened?'

'Have I ruined things with Andreas?'

'No, it's *great*. So great I had to sit sideways on the plane.'

Rachel cocked her head, squinting at him, then got the joke.

'Spence!' she cried, slapping his arm. It felt like it had been years since she'd laughed.

He went to pick up his coffee, then took another look at the surface and nudged it further away. 'Now, are you going to tell me what's going on?'

Before this week, she hadn't told anyone what she'd done to put Griffin in prison. Was she really going to tell two people in the space of as many days? What next? Hire a bus and tour Oxford Circus with a megaphone. If the wrong person found out, despite everything Griffin was doing to her again, she would still be in a lot of trouble. But Spence had come all the way back from Greece to help her. And anyway, who else could she trust?

'Buckle up,' Rachel said. 'I'm going to tell you *everything*.'

'Yikes. Should I be looking for the emergency exit?'

'If you find one, make sure you come and get me.'

Spence listened to it all – the hacker, the planted photos, Griffin's prison sentence, and everything he'd done to her since getting out – only interrupting to mutter *Oh my god* or to make a noise of disbelief. The one thing she left out was the photo of Becca. She didn't want to risk making him feel guilty, even though he'd probably find it hilarious. When Rachel finished, he slumped back in his chair and wiped his forehead.

'Well?' she asked.

'You've got to go to the police.'

'What if they arrest Konrad?'

'Are you going to wait for him to actually hurt you?'

'I don't know what to do.'

'This may seem like a dumb question,' Spence said, leaning forward. 'But how do you know Griffin's out of prison? He could be paying someone to do all this. You know, from *inside*.'

'Wait here,' Rachel said, and hurried into the living room. Lily was lying on the sofa, transfixed to Peppa splashing in muddy puddles. TV before breakfast – how could that be good for her? Why not go the whole way and feed her Haribo for dinner? Rachel sighed and grabbed her laptop from the coffee table.

'You're not showing me porn, are you?' Spence asked. 'It's the only time I ever look at my laptop.'

'Sorry to disappoint you,' she replied, opening a web browser and typing www.paedo-hunter.net. She was still logged into the forum, and went straight to the thread for Alan Griffin. She scrolled to the bottom, looking for the post saying he'd been released.

Spence touched her arm. 'Everything okay? You've gone pale. Even paler, I mean. I've got two words for you – sun and bed.'

'No way,' she said, shaking her head.

'What? *What?*'

She pressed her finger to the screen. 'Look.'

A new user called *JustForYou* had posted an update last night, at eight o'clock. That was around the same time she'd found the camera. It contained a single line.

18 Drayton Road, Norcot RG30 1EL

CHAPTER THIRTY

Reunion

Spence didn't want her to go, not on her own, but she was sick of being the target. Griffin had stolen her money, her boyfriend, her job – and with that hidden camera, her dignity. Enough. She wasn't a five-stone nothing starving herself in a hospital bed. If she had to fight to keep him from kicking her life around, she would fight.

'I hope it won't come to that,' Rachel said, demonstrating the block and punch she'd learned in a self-defence seminar. 'Although I'd love to spend a few hours kneeing him in the groin.'

Spence threw jabs at the fridge. He had a wiry welterweight physique honed from circuit classes at the gym. 'At least let me come. I'll wait outside.'

'I need you here with Lily.'

'It's a trap.'

'Or a lucky break. Someone usually posts the address within a couple of weeks.'

Spence opened his hands to her. 'Who's this *JustForYou*? It was their first post.'

'People open an account and post once, especially with an address. Could even be a copper.'

'It's too much to be a coincidence.'

She gave him a look that said she didn't want this discussion again. 'Are you sure you're okay looking after Lily?'

'All my nieces say I'm the best uncle ever. But seeing as I'm their only uncle, that's probably not saying much.'

'Do you think I'm crazy for doing this?'

Spence nodded. 'Yes. I've told you that already, but you're as stubborn as a week-old cum stain.'

Rachel took his hand. 'I'll call before I go in. I'll tell him there are people waiting to hear from me.' She unlocked her phone and tapped through to the voice recorder. 'I just want him to say the wrong thing, to incriminate himself. He may hate me, but he won't want to go back inside. It's time I called his bluff.'

'What about... a weapon?'

She'd thought about that – a knife in her bag, perhaps – but was worried that might invite violence. And that she'd slice off the tops of her fingers rooting around for a hair band. 'I think it's okay.'

'Pepper spray?'

'Don't have any.'

Spence grinned. '*That* is something I might be able to help you with.'

While she showered, he filled the miniature plastic spray bottle she used to make paint silhouettes with Lily with a mixture of water, ground peppercorns, and Tabasco sauce. 'Where'd you learn how to do that?' she asked, back downstairs and ready to go.

He handed over the bottle ceremonially. 'Try having as many dodgy Grindr hook-ups as me.'

Rachel took the quiet eleven fifteen from Paddington to Reading, and came out of the station to a line of taxis at the rank. Even though she'd planned the route to Griffin's by bus, it would take another hour, and that was too much; she wanted to finish this. She still had twenty pounds cash, and had dug her emergency credit card from its hiding place at the back of the wardrobe, so she climbed in the back of a rusty blue Vauxhall with plastic-covered seats, driven by an unshaven man who nodded tiredly when she gave the address.

She watched the high street roll past. Such a dismal place – damp, faintly smelling of fried chicken, with the same grim mix tape of Greggs, Boots and Costa Coffee as every other town. God, she hated this country sometimes. *Australia*. That's where she needed to be. Glittering beaches, turquoise skies, summer nights sitting with fun, tanned friends outside some hip bar. As soon as she got home, she was looking into flights. Maybe even send Rowena a message.

The buildings fell away to reveal the countryside. Wooden fences, meadows, the occasional sheep winsomely chewing the grass. She wound down the window and stretched her lungs with cool air. What if it *was* a trap? What if she stepped in his front door, got bashed over the head, and woke up strapped to a table in the basement? If she told him people knew she was here, would he let her go? But if he wanted to hurt her, he'd had plenty of chances already. Yesterday, for example, when she was flaked out on the sofa for the whole day. He must have been watching her sleep. How easy would it have been to–

'Lady? *Lady?*'

The taxi driver was talking to her. They were stopped outside a depressing semi-detached midway along a miserable street. She apologised, paid, and got out.

Rachel ducked into the shadow of a scrawny elm and took in Griffin's house. It was in worse condition that the ones next to it, with peeling paintwork, rotten window frames, and fissured pebble dash; chunks had come away near the door, showing the dull brown bricks behind. She called Spence.

'Ten minutes, or I'm ringing the police,' he said.

'Make it twenty,' she replied.

After she hung up, she moved the tiny bottle of pepper spray to her back pocket, and crept up to the front door. She heard the television coming through the window, a game show, judging by the excited presenter and audience applause. *Someone* was in. She started the voice recorder on her phone and put it in the pocket on the front of her jacket, which she hoped was the best place to catch their conversation. Heart pounding, she pressed the bell. A sharp trill sounded. She held it for a second, and stepped back, hand midway to the pepper spray, like a gunslinger ready for a showdown. Nothing.

He'd fooled her. He didn't live here at all. He just wanted to lure her here so—

So nothing. Perhaps he was on the toilet, or having a nap, or reckoned it was Jehovah's Witnesses at the door and didn't want to get into a big theological discussion about why evil shits like him got to terrorise young women. She pressed the bell again, keeping her finger on it, for three seconds, five seconds, ten.

The door swung open. Staring out was a scrawny man in blue tracksuit bottoms and a stained England football shirt. Late fifties, maybe early sixties. Six weeks into stubble, hair thinning against his scalp, red eyes couched in saggy grey bags. He looked like a park bench drunk on his day off. From inside the house came a *ding-ding-ding*, cheers from the crowd, someone winning the jackpot.

This couldn't be Griffin. The well-fed well-heeled middle-aged man who'd followed her home from school bore little relation to this scraggy scrote in the doorway. Yet there was something recognisable in the shape of his eyes, the set of his mouth. It looked like his sick brother, perhaps six weeks into a course of chemotherapy.

'Whatever it is,' he growled, going to shut the door. 'I don't wa—'

Rachel jammed her foot in the gap. 'Wait.'

She put her shoulder to the door and pushed. He tried to resist, but quickly relented, and Rachel stumbled into the dark hallway. It smelled of stale beer and damp clothes left in a heap.

'Get out,' he said, breathing hard, looking over his shoulders as he stepped backwards, like he expected someone to be coming from behind. 'Leave me alone.'

Now she was inside, even in the murky light, she knew it was him. It was the voice. After years of playing *I am going to ruin your life* on repeat in her mind, she'd recognise it anywhere. 'What's wrong, Griffin? Didn't think I'd come?'

He pulled the lounge door closed, muting the jangling theme music. 'I know you.' He shook his fingers by his head. 'You're...'

Rachel widened her stance. She had at least three inches on him. He looked so weak, so *wrecked*. 'Don't play stupid.'

Griffin nodded, his smile spreading. His once-white teeth were grey as dishwater. He started a laugh that became a cough, and wiped the flecks of spit from his lips with the shoulder of his shirt. 'I got you now. Fuck my face. I never thought I'd see *you* again. What you doin' here?'

The smile. That's what propelled her. He was destroying her life, all over again, this pathetic piece of... *scum* – and grinning about it! Like she was powerless. Like she could do nothing to stop him. He was wrong.

Rachel rushed him, hooking him round his neck, and slamming him against the cupboard under the stairs. He staggered sideways. It felt good to hurt him, to see the shock of pain pass across his disgusting face. She grabbed his hair, the grease in it oozing between her fingers, his musty, unwashed stink in her nose, and yanked back.

'Give me one good reason,' she snarled. 'Why I shouldn't snap your neck?'

His smile faded, leaving his capillary-strewn eyes, his sour breath, the sad sink of his cheeks. She got an image of him waiting outside the school, clean-shaven, filling out his smart suit. How solid he'd looked back then. Impenetrable. He'd lost a third of his body weight. Scores of pale curling scars, white like maggots, writhed over his neck, going past the collar of his England top.

'Death by a thousand cuts,' he said. 'They don't much like paedos inside.'

Rachel pushed him away. 'You expecting sympathy?'

'You want to talk like *civilised* people?' he asked, rubbing the back of his head.

She paused, adrenaline twitching her fingers, then nodded. He gestured to the lounge door.

'After you,' Rachel said.

Griffin shrugged and pushed it open. 'I've been shanked in the arse more times than a choirboy in the Vatican.' He leaned towards her – she reared back. The look he gave her could almost be called earnest. 'If you're here to *do* something,' he said. 'It doesn't bother me much.'

Rachel let out a shaky breath, and followed him in. The lounge was even more desolate than the outside of the house. This was *not* what she'd expected. Aside from the armchair, a squat brown corduroy lump that wouldn't look out of place poking from a skip, a beer crate for a footstool, and a small flat screen TV, the base of which seemed to have been built from duct tape, the room was bare. No photos, no ornaments, no niceties at all. Just cobwebs in the corners, bare plaster walls, and a dun green carpet, worn through to the underlay, scattered with cigarette butts and fungal take-out trays. Even the air was sad, like it had been made from lonely sighs. A space heater old enough to have been on an Apollo mission sat in the corner, though judging by the temperature in the room, it didn't work.

'Quite the reunion, eh?' Griffin gestured to the chair. 'Take the weight off.'

Was that a joke? His expression was peculiar, his fallen-in face tricky to read. A scar coming off the bottom left of his lip gave him a permanent smirk. He waited a moment longer, then took the chair for himself, groaning like he'd finished a fourteen-hour shift.

'I'd offer you a drink,' he said, waving behind to a door, swollen with damp, that she supposed headed to the kitchen. 'But unless you want to squeeze a piss out of one of the mice, you're out of luck.' He retrieved a can of Special Brew from beside his chair and shook it at her. 'Got a few gulps of backwash.'

She stayed tensed, hand hovered by her waist, in reach of the pepper spray. What was his game? Where was the trap? He looked barely strong enough to beat Lily in an arm wrestle.

Griffin clicked off the television with the remote and chucked it on the floor. The batteries bounced out of the back, and he mouthed *my life*. He drank from the can, slurping louder than he had to, like he was taunting her.

There wasn't any joy, or even satisfaction, at what prison had done to him; it was a Wizard of Oz moment, the curtain pulled back, but instead of a god there was a feeble old man.

'I'm not scared of you,' she said.

He held the can upside down over his mouth, his tongue worming around the hole for the last drops. 'Why should you be?' he asked, casual.

'You didn't think I'd come,' she said. 'You thought I'd be too scared to leave the house. You thought...'

He lowered his can. She didn't like the way he was appraising her, his head to the side, like someone watching a rare insect trapped in a jar. 'Go on,' he said. 'What else did I think?'

'I'm not going to let you ruin my life again.'

He dismissed her with a wave and an eye roll. 'Trust me. You are of *no* interest.'

Something wasn't right. He'd stolen over two thousand pounds from her, so why was he in this horrible house? Why was he dressed like a hobo fallen on hard times, searching for the last dregs of beer in an empty can? Even if he didn't want to spend it on fast cars, loose women, and at least one clean change of clothes – although more than likely he used it to pay the hackers to delete her eMAR records – he would surely have at least enough put aside to buy a four-pack when he wanted. It wasn't just the money, but his attitude too. Of all the scenarios she'd considered, an amused dismissal of any involvement was not one she'd planned for.

Unless... he'd guessed she'd be recording him, and this was part of the act. If anyone listened to it afterward, they'd say she was the aggressive one, that he was being harassed by *her*. What now? *What now?*

'Uhh, shit,' said Griffin. 'I really did a number on you. Look...' He made a noise like a groan, but more strangled, his fingers going to the scars on his neck. 'Maybe it's not a bad thing you're here. I know the importance of closure.'

'What *closure*? I want you to leave me the fuck alone.'

He glanced at her like he hadn't caught what she'd said. 'I don't blame you for hating me, you and the rest of them. I deserved it. Prison, everything.' He lifted his beer, but stopped halfway, remembering it was empty. 'There are no excuses, but you can hear them anyway. It's the least you deserve.'

Griffin pushed his filthy fingers to his eyes and sniffed hard.

Was he *crying*?

'I've got girls of my own,' he said, and gulped down a quivery breath. 'Carrie and Fran. Carrie's about your age. You look... she's tall as well. Maybe that's why I chose you. I'm sick, I know that. My wife left me when they were young, and she turned them against me. By the time they were teenagers, they wouldn't even see me. I... I was depressed. The doctors tried me on all kinds of drugs, but they didn't do much. For years I held it together, but then I read about these new pills you could get in America, and like an idiot I bought them online. I don't know what they were, but they fucked my head something proper. I wasn't me anymore. Totally psychotic.'

He caught Rachel's eye. It felt as though she were in a boat, gripping the sides as it tilted viciously in the water, threatening to capsize. What was he doing? Was she supposed to *feel sorry* for him?

'You got it worse than the rest,' Griffin went on. 'I saw that picture you put online, you know, the one in your room, and... I fell for you. I was in love. Then you rushed out of the house, screaming how I was a dirty pervert, and I thought, what a bitch. What a prick-teasing bitch. I hated you so much. Pathetic, I know, but, well...' He tapped his chest. 'I am pathetic. Don't you think?'

He paused again. Did he want her to agree with him? She

couldn't believe what she was hearing. This... this ridiculous *confession*.

'Here's the thing,' he went on. 'Someone set me up with that kiddie porn, but what got me sent to Broadmoor were things I wrote, these stories about torturing young girls. Those were all me – I was having terrible thoughts. I was even thinking about... doing some of it. Whoever stitched me up did the world a favour.' He fingered the rim of the can. 'If I could find out who got me sent down, I'd thank them.'

So that was it. He wanted her to admit she was involved in planting the photos on his computer. This place, his dishevelled state, they were part of the ruse. The whole place was probably wired for sound. Well, she'd turn his little trick back on him.

'I know you stole my money,' she said, voice raised. 'And hid a camera in my house.'

'Hid a what?'

The incredulity on his face couldn't have been more fake if he were wearing a rubber mask.

'I know what you're doing,' she said. 'And I have evidence.'

'Evidence? What evidence?' He tensed his fingers on the arm of the chair. 'What the fuck do you want with me?'

His hapless air had gone. He was looking at her sharply, as though timing his strike. Spence was right – she was crazy coming here. What was she thinking? Griffin had been in *prison*. She took a step back, going for her pocket, feeling the outline of the spray bottle. 'I want you to leave me alone.'

'Are you fucking mental?'

She held out the spray bottle. 'Stay out of my life. I'm warning you.'

'Oh, you're *warning* me now, are you?'

'If you do anything else to me,' she said, hearing the hysteria in her voice. 'I'll kill you. I swear I'll kill you before I let you ruin my life again.'

Was this what he wanted? For her to assault him? So he could go to the police to have her arrested? She scanned the walls and ceiling for cameras. Was he filming her now?

'Get out,' Griffin said, pulling himself up. She saw something glint in his hand. 'Get your crazy fucking arse out of my house. Or *I'll* get the police.'

'I want my money back,' she said. 'And I want you to *leave me alone!*'

He swung his arm around. Razor blades, melted in the head of a cheap toothbrush. 'Make me, cunt.'

Rachel pushed down on the spray, sending an arc of liquid into his face.

Griffin shrieked and covered his eyes. 'You fucking bitch! You crazy fucking bitch!'

She turned and ran into the hallway, and out the open front door – behind her, he was hollering, 'And if I ever see *you* again, I'll...' – but she was already down the street, breaking into a sprint before she could hear the rest.

CHAPTER THIRTY-ONE

JustForYou

Rachel clung to the bus stop, sucking in breath. Where was she? A road beside a field, the air thick with the smell of waterlogged mud. What if she'd gone the wrong way? What if there was no bus back to Reading? She scanned the timetable, looking for clues, but the plastic covering was scratched, as though rubbed with wire wool, and she couldn't even see what time the next bus was coming, let alone if it was going the right way. She pulled out her phone, hoping to load a map, but she had no Internet. It was after one, over half an hour since she rang Spence.

'Oh my god,' he said, his voice agitated. 'I was calling nine nine nine when you rang. Missing, presumed *dead*.'

'Thank heavens for Spence's home-made pepper spray.'

'*No!*'

She smiled at the memory. It'd been pretty much the only thing she did right. 'Between the eyes.'

'Money shot!' Spence's laugh sounded more like a yelp. 'How are you?'

Rachel glanced around. The sky was miserable, but not falling in. As long as she got to the train station by three, she'd miss the commuter rush and be back in London at a reasonable hour. 'As well as can be expected. Lil okay?'

'If by okay you mean filling my phone with pictures of us as every known animal in the ark, and some that should have drowned in the flood, then yes. She's okay.'

'Have you put on *Frozen* yet?' As Rachel asked that, she heard the orchestral opening.

'This time I get to be Anna,' he replied. He lowered his voice. 'Get home safe, okay?'

She told him not to worry and hung up. The dark clouds over the nearby hills were approaching fast. Rachel zipped her jacket to her chin and prayed for luck. Or failing that, a bus.

Forty-five minutes later, soaked and desolate, she got on the bus, a cold shuddering strip-lit throwback to a time when such journeys were a test of endurance as well as a way to get somewhere. She sat down shivering, and stayed that way as they meandered past dry-stone walls, brown pastures, farm buildings rising in the distant murk. On the front it had just said *Reading*. She'd asked the driver if they were going to the train station, but his grunt and muttered 'near to' didn't fill her with confidence.

She put her head against the cold window and watched the thick lines of rain roll down the glass. Her phone – it was still recording. She played back the audio, holding the handset to her ear like she was on a call. Her voice was clearer than his, but she caught most of what he said. It only worsened her mood. He just didn't sound guilty. It was only at the end, when he threatened her, that he showed what he was really about. And that story, those pills from America. *If I could find out who got me sent down, I'd thank them.* Did he think she was so stupid as to come out and admit what she'd done? Then again, hadn't she wanted him to do the same?

Still, it didn't feel right.

. . .

Considering how the day was going, it was no surprise that the driver's definition of *near to* was different to her own. Radically different. Emmers Green, the last stop, while technically in Reading, was three miles from the train station. Rather than risk another bus, Rachel jogged along the A road to the city, jacket clasped at the neck, the rain whipping through the gap in her hood.

She hit the station after half three, exhausted, stomach squirming with hunger. The back of her head had begun to tingle and she stumbled on the curb. Something seemed to be approaching very quickly from behind her eyes. She staggered into Boots, looking for a protein drink, but they only had Slimfast shakes. She bought a strawberry one, although it tasted more like fusty cardboard than fruit, and sipped it while searching the Departures board.

Her phone vibrated. Probably Spence shrieking with horror at the Disney overload. She checked the screen – *No, it couldn't be.* A LinkedIn message.

She opened the app. It was from him!

Hi Sophie,

Thanks so much for getting in touch. Sorry for not replying sooner, but I don't have a phone at the moment, and it's not always easy to get online. Let me know where and when to meet for an interview, and I'll be there.

I appreciate this chance more than you could ever know. I promise I won't let you down.

Alan Griffin.

Even after the third read, Rachel didn't get it. Was he being sarcastic? Or did he really not know it was her? Perhaps he wasn't watching when she wrote the message.

The crowd in the concourse was clearing. Rachel checked the board – her train was leaving in three minutes. She raced to the platform and managed to squeeze on. Perfect. Just perfect. Packed in a scrum of suits and office skirts, close enough to inhale sweat and perfume and stale coffee with every breath. She grasped a ceiling strap and tried to keep it together. Today had solved nothing. If anything, she'd made it worse – he knew he was getting to her. Condensation ran down the inside of the windows; the bodies pressed against her gave off a suffocating heat; the Slimfast shake lurched around her stomach as though it had come alive and was looking for the exit. Would she ever get her life back? Or was this it? Endless terror until she snapped. It felt as though it had been her world forever. There was no way out. She squeezed her eyes shut; the tracks clattered, *don't pan-ic, don't pan-ic, don't pan-ic*; the brakes screeched and she glanced around. Everyone seemed to be looking away, but she knew they'd been watching her, amused by her performance. They all thought she was mad.

From Paddington, it took another hour to get back. By the time she barged through the front door at home, it was six. Spence had been looking after Lily for eight hours. A huge amount of time to fill with someone else's kid – a huge amount to fill with your *own* kid.

'Lily!' she cried. 'Mummy's home!'

Dread flooded her body so fast it felt like drowning. The lights were off upstairs. No sounds from the kitchen. Were they playing hide and seek? She called again, and waited, not moving. Silence. She touched the back of the television. Cold. *That was the trap. Spence was in on it. They wanted to lure her away so he could take Lily.* She fumbled out her phone. A couple of missed calls from Mark, and a WhatsApp message from Spence. They were in the park. He'd sent a picture of Lily by the small algae-filled duck pond, dropping sunflower seeds into the water. Rachel flung the phone onto the sofa and slumped against the wall, hands to her chest.

The phone leapt to life. Mark's name flashed on the screen. She debated whether to take it – she was desperate for a glass of warm milk, a hot shower and a change of clothes – but she'd put this off long enough. After what happened today, Mark had to know about Griffin.

'Hey,' she said. 'I need to tell–'

He cut her off. 'You at home?'

'Sure, I–'

'Do *not* move. I'm coming over. Right now.' He hung up before she could reply.

Rachel went through to the kitchen and got the milk from the fridge. It splashed over the side of the glass as she poured. She heated it for thirty seconds then drank it slowly, waiting for it to settle in her stomach between sips. The slow hand-to-mouth motion was calming, although her head still hurt like someone was forcing their thumb into the soft matter at the front of her brain. She was seriously dehydrated.

She heard the front door open and froze. Lily's high childish laugh came from the living room. Rachel rushed through and grabbed her into an embrace, holding her as tightly as if she'd nearly been hit by a car.

'I fed the ducks,' Lily said.

'I know.' Rachel smiled at Spence. 'I saw the photo.'

'Do you know what ducks say when you feed them?' Lily asked.

'What's that, sweetness?'

Lily reared back and gripped her mother's cheeks, squeezing the skin hard enough to hurt. Her face was cold and serious, like something from a horror film, the moment before the cute little girl explains in a demonic voice how great it is to love Satan. Lily leaned in, until her nose was touching Rachel's and, eyes unflinching, screeched, '*QUAAAAAAAAK!*'

She let go and fell back, laughing. Rachel touched her cheek. Her hand was shaking. That was it, she'd broken her daughter. She'd tried so hard, she'd wanted so much to be different to her parents, but the evidence of her failure was right there, screaming in her face.

'Say sorry to Mummy,' Rachel pleaded, but Lily was caught up with trying to look at the heel of her wellington boot. Rachel grabbed her arm. 'I asked you to–'

'No!' Spence tried to release her grip. 'It's a joke. You're hurting her.'

Rachel shot him a look. 'It's not a joke.'

He worked her last fingers free. 'It's something I used to do with my brother as a kid. I just—'

The front door flew open. Rachel scrambled to cover Lily, pushing her to the carpet and lying on top, as though the entrance had been blasted off.

'Oh, you *are* alive then?'

Mark's voice. Rachel glanced around. He was edging towards them, each step dropping him lower into a crouch. Spence backed out of the way.

'Let go of Lily,' Mark said, gently. 'Please?'

Rachel lifted her hands, and Lily crawled from under her. Whimpering, she ran to her father, who hoisted her up. He turned her around, as though inspecting her for damage.

'I'm sorry. I — I thought...' Rachel shook her head. 'I just thought...'

Mark deposited Lily onto the sofa, then held his hand out for Rachel. 'Can we have a chat?' he asked, helping her up. 'In the kitchen.'

She followed him through. He went to lean against the counter, but seeing the mess of spills and crockery, thought better of it and stood with his hands on his hips. 'What the actual hell?'

'She screamed in my face,' Rachel muttered, more to herself than Mark.

'What are you talking about?'

'Lily, before you came in.'

'What are you *talking* about? God, you're driving me nuts. What's happening to you? Do you have any idea how worried your dad's been?'

Rachel's face was humming, her throat prickling. She groped for the edge of table. Did she have an Oxy on the train back, or was she just exhausted? She couldn't remember. 'I don't... My dad?'

'He was supposed to pick up Lily? From nursery?'

'Oh, no. I meant to call them, but–'

'When they said she hadn't been in, and they hadn't heard from you, he came round here and found the place empty. He was frantic by the time he got to mine. I know...' Mark scratched the back of his neck. 'I know you've got your, you know, with your dad. I get it. But don't punish the old bloke.'

She shook her head. 'I wasn't... I didn't...'

'*Really?*'

'I promise.'

He went serious. 'You know he thought... And when I rang and you didn't answer... The way you've been acting, we were worried you might have, you know, done something.'

Done something. How crazy did he think she was? Enough to jump in front of a train with Lily in her arms?

This had to stop.

'Listen to me,' she said. 'It's Alan Griffin.'

Mark stepped back. '*What?*'

Rachel nodded carefully.

'Oh, shit.' Mark grabbed his chin. 'Oh shit, shit, shit... Why didn't–?'

'I know, I'm sorry. I'm so, so sorry.' It was such a relief to tell someone who knew what Griffin was capable of doing; it felt as though a fist gripping her lungs had let go, allowing her to breathe freely for the first time in days. 'I should have told you – I *wish* I'd told you.'

'Oh, wow. Oh, God. Alan Griffin. Already? I thought he got–'

'Out early.'

'So what–'

'He got me suspended from work.'

'How did he–?'

'He stole my wages.'

'He did *what?*'

She was trying to remember all of it, but her mind had become a sinkhole, and she could only reach inside to grab random thoughts. 'The photo – *the photo!*'

Mark looked confused. 'What photo?'

'The one of me as a teenager.'

'*That* photo?'

'*That* photo.' Rachel licked her lips. She knew this wasn't coming out right, that it wouldn't make complete sense, but telling him was like vomiting poison. She couldn't stop. 'I was at the gym, and Griffin sent it to Konrad's mate Pete on Snapchat. He got into my account and sent him that photo of me. So that it looked like I did it.'

Mark's nod was warier than she hoped. 'Griffin had your phone?'

'No, he hacked my phone.'

'Right.'

'Then he broke me and Konrad up.'

'But how–?'

'He set him up with loan sharks, then stole my money from my account, so it looked like–'

'Hold up,' Mark said, waving his hands. 'Who stole money? Konrad?'

'No, Griffin. From me, *and* Konrad.'

'Whaaaaa?'

Mark looked lost. She was about to begin again, but he cut her off. 'Stop, stop, please. I can't... *process* what you're saying.' He paused for a long breath, his fingers pressed back to back in the middle of his chest. 'Let's start from the beginning. Okay. How do you know Griffin's out?'

'Look at this.' Rachel opened the laptop on the kitchen table and slid into a chair, trying not to notice the way Mark was grimacing at her, like she had something gross smeared on her cheek, but it was too far into the conversation to say anything. She loaded the paedo hunter website.

'Not these again,' he groaned.

'Hold on.'

'You know this is how–'

'Wait!' She patted his forearm, softened her voice. 'Just wait, okay?' She moved down Griffin's page until she got to the post saying he'd been released.

'Oh, Jesus,' Mark said. 'What else is there?'

'You'll like this,' Rachel said, scrolling to his address, pleased he finally sounded like he believed her. 'I think he posted this himself, to mess with me.'

Mark frowned as he looked at the screen. A moment later, his head began an apologetic, but still definite, shake. She was wrong. He didn't believe her. Same as Becca, he thought she was making it up to get attention. How else could she prove it? The hidden camera! Where did she–?

'Tell me the truth, Rach,' Mark said, his tone measured, careful rather than accusatory. 'Are you stalking Alan Griffin?'

Rachel felt her shoulders twitch. 'Am I what?'

Mark tried for a laugh, but it flatlined into a nervous *ummmm*. 'You posted his address online. Now you're trying to tell me you found it. And you've–'

'Wait – *what?* You think I posted his address. It was...' She leaned forward to read the name. 'JustForYou. But I think that's Griffin. I think–'

'Stop, Rachel – *stop!*' He jabbed the login name in the top right corner of the forum page. '*You're* logged on as JustForYou. Right now. On *this* computer.'

How was that possible?

'He must have been here, when I was out,' she said, but even she wasn't convinced. 'Maybe he drove.'

She sparked on an image of Griffin, sad and scuzzy in his hovel, his slug of a tongue feeling around the beer can lip for the final drops.

Something wasn't right.

Mark clicked on JustForYou's name to open the profile. The

fields were bare, no personal details or interests, no signature set up to go on the bottom of posts. He pointed to the session details.

'You've been logged into this account since seven thirty last night. Alan Griffin's address was posted straight after.'

She stared at the screen, stunned. Could *she* have done all this to herself? Sent that photo from Snapchat, transferred the money to Konrad's account, deleted her patient records and posted that fat-shaming picture of Becca. The text she received when Konrad left – *YOU'RE ALL MINE NOW* – had she sent that from a burner phone hidden down the back of the sofa? Was that possible? Had she plied herself with too many painkillers and starved herself too many times that she'd actually broken her brain?

Mark was rubbing her arms, like she'd told him she was cold. 'We'll get through this, okay? I'm here for you. You're not alone, Rachel.'

She wasn't listening. Her headache had gone scalpel sharp. She needed to get some sleep, let her subconscious sift through it all, come to it tomorrow with fresh eyes. It'd be better if he took Li–

A shrill scream from the living room. Mark bolted out of the kitchen. She lumbered after him, moving so slow it felt as if she was wading.

Mark was on the floor, rocking and shushing Lily. Spence was back on his heels, mouth wide and hands to his head, like he'd been frozen mid-scream. Rachel saw the blood. So much blood. Covering Lily's little arm and spilling onto Mark's neatly pressed jeans. Beside them was the ceramic vegetable knife, the white blade stained red. 'You're the bloody nurses,' he said. 'Do something!'

CHAPTER THIRTY-TWO

Blood

L ily had been reaching under the sofa for a dropped crayon, and instead found the knife. The wound stretched across her palm, from the base of her little finger to the soft pad of flesh beside her thumb. Although not deep, it bled like a slashed artery.

Mark wrapped Lily in his beige raincoat, which, Rachel noted through her numbness, was as smart and new as the rest of his wardrobe. Clutching his daughter to his chest, he ran the mile to Whittington Hospital A&E. Rachel lumbered through the wet streets, unable to keep up, her legs stiff and unwieldy.

She staggered past the ambulances, through the sliding doors, and into the strip-lit hell of a busy emergency room. Like all nurses, as a student she'd done a stint in A&E, a two-week placement in The Dungeon of Torment, otherwise known as Ealing Hospital. And like all students, Rachel had found the experience exciting, dramatic, but more than anything, terrifying, especially the Friday night shifts where the smell of bleach, beer, and kebab burps had her retching into the toilet for half the night. Rarely had the term "never again" been more apt.

She scanned the coughing groaning contents of the plastic chairs in the reception. No sign of Lily or Mark. The receptionist, an older woman with a receding hairline and an aura that suggested she'd been asked a thousand stupid questions in the last hour alone, told her they were in triage, but said she couldn't go in.

'I'm her mother,' Rachel moaned.

'I don't know that,' she replied.

'I'm a nurse.'

'So you should know better than to ask.' Her expression softened a touch. 'Take a seat. They'll be out soon.'

Rachel perched on the last of a crooked line of grey chairs. She stared at the wall-mounted television, where a brassy blonde girl was letting rip at a smirking lump for kissing her best friend, but it failed to distract Rachel from the awful truth: she was a terrible mother. If ever she needed proof of that fact, this was it. Who left a sharp knife under the sofa when there was a child in the house? Worse, she didn't even remember putting it there! She thought it was in her bedroom, although that wasn't too much of an improvement. Some parent. Pathetic.

Eventually, Mark came out, Lily clinging to him like a koala, his stained raincoat folded into a pillow on his shoulder. Rachel sprang from her seat, but he pressed down with his hand and came to her. She wanted to rip her daughter from his arms – *She's mine, she's MINE!* – but it was as if she'd forfeited some primal right of motherhood. Why should she be the one to comfort her when she was the one to blame?

Twenty minutes later, a junior doctor was stitching the wound. Rachel wept as the needle pierced the pink ridges of skin, crushed by the knowledge that whenever her daughter looked at the scar, she'd be reminded of her mother's negligence. Lily sat on Mark's lap as it was being done, shrugging off Rachel's hand when she tried to place it on her shoulder, turning her head when she went to kiss her cheek.

'She's tired,' Mark said after Lily was discharged, but the resigned look on his face told the real story. In her core, in her very being, Rachel was broken. It emanated from her like body odour, a pheromone of failure. She tried to cover it up, but if anyone stood too close, then sooner or later they got the stink of her real nature and couldn't wait to get away. First her parents, now Mark and Lily, with every friend, colleague and acquaintance along the way. Who did she have left? No-one.

She was alone.

Always was, always will be.

Back at Mark's apartment, once he'd put Lily to bed, they stood together in the hallway. He asked Rachel to come and sit in the lounge, but she said she wasn't stopping long. The place stank of dehydrated broccoli; he must have been steaming vegetables when he left and forgot to turn them off.

'I'm not taking Lily away,' Mark said. 'It's just until...'

He left the words hanging. Until when? She sorted her head out? Until Griffin was gone? Until hell entered the next ice age? Rachel nodded, glumly rubbing at a bead of dried paint on the wall, lips bitten into her mouth to stop the tears. She didn't want to be there. She didn't want to be anywhere. She wanted to be blank and lost, to disappear completely.

'Tell me you understand, Rach.'

'I understand,' she replied, but she couldn't look at him.

'It's just after what you said. Yesterday...'

Was that only yesterday? It seemed like a year ago. 'It's okay.'

'I don't want you to go home and dredge through everything and pull out some paranoia that I'm trying to steal Lily from you.'

'I won't.'

'Right. Okay. Good. It's a cut – fine. But if something else happened... Social services, you know?'

Yes, she knew. She'd been trained to look for the signs, had seen child services come onto the ward to interview parents accused of neglect. With the superiority of the flipping ignorant, she'd assumed it would never happen to her.

Mark put his hand on her shoulder. 'Stay as well. Long as you like.'

'What about your girlfriend?'

'You're still my friend. My best friend.'

The kindness in his face cracked her defences, and she started to cry. 'I'm sorry. I'm so sorry.'

'I wish you'd told me. You really think it's Griffin?'

'There's no other explanation.'

Wasn't there? The unsaid hung between them like a ghost, chilling the air. Who was signed in as JustForYou when Griffin's address appeared on paedo-hunter.net? Who was signed into Snapchat when that photo was sent to Konrad's mates? Whose Insta account was Becca's photo posted on? Wasn't the simplest, most convincing, explanation for all of this that she was doing it to *herself*? That she'd hunted Alan Griffin in some mad amnesiac fugue and posted his address online. By day, a nurse and mother, by night a stalking self-destructive lunatic.

'So what we going to do about it?' Mark asked.

'I don't know.'

'The police.'

'I can't.'

'I know last time they—'

'*No*, Mark. Please.' She gripped her fingers guiltily, as though she'd given something away. 'You don't know the full story. He set up Konrad, made it look like he stole the money from my bank account.'

'And you don't think maybe...'

She saw Konrad at her bedroom door, struggling to contain his tears. 'It's not him.'

Mark shrugged out an okay, but she could see he wasn't convinced. 'Get some rest. Let's talk in the morning.'

What she wouldn't give for a good night's rest, to wake fresh and alert and ready to face the horror her life had become, but she knew it wouldn't happen. She started for the door but stopped and tried for a smile. 'Is it... you know, serious? With this girl?'

'I think it just might be.'

'I'm – I'm pleased. About time, eh?'

He stepped towards her and they hugged again. 'Thanks,' he said. 'Maybe, you know. You'd like to meet her? When all this... you know...'

'I'd like that.'

'Oh, and Rach?'

'What?'

'*Eat something.*'

Spence was still at her place, as he said he'd be, eating chow mein from a silver foil tray. When she opened the door, he rushed to help her, taking her arm and encouraging her back to the sofa, as though she were an aged relative who'd been gone for hours without telling anyone.

'How was it?' he asked.

The soy and ginger smell of his breath made her stomach spasm, and Rachel had to hold back a heave. She glanced at where it had happened, remembering the pool of blood on the blue carpet. Spence had scrubbed it into a faint rusty smear. Lily's blood. *Lily's blood.* There forever for her to see. Something seemed to give in Rachel's mind, like the slats of a bed breaking beneath a mattress that had been jumped on too many times. She pitched forward and let out a wail.

'It was a mistake,' Spence murmured, rubbing her back. 'People make mistakes.'

'What kind of mistake scars your child?'

'You've been under a lot of stress. It was–'

'She's better off away from me. I – I don't want her turn-turning into me.'

'There's nothing wrong with you. You're amazing. You're fabulous.'

'I should have known the knife was there.'

'It was an accident.'

'An *accident*? An accident is when you trip on a curb, or spill your coffee down your front. An accident is when you put your whites and colours in the same wash. An accident is not when your child slices her hand open on a knife that *you've* left hidden around the house.'

'It's as much my fault. I was on my phone, I wasn't watching.' Spence nodded to his half-finished tray of noodles. 'You want some food? I've chowed my last mein for today.'

She shook her head. 'My stomach's off. I'll have a glass of warm milk in bed.'

'I'm worried about you.'

'Please, don't be.'

'I'm not stupid, Rachel. You could carve up a supermodel's face with those cheekbones.'

'Listen, you go. I'll be—'

Spence shut her up with a sassy snap of his fingers. 'Nu-uh, girl. Spence is stayin'.'

'You really don't—'

'And if anyone comes knocking, I'll give them a — *hiya!*' He executed a set of mid-air chops. 'Unless it's a hot guy, in which case it might be *hey ya!*'

She could see how hard he was working to cheer her up. How could she be so selfish, keeping him here? He should be in Greece, sipping champagne from the dimple of some hot bloke's bum cheek, not crashing on her cold sofa. 'Have you spoken to Andreas? Have you explained—?'

'Plenty of time to hear my latest love woes tomorrow, missy.'

'Oh! Does that—?'

Spence clapped his hands. 'Bed — *now*. I'll be up in five with your milk.'

. . .

Rachel jolted awake in the dark. Someone had screamed.

Lily? Where was Lily? Her mind sprinted back – *oh God.*

The knife.

Her baby's blood.

Rachel patted for the lamp on her nightstand. She probably woke herself with her own shrieking, like a soldier with PTSD. The bed felt solid, the sheets rough, fibrous. This wasn't her bed. It was the floor. Whose floor? Had she been kidnapped? She rolled onto her front, groping in the dark, an electric fizz of fear going from her neck to her heels, until the back of her fingers rapped something wooden. She felt furniture, the leg of a dressing table, and groaned. It was *her* dressing table. She was on the floor of *her* bedroom. Okay, she got it now. She'd smashed herself unconscious with sleeping pills, climbed out of bed, and went for a crawl. As you do. If you're deranged.

Footsteps thumped up the stairs. The hallway light came on. Rachel scrabbled backwards, smacking her head on the radiator.

'Rach – *Rach!*'

'I'm here,' she called, rubbing the back of her skull.

The door opened. Spence stepped in, his silhouette facing the bed. 'Rachel?'

'Here,' she replied, dragging herself up with the table.

He felt around for the light and turned it on. 'What are you doing down there?'

'I don't...' she began, shielding her eyes, but then she saw his legs.

Was she still dreaming? Stuck in a nightmare where you think you wake again and again but never actually do?

It couldn't be there, all that blood.

Below his Mykonos T-shirt, past his grey checked hipster trunks, crimson rivulets ran from his thighs like a gory barcode. She opened her mouth to speak, but nothing came out. This wasn't real.

'It's okay, Rach. Stay calm. It looks worse than it is.'

'What – what...'

'I was asleep,' he said, crouching beside her. His skin was clammy, his chin quivering. Scores of tiny cuts covered his legs. 'I heard a crash, and...' He shut his eyes and winced. 'Someone threw a *brick* through the window.'

She followed him downstairs. The curtain had caught most of the bigger pieces, but shards still covered the sofa.

'We can't stay here,' he said. 'Let's go back to mine.'

While Spence covered the hole as best he could with cardboard and tape, then stuffed her an overnight bag, Rachel rocked in the armchair, holding her head with her fingertips, as though it were broken down the middle and she had to keep the two sides together until they got help.

They got out just before six. It was still dark, the air chilly, the first edges of dawn worrying the horizon. Ducked low, as if the pavement was being swept with searchlights, they weaved through the back streets, glancing round every few seconds to see if they were being followed, coming out on the Holloway Road in time to see a black cab pulling up by a bus stop. Spence hurried to it, arm out, and they clambered into the back. Spots of blood were coming through his skinny jeans. He leaned forward to talk to the driver through the partition. 'Head down Seven Sisters to Tottenham. I'll direct when you're close.'

Rachel clawed at her throat. It had closed up so tight she couldn't breathe. Terror after terror after terror, her life a series of jump scares. She doubled over, hands pressed to her chest, sure she could feel a leaden sensation spreading around her ribs. *When would it end? Was he not going to stop until she was dead?*

'It's okay, it's okay,' Spence said, rubbing her back. 'You're safe. You're with me now.'

CHAPTER THIRTY-THREE

Nurse

First he called the ward.

'St Pancras, Oakwood.'

'Good morning. May I ask to whom I am talking?'

'Oh, okay. I'm Hannah. I'm the... student nurse. Do you want me to get–?'

'No, no, it's okay. It's nothing bad! My name is Phil Jenkins, and my father, Michael, was recently with you, recovering from a problem with his hip. He's feeling much better now and has asked me to get in touch so he can send a little something to the kind nurses who cared for him. May I have your full address please?'

'Sure, of course. Just address it to the ward. We're at four St Pancras Way, Kings Cross... Hold on a sec... Okay, here we are. NW1 0PE.'

'Wonderful. Thank you, Hannah. One more thing. My father said one of the nurses there was especially helpful to him. Spence... errr... something.'

'Spence Borrowman?'

'Yes, that's right. How do you spell that?'

'B-O-R-R-O-W-M-A-N.'

'And who is actually in charge – I'd like to include them in the thank you.'

'You mean Linda?'

'Linda...?'

'Linda Green. The ward manager.'

'That's perfect. Thank you, Hannah. You've been a great help.'

Then he called the manager.

'Linda speaking.'

'Is that Linda Green, manager of the Oakwood ward at St Pancras Hospital?'

'Yes. Yes it is. Has something happened?'

'My name is David Steer, and I'm calling from the Department for Work and Pensions. I have to start by informing you that this call is being recorded. We're investigating a possible illegal worker, a Spencer Borrowman. That's B-O-R-R-O-W-M-A-N. Are you able to assist with this?'

'Oh my word, Spence? But he's English.'

'It's not his nationality we're concerned about. We have reason to believe his nursing credentials are false.'

'No, I can't believe–'

'If you'd prefer, we can bring you into the office for a formal interview.'

'Well... I...'

'Do you mind if I ask you a few questions?'

'Yes, sure, of course. I'm sorry. I want to help. We're having all sorts of problems at the moment. Another nurse is suspended. Never rains, does it?'

'Can you confirm how long Mr Borrowman has been with yourself?'

'Well now, he started as a bank nurse – that's an agency nurse – to cover Rowena Feldman. She eventually moved–'

'How long ago was that?'

'Less than a year, maybe eleven months. I can—'

'And prior to that he worked as a bank nurse, for different hospitals?'

'I assume so.'

'And do you have the details of where he trained? According to our records, it was at Lincoln University.'

'Hold on, please, let me check... Okay, here it is. Coventry, that's what we have.'

'Dates?'

'2005 to 2008.'

'Hmmm... Just as we thought. Okay, that's it for now. We'll be on site in the next few weeks to interview the rest of the staff.'

'Great. Great.'

'My name's David Steer, extension four-three-four. If you need to get in contact.'

'Thank you, thank you.'

'No, thank *you*, Linda.'

PART THREE

CHAPTER THIRTY-FOUR

Recovery

Why did they call them reality shows? When, in the real world, were you forced to live with a bunch of loud, fun people, and vote them out week by week? When, in the real world, were you able to compete against a coven of beautiful but catty rivals for the affections of a handsome millionaire who, for unconvincing reasons, couldn't find a date on his own? They should call them fantasy shows, dream shows. Shows to take reality away.

Rachel's favourites were the ones with the twist at the end. The millionaire's a pauper, the model's a cleaner. That bloke playing the piano was actually, only a month ago, a pig farmer from Uzbekistan. She liked to see the moment the truth was revealed, the surprise growing on the faces of those who'd been duped. Nested in the corner of Spence's sofa, the duvet pulled up to her chin, still cold despite her layers of clothes – a chill had seeped like winter frost into the foundations of her body – she sipped herbal tea, dipped celery sticks in salt, and waited for the big reveal.

'I hate Georgie,' Spence said. 'That orange bitch. She looks like she exfoliated with Wotsits.'

On the screen, a beauty-pageant brunette in a black cocktail dress was conspiring by the swimming pool with Danielle, the ginger human rights lawyer with the sparkling smile, their dark horse to win the whole thing.

'Cameron doesn't like fakers,' Rachel replied. 'If Danielle tells him Georgie lied about being a vet, he'll vote her out.'

'That's the problem with Danielle. She won't betray anyone's trust, even a scheming bitch like Georgie.'

'She's got to get her head in the game.'

Spence leaned over Rachel's piled-up duvet, ready for a high five. 'Go Team Danielle!'

She slapped his palm. Oh, Cameron. The perfect man. Six feet of broad muscles and graceful gestures, with the brooding eyes of a soap star and the heart of a Médecins Sans Frontières doctor. His secret: once a tech millionaire, he'd donated his entire fortune to malaria research and now worked as a handyman in a Mexican orphanage. Out of all the sneaks and snakes vying for his attention, Danielle was the only one worthy, the only one who'd stick on dungarees, grab a mop, and follow him to Oaxaca.

At the end of the episode, Rachel and Spence applauded as Cameron dismissed Georgie from the mansion.

'Saw right through her,' Spence said.

'Fake as a pair of silicone tits.'

He pushed off the sofa, laughing. 'You're such a grade-A bitch. But I love ya anyway.' He stretched, pumping one fist in the air then the other. 'Better get dinner on.'

'What's on the menu tonight, chef?'

'Carbonara?'

'Mmmm... can't wait.'

She'd been staying with him for a week, and in that time he'd shown himself to be as deft at rich Italian food as he was at sharp Asian flavours or dusky Indian spices.

Spence's apartment was open plan, so from the corner of his grey suede sofa, she could watch him cook. While he poured boiling water into the spaghetti-filled saucepan, humming a jaunty tune that sounded like something from a musical, she flicked through the channels, settling on Good Food+1, where a manicured hand was sliding a silver peeler along the side of an asparagus tip. A voiceover explained about the wonders of spring veg.

At first, repelled by the thought of someone watching her eat, Rachel didn't want him to make meals, saying she'd rather graze, but he'd insisted.

'You don't have to eat any of it,' he'd said. 'But it'll be there if you do.' He'd been so good to her, insisting she stay for as long as she needed, even giving her his room, with the double bed and the en suite bathroom, that she didn't want to disappoint him. Besides, by trying to get her to eat at meal times, he was doing the right thing to help her recovery. They'd do the same in a clinic. And she wanted to recover, of course she did – she was on her knees and had to get back up. She just needed more time. A few more days.

Spence's apartment was perfect for hiding out. On the fourth floor of a windswept new development near the North Circular, towards the back of a gated complex, it was buried in the London hinterlands. Griffin would never find her here. It helped that it was such a great place to hang out – she didn't know why Spence talked it down so much. In the past, whenever she'd suggested coming over, he'd waved her away, as though it would be embarrassing for her to see where he lived.

Yes, it was small, only the kitchen/lounge and two bedrooms, and the local area was never going to be featured in the *Evening Standard* as a cool new hipster neighbourhood, not unless someone opened a line of beard-shaping salons by the Esso garage, but the decor was so elegantly stylish. The white feather lampshade, the monochrome Parisian prints, each in their own box frame, spaced along the back wall, the inset shelves lined with interesting books, wide candles, and polished wooden stickmen sculptures that looked like they might come from Africa. It was so different from the jumbled clutter she spent half her time rooting through at home.

On the television, the asparagus was being fried on a griddle pan, one side already scored with thick char lines. The manicured hand tossed on rock salt. Rachel stretched her leg, massaging the growing ache in her thigh. The warm feeling in her head was fading too. The Demerol wearing off. *Damn it*. She shivered and pulled the duvet over her mouth, hoping her breath would rebound and heat the top of her face. Was it getting colder? That last dose hadn't lasted long, maybe a couple of hours. They were strong too. Opioids. Maybe they were old, out of date. She hoped so. With resistance came physical dependence, and *that* was one thing she didn't need, not on top of everything else.

When they'd first arrived at Spence's a week ago, she'd panicked. She'd forgotten to tell him about the money box, and as awful and addicted as it sounded, she didn't think she'd cope without it. She was swaying on the edge, could feel her toes hanging over the abyss, and feared the next shame spiral might send her all the way to the bottom. In the end, it wasn't an issue.

When she'd broached the subject with him, thinking maybe they could make an emergency appointment with a GP, he rather guiltily admitted to a sizeable pharmaceutical stash of his own, pilfered over the years, mostly from dead patients. It wasn't an uncommon thing for hospital workers to do – doctors, orderlies, and cleaners alike all did it – and it wasn't something she condoned, but neither was she going to be a prig about it, especially as she helped herself to his hoard as soon as it was offered.

The first few days, Rachel had stayed in bed. Lights off, door closed, duvet pulled up, she'd focused on the hunger; it was like the tide, sometimes high, sometimes low, but always there, going round and round her world. She ate nothing in that time, sipping only water when her throat became too raw from crying, refusing Spence's pleas to have a glass of warm milk, a bowl of vegetable soup, half a banana, something. She didn't deserve to eat.

She didn't want to talk about what to do next, how to deal with Griffin, or what new piece of her life he was feeding through the shredder while she wasn't there. The only blessing was that the brick through the window at least proved she wasn't some deranged schizophrenic trying to sabotage her own sanity, not unless shimmying up a drainpipe was one of her subconscious's superpowers. As far as comforts went, it was about as useful as a blanket on a bed of knives. Her world was still in tatters.

Meanwhile the anorexic voice, constant as tinnitus, had set up decks in the shadows of her mind and was playing horror noises – rending metal, women screaming, demonic laughter – behind worried sound-bites. *You can't eat. You won't eat. You'll never eat again.* The painkillers had helped, softening the sounds to a whisper, and sometimes she tried confronting the voice, shouting it down with *I know you!* and *I won't let you win!* But most of the time she had to listen. And the more she listened, the more the voice made sense, especially when it talked about Lily.

There *were* many arguments to be made for Lily being better off without her. Looking at it objectively, as an outsider from the situation, no-one could be blamed for coming to that conclusion. Where would Lily be safer? Where would she be happier? Where would she get the chance for the best possible life? On the one side, there was Mark, stable, with money, and a new girlfriend he was serious about, who loved his daughter as much as she did, and on the other there was Rachel: a jinx, a liability, an anxious depressed anorexic whose very gravity seemed to attract bad things. Maybe years from now, while being wheeled back to the psych ward after another round of electroshock therapy, she'd look back at what Griffin was doing to her as the best thing that could have happened. It got Lily away before she soaked up any more of her mother's madness.

Eventually, Rachel realised she couldn't hide in Spence's bedroom forever. Whether she wanted to or not, she had to kick off the process of recovery. So she crawled out of bed, sat on his sofa instead, and tried to eat – although perhaps not as much as she made out to Spence, who always looked a little too much like a proud parent watching their kid go potty whenever Rachel took chocolates from the offered box of Cadbury's Celebrations. She felt guilty and a little pathetic unwrapping them, pretending to put them in her mouth, then hiding them in her pocket – and later, unsure whether they'd flush down the toilet, beneath her mattress, rewrapped so they didn't melt and make a mess – but the shame and the secrecy, the whole exhausting palaver, were as much a part of it as the illicit thrill of pride at her powers of denial. She took great and constant comfort in the fact that she was stronger than anyone would ever know.

Rachel yawned and opened her arms wide until the joints cracked along her spine. Without daily exercise, her muscles had stiffened and her bones felt brittle as thin ice. That wasn't all. She had pain in her kidneys and chest, and a permanent dull throb deep in her pelvis, just above her uterus. Her period, which was due to come on days ago, showed no signs of starting. She dug the amber plastic tub of Demerol from between the sofa cushions and fingered the screw cap. Normal people didn't live this way. But what else could she do? She was here. This was happening. She could no more change her immediate situation than she could turn herself into someone else simply by looking at her reflection and willing it so. Recovery was a process, as much as the starvation itself, and couldn't be rushed.

The cookery programme cut to a commercial break. She clicked off the television and rubbed her eyes. From the kitchen came a deep-meat aroma of sizzling pancetta that made her mouth water and her stomach pulse. What was her calorie count? The lower it was, the more she could eat tonight. She'd set herself a target of five hundred, big enough to be a ledge to four digits, but not so big as to be intimidating. A nice round number that she could achieve over the day. She worked through it from the morning – glass of semi-skimmed milk, a hundred millilitres exact, forty-seven calories. Seven carrot sticks, six calories each, more or less, another forty-two. Forty-nine total. No, eighty-nine. She rubbed her eyes. Her head was too swampy, so she called to Spence in the kitchen to throw her his phone. In the rush to get away, she'd left hers at home. At first, she'd freaked out, not having it, but now it felt like more of a relief, not being lured to look at the screen every few minutes.

He turned off the extractor fan above the cooker, stopped stirring and put his hand to his ear.

Rachel made her hands into a cup and mimed a catch. 'Phone?'

'Not if you're going to zombie out looking at Insta pics of cakes again.' He slacked his jaw and lolled his tongue. 'Just creepy.'

'Gotta add something up.'

He shrugged, slid it from the counter, ran his finger along the screen to unlock it, and tossed it to land on the cushion beside her. When she reached for it, the muscle covering her ribs went into spasm. Fortunately Spence had turned the fan back on, so he didn't hear her whimpering. She wasn't supposed to have the next Demerol until after dinner, a double bedtime dose to get her through the night, but she didn't think she could wait that long. Besides, why did it matter? How was it any better to be in pain?

She found the calculator and started to input the calories, but a wave of sadness swept through her and she pressed her fingers to her eyes, trying to stop the tears. What was she *doing*? She closed the calculator and went to his texts, opening the one from Mark last night, a close-up photo of Lily's grinning face with the words: *don't worry about me, Mummy. You just get better soon x.*

Rachel thought about her high sweet voice, her beautiful little smile, the way she clung to her as she carried her downstairs for breakfast. Even now, when Lily could run up and down the steps without touching the banister, she insisted on the morning Mummy Train. The best part of the day was the feel of her daughter's arms wrapped tight around her. In those moments it all made sense, her being a mother.

Everyone else in her life, Konrad, Becca, even her dad, had given up on her – they all had or could easily get Spence's number, but none had bothered to get in touch, to check she was okay – but Lily loved her, she was sure of that, despite how she'd been at the hospital. How could she desert her daughter? How could she leave her behind?

Rachel remembered her father in the kitchen talking about her mum. *She got rid of me, then she got rid of you...*

Was that really what happened when she went to live with her gran? Did her own mum send her away so she could starve herself to death? Was she doing the same thing? Spence was bound to get sick of her being here, sooner or later, and she'd have to go home. Lily wouldn't be able to live with her, not in the state she was in. What would happen then?

You know what will happen then.

Rachel locked Spence's phone, her heart wrenching as Lily's face disappeared into the darkness, and Rachel pressed her fist to her mouth. She needed to calm down. Everything was beginning to whip around inside. Her mum must have felt like this – like she'd failed, like there was no other way, like her daughter would have a better life far from her. Rachel twisted the lid off the Demerol and tipped two of the small white pills into her palm. *Fuck it.* She shook out another and pushed all three to her mouth, grinding them between her teeth, shuddering at the bitter taste.

From the kitchen came the sound of a cork being eased from a bottle of wine. 'Ready!' Spence called.

She padded over to the table. 'You really don't have to go to all this effort every time,' she said, as he pulled out her chair.

He always made it look so special for dinner. On a white tablecloth, washing-machine clean, he'd laid out black woven placemats, the cutlery precisely straight on either side, their wine glasses waiting a barely respectful distance from the last tines of their forks. Between their settings sat a dainty green seawater bowl, heaped with fresh grated Parmesan, the tiny silver spoon buried into the side as though it'd been thrown at the cheese like a dart. The line of chunky tea lights sitting deep in their smoky glasses on the counter gave the kitchen a romantic glow. He didn't have to do all this, but she appreciated his efforts to make it nice for her, to make the best possible ambiance for her to eat.

'Cheers,' Spence said, tipping his wine glass towards her.

Rachel toasted him and took a ten-calorie sip, savouring the dry oaky flavour. 'It smells amazing,' she said, lowering her nose to the graceful swirl of creamy pasta, speckled with black pepper and pancetta, on her plate. The muscle in her ribs seized again, but she kept the pain off her face and carried on pretending to sniff while frantically massaging the area with her fingertips until she was able to sit up straight. She prayed those pills kicked in soon.

'Boner appetite,' Spence said.

'Boners to you too,' Rachel replied, separating out a strand of spaghetti. She twirled it with her fork, smothering it with sauce, and lifted it into her mouth. She chewed slowly, methodically, taking minutes to finish. And repeat.

To his credit, Spence didn't stare. Instead, he ate his food like a normal human being, dabbing with a napkin between bites, and carried on the conversation as though he weren't sharing the table with an actual mad woman. She didn't deserve to have such a good friend, someone who'd come back from holiday to defend her at work, who put up with her mooching miserably around his apartment, who had his legs shredded for her, although thankfully it had looked worse than it was, and none of the cuts needed more than a plaster. How much longer would he put up with her? A week was a long time to babysit even the best of friends. Whether she wanted to go or not, she needed to pull herself together and get out of here, before this relationship became as ruined as the rest in her life. She couldn't bear the thought of that happening.

She cleared her throat. 'Spence?'

He paused, fork halfway to his mouth. Seeing her face, he frowned. 'Pasta no good?'

'This last week... You could have done so much with the rest of your time off – you could have flown back out to Greece. But instead you've put your life on hold to play nursemaid to me.'

Spence eased his smile into something a bit more relaxed. 'It's been such a pleasure, really. How often do we get to hang out? It's always work, or a quick drink.'

That was true, and if any positives at all could be gleaned from this horror show, it was that their friendship had deepened from the time they'd spent together. Who knew, for example, that he dressed as smartly sitting around watching morning telly as he did when he was off for a night out? Meanwhile, she hadn't changed out of her trackie bottoms in days. Every time she saw herself in the mirror – hair like an eccentric scientist, the same complexion as someone slid out on a tray in a morgue – she shuddered. Although, thinking about it, perhaps he was trying to make the same point. All the more reason to go before her stay became unwelcome.

'You've been so kind to me,' she said. 'But I really think–'

'The worst thing you can do is rush back before you're ready.'

'What about work? Aren't you due in tomorrow?'

'Fuck them. For how they're treating you. I was thinking of leaving anyway.'

Spence had spoken to Linda a few days ago, but it didn't look great. Somehow, all the backups for the eMAR records had become corrupted. Of course, the tribunal could see this as evidence the whole eMAR system was faulty, but Linda had checked the records of pretty much every other nurse who'd worked at the hospital, even the bank nurses who'd only been there days, and no-one else had such inconsistencies with their paper records.

'It's not their fault the backups got corrupted,' Rachel said.

'You've worked there *two years*.' He forked some pasta into his mouth, covering his lips as he chewed. 'Isn't that worth something? And I told Linda all the Griffin stuff was true. So not only are they calling you incompetent, they're calling me a liar!'

Rachel shook her head. First his relationship, now his job. No way was she going to be responsible for *that*. She was like a vortex, sucking anything good from people's lives. 'I've got to get out of your hair.'

'I like you in my hair. You're fine in my hair.'

'But what about Lily? I need–'

'She's *fine*. You saw the text from Mark, she's doing great.' Spence gave Rachel's hand a reassuring squeeze. 'Focus on *you* for a change.'

Rachel thought of trawling through the mess waiting for her at home. The unpaid bills, the investigation at work, the dying relationships littering the battlefield of her life.

Spence picked up his wine, took a thoughtful sip, then put it back down again. 'Let's be honest, Rach. The state you're in, I wouldn't be able to let you go home. I'd have to take you to a hospital. You know that, right? So you either recover here, watching *Millionaire's Secret* while your fabulous best friend takes care of you, or you go to some cold miserable clinic where they prod you and weigh you and threaten to stick tubes in your tummy. Okay?'

The first warm flickers from the Demerol started in her chest. She breathed out, her eyes slipping closed. Why was she always fighting herself? Why did she always have to make it so *difficult*? Wouldn't it be nicer to hang around here for a bit longer, until she felt ready to face Griffin again?

'I mean, you're eating, right?' Spence said. 'I've seen you scoffing those chocs!'

It was true – she was eating. Maybe not as much as he thought, but a little, every day. That was a big part of recovery, and couldn't be dismissed.

'You've been here before,' Spence went on. 'This isn't the first time you've beaten this thing.'

'You're right,' she murmured.

'Allow yourself the time and space to recover. Griffin will still be there when you go home, so give yourself the best possible chance of beating that bastard. Okay?'

'Okay.'

'Don't let him win.'

She opened her eyes, and smiled. 'I won't.'

Spence nodded to her plate. 'Now go on, do your wacky eating thing.'

She laughed and picked out a strand of spaghetti with her fork. 'Yes, master.'

As she twirled it, carefully, her vision splitting a little, she glanced at the tall pepper mill and the short salt grinder beside the Parmesan bowl. Something in the angle of the three made her remember her parents, an argument, her father pacing the kitchen, hunched, head down, her mother in pursuit, barely up to his shoulders, her fleshless lips flapping as she shrieked insults. Round and round they went, hating each other, while she, six if that, stood and watched.

You were the cheese. Worthless calories.

Spence lifted the Parmesan bowl and offered her a spoon. 'You want?'

'No thanks,' she replied. *Push those thoughts away. Take a leaf from Spence. Positive, positive, positive! Enjoy the Demerol buzz. You might as well.* Rachel smothered her spaghetti strand in sauce and – *Go on! Live a little!* – speared a cube of pancetta. At least twenty calories, but worth it. She grinned, her brain feeling floaty. 'How about we lock the doors, block out the windows, and stay here forever?'

Spence dabbed his mouth. 'What happens when we run out of *Millionaire's Secret?*'

'There's a new one, I think. These hot blokes compete to date a woman who turns out to be trans.'

'Sold to the hot momma in the ten jumpers!'

'How do you know I'm a momma?' Rachel took a reckless swig of wine. 'What if I told you I had a foot-long salami down here?'

Spence cackled with laughter. 'I don't know... *Marry me?*'

CHAPTER THIRTY-FIVE

Lily

It wasn't a dream, Rachel wasn't asleep. It was more a spaced-out scenario, her thoughts playing through a fantasy, one she used to have all the time in her teens.

She was a young girl, curled in bed, hands folded beneath her pillow, pretending to be asleep. The bedroom door opened, and her mum – she could tell by the weight of her footsteps, the perfume of her soap – came into the room. Rachel's heart beat faster. She'd come back. Finally, after waiting for so long, she was back.

Her mum lay on the bed behind her, weighing so little that she barely caused a dip in the mattress. Rachel felt the press of her body, the soothing flow of her breath on her neck, and a sense of deep contentment, one she could not remember experiencing before, settled in her chest.

'It's time for me to go,' her mum said, her voice already far away.

No, she thought. *Not yet. Please not yet. Please, please–*

She tried to say something, but she couldn't speak. She tried to turn around, to face her mum, but she couldn't move. As the image faded to black, she screamed and thrashed in her mind, although her body remained perfectly still.

Rachel opened her eyes. The vision had been so vivid, the loss of her mum so acute, it brought to her heart such an aching grief that she was suddenly back to being ten years old, lying in her bedroom on the evening of the funeral, weeping by herself.

This will be Lily soon. Yearning for the mother's love she will never have, because you'll already be dead.

What time was it? She didn't have her phone, and the echo of moonlight coming through the curtains held no answers. Her head was pounding and her sheets were wet from the melancholy fever dreams, each more heartbreaking than the last, that had been coming and going for hours. She shouldn't have had three Demerol, they'd smashed her sideways, but it had been fun at the time, a welcome release, sitting up with Spence, finishing the bottle of wine, listening to MistaJam play dance anthems on Radio 1 and swapping jokes about some of the crazies on the ward. But worse than the comedown, that last dose had pushed her body into dependence. She could tell from the withdrawal twitches in her limbs, the sensation of insects crawling over the surface of her brain, the nervy edge to the voice telling her she really should take some more, because she was in pain, right? Every part of her body was hurting, and what good was it doing her lying here hurting like this?

She turned on the bedside light, gritting against the jolt of agony in her shoulder. Even pressing the button made her finger hurt. Was it any surprise? She knew she needed to stay active, that her muscles seized up if she didn't, but instead of listening to her body she'd shut it up with sedatives, and now look at her. She couldn't blink without wincing. Her skeleton felt like it was made of cracked glass, with every movement causing more fractures.

Recovery?

Such bullshit. She was getting weaker by the day.

Her hand went to the nightstand drawer. The plastic bottle of Demerol was inside. Why not admit the truth for once? She longed to be back in the hospital, back on the psych ward, locked away from the world, where all her failings in it no longer mattered, where she could drift light as a ghost through the pale corridors, mind effortlessly blank, a hazy smile touching her lips. So at peace, so relaxed. That was why she had the stash at home. That was why every time something went wrong, her first reaction was to not eat for a day. That was why she was allowing herself to wallow at Spence's place when she should be at home, fighting Alan Griffin.

She slammed the drawer shut and tossed onto her other side, the wrought iron bed frame squealing in protest. Look at what she was doing to the people who cared about her, to Lily, to Mark, even her dad. Wasn't a sad masochistic part of her secretly pleased she'd driven them away?

She got rid of me, then she got rid of you...

And she was doing the same to Spence, imposing on him. She'd even stolen his bedroom! It should be *him* in here, lying awake in the middle of the night, maybe sharing sweet words with some hot new stud, not his fucked-up mate sweating out her opioid addiction after ditching her family.

She turned back to the drawer, yanked it open. She shook out two Demerol, picturing herself lying back and waiting for the warmth to come in and smother the hunger, the pain, the panicking voice. She stared at the small white pills in her palm.

Maybe it would be better for everyone if you just went home, and waited for the end.

Something inside Rachel seized at that thought – not out of the horror of it, as she would have hoped, but out of excitement. She could go home, lock the door, and let nature do what it does best when it's deprived of sustenance. Who would be there to stop her?

No-one.

An urgent queasy feeling swamped her stomach. She saw Lily as a teenage girl, tall as a willow, with a slender serious face. Her long brown hair was side-parted, a single braid going past her exposed ear. She was crouching by a gravestone, frowning but sad, like she'd been told something important, and she'd said she understood, but really she had no idea what they were talking about, and knew she never would.

She's too young to remember you. Probably best to do it now, rather than wait.

What, like it'd been for her? Not knowing whether her mum died because she was ill, or because she didn't love her enough to stay alive? Haunted by her skeletal presence in every fucking thing she did. Is that what she wanted for Lily?

That was if they even let her die, which they wouldn't. Mark would burst through the door, call the ambulance, and she'd be dragged off to the hospital, cast into the wilderness of shrinks and psychiatric wards. Committed for what, five years? Ten? Before they deemed her sane enough to live unsupervised. She'd be huddled in some damp council hovel, weathered away from years of starvation, fingers creaking as she logged into Facebook to see what Griffin had posted on her timeline today.

She'd be absent from Lily's life, desperately wanting to be a part of it, but not able to be because she'd messed it all up. And by the time she was out and ready to reconnect, to say sorry for all the lost years, Lily wouldn't want to know her, same as she didn't want to know her dad. Imagine what that would be like. A living hell. A living death. She saw it, the two of them meeting, the same disgust in her daughter's face that her dad no doubt saw in hers. No matter how many times she'd try to apologise, to explain her absence, to plead for another chance, Lily wouldn't want to know. She wouldn't want anything to do with her.

Rachel pushed out of bed, her body in agony, but she had to do this. If that were true, if that was how her life played out, then it would be worse than anything Griffin might do to her, worse than any torture she could imagine.

She grabbed the Demerol from the drawer, hobbled to the en suite, and flushed them down the toilet. As the pills disappeared into the u-bend, she knew it was a stupid gesture, that Spence had plenty of other pharmaceuticals to pilfer in the morning, but she also knew that didn't matter. There'd always be more drugs. There'd always be more reasons to punish herself. That had nothing to do with Griffin. So many excuses, and she was sick of them. *Sick* of them.

Even if she did somehow get rid of Alan Griffin, even if she managed to make Mark and Becca and Spence see her as a normal human being again, and not some mental case they've been lumbered with, even if Lily wasn't so scarred already, inside and out, then something else would happen, some other *drama*, and she'd be right back here again. Alone and miserable in the middle of the night, starving.

This was the last time. This had to stop.

In the morning, she was going back to the clinic, to check in as a day patient. She needed to accept she still had a problem, that if she didn't understand this fact and take the appropriate steps then, like a cancer, it would keep coming back and coming back. No-one should lose their mum so young, but it had happened, and she had to come to terms with that. Finally, that had to happen.

Mark wasn't like this. He'd not had a relapse in over three years. Maybe there was something in his food diaries, his mindful meditations, his claims that he welcomed anorexic thoughts instead of beating them down. Who was she trying to beat anyway? Herself? No wonder the battle was futile. All that happened was one side, her good side, her conscious mind, got tired and gave up, letting the bad side win.

Most people could laugh it off when their bad side won, but her bad side was a fucking psychopath intent on destroying her life.

Rachel climbed back into bed. Her flesh felt made of freezing ridges, like a radiator in an abandoned building, and she shivered uncontrollably. As for what to do about Griffin? She had no idea. At least Mark knew now. Maybe he'd already come up with a plan? Or if not, maybe the four of them, her and Lily, Mark and his new girlfriend, could move out to Australia. It'd be like a sitcom – *My Two Mums*. She allowed herself a smile as she imagined Rowena opening the front door of her swanky Sydney apartment to find them waiting there, dishevelled from the flight and screaming at each other, with a stack of suitcases behind.

The truth was, it didn't matter what she did about Griffin.

What mattered was that she didn't do *this*.

Everything hurt, but she tried to welcome the pain. It was the only thing she could do. She pictured the sources as massive storm systems, swirling around her body, and she was watching them from above, seeing the ebb and flow of intensity. She slipped into thoughts about her dad, going over some of their exchanges again, and realised that perhaps the greatest gift a parent can give is to make a mistake so bad that their child will do anything not to repeat it.

As the first hint of morning came through the curtains, she drifted into a dreamless sleep. She still woke every twenty minutes or so to turn, when the pain of her position became too much, but she always fell back into the dark, but thankfully empty, cave her subconscious had kindly created for her.

Soon she opened her eyes and the gloomy light suggested it was maybe seven. No point hanging around. She threw off the duvet, sat up and twisted her torso one way then the other. She still ached all over, but surprisingly, it was the most refreshed she'd felt in weeks. She slid off the bed and went to slap on the light.

First food, then Lily. Then the rest of her life.

But when she pressed down the door handle, she found the bedroom was locked.

CHAPTER THIRTY-SIX

Rowena

Mark checked Rowena's profile on Facebook for the tenth time that day.

She hadn't accepted his friend request, or responded to any of his messages – she didn't know him, so why should she? – but still, something felt off. He opened a spreadsheet and made notes about her updates since she'd emigrated, when they were posted, what they were about, whether there was a photo attached and who was in it.

The more notes he made, the greater his feeling of dread grew.

What if...

He looked around the Australian government's website, found the right number, and called.

'G'day, Barry speaking.'

Mark cleared his throat. 'Oh hi, Barry. Hello. Is this the Australian Department of Immigration and Border Protection?'

'Department of Home Affairs. Sure is. You're through to customer relations, New South Wales.'

'Okay – great! I really hope you can help. I'm a writer. I'm researching a novel. I've got a couple of quick questions, about border security–'

'I'm not sure—'

'Nothing sensitive! Promise. They're general questions. You'd really be helping me out *a lot*.'

'I—'

'Before you say no, let me ask them. If you can't answer – no worries!'

'...Go on then.'

'Thanks, Barry, you're a star. Okay, first one. It's pretty straightforward. Say I was calling from the British police, and I wanted to find out if someone came through immigration on the day they were supposed to. What department would deal with that?'

'Is it recent?'

'Let's say about a year ago.'

'That'll be the archive department you need to speak to.'

'Archive department. Got it. And is that in just one place? Or are there different archive departments round the country?'

'I believe it's based in Queensland.'

'Queensland. Great. Thanks, Barry, I really appreciate your help.'

'Is that it?'

'That's it. You've been a great help. I'll even put you in the acknowledgements. It was Barry...?'

'Mallory. That's M-A-L-L-O-R-Y. What's the book called? So I can look—'

Click.

'HR.'

'G'day. Barry Mallory here. I'm calling from customer relations in Sydney.'

'Hey, Barry. How can I help?'

'My computer's gone on the blink and everyone's buggered off for lunch. Who do I speak to about getting it fixed? I've only started this week. I don't know who to ask. Have we got an IT department? Or do we outsource it?'

'It's a problem with Windows?'

'That's right, mate.'

'We use a company called Centrix. Do you need their—?'

Click.

'Archives, Tracy speaking.'

'Hi, Tracy. My name's Ralph Lum. I'm calling from Centrix. We look after your IT systems. Have you got a few moments?'

'Sure, love. How can I help?'

'You're based in the Queensland office, right?'

'That's right, love.'

'We've received quite a few service request calls from the Queensland office in the last week. Problems logging into applications. You had any issues?'

'Can't say I have.'

'No problems connecting to the network?'

'None at all.'

'That's good news. And you're in the archives department, right?'

'That's right, love.'

'Would you mind doing a couple of quick checks? Take two minutes, promise.'

'Sure. What do you need me to do?'

'First up, log off and on again. I can see on this end when your computer comes onto the network.'

'All right, let me save my work... There. Logging off now... Okay, I'm off.'

'Great. Go ahead and log on.'

'Logging on... It's just starting up.'

'Okay, I can see you now. Brilliant, thanks Tracy. When you log in, what applications do you open? Outlook?'

'That's right. Outlook for e-mail. We've got chat as well.'

'Any other applications?'

'I usually log into ArcNet. That's what we use to check records and stuff.'

'Is that a web-based application?'

'A what?'

'Do you access it through a web browser, like Internet Explorer?'

'That's right.'

'Can you start it now, please? I want to make sure you can log in okay.'

'Sure. One second... Internet Explorer's just loading... There we go. You want me to log in?'

'Can you give me the URL? That's the address. It should start with https.'

'It's https, colon, forward slash, forward slash. Arcnet-dot-adibp-dot-com-dot-au. Do you need me to log in?'

'Go for it, Tracy.'

'All right. I'm in.'

'And I can see you logged in. That's perfect. Thanks for your help today, Tracy.'

'No problem, love. Have a great day.'

'You too.'

Click.

Mark ran a port scan on the server arcnet.adibp.com.au. As expected, the common ports like FTP, Telnet, and HTTP were well protected. Port 22 was open, which probably meant a secure shell service was running. If all else failed, that could be forced, but that might show up on monitoring.

Fortunately, that wasn't necessary. The Simple Network Management Protocol, used for network management, was open on the default UDP port, 161.

The next part was easy. It was only SNMPv1, not the harder to hack SNMPv3. He spoofed some UDP packets to get round the SNMP access list and find the name of its router, then brute attacked with thousands of passwords per second to get the SNMP community string, its version of a username and password. He embedded in the attack a command to upload a new configuration file from an FTP site to the router, which imported that file back to the server using running-config.

In this configuration file was a new login for arcnet.adibp.-com.au. He used that to search for when Rowena Feldman entered Australia.

If she ever did.

CHAPTER THIRTY-SEVEN

Andreas

Rachel stared at her hand, still on the handle. The sound of her thumping heart filled her head. *Don't panic.* It was probably just stuck. She pushed down again. The door didn't move. *Griffin was here. He'd tracked her down, got rid of Spence, and locked her in.* The door looked new, solid. She slapped it, the noise echoing off the walls, her palm stinging. She slapped it again and again, calling, 'Spence? Spence? *Spence?*'

A key rattled in the lock. The door was pulled open. Spence stood on the other side, sweat on his face, breathing hard, looking at her like she'd just crawled out of the ground. Rachel barged past him, grabbed a juice glass from beside the kitchen sink, and filled it with cold water. Spence came up behind her. She turned to face him. He looked more apologetic, but something was wrong. He was normally so... *neat*, his clothes smart to his body, his hair waxed, but his burgundy dressing gown was skewed, and blond tufts sprouted from his scalp at weird angles.

'I thought he was here,' she said, and swilled the water she'd managed to get in the glass, thankful for the sudden cold in her mouth to snap her back to reality. 'I thought...'

Spence covered his face and stood motionless. After a pause, a long groan rose from deep inside his chest, coming out of his mouth as a muffled sob. His hands began to shake, and when he lowered them, his cheeks were wet with tears.

'I'm sorry,' he said. 'I'm so sorry.'

Rachel glanced into the lounge and saw his MacBook open on the glass coffee table. 'What's going on? What happened?'

'He dumped me. Andreas *dumped* me.'

'*When?*'

'Last night, really late. I've not slept. He was with someone else. He told me they – they were...' A wail mangled the rest of his words. He buried his head into Rachel's shoulder. She shushed him and stroked the back of his head, her insides twisted. This was her fault, she'd done this, another car crash to add to the growing pileup in her conscience. If he hadn't come back, they'd still be together.

'Go to him,' she said. 'Fix it. In fact, I've made a decision.'

Spence pulled his head back and looked at her suspiciously. 'What?'

'Let's sit.' Rachel gestured to the sofa.

He glanced at the laptop. 'Let's sit at the table.'

So that was it. He'd probably been watching porn. That would explain why he'd locked her door – no-one wants to be caught with their hands down their pants. 'Promise me one thing first,' she said, pulling out a chair. 'Please don't lock me in a room again. I know this is your place, and you want your privacy, but it frightened me.'

'I – I was just trying to keep you safe,' he said, the words coming in a rush. 'You told me about the knife, and I found you on the floor in your bedroom. And I didn't want to say anything, but you're really nailing the meds, and I know things are stressful, but–'

'Oh my god,' she said, laughing it off. The last thing she wanted to do was embarrass him. 'It's not a big deal. You didn't go away for the weekend or anything and leave me in there.'

'Okay, good,' he said, seemingly reassured. He turned to the counter. 'Coffee?'

'Wait. Come sit.'

He took the chair next to her, facing out, so they were almost knee to knee. She reached forward and squeezed his hand.

'You've been amazing,' she said. 'I couldn't − I mean, this last week, I can't begin to thank you enough. But I'm ready to go back now. I need to get help. Real help. I can't...' She felt herself welling up, and glanced at Spence, expecting to see him looking sympathetic, but instead his eyes were hard.

'You can't go home.'

'I've got to.'

Spence shook his head. 'You're sick.'

'I know, and I'm going to get help.'

'You're going straight to hospital to have yourself committed?'

'What? No, of course not.' Was he joking? She searched his mouth for the trace of a smile. 'But I will go back to the clinic, maybe as a day−'

'I can't let you go home on your own.'

He was right. Being in that house, with the broken window, Lily not there, could destroy her resolve. 'Let me give Mark a call,' she said. 'See if his offer of a bed is still valid for a few days.'

'If you're going to stay there, you might as well stay here.'

'I've already outstayed my welcome.'

'That's not−'

'Please, Spence. I've made up my mind. I need to speak to Mark anyway, I need him to help me become more... like him. You know? More together. And to work out what we're going to do about Griffin. Can I use your phone?'

Spence was chewing the side of his nail and frowning, like he'd been distracted by a distressing thought.

'*Spence?*'

'What?'

'Can I use your phone? To call Mark?'

He shook his head. 'Out of battery. Just charging it.'

So what if it was out of battery? All she needed was to make a quick call. It could stay plugged in. Perhaps he was worried she'd snoop around, and he didn't want her to see any texts between him and Andreas? She'd never do that, but he clearly wasn't thinking straight. She decided to leave it. With Lily staying, Mark would probably be working from home, so she could call him any time. Breakfast first, then she'd badger Spence again for his phone. Maybe get him to book her an Uber.

'So,' Rachel said, brightly. 'Eggs?'

Spence waved towards the fridge. 'Yeah, whatever.'

Among the healthy food – salads, vegetables, low-fat yogurts – she found a yellow carton of Happy Eggs, and a block of mature cheddar. 'I'm making scrambled. That okay?'

'So what's the plan?' he asked. 'When you get back. You know, Griffin.'

She got a bowl and began cracking. 'I don't have an actual plan, *per se*. More a different way of looking at the problem.'

'What way's that?'

'One that doesn't involve starving myself into an early grave. Although I do owe you a batch of stolen Demerol – sorry!'

'Right,' he said.

She splashed in milk and whisked the eggs with a fork. 'I just... I don't want to do this anymore. There had to be way out. If Mark can do it – if my *dad* can do it, and he's the biggest...' She was about to say *the biggest waster going*, but stopped herself. When she got back, she was going to get him to come round, hear his side of the story. Really listen to what he had to say. 'And if he can do it, then why not me as well.'

'What about Griffin?'

'Not sure yet,' she said, getting a frying pan from the cupboard under the sink. She turned on the electric hob. 'I'm hoping Mark might have some ideas. Or... I'm thinking about maybe starting fresh, in Australia.'

'*Australia.*'

Rachel poured in the eggs. 'I know someone there.'

'What if he finds you?'

She gave him a what-you-going-to-do shrug. 'Least it'll be warm.'

'But...' Spence threw glances around the room, like he was looking for clues to a puzzle. He covered his face again. 'I need you here... Andreas...'

Spence was obviously upset and couldn't bear the thought of being alone. She didn't want to add to his misery, especially after he'd been so good to her, but she needed to think of herself. She needed to think of Lily. She needed to sort out her life.

'Come on,' she said, gently. 'You've only known him a few months. Next week there'll be someone else, and—'

'I don't want anyone else,' Spence muttered. 'I'm in love.'

'You can't fall in love with someone that fast.'

He dropped his hands and laughed, but the sound was awkward and forced. 'We should be together. Wouldn't that be great?'

'I may look a bit like a man,' she said, pushing the eggs with a wooden spoon, the smell causing her stomach to make a yawning noise. 'But I can assure you, the plumbing is all wrong for you.'

He lifted an eyebrow and cocked his head towards the bedroom. 'How about we go and find out?'

As much as she didn't want to upset Spence, his joking around was hard work. Andreas or not, he could at least be a little happy for her, that she felt strong enough to go back and face Griffin. She got two plates, portioned the eggs equally, and grated cheese over the top. He never said he loved Andreas, never even hinted it. She didn't think Spence would be so heartbroken about them breaking up.

When she turned back with the plates, he wasn't at the table, but had moved to the sofa, shut the laptop, and clicked on the television. The channel was set to The Food Network, where a bald fast-talking black bloke in army fatigues was demanding to know what kind of sorbet you like to have as a palate cleanser.

'Can we put something else on?' Rachel asked, bringing the plates over. 'I can't watch this anymore. How about the news?'

Spence stared at the screen as though she hadn't said anything.

She held a plate out to him. 'Spence?'

He carried on ignoring her. Was it because she'd mentioned Australia? More likely it was because she'd dumped over his proclamations of love. As selfish as it sounded, she couldn't handle his tantrum, not when she needed to focus on eating. She didn't expect it to be easy to get these eggs down, nearly as much food in a single meal as she'd been eating in a whole day, and she wasn't sure if her stomach had arrived at the same place as her mind last night. Her body rebelled against her on a daily basis, so why should she expect it to be any different now?

There was no point in putting it off. She put his plate down, perched on the edge of the sofa, loaded her fork and lifted it to her lips. *Start with one mouthful,* she thought. *See how you get on.*

Although the cheese was a mistake, the texture too claggy, the heat of the eggs was welcome on her tongue. On the screen, Sergeant Sorbet had been replaced by a hipster chick with a pierced bottom lip, whipping a bowl of luminous pink frosting for a tray of cupcakes. Utter garbage, but Spence was watching like it was his favourite programme and didn't want to be disturbed. Rachel took another bite, more confident now. The food felt warm as embers going down her throat.

'Look, Spence,' she said. 'I'm sorry if I upset you, okay? I didn't mean to doubt your... feelings for Andreas.' She wanted to cross the sofa, to sit next to him, but something about the stiff way he was sitting, like a bird on a wire, told her that if she did then he'd get up. 'And even if I *did* decide to go to Australia, an idea which, I might add, I concocted after being out of it on painkillers for the last week, it won't be for ages yet. I just need to get my head around stuff at home. But I'll be here for you, like you were for me. I promise.'

Still not looking at her, he asked, 'How're the eggs?'

'They're going,' she replied, tipping her half-finished plate at him.

She waited for him to reply, but instead he remained transfixed to the stupid cupcakes. What was with him? At best, he'd been ambivalent about her watching cooking shows – usually when she put them on, he fiddled on his phone. Did he think it was healthy for her to watch them? Did he think it helped her in any way? She forced herself to calm down. This was *her* fault, not his. She'd brought her crazy into his house, and now he didn't know which way was sideways. Perhaps he thought she found staring at food and starving herself relaxing? How was he to know the screwed-up machinations of an anorexic?

'Listen,' she said. 'I just... I think I need to go. Can I use your phone now? Or maybe better, can you book me an Uber? I've got an emergency twenty in my wash bag, so take that. Okay?'

He flipped off the television and threw down the remote. '*Fine*,' he said, shoving off the sofa.

She watched him slouch away with all the endeavour of a teenager told to clean his room. Why was he being like this? If she needed one final clear indication that she had to leave to salvage their friendship, then this was it.

She scooped the last of the egg into her mouth, pushed her plate aside, and stood up – then sat down again, her hand going to her middle. The food seemed to be expanding by the second, like someone was inflating a balloon in her belly.

Spence rushed to her side. 'Are you okay?'

'I think I ate too much.'

He helped her to the bedroom. 'Take five, let it digest. You don't have to rush off this minute, do you?'

She felt better lying down. A quick rest, then she'd be up and out of there. As soon as the pain passed.

'I'm sorry for being such a prick,' Spence said, tucking her in. 'This thing with Andreas has really knocked me.'

'Don't apologise. I'm a *long* way from perfect.'

'I don't think so.'

'You're too kind.'

'Let me get you a glass of warm milk to sip,' he said, getting up.

The thought of ingesting anything else sent waves of nausea through her. But also she'd not eaten that much, the food was just a shock to the body, and warm milk did always settle her stomach…

'Sure,' she said. 'If it's not too much hassle.'

He headed out the room.

Moments later, he leaned back in. 'I fancy a coffee as well, and there's not enough milk,' he said. 'I'll nip to the garage, be back in ten. Don't go anywhere!'

CHAPTER THIRTY-EIGHT

News

Less than a minute after Spence left the apartment, Rachel broke wind like you can only do on your own. Straight away the pressure in her stomach eased, and she sent thanks down to her bowels. She'd worried this was some new rebellion, another subconscious stranglehold on her sanity, but no, she just had gas.

She paused with her hand on the corner of her duvet. Would it be so terrible if she left? She had that twenty, enough to get her home, even in a black cab at morning rush hour. It was a pretty shitty thing to do to Spence when he was this upset about Andreas, especially as he'd gone to get her milk, but she was either going to put herself first to get her life together, or she wasn't. And besides, it would save another round of discussions about it. He made some compelling arguments for why she should stay, and she could see herself being swayed. It wouldn't take much to pull the lid off her doubts and set them free. She dredged an image from last night – the teenage Lily greeting her emaciated mother with disdain – and threw back the covers. No way would she let that happen.

She limped around the room, stuffing her bag, then headed to the kitchen. She grabbed a notepad and biro from beside the kettle. What to say? *Thanks for dropping everything, including the guy you were super keen on, who probably only cheated on you because you left him in the lurch, to look after me. To repay you I'm going to do a runner while you're at the shops buying me milk. Cheers!*

She needed to stop stalling – he'd be back in a minute. She settled for a scrawled *sorry* and a load of kisses. As soon as she got home, she'd call.

She shouldered her bag, went to the front door, and took one last look around. One day she'd make it up to Spence. He'd really saved her. When she was at the bottom, with nowhere else to go, he was there for her in a way that no-one else in her life was, not even Mark. Spence never once doubted her, never once questioned her sanity. He was a better friend than she could have ever expected.

She went to open the front door, preparing to step outside, to feel fresh air in her lungs for the first time in a week. Except, the door didn't open. She tried the handle over and over, twisting the latch as well, the realisation frothing in her that, yes, he really had locked her in – *again!* No way. That wasn't possible. Not after what she'd said to him that morning. She slapped the door, wondering for a crazy moment if she could charge it, but saw herself crumpled on the floor, her collarbone shattered, and thought better of it.

She ducked her head under the curtain, looking past the walkway that ran along the front of the apartments, leading to the lifts. She looked to the car park, and further on to the gates, but couldn't see him. The twenty-four-hour Esso was outside the estate. He was probably in there now.

Clearly the cosmos was telling her something. Yes, she wanted to get home, to see her daughter, to find the help she needed, but that didn't mean she could be so rude to someone who'd been so kind to her.

She dropped onto the sofa. He'd been gone five minutes, and at most he'd be five more, so she'd wait. Not even mention the locked door. When he got back, she'd say she was feeling better, that she still had to go, but she'd give him a call later on. See, was that so hard?

Rachel clicked on the television with the remote. The sorbet dude was jabbering about adding glucose powder instead of sugar for a dessert that could be used as part of a fitness regime. She flicked to BBC News, needing to reconnect with the world. Live footage from Afghanistan showed buildings bombed to rubble. Rebels had been hiding in schools, using children as human shields. Now, there were people with *real* problems!

The note on the kitchen table. She considered leaving it there, maybe having a laugh with Spence about him locking her in again, but didn't want to risk upsetting him, not after how he was acting before, so she pushed off the sofa to get it. As she was ripping the page from the pad, the Afghanistan report ended.

And now back to our main story, the suspected kidnapping of twenty-seven-year-old nurse Rachel Stone.

Rachel looked at the television. Her photo filled the screen, the same one as on her hospital ID badge, hair scraped back, lips tugged on the left side into a slight smile. Couldn't they have found something a little more flattering? Not one that made her look like a serial killer remembering her favourite joke. Right, because that was the important thing here. The quality of the picture, not the fact that her *kidnapping* was the lead story on the BBC. That's what it said in the caption – *London nurse kidnapped* – even if she had, somehow, misheard the newscaster.

The picture changed to St Pancras hospital. Was she hallucinating? Dreaming? Lying in bed trapped in a lucid fucking coma? A male voiceover started.

He said his name was Spencer Borrowman. He said he was a nurse from Coventry. Neither of these things were true. But what is true is he worked alongside Rachel Stone at this North London hospital, in the psychotherapy recovery ward. What is also true, is both they – and another nurse, fifty-five-year-old Rowena Feldman – are now considered missing.

Rachel felt around for a chair. This couldn't be happening. The image cut to a ward. She recognised the nurses' station, the leaning tower of folders listing against the ancient Dell desktop, the whiteboard with their phone numbers on, written in Linda's neat curved letters, the filing cabinets with the peeling sticky labels, the TV card vending machine. That was *her* ward. That was Oakwood!

When Rowena Feldman made the spur of the minute decision to take a sabbatical from St Pancras Hospital, no-one questioned it. When she got to Australia and updated her social media with pictures of her new life, friends back home were happy for her. But investigations have uncovered an increasingly sinister situation. The Australian government have now confirmed she did not even enter the country, and early signs show none of these updates were, in fact, posted by her.

Rowena wasn't in Australia? But they'd swapped messages. Rachel had seen photos. Except when she thought about it, hadn't most of the photos been of landmarks? Or other people, new friends she'd made out there. So who was sending her messages? Griffin? No, that was ridiculous. Alan Griffin had no way of knowing Rowena. And how could he possibly stop her from going to Australia?

This whole thing had to be a mistake, a misunderstanding. There had to be a rational explanation. Griffin was behind it, somehow...

But what about Mark? He knew she was here. He'd been in touch; she'd seen his texts. Why hadn't he told them where they were? Linda too. Spence had spoken to her. Why hadn't she told the police they were safe?

The screen cut to a shot of Spence, his slender features and bleached hair, again from his nurse's ID badge. The same face she'd seen almost every day, for how long? Eleven months?

Spencer Borrowman began working at St Pancras hospital after Rowena Feldman left for her sabbatical. As described by Linda Green, the ward manager, he was a hard-working conscientious nurse. Well loved by the patients. Except, he wasn't a nurse at all. University records were faked, as was the scan of his passport on NHS files.

But he hadn't kidnapped her. She'd come of her own accord. This *had* to be a mistake.

The screen changed again, this time showing a picture of the two of them from last year's Christmas party, one of the few times she'd been drunk enough to allow someone to take a photo of her on their phone. They were by the roster, wearing Santa hats and toasting mince pies. She'd been so drunk that he'd bundled her into a black cab and shoved money in the driver's hand to get her home. If he was really a kidnapper, then why not take advantage of her then? Or any of the other times they'd gone out? They'd been alone together a hundred times.

Mr Borrowman worked at the hospital for nearly a year, becoming especially close with the second nurse, Rachel Stone, a single mother from Hornsey, North London. Ms Stone was last seen on Thursday the fifteenth of October, heading back to her house, where it is presumed Mr Borrowman was waiting.

The screen cut to her house – *her house*. Cordoned off with blue and white *Police Line Do Not Cross* tape. The window had been properly boarded.

What happened after, no-one can say. A window was broken in the night. Some residents of this peaceful street remember looking out, but saw nothing. Police found signs of a struggle, traces of blood, but no clues as to where they are. And nothing, yet, that suggests... murder. One thing is for sure, something happened here, and all three people involved are still missing. Back to you–

Rachel turned off the television. A high-pitch whine filled her head, like she'd been standing next to loud speakers for too long. She checked the front door again, opening the latch and pulling. It wouldn't budge. He'd locked the mortise. Why would Spence do that if he was nipping to the shops? No-one would be able to open the door from the outside, so why do that? She dragged open the curtains. The window to the walkway was also locked, the keys not there.

If he hadn't kidnapped her, why could she not get out? She looked around again, a cold sensation spreading through her.

This wasn't an apartment. It was a prison.

CHAPTER THIRTY-NINE

Milk

His phone. He'd been about to get it when she started feeling sick. He helped her to bed, went to get a glass of milk, came back to say he was going to the shop, and that was it. So it should still be charging. She raced to his room, fumbling the handle, her breath becoming a whimper as she thought that it too was locked, but it turned out to be just her inability to work a bloody door. At the second attempt it flew back, banging against the wall.

Rachel paused. Before she violated his privacy, shouldn't she be sure it was him? Was it such a stretch to imagine Spence was being framed, like Konrad? And she was buying it, without question.

After everything she'd been through, shouldn't she be giving him the benefit of the doubt?

But what if it was him, and this was her one chance to get away?

She stepped uneasily into the room and stood by his bed, scanning for the plug sockets. Just find the phone. It'd be locked, but she'd be able to call the emergency services. What other choice did she have? If Spence were being framed, it would clear his name.

But why don't they know where he lives? Won't the hospital have it on file? Or his bank?

Nothing in the plug sockets, so she pulled open the drawers of his bedside cabinet, looking for spare keys, he must have spare keys, everyone had spare keys, but they were empty. She went next to his dresser, expecting it to be full – she'd assumed he'd moved his things out of his room those first catatonic days – but the top drawer aside, which held his folded clothes from the last week, the rest contained nothing, not even lint. He needed to have more stuff than this. It was all wrong.

The windows. They were on the top floor, but maybe she could bang and get someone's attention. She ran out of his bedroom, swinging around in the kitchen and going back to close his door. He didn't know that she knew. That was her only advantage. If she couldn't get out before he got back, she didn't want him thinking she'd snooped around.

No sign of Spence in the car park, or further out by the gates. Maybe he'd seen the news, got scared, and bolted. Maybe that was the real reason he'd locked her in the room. She gave the glass a tentative slap, but the sound was muted and echoed back. She examined the window – her spine chilled. It was triple glazed. She could run an airplane in here and you wouldn't hear more than a hum outside. The way the apartment was set back, the chance of someone seeing her from the car park was minuscule. That didn't stop her banging the glass and screaming for help.

She wheeled away, sobbing, the initial shock of the truth, that it was Spence, *Spence,* that he'd done all of this to her, finally subsiding, leaving only the terrifying reality that she was trapped. He was going to be back any minute. To do what? Kill her. *Not Spence!* Or he wasn't coming back at all, at which point, once the food was gone, she'd starve to death. Oh, great. *Fuck you, irony.*

She needed to find a weapon. The chopping knives weren't attached to the magnetic strip beside the fridge. He must have taken them. She pulled out the drawers under the kettle. At home, hers were crammed with bills, batteries, Post-it notes, copper change, half-finished packets of paracetamol, and a million other bits of assorted crap, the detritus of everyday life, stuffed in there when there was no more logical place for them to go, but aside from four sets of cutlery in the top one, they were as empty as the ones in his bedroom. She checked the cupboards next. Any packaged food, like pasta or rice, had been barely used. Same for the cleaning products under the sink. On a whim, she wedged her shoulder behind the fridge and pushed it out a few inches. She dropped to her knees and ran her hand on the laminate underneath. Not a crumb. Spence was tidy, but no-one was *this* clean. Especially as she hadn't seen him do more than load the dishwasher in the last week. Did he even live here? No wonder no-one knew where they were.

Rachel gripped her head. It was too much. She couldn't take it all in. *He did live here* – she couldn't clear her mind of that fact. But why did she think that? Because he said so? Because he had a couple of photos of himself on the shelves? Because he owned some books? She remembered thinking how they had such similar tastes. And right then, she saw it, all of it. They *always* had so much in common. Not just books, but music, and food, and television. They bitched about the same celebrities, swooned over the same soap stars, but they were all lies, every one. Same as this place. This wasn't someone's *home*. It was an approximation of a home, no more real than background scenery on a stage. And she'd been locked in it by a lunatic.

She checked the window again – he must have been gone twenty minutes – and caught her breath. He was walking fast across the car park, hood up and coat zipped high to cover his face, clutching a brown holdall by the straps over his shoulder. What the hell was in there? They didn't give you brown holdalls at the garage to carry your milk home.

She wouldn't have to wait long to find out. He'd be here in minutes.

She pulled the curtains back and scanned the room for evidence that she'd been looking around. She had to pretend she knew nothing, that she'd been too ill to get out of bed, let alone leave the room, switch on the television, and see she was the subject of a national manhunt. Everything looked the same as after breakfast, tidy but for a few plates and glasses. *Oh, shit.* The fridge was still pulled out. *Stupid, stupid, stupid!* She rushed to it, pushing it back, but without the wall for leverage it wouldn't move. She pressed her shoulder to the door and jerked her body forward, her heart stopping for two whole beats when it tipped back on its legs, but she got a hand round to steady it, and used the momentum to swing it towards the wall. She jumped back, sweating, shaking, trying to assess if the fridge was straight, realising that if she couldn't tell then it was probably okay, and dashed for her room, hearing the front door opening and clunking closed, kicking off her shoes and diving under the duvet and trying to steady her breath as she heard him step into her bedroom.

'Rachel? You awake?'

Her bag! It was in the lounge, near the window. That was okay. She could say she packed it in preparation to go, but felt so bad she had to come back to bed again. That wasn't terrible. As long as she had her story straight now, not when he asked her about it.

His footsteps padded across the carpet. 'Rachel?'

Just pretend to be asleep. She'd spent her whole life lying to people. This was one more time, one more performance.

She moaned and eased the duvet down from her face, as if rousing from deep sleep. 'I must – I must have nodded off,' she croaked, smacking her mouth like it was parched. 'You've been gone ages.'

'I'm sorry I took so long,' he said. 'I had to grab a few other things.'

His voice was calm, measured, giving nothing away. She wished she could see his expression, but with the only light coming in from the hallway, his face was dark.

'I shouldn't have eaten so much,' she said. 'I got up to pack, but I felt so dreadful I had to come back to bed.'

'I'm sorry for how I was acting,' he replied, although his tone carried no apology. His pitch was flat, a little weary if anything, like a taxi driver asking *where to* at the end of a twelve-hour shift. 'I freaked out about Andreas. I really miss him.'

Yeah, right. He sounded like he missed Andreas as much as what? Having his teeth drilled at the dentist? This was all wrong. He was all wrong. No doubt now. He was behind it, and he had her trapped. She needed to buy time to think of a plan.

She made to turn away. 'You mind if I get a bit more sleep? I'm still not feeling too good.'

'Why don't I get you that glass of warm milk?'

'I'm not sure my stomach's–'

'It always settles your stomach. You said so.'

'I don't want you running around anymore. I'll have a sleep, then–'

'I went to the shops for you. You don't want to disappoint me, do you?'

She heard the edge in his voice, the threat. 'If you're sure you don't mind. Thank – thanks, Spence.'

He turned and left without a word. Did he know that she knew? Clearly he wanted her to drink the milk. What was he going to do? Poison her? But why go to all this trouble, creating a fake life, luring her here, just to end it like that?

From the kitchen came the sucker sound of the fridge door opening. And she'd left her daughter with him for a *whole day*. She remembered Lily squeezing her cheeks and screaming into her face – *the cut!* The knife was sharp, she'd even hurt herself with it, but thinking about it again, Lily would've had to really grab the blade to cut herself so badly, and how likely was that when she was looking under the sofa for a crayon? Spence must have done it to her and told her not to say anything. She'd learned that in a seminar on how to spot abuse, how the abuser may threaten to kill the child's parent if they told them the truth. That must have been why Lily was ignoring her outside the hospital. Not because she hated her, but because she was scared for her.

A click then the microwave door slammed shut. It beeped as

Spence set the timer. Rachel bit down on her anger, thanking everything holy he hadn't done anything worse to Lily.

Could she run? Make a break for the front door? Rachel couldn't imagine he'd locked it again after coming home.

The problem was she felt so drained. It'd taken all she had to move a mostly empty fridge a few inches. Weeks ago, she'd have fancied her chances, but now even lifting herself out of bed would expend most of her remaining energy. There wouldn't be much of a fight.

No, the best plan was to play along as if nothing had changed. She needed to convince him that she hadn't seen the news, that she didn't know the police were looking for them.

Spence came back in the room and made his way to her bed, glass of milk held out as though it were an offering.

'Thank you,' she said, taking it, hoping he'd go so she could flush it down the toilet. She didn't trust anything he gave her. She went to put it on the bedside table. 'I'll have it in a bit.'

He didn't move. 'You should drink it now, before it goes cold.'

She took a sip, and went again to put it down.

'Now come on,' he said. 'You know you need to drink it all to settle your stomach.'

What choice did she have?

Rachel lifted the glass to her lips, and drank.

CHAPTER FORTY

Search

Two in the morning, Mark's face lit up by the monitors set up in a wide semi-circle on his desk.

Rachel's dad stopped pacing behind him. 'Why we looking at these again? What are they going to tell us that we don't already know?'

'What else can we do?' Mark sighed, eyes scanning the rows of text – usernames, sessions times, IP addresses – from the paedo hunter website log files.

'We can get out there–'

'And do what? You could knock on every door in the country and still not find her.'

'Better that than sitting here twiddling our bloody thumbs. My whole life–'

'You've got to check everything. The smallest detail–'

'I've let her down, and now I'm losing her forever.'

'–could lead us to him.'

'She's my *daughter*, Mark. Imagine it was Lily. Would you sit here staring at a screen?'

Mark swivelled his chair. 'We'll find her, I promise.'

'What if we don't?'

'I found out Spence faked his university records, didn't I? And that Rowena never entered Australia. Right?'

'Someone must have seen her – or *him*. I'll print posters. I won't stop until the whole of London knows about her.'

'They might not be in London.'

'They're here. I can feel it.'

'Look, Jim. I know you're upset–'

'I can't do nothing.'

'I just need more time.'

'What time, Mark? That copper said the first forty-eight hours–'

'Why would Spence wheedle his way into her life for the last year just to kill her?'

'Who knows what that lunatic's doing to her!'

'Keep your voice down, will you? Lil's already been up with nightmares.'

'I'm sorry, I...'

'You know I'm doing everything I can.'

'I know, Mark. I know.'

'So sit down. There, okay? He's clever, but everyone makes mistakes. Let's start again. What have we got that's *not* a dead end?'

'His wages?'

Mark changed tabs on the right-hand screen, bringing up a spreadsheet. 'The HSBC account, registered to the... Luton address, name Kate Smith on the deeds. Could he make it any more generic?'

'Should we go over there again?'

'Police have already got it under surveillance. Besides, it's a shell. There's nothing there.'

'I don't bloody know.'

'There's got to be something in these logs. I know how he did it – I can see where he made the changes to the data. I just need more–'

'We don't have *time,* Mark.'

'He would've connected through an SSL tunnel to a Tor router, but maybe... Who you calling, Jim?'

'Konrad.'

'Let him sleep.'

'He'll be up.'

'You need to rest, Jim.'

'You stay here, carry on doing what you're doing. We'll go to the printers. I'm going to get posters made, leaflets.'

'It's the middle of the night!'

'We're in London. There'll be somewhere open.'

'Sit back down, let's keep going. Jim? *Jimmy*? Come back!'

CHAPTER FORTY-ONE

Spence

White. The whole world, white. And in the background, a low mumbling, like someone in prayer.

Was this Heaven?

Rachel shifted her head and saw a grey pendant light shade. *It's not heaven, you dummy. It's the ceiling.*

A number of things came to her at once – her bladder felt about to burst; her headache was a gloaming migraine of misery; her mouth was as foul and sticky as used flypaper; the low mumbling was coming from a portable television positioned in the corner of the room, tuned to The Food Network; finally, but perhaps most importantly, she'd been drugged by someone who, until that morning, she'd considered to be one of her closest friends.

Spence knew that she knew. But how much? That her disappearance was being investigated? That she wasn't free to walk out? What did it matter – he'd played his hand. Spiking her milk with knockout drops was pretty much a statement of intent. The statement being, she was fucked.

How long had she been out for? The clock in the corner of the screen said six thirteen. Ten hours! What had he given her? She rolled her shoulders and the numbness evaporated from her body, only to be replaced by a dull energy-draining pain, as though someone had gone at her flesh with a tenderising hammer while she slept. Without doubt her legs would be worse. Bracing herself, she bent them at the knee. At least she tried to. After a few inches, they stopped. She dragged up the duvet and let slip a moan.

Now *this* was bad.

If she was fucked before, then she was double-fucked now, with a nice cherry of despair on top. A leather cuff, padded with black faux fur, enclosed each ankle, and a chain thick enough to tow a car connected them. Another chain led off that one, going past the bottom of the mattress. Rachel pulled again, watching it go taut. It was attached to the wrought iron bed frame.

Her first reaction was to lose her shit, to scream and plead and offer anything for him to let her go, but a somehow-still-rational fragment of her mind reminded her that she wasn't dead yet. He wanted something from her. There was hope. *Yeah, sure. Wonder what that could be?* She felt her crotch, relieved to find no soreness. Another thing, her manacles were padded, which meant that despite knocking her unconscious and chaining her to the bed, her comfort was important to him. He'd even given her a television! So yes, Spence was crazy, probably flay-your-skin-and-wear-it crazy, but he wanted her alive, he hadn't raped her, and he kind of cared whether she was happy. It wasn't much, admittedly, but it beat being chopped up and dissolved in a bath of sulphuric acid.

Rachel worked her mouth to get enough saliva to talk. Trying to keep the hysteria out of her voice, she called, 'Spence? Are you there?'

The remote was on the bedside cabinet, so she switched off the TV. The sudden silence increased her fear, as though the cheery patter of the presenters had stopped her brain from fully realising the true horror of her situation. She called for him again. Nothing. He'd gone. He'd left her here to die. She scrabbled at the cuffs, probing them for weakness, but they were heavy duty, the leather covering a metal core, and locked with a key. She went at the chains, seeing if she could slide them around the bed frame, shaking them with frustration when they wouldn't move.

'The bed's specially made.'

Spence was by the door. He was holding a tray, smiling like he was surprising her with breakfast in bed on her birthday.

'So you might as well relax,' he said.

Except, it wasn't Spence, not really. Gone was the bleached hair, the skinny jeans and trendy T-shirt, replaced with a chestnut-brown matinee idol side-parting, a tailored black shirt, open two buttons down from the collar, tapered at the waist, and a pair of stylish grey trousers, the material slightly furred. Suede or moleskin. Smart black leather shoes, neatly laced, of a kind that Spence would routinely mock as being "boring office blah", completed the transformation. Even his smell was different, his cologne light and icy, not too dissimilar to what Konrad would wear... oh, *shit*.

She bit the inside of her cheek to keep her shock in check. He didn't just smell like Konrad, he *looked* like him as well.

The times they'd been for a romantic meal, that was how he'd styled his hair. He'd dyed it the same colour as well. And that outfit. Konrad wore the same one on their night out at St John in Spitalfields, when she thought he was going to say he loved her. She remembered the camera she'd found in the living room, what she and Konrad did on the sofa when they got home that night, and shuddered. How long had Spence been spying on her?

A chair from the kitchen had been placed near the bed, but not quite close enough for her to reach. He'd done this before. How many people had died here? Spence placed the tray on the chair and stood with his hands resting on the back. When Rachel saw what was on the tray, a chill crept up her neck and over her cheeks.

This was it, she was going to die.

The next thought hit her like a bare-knuckle punch. *I'll never see Lily again.*

All notions of keeping herself together disappeared. 'Spence, listen to me, please – please, I'll do anything. Anything you want.' Tears spilled from her eyes. She gulped down the sob battling up her throat. 'Don't do this, Spence. Please, please, *please*. Don't do this to me.'

'Hey. Come on, Rach. It's okay. You're safe. I'm not going to do anything to you.' He gestured to the tray. On it was a needle, prepped with a clear liquid, a shallow paper cup of pills, the kind she would dispense on the ward fifty times a day, and a glass of water. 'This is for *you*.'

She swiped her eyes dry with her sleeve. 'For me?'

'This is probably all coming as a bit of a shock to you.'

No shit, psycho.

'But I want you to know,' he went on, 'that you don't have to stay here. You can leave any time.' He pushed off the back of the chair and came round the side, crouching beside it. 'And this is your way out.'

'I don't– I–'

'Let me explain. In the syringe is potassium chloride. Hurts like hell, so I hear, like having your insides melted, but over in minutes. As luck would have it, as a nurse, you'd be able to administer this correctly. You don't want to get *that* wrong.' He grimaced at a memory and moved his finger to the pills. 'Amitriptyline and Doxazepam. It'll take longer, maybe a few hours, but it's a lot more relaxed. You can chill out, mix it with some Demerol, or whatever you haven't flushed down the loo, and enjoy the buzz.'

'Enjoy the *buzz*?'

Spence straightened, his stance wide and hands resting behind his back, his chest pressing against the fabric of his shirt. Even his gait had changed, going from a slightly camp slouch to something altogether more masculine, even a bit military. He lifted his chin. 'Lastly, you can tell me to go, and I'll go. Then we wait for nature to run its course. I can leave you more water, if you wish, and then you can take as little or as long – relatively speaking – as you liked over it.'

'You're saying you'd leave me to starve,' she said slowly.

'If you'd prefer.'

'If I'd *prefer?*'

This wasn't happening. It had to be a hoax, some messed-up joke. What if it was one of those sinister Internet sites where rich people paid to watch someone being tortured?

'Please, Spence,' she whispered, looking in his eyes. He stared back, unblinking. 'We were friends, weren't we?' She waited for him to reply, but he remained so unflinching that she pictured him fleetingly as a robot, with a circuit board behind his face. 'Let me go. *Please.* I– I won't tell anyone.'

Fast as a flicked switch, his whole demeanour changed, his shoulders relaxing, his body turning side on, a little like a model at the end of the catwalk – and it was Spence, right there, *her* Spence, the friend who started work early to help out with her shifts, who regaled her with tales of his hedonistic lifestyle, who came round on Friday nights to watch rom-coms and moan about the happy-ever-after endings. Not that weird masculine version of him.

He gave her the same smile and wink as he had a hundred times on the ward.

It's him! He's still–

Just as quickly, his posture changed back. He shook a playful finger at her. 'Had you going there, right?'

'Why– why are you doing this to me?'

He paused, considering her, then took the tray from the chair and placed it on the floor beside the bed. He sat down, crossing his leg, ankle to knee, lacing his hands behind his head. She got an image of a tropical bird, something from *Planet Earth*, strutting around and making himself big to attract a mate. *That's what he's doing, the little man. Trying to make himself big.*

'Why else?' he said. 'Because I love you.'

'You need help,' she said, shaking her head.

Spence looked her up and down. 'I'm not the one chained to the bed.'

'So you did all of it? You sent that photo to Konrad's mates? You stole the money from my account? You got me sacked from work?'

'Technically only suspended.'

'You knew what that job meant to me.' She bit on her lips to stop them from trembling.

'You're looking at it all the wrong way.' His expression was exasperated but amused, like she was a child asking the same stupid question for the hundredth time. 'Try seeing it more as a grand romantic gesture.'

'What about some flowers? Or a box of fucking chocolates?' She began to cry again. 'How could you do this to me, Spence? How could you...?'

'Here,' he said, reaching into his back pocket. He held out a folded handkerchief.

'No *thank you*.'

He drew his hand back. 'Try not to blow your nose on the sheets. It's not very ladylike.'

'Fuck you.'

'Neither is that.'

'Fuck you.'

'I think you're a bit tired.' He started to stand.

She looked at the pills and needle on the tray. Was he leaving her here to die?

'*Wait!*'

Spence casually lowered himself down. 'Yes?'

'What do you want from me? Is it sex? You want to have sex with me? I thought you were *gay*.'

'Have you ever, in person, seen me so much as kiss a man?'

It was true, she hadn't. She'd been shown a parade of boyfriends in photos, lapped up lurid stories of late-night encounters in night-clubs, but had never actually seen proof of his sexuality beyond what he'd told her. Rachel slumped back against her pillow. The full realisation of her situation hit her – that it was Spence all along, her friend Spence, and now he had her chained to his bed – and she let out a disbelieving laugh. 'But why all the charade? Why get to know me? Why not just beat me over the head in a dark alley and drag me here?'

'You don't capture birds of paradise by beating them over the head.'

She kicked her legs, shaking the chains. 'What difference would it have made?'

'I admit, things haven't gone exactly to plan.'

'*To plan?* What plan was that?'

'I'd have liked the honeymoon period first, before we got to this stage.'

'*Honeymoon period?* But I didn't... I don't...' She stopped herself, knowing it'd do no good saying she didn't find him attractive. 'But we were *friends,*' she finished, lamely.

'We'd have got it on, eventually. Maybe after you heard about Mark's engagement.'

'His *what*? They've only been together a few weeks!'

'Visa issues with his Vietnamese honey trap, I believe. From what I hear, all you have to do is touch his penis and he'll say yes to anything.'

Rachel rattled her head, mouth loose, speechless.

'Who else would you have turned to?' Spence carried on. 'Your dad? That old drunk's probably hitting the bottle as we speak. How about Becca? She's one cosmo from a breakdown. Konrad? God, I hate that butch handsome type – so derivative. That *worscht* is lucky he's not doing five years in Pentonville. No, it'd be me. I'd be there, looking after you, caring for you, as you got thinner and thinner, weaker and weaker.'

'But... but I thought...'

'I know, I know, you thought he was gay. But it's not as though the queer hadn't been with a woman before. You know that, right? He'd opened up to you about his past, how he was unsure for many years, and had even been engaged to a girl at one point. Twenty-one, I think he was, if I remember the story correctly. And he was *so* hurt by the whole Andreas debacle. Men are so callous, so heartless... One night you'd have sunk a bottle of something seriously alcoholic together, and he'd have woken in your bed.' He gave her a seductive lift of the eyebrows. 'And you would have asked him to stay.'

'So– so that was your plan? Ruin my life so much that I wouldn't be able to live without you?'

'I prefer to think of it more as boy meets girl, boy falls in love–'

'Boy chains girl to bed? I don't think I've seen that one.'

'Like I said, we weren't supposed to get to this stage for a while, but what can we do? You're here now. That's the important thing.'

The way he was being with her, calm, almost dignified, while she carried on hysterically, was too much. 'What can we *do*? I'm chained to the bed, you maniac!'

He rolled his eyes as if to ask, *Why are you always so dramatic?*

'Look,' he said, reasonably. 'You've just said nothing would've happened between us. We were *friends*, right?'

She nodded, warily.

'I wanted you,' he went on. 'You'd never have come to me willingly – even if you thought I was straight – so I took you. It's not rocket science. Everyone can do the same as me. The world is there for the taking, you've just got to have the balls to grab it.'

'And you don't care if I don't feel the same way.'

Spence lifted his spine, and straightened his shirt. 'Does the king care that the young girl brought to him in the night would rather still be asleep in her bed? Does a village chieftain worry that the beautiful tiger he captures would rather be roaming the jungle?'

'I'm not an animal. I'm a human being.'

'Please. If I saw people that way, I'd never get anything done.'

'Why me? Of all the people you could have done this to, all the hot celebrities–'

'*Pfft.* Plastic.'

'But why pick *me*? What did I ever do...?' She felt herself losing it again, and fought back the tears. *Hold it together!*

'Wow, you're really fishing for compliments now! Okay, I'll bite. You're tall, I like that. And you're very attractive, physically I mean. You'd certainly never go for someone who looked like me.'

Rachel opened her mouth to speak, but his shake of the head shut her up.

'Don't deny it,' he said. 'One thing I can't stand is liars. What else...? You're intelligent – and strong-willed, I admire that. I hate weak people.' He shook the bed frame. 'This right here would be no fun if you were weak, and this is usually the best bit. Shit gets *real* in this room. But I guess the main thing is, I don't know... you *intrigue* me. Which is not something that happens very often. We've actually got a lot in common. There's this darkness inside you, it goes right to your core. I can see it. And it *really* gets me going. The whole starvation thing is incredibly sexy.'

'Go for anorexics, do you?'

'Never had one before, but I'm a convert.' He leaned forward, eyes sparking, Spence again. '*Very* heroin chic.'

When he sat back, all trace of her friend was gone.

How had she brought this *thing* into her life? Was it the doxing? Had he been stalking her for years, waiting for the right moment to strike? 'How long have you been... watching me?'

'If you must know, I've been *interested* in you for a while now, but the timing was never great. Either you were too young, or I was with someone else, then you got pregnant with Lily. I didn't want to interrupt that. I'm not a monster!' He looked in her eyes, as though waiting for her to agree, and she quickly nodded. 'I was keeping tabs on that sap in prison, saw he was up for parole. And you had a new boyfriend, so I could work with that – I was single myself and looking for a new project. So I guess it all just fell into place.'

The way he was talking, as if he were relaying some vaguely interesting anecdote about how he landed a new job, instead of the nuts and bolts of why he had destroyed her fucking life, was too much. She failed to keep the sarcasm from her voice. '*Fell into place?* How is tricking your way into my life for nearly a year – you're not a real nurse, I take it?' Spence gave her a little *caught me* pout. 'So you pretend to be a nurse—'

'How do you think I'm such a good chef? Or interior designer? One of the things I love most about my romances is the opportunity to broaden my skill sets, and being with you gave me a chance to get some real-time medical training. There's only so much you can learn from skimming text books and binge watching *Casualty*.'

'But the patients... You could have killed someone.'

'More than one.' He waved dismissively. 'Ehh, they were old.'

Rachel tried to keep her face blank as she processed what he was saying. How many times had he appeared in someone's life and destroyed it to the point where they'd turned to him for comfort? How many people had ended up chained to the bed like this? And no-one had ever found him out, otherwise she wouldn't be here now.

'Is it so hard to understand?' he said. 'I saw you, I fell in love with you, so I took you. That's what love is, right? Taking what you want and making it your own.'

How he was speaking reminded her of the psychopaths she'd met during her stint at The Northside Centre, the kid who stabbed the other boy in the throat for sitting in his chair. She needed to stay calm, humour him. He was liable to be unpredictable. Prone to sudden violence.

'Okay, you took me,' she said. 'So what are you going to do with me?'

'*That* is up to you.'

'What do you want?' she asked, cautiously.

'Straighten that out,' he said, nodding to the duvet. 'Cover your legs.'

She did as he asked. 'That better?'

Spence leaned forward. 'Make it real. As long as you make it real, I'll stay. If you don't, I'll go. It's that simple.'

She couldn't reason with him, that much was clear, so instead she needed to bide her time, see what he was going to do next. Maybe, when he eventually got round to raping her, she could convince him to unchain her legs, then overpower him.

'I'll make it real,' she said, and forced her lips into a smile. 'If that's what you want.'

He pushed the cuff of his shirt back, and setting his shoulders like a catalogue model, checked his watch. 'I'd say it was nearly time for dinner. You must be hungry.'

That was an understatement. It felt like her stomach was turning itself inside out, looking for scraps of food in its pockets. But she could handle that. More important, he needed to think she couldn't eat, that she was getting weaker. Too weak to try to escape.

'I don't think...' she said.

'I'll make it, so it's there if you want,' he replied, his smile impish – "her" Spence used to say the same.

At the door, he turned back to her. 'One more thing. It's perfectly natural for someone in your position to try to think of ways to get away, or to bash something over my head when I'm not looking. If that's what you're thinking of doing, then let me tell you one of my favourite sayings. *There's nothing worse than knowing what you had, but lost forever.*'

He fixed his eyes on hers, his stare cold, and mimed slicing across his palm. 'You still have your daughter at home. I'd hate for something *else* to happen to her.'

When he was gone, Rachel covered her face and started to cry. *Oh, Lily.* The thought that she'd never–

She lowered her hands, her eyes widening.

She saw herself as a teenager in the eating disorder clinic, laptop balanced on her legs, Mark beside her as they trawled the dark web for someone to help frame Alan Griffin. She saw the chat window, the name flashing as words appeared.

There's nothing worse than knowing what you had, but lost forever.

That was how this *thing* had appeared in her life – she'd invited him! He was the hacker they paid on the dark web to plant the pictures on Griffin's computer.

He was Regret.

CHAPTER FORTY-TWO

Date

Was it so strange what Spence was doing? Did a dictator think the people waving in a crowd were his loyal and loving subjects? Did a pop starlet believe the sycophants in her entourage cooed at her every utterance because she was smarter than the Dalai Lama? Did the sleaze handing over fifty quid in a Soho bedsit reckon the prostitute reclining on the plastic-sheeted bed liked having sex with lonely overweight losers who probably hadn't washed their balls in a week?

No, no, and absolutely no.

All the punter, the dictator, the starlet wanted was the *performance* to be convincing. It was the same with Spence – in his own screwed up way, he wanted them to be together. Despite keeping her chained to the bed, he thought they could somehow have a relationship.

If that's what he wants, that's what he'll get.

She had to be like a Geisha, smiling even while some saggy eighty-year-old thrust his liver-spotted junk at her mouth. If she didn't, she'd never see Lily again.

It helped that he'd given her more pills, so she could pretend to be out of it, less of a threat. Sendorax, that was the name stamped on the strip of ten. Probably another opioid. The easiest thing to get her hooked on. She'd even made a joke – *Least I won't be able to flush them away this time*. When he handed them to her, she popped two and put them in her mouth. After he left, she took them out and hid them under the far side of the mattress, beside the squashed chocolates she'd been too scared to throw down the toilet, in case they didn't flush. How ironic they might now be what saved her. She was going to need her strength for when she tried to escape.

Propped with pillows into as much of a sitting position as her chain would allow, her cheeks slack and eyes glazed, Rachel watched the television. *The Naked Chef* on Food TV+1, Jamie Oliver flapping his lips over a cottage pie. She needed to keep up the pretence of being spaced out, even when Spence wasn't in the bedroom with her. Especially when he wasn't. Unlike *her* Spence, who couldn't take his coat off without a fanfare, this new incarnation moved as stealthily as a panther hunting prey. Once, he was two steps into the room, checking if she wanted a drink, before she realised he was there.

She reached beside the mattress, eyes flitting to the door, leaning slowly, ready to make out she was changing positions if he caught her. Her fingers found one of the flattened chocolates. A Bounty, nice. The coconut could count as one of her five a day. She held it under the duvet, trying to time the crinkling of the wrapper to Jamie bashing his spatula around the frying pan. When to make a move? Now, when she had the most strength? Or in a few weeks' time, when she'd earned Spence's trust and his defences were down?

She slipped the chocolate into her mouth, chewing fast, swallowing as soon as she was able and making her face slack again. No, it had to be soon. All his bullshit about love – more likely he'd fuck her a few times then leave her here to die. Even if he kept her longer, trapped in his sociopathic version of a honeymoon couple, she'd only get weaker, her body becoming frailer and more painful the longer she was chained to the bed, and he'd still get rid of her in the end. What then? After he'd left her here to die? She wouldn't put it past him to spy on Lily for the next twenty years, then do the same to her, going through them like some macabre mother/daughter fantasy. She could not risk that happening.

Should she tell him she knew he was the hacker they paid to frame Griffin? He hadn't offered that information himself, so maybe he didn't want her to know. Could she use that, somehow? Why hadn't he told her? He was keen enough to mention the other women he'd done this to – a chef, an interior designer, and who knew how many more.

This is where shit gets real.

She shuddered. That did not sound good.

From the kitchen came the dairy scent of melting butter, and behind that, a back-note of brine. Seafood. Her mind flitted with images of poaching salmon, fillets of sea bass browning in the pan, golden crab cakes garnished with herbed aioli, whetting her mouth in anticipation. She reached for another chocolate, a caramel. Somehow, she needed to convince Spence to unchain her. It wasn't going to be easy. He'd already refused one request, when she asked to go to the toilet; he told her to wait, then came back with a bedpan. When she moaned of the indignity, he reminded her he'd been working as a nurse on a geriatric ward for the last year, so had seen every conceivable type of waste producible by the human body. In vast quantities too.

'You haven't seen mine,' she replied, petulantly.

'Not yet,' he grinned, and left her to it.

She needn't have worried – she was as clogged as a London gutter. Although, for perhaps the first time in her life, she was happy to have constipation. The one thing that could make this situation even worse would be interspersing it with moments when she handed him a pan full of her own poo. Hopefully she would be out of here before that ever happened.

. . .

Two chocolates later, Spence appeared in the doorway. Rachel caught the movement out the corner of her eye, but stayed glazed to the television, where Jamie was blackening some broccoli to go with the cottage pie.

'Rachel,' Spence said softly. 'Sweetness?'

That's what she called Lily. *You bastard, you can't have that!*

She swung her head around, heavy-lidded, blinking like she was struggling to stay awake. 'Hey... What's...'

'Let's have dinner, eh?' His voice was soft, compassionate almost, as though they were trapped here together, and he were as much of a victim of these circumstances as her. 'I made something special.'

'Smells lovely,' she mumbled, not wanting to open her mouth too much in case he smelled the chocolate on her breath.

'How are those painkillers?'

'It's nice.'

'Thought you'd like them,' he said, coming into the room.

She rubbed her face, making her eyes wide, like she was trying to wake herself up, but froze when she saw he was holding another tray. 'What's on that?'

'Oysters,' he said, putting it on the side. 'I know you love them.'

She felt her throat seize. *Keep it together. Don't show anything.* Not only was he *wearing* what Konrad wore on their Spitalfields date, he'd made the same food.

'I do love them,' she murmured, and placed a hand over her stomach. 'It's just... it's not...'

'Have as much or as little as you want,' Spence said, giving her a coy glance. 'I would never dream of telling you what to eat.' He switched off the television, took some tea candles from the tray, and spaced them around. When lit, they made a soft orange haze in the room.

'Romantic,' Rachel said, dreamily.

'I want things to be special. On our first date.'

The same clothes as Konrad, the same hairstyle, the same food.

What did Spence think would happen? That the candles would soften the light and the pills soften her mind so much her eyes would forget the fifty kilos separating the two men? That she'd *actually* think she was back home with her boyfriend, and not chained to some lunatic's bed?

A cork popped in the kitchen. Spence returned with two flutes of sparkling white. *Some celebration. Not even Becca would be pleased to see a glass of fizz right now.* He paused by the chair, then stepped deliberately towards her and held out a glass.

The muscles in her forearm twitched. He was close enough to grab, to get his balls and give them a twist.

You still have your daughter at home. I'd hate for something else to happen to her.

No, it wasn't the right time. It would be too easy for him to pull away. Also, even if she did somehow overpower him, how would she get out of her restraints?

Rachel reached for the glass. As she took it, he resisted, laying his finger over the back of her hand. A sharp jolt at the physical touch raced up her arm. He looked in her eyes, and let go. She felt shaken, violated, as she sat back. *Stay calm. Don't give anything away.*

Spence got the tray from the dresser, put it on the bed, and drew the chair closer. A circle of garlic butter oysters, served in half shells and sprinkled with parsley, lay on a bed of crushed white crystals in a silver dish. He'd cooked and presented them identical to that night. How did he know that? Had she told him about them? Or had he been spying through the restaurant window? Despite everything, she couldn't help but be impressed by his attention to detail. No wonder he was able to pass himself off as a nurse.

He lifted his drink. 'What should we toast?'

Your slow and agonising death?

'How about... to the truth?' she replied, touching her glass to his.

'I like that. The truth.'

Rachel made an appreciative noise, even though the wine was as sharp and uncomfortable as needles in her gut, and put her glass on the bedside table. 'These oysters look amazing,' she said, trying to stop her hand from trembling as she reached for one.

'I prefer them raw,' he replied, smiling suggestively. 'No lemon, no garnish at all. Just the fresh taste of the sea in my mouth, grit and all. They say Casanova ate fifty like that every morning.'

'I'll start with one.'

He lifted his oyster to her like a salute. 'Everything has to start somewhere.'

She tipped the shell into her mouth, not wanting to like it, but the taste of the butter, touched with pepper, and the soft, almost creamy, texture of the oyster, lit sparklers on her tongue. They were exactly the same as in the restaurant, if not better. She wanted to slug them all, faster than tequila shots at a hen party. Instead, she put the shell next to her glass, face scrunched like the food had got stuck on the way down.

'No good?' he asked.

'They're amazing,' she said. 'I'm just... It's hard to...'

He leaned forward and put his hand over hers. 'Hey, it's okay. As much or as little as you want. No judgement. Not here.'

Forgive me, Lily.

'Can I tell you something,' Rachel said, speaking quietly, as though revealing a secret to an empty room. He nodded, shifting his body forward, keeping his hand on hers. 'You've heard me moan, right? Working full-time, then coming home and being a parent. I love my daughter. You know I do. But it's hard. Every day is a battle. And – and I'm just so tired. All the time.' Her chin quivered, and she took a breath. 'My mother was the same. She loved me, of course she did, but she couldn't cope, not after my dad left. If I hadn't watched her waste away, I wouldn't have seen how to do it *myself.*' She choked out a sob. 'I'm so scared I'll pass it onto Lily next.'

'It's okay,' Spence said. 'I understand.'

'I'm going to tell you something I've never told anyone. Something I... I struggle to admit to myself.'

He sat back, his smile deepening. 'Go on.'

'The first time my eating got really bad, with the whole Griffin thing, they sent me to the psych ward. You know, with the real nutters.' She tried to swallow and lick her lips, but her mouth was too dry to do either. Spence was watching her, motionless, like a cobra waiting to see if the mouse in its sights was about to make a sudden move. 'You'd think I would've hated it there, but... I didn't. I liked it. Life was so *easy*. Sometimes I even wish I was back there. No job, no bills, no kid. No responsibilities at all. Just watching telly, resting – as much rest as I want. And reading too. I loved reading, but I've not picked up a book since, well, I don't know since when. And not having to worry about what I ate, because I could eat what I wanted, when I wanted, even if that was nothing. And if the doctors weren't thrilled about it, they could just feed me through my stomach and leave me alone! That was... That was the happiest time of my life.'

Spence had been nodding as she spoke, and he carried on for another few beats after she stopped. He sat back and blew out his cheeks, looking unsure, like he was trying to work out the moral of the story.

'This last week, being here, it's the happiest I've been since then,' she went on. 'I didn't want to leave. It was duty making me want to go. And if you tell me it's okay not to feel like that, that I can just be here and live the life *I* want, then I... I *believe you*. Is that crazy?'

He took a sip of wine. 'It's not crazy.'

'Are you sure, because it sounds crazy to me.'

He grinned, going for another oyster, but paused and instead offered the dish to her. 'Maybe we can be crazy together?'

She reached for a shell. 'Maybe we can.'

CHAPTER FORTY-THREE

CCTV

'God, I wish it was closer,' Mark said, zooming in on the image. 'There's another camera that's much nearer, but it's been out of service since last year.'

Konrad rubbed his eyes and focused again on the screen, where grainy footage showed a couple, blown up to blocky pixels, getting in what looked like a black cab. 'And you think that's them,' he asked.

'I do. I really do.' Mark tabbed to the rightmost screen, and pressed start. 'Look. This is Sussex Way, five forty-seven. I know it's dark, and they're bent over, but look at their heights and tell me that couldn't be them.' He went back to the first screen, wound it back. 'And they're the same ones who come out... here, at the top of Tollington. Four minutes later. How many people are rushing through the back streets of Holloway at that time of the morning? It's got to be them.'

'So they got a taxi? So what? We can't see the number plate.'

'Sure, but if we can find the driver, then it would be possible to check the GPS history.'

Konrad grinned and slapped him on the back. 'You genius! How many black cabs are there in London? There can't be that many. We need to get it in the papers, maybe today's *Evening Standard*. Should I call them?'

'Might not be the best idea. Hacking into the council's CCTV is definitely on the illegal side of the law.' Mark retrieved a scuffed laptop the size of a hardback book from a desk drawer. He opened the lid and typed straight onto the screen. 'There's a whistleblower's dropbox on the dark web. I can leave the footage there.'

'Is that safer?'

Mark gave him a grim smile. 'It is for you.'

CHAPTER FORTY-FOUR

Real

Rachel palmed the oyster obviously, but hopefully not so much that Spence realised it was staged, into the handkerchief he'd given her earlier in the day, then watched him finish the rest. After he tidied, he pulled his chair round to beside her bed and turned on the television. *Secret Millionaire*, which he endured with noticeably less interest than before, even towards the end, wondering aloud how she could sit through this rubbish. They followed that with the first episode of *Breaking Bad*, Konrad's favourite show. Spence thought it was a classic series they could enjoy together.

Midway through it, twenty minutes after popping a couple of Sendorax in her mouth, Rachel slid down the mattress, placed her hands under her pillow, and faked falling asleep. Spence continued to watch for a while, then clicked off the telly. She heard his breaths getting nearer, could feel the warmth of his body as he leaned close to her, and wondered if she should lash out, go for his eyes, but then he was pulling away, light-stepping to the door. She waited until she heard the quiet click of the lock, then spat out the pills, putting them with the others under the mattress, and forced down the cold chewed remains of her second oyster.

Through the night, she nibbled on chocolates, wanting to eat them quicker, the hunger was tormenting, her stomach snarling, but anxiety made her throat feel as if someone was gripping it like a rope over a bear pit. She was weak. She could feel it. All the work she'd done to rebuild her body, and it felt just as shot as before, her flesh like the layer of quilting on a cheap hotel mattress, her bones sharp as springs. She'd dropped a stone and a half, maybe more.

Without knowing the time, the night seemed to go on forever. It became a moment-by-moment struggle not to take the painkillers. The thing that shocked Rachel most was how much she wanted to live. Forget the imagined funerals of her childhood, the remorseful eulogies, the finessed scenarios where her father burst through the mourners, dropped to his knees by her dirt-splattered casket, and begged the world to spin back around, so he could see his daughter one more time. Nothing could be further from how she felt. She was going to get out of here, get back to Lily. Be the mum her own one should have been.

But how? *How?* She reached beside the bed, very carefully patted the floor, and came back with the euthanasia tray. When he was clearing dinner, she'd asked him to take it, its presence creeped her out, but he'd thought about it, looking from her to the tray and back, then said it was for the best if they kept it there.

'You're free to leave any time,' he'd said.

She picked up the needle. What if she hid it under the duvet, facing away, feigning death? The tray could be spilled on the floor. When he came close, to check if she was dead, she could wait for him to lean in and stab him in the neck with the potassium chloride. But what if she missed? If her reactions were too slow? What if he was waiting for her to mess up so he could do something horrible to Lily, leaving Rachel to live with the guilt that it was her fault, as though she were a subject in his psycho thesis on regret?

She put the tray back on the floor and massaged her thighs.

What the fuck was she going to *do*?

. . .

By morning, Rachel felt as haggard as she was supposedly pretending to be. When Spence came in around eight to see if she wanted a coffee, or something to eat, her grunt to be left alone from under the duvet wasn't an act. She'd started to doze at sun up, and was desperate to hold onto the sleep. What else was she going to do? Sit in bed and watch television like she'd sneaked a sick day from work?

Eventually, Spence dragged the curtains open, filling the room with murky light. 'You'd hibernate like a bear if I let you.'

'Oh, hey,' she said, coming around.

Even though he was again dressed like Konrad, this time in the black polo neck/beige linen trouser combination from their three-month-iversary, when they had smoked salmon blinis and chilled white wine in bed, Spence's demeanour was all wrong. The roll on his polo neck was skewed, his hair came up in little crests where it should have been flat, but it was more in the way he was holding himself, as though he could sense someone standing behind him.

Then she realised. He was *flustered*.

What had happened? Had he seen something on the news?

Rachel cleared her throat, unsure whether to ask him what was wrong. To buy time, she poured herself a glass of water from the jug on her nightstand. The painkillers. They were gone from beside her bed. She pulled open the drawer.

'You can have them back after,' he said. There was an edge to his voice, an urgency. 'I don't want you falling asleep on me this time.'

This time. That didn't sound good. In fact, his whole manner was worrying. Last night, she thought she had a handle on him, but now he seemed harried, unpredictable. She needed to find a way to cool him down, get him back to the same mood as before.

He drummed his fingers on the iron bed frame. 'Food? You want? Or should we not bother? You're not going to eat it anyway, right?' He nodded, like he was agreeing with the voice in his head. 'Okay, let's just get to it.'

Rachel tried to pull her legs to her chest, whimpering when she realised she couldn't. 'Food is good. Can we have some food? *Please?*'

Spence sucked his teeth, regarding her. '*Fine,*' he said. 'Why not, eh? We've kept it going this long already.'

She didn't like this. How he was talking, how he was acting, like she was a chore that had to be dealt with. In the kitchen, plates clattered, cutlery crashed, cupboard doors banged shut. Whatever it meant, it wasn't good. The silent seducer from last night was gone. What had happened? Some new development in the investigation? Were the police closing in? Was Spence in such a rush because they'd almost tracked him down, and he wanted to get out of here?

But not before he'd finished with her.

When he returned, he handed Rachel a plate of crude smoked salmon blinis, the fish so rough around the edges it looked torn by hand, and opened a screw top bottle of white wine.

'You need a glass?' he asked, tipping the neck to her, as if they were winos sharing it in a bus stop.

'Might be nice.'

'*Fine.*'

He handed her the bottle.

A slammed cupboard later, he returned with two glasses, snatched the wine, and poured both near to the brim.

'Cheers,' he said and downed his glass in one. 'Well, I'm ready.'

This was happening too fast. She had to slow it down. 'Please, sit. You said last night this would be nice. You said–'

'Okay, *okay*. I'm sitting.' He plonked himself onto the chair. 'Happy?'

'I thought we could talk for a bit,' she said, lifting one of the blinis. 'There's so much I want to know.'

'To know? What do you need to *know*?'

'Some of the stuff you did to me. I'd like–'

'What does it matter?'

She scrabbled around her brain for reasons. 'Because... I'm *impressed* with how you managed to do it all. I mean the Snapchat thing, sending the photo from my account. Becca said that was impossible. That you couldn't log into Snap from–'

'Oh yeah, Becca. That fountain of computing wisdom. She wouldn't know a UDP connection from a kick in the cunt. I just copied the user file from the install folder on your phone, put it in mine, then logged in with your password. Too easy.'

'Okay, okay. But what about the forum? That user, *JustForYou*, was logged in on my laptop when Griffin's address was posted. But that's impossible because I was logged on as me.'

He shoved a blini into his mouth whole, and continued talking as he chewed. 'The login time on your profile page. Where does that come from? It's data, that's all it is. So I changed it.'

'But it was a secure site.'

'Pur-lease, a tap-dancing monkey with a keyboard could clickety-clack its way through that website's idea of cyber security and no-one would notice a thing.'

'What about the NHS? They must have had–'

'Whatever. I mean seriously, why does it matter? You're mine. End of story.'

'But I–'

'But you nothing.'

'I – I want to know the real you.'

'The *what*?'

She shrank back on the bed. 'I thought...'

'Who cares what you think? Who cares what any of you think?'

'Please, Spence, don't be like this.'

He gestured to the window, expansively, like an emperor about to address his kingdom. 'And one of you... lacklustre, unimpressive *people* thinks you can do what I do? *You can do what I do?*'

'Stop it,' Rachel wailed. 'You're scaring me.'

Spence looked at her, eyes cold as machinery. 'You should be scared of me.'

He pushed off the chair, coming at her. Rachel held up her hands, pleading. 'Wait, please, not like this. Please don't do it like this.' He grabbed her wrist, pulling her arm aside, his strength surprising. 'You said it would be nice, Spence,' she said. *'You promised it would be nice.'*

He pushed her back on the bed, pinning her wrists each side of the pillow. His eyes drifted down her body.

'It can be still good,' she pleaded. 'I can make it good for you. It's what you want, isn't it? For it to be good, you know? For it to be *real.'*

His eyes came back to meet hers. She searched them for the smallest glimmer of compassion.

'*Please,'* she whispered.

Spence pushed off from her. He cleared his throat, straightening his jumper and smoothing his hair. He shifted his torso one way then the other, like he was imagining a dance move, lengthened his spine, positioned his hands behind his back, and, in an instant, became the Spence from last night.

'All I ever want,' he said, smiling casually, as though the last few minutes had only happened in her mind, 'is to make *you* happy.'

'And I'm ready to make you happy,' she replied. This was her chance, her *one* chance. 'I just need you to do one thing for me.'

CHAPTER FORTY-FIVE

Key

'I got you the bed pan,' Spence snapped. 'That's what it's there for.'

'I've tried so many times,' Rachel moaned. 'I can't get comfortable on it. It's hard enough when I'm this... blocked. I need to sit on a toilet. *Please.*'

She hadn't wanted to ask when he was in this mood. Guarded, suspicious. She wanted the Spence from yesterday, the one who talked about being in love. But what choice did she have? It was clear now that once they'd *slept together*, as he would no doubt describe the rape to himself, he was leaving, getting out, before the police traced him here. She needed to do something.

Now, or never.

'I can't let you out,' he said.

'I won't *try* anything. You warned me what you'd do to Lily.'

He started on the buttons of his shirt, opening them from the collar, slowly, his mouth pushed into an appreciative pout, like she was waiting willingly for him on the bed. Was he even listening to her?

'Spence? *Please.* You said we could enjoy it. I just want to be comfortable – my stomach hurts so much.'

'We've talked enough,' he said, slipping his shirt off one shoulder, then the other, tensing his chest with every movement. She'd never seen him with his top off, and although his muscles didn't bulge from his body like Konrad's, they had a steel-rope tautness that wilted her confidence.

Her eyes roamed the room. Even if he did let her use the loo, was there anything she could grab as a weapon. The water jug by her bed? The needle of potassium chloride on the floor? She felt slow and frail, her muscles so weak he'd probably be able to pluck whatever she grabbed from her hand before she could strike. What if she gave up on him letting her out, and waited until they were in the middle of it to catch him unawares? Jamming her thumbs into his eyes at the moment of orgasm, pushing until her nails dug into his brain. Then what? She'd still be locked to the bed, starving to death, but this time with Spence's corpse for company. Scratch that.

Get free first, then worry about what to do.

She needed to change tack. 'Here,' she said, shuffling to the end of the bed. She reached for him. 'Let me.'

Spence looked from her hand to her face, and smiled. He stepped forward, close enough for her to slip her fingers into his waistband, pull him towards her, and slide the slick leather tongue of his belt free from the loops. She kissed his taut tanned stomach.

'I can make it amazing,' she said, tracing the groove in the centre of his abs with her tongue.

She felt the slow rhythm of his heart. He looked down at her, his expression impassive, and placed a hand on the top of her head. *Oh god, here it comes.* But instead of pushing down, he stroked her hair, tentatively, like she was a cute dog he thought might have a touch of mange.

She kissed around his belly button, hard as a coin in his six-pack. Breathing hard, like she was getting into it, she whispered, 'I can make it so good for you.'

He tipped her chin up with his finger. 'You'll make it good?'

'I'll make it so good.'

'If I let you go to the toilet, you'll make it *real*?'

'You can do anything to me, and I'll love it. I'll love *you*.'

'Anything? Well, that is in an interesting proposition,' he said, his smile going sharp. 'I've always wanted to be in an *experimental* relationship.' He rocked his head from side to side. 'Okay.'

When he returned, he stayed by the door and showed her the key. 'Here's how it's going to work,' he said. 'I'll unlock you, but you're not going to move, not until I say. So much as twitch, I'll be out the door, and you can sit here for as long as it takes to die wondering what I'm doing to your daughter. Understand?'

Rachel nodded. She felt strung out on adrenaline, her thoughts escalating like a panic attack. How was she going to get close to him, let alone overpower him? What if this was her only chance to get free and she blew it?

What was she going to *do*?

Spence moved towards her, watching her face. At the foot of the bed, still holding her gaze, he lifted the padlock where the chains connected. 'You won't get a second warning,' he said, and slid in the key, turning it and stepping away with the lock in his hand. Holding a finger up, he moved backwards until he was by the bedroom door again.

'Please,' he said, extending his arm towards the en suite. 'Take your time.'

This was it. She was free. But to do what? Rush him? Even turning sideways off the bed and bending her knees to put her feet on the floor sent debilitating ripples of pain though her bones. Her muscles felt like wrung-out dishrags, stapled badly to joints that seemed entirely made of rheumatism. Meanwhile, he had the ripped torso of a martial arts champion. She shuffled across the carpet, the chain attaching her ankles clumping with every step, her legs moving like engine parts that hadn't been oiled for years, wishing she was exaggerating how much everything hurt, but every operation of her lower limbs really was agony. His eyes followed her all the way; even when she couldn't see his face anymore, she knew they were on her.

She opened the bathroom door and stepped inside. She glanced around, feet cold on the tiles, taking stock, but everything had been removed – soap, toothpaste, shower gel. The shelves above the sink were bare, even the cistern cover was gone from the toilet. She pressed the handle to close the door.

'Leave it open,' Spence said. '*Please.*'

Rachel eased herself onto the toilet seat. This was hopeless. She wasn't quick enough, or strong enough, to attack him. She had to convince him to let her stay unchained. Maybe over time she could get him to trust her. *What time? You think he's going to sit here while the police are hunting for him?* He probably had fake papers and a prosthetic face waiting in the front room. Bang, bang, thank you, ma'am, and then off to the Caribbean to celebrate another successful destruction of someone's life.

'You said two minutes,' Spence called, cheerfully. 'You know what they say. Shit, or get off the pot.'

'Jus-just one more...' She bit her lips and squeezed her eyes, trying to keep back her tears. *Hold it together!* 'One more minute.'

One more minute for what? What could she do?

Nothing.

She dragged herself off the toilet.

When she came out of the bathroom, the sight of it all – Spence, shirtless, his belt undone, watching her from the door, the mattress with the chain at the bottom, thick as a snake, waiting for her to be restrained again – sent a tremble of something close to grief through her.

'All good?' he asked.

Every step to the bed felt like struggling in a headwind. There was no way out. She couldn't come up with how to beat him. He was going to rape her and leave her here to die.

'Pull yourself together,' he said. 'You said you'd make it nice. You don't want to know what I do to liars.'

Rachel stumbled, her feet getting tangled in her chain, and fell against the mattress. The tray was in reach. But even if she grabbed the needle, he'd be out of the door before she got close. She didn't want to cry in front of him, knew it wasn't what he wanted to see, but she couldn't stop herself. 'Don't make me go back. Please, don't make me. We can make this real. We can be a proper couple. I'll love you, I really will. Just don't make me go back.'

'Real girlfriends don't make this kind of scene before... *making love*.' He shook out his shoulders. 'Look, you're ruining this for me now. I've put a lot of effort into this and you're ruining it, and you don't want to see what will happen if you ruin it for me. Do you understand?'

Something about the dispassionate way he was speaking to her, like she was an extra requiring minor direction in the film of his life, was more chilling than if he were standing over her with a knife. She nodded quickly, and scrambled onto the bed.

'Good,' he said, tossing the open padlock so it landed next to the chain. 'Now if you don't mind...'

Oh, great. As good as digging her own grave. She looked for a weak link in the chains, but they were both heavy duty. She clicked the lock shut.

And that, was that.

He started towards her, unbuttoning the top of his trousers. 'How about we lose the jumpers. Finally.'

By the time she'd lifted them off, he was down to his boxer shorts, the kind of tight black trunks Konrad used to wear. They weren't so flattering on Spence's spindly legs.

'T-shirt too,' he said, motioning for her to lift it off. 'I want to feel your *skin*.'

He mounted the bed like a stalking tiger, moving with his shoulders, intent on her. She needed to do this, she needed to make it good, whatever he wanted to do to her, the weirder and the freakier the better, as long as she stayed interesting to him, so that he didn't leave her here to die.

She reached for his shoulder, slowly, like she was worried he'd turn his head and snap at her hand, and guided him towards her. Then they were kissing, Spence on his elbow and leaning over her, his body pressing her down, one hand fisted in her hair so she couldn't move her head much if she wanted. His other hand roamed her front, stopping to roughly squeeze her breast, to grab what flesh remained on her flank. She didn't know what she expected, some tenderness maybe, after what he'd said about *love*, but there was none.

His mouth worked at hers as if it were opening a puzzle, his tongue darted between her lips like a predatory fish examining a dark cavern for prey, his saliva carried the salt-fish taste of smoked salmon. When her fingers stroked his back, he tensed to her touch wherever they went, as if to prove his physique to her.

Then she got it. He didn't care about *her*, how she felt, but he did care about what she thought of *him*.

And something else – the key to the padlock was in his trousers.

Next to the bed.

Spence tightened his grip on her hair, pulling back so she had to tilt her chin up. He slid his lips over her cheek, nibbling her skin, then ran his tongue down the side of her neck. With his other hand, he rubbed between her legs, through the thin material of her knickers. He pulled his head back and, looking at her coldly, put his first two fingers deep into his mouth. When he took them out, they glistened in the light. Tugging her knickers aside, he thrust his fingers deep into her. Rachel bucked, arm around his neck, catching herself in time to make it look like pleasure instead of alarm. She moaned in his ear, 'That's it. That's how I like it.'

He grunted, pushing his fingers into her hard and fast, his face tight and intense as she turned his cheek and licked his neck, dipping her tongue in the hollow beside his trachea, her hands going up and down his back, his carotid artery throbbing against her open lips – now, *now*, *NOW!* She wrapped both arms tight to his neck and clamped her teeth.

He pushed against her chest, unsure, for less than half a second, but it was enough time for her to lock her arms, her mind going white and blank as she pressed down her jaws with all that she had, every inch of muscle and sinew working together, and he became everything she'd ever deprived herself, every pain she'd inflicted on herself, every bite of self-loathing she'd taken from her soul.

Her mouth filled with the taste of rusty metal as her incisors broke through his skin, tearing through the thin muscle beneath. Spence beat at her side and chest, but it was as though she possessed superhuman strength, like a mother who rips the door off a burning car to get to her baby, and he couldn't work his way free of her grip. She forced her jaws harder, biting deeper. The blood became a torrent, firing into her mouth, hitting the back of her throat. She twisted away, coughing up thick red gluts.

Spence rolled off the bed, landing in an ungainly crouch, his expression more confused than anything else. He touched his neck and frowned at his crimson fingers. The wound was deep and ragged, and pumped blood like a burst water pipe onto his bare chest. His tan had gone pale yellow, like sand.

'You stupid...' he began, trying to stand, but seeming to go dizzy. He took a fast step to the side to regain his balance. 'You stupid fucking bitch. How – how are you going...?'

They both looked down at the same time. Spence dropped to his haunches as Rachel lurched from the bed, her arms hitting the floor where the trousers had been, a moment after he'd snatched them.

His leg was close enough to grab. 'Please. Think of Lily. Don't do this to her...'

Spence was looking down at Rachel, eyes unfocused, swaying slightly. The blood seemed to be coming out slower. What if he staggered backwards, died out of reach? Taking the key with him.

Grab him – *grab him now!*

She shot out her hand, her fingertips grazing the hairs on his shin as he stepped smartly to the side.

He went down on one knee. When he looked up with his hopeful promising smile, it almost looked like he was proposing.

'Have fun,' he said, and pitched forward.

CHAPTER FORTY-SIX

Starve

Rachel stared at Spence's body. She knew what this meant, the finality of her situation, but the knowledge seemed to sit on top of her mind, and a deeper part of her still expected him to move, to sit up, to laugh like The Joker, and suggest she was a fool for thinking she could get rid of him that easily. She was sorry when this expectation, however absurd, faded away, because what came after was so much worse.

She scrambled forward, the manacles straining against her ankles, fingers outstretched, trying to reach his arm. He was maybe only ten centimetres away in the end, but it might well have been a thousand because, unless she was going to gnaw both legs off, it wasn't going to make a difference how far he was, any distance was too far. Besides, if she chewed her way out she wouldn't need the bloody key!

Once she'd finished screaming, cursing and banging the floor, she got back on the bed and took stock. She had maybe a litre of water in the jug, plus whatever was in her bladder. Over half a bottle of white wine, and what was left in her glass. Some chocolates, but not as many as she could have had – why had she eaten so many last night? Oh, and her death tray. She couldn't forget that. She took a swig from the wine bottle and smiled grimly.

Cheers to me!

Then she broke two fingernails trying to force open the restraints.

Spence was right about one thing though, that crazy psycho fuck. Regret, it was the worst. Questions tormented her, day and night, tearing at her sanity. Why hadn't she held on to him tighter? A few more seconds, that was all, and he would have been too weak to get free. Why had she allowed him so easily into her life anyway? Had she been so starved for attention that she'd had to offer her friendship so completely to someone she barely knew? She lost count of the times she beat the heel of her hand against her forehead, before realising she was wasting precious energy doing that when she could quite as easily berate herself using her inside voice.

More than anything, she wished he'd left the television switched on, so she could check the news, see if they were still looking for her.

As the days passed and the chocolates disappeared, along with most of the clean water, so did the last of her hope. She tried to keep it alive by fanning the flames of interest in her mind – *What had made Spence so flustered? Could he have left a clue to where they were?* In her dreams, she watched the case being cracked, seeing the scenes play out like she were a ghost in the room, convoluted discussions about who she was last seen with, wild madcap chases that ended in bizarre anxious loops where things weren't being slotted in the right places.

On day six, she ran out of water. Not that she was too bothered by that point. She was already drinking the piss of her piss, and it didn't taste any nicer after the second run through her bladder. The full doom of her situation sank deep into her, but, perhaps surprisingly, as it was absorbed, it seemed to lose its potency; it no longer carried the same sucker punch to her spirit as before. All the questions, all the recriminations, all the fears fell away. What was the point? No-one was coming for her. No-one would ever find her here.

She started seeing the positives. If she had to choose a way to die, to pick just one, then starvation would probably be high on her list. She didn't mind the Chinese water torture accumulation of ache in her stomach, or the primal sensation of raw hunger surging from her chest to her groin that she had to grit her teeth to bear. For others, it would drive them crazy, they wouldn't be able to think of anything worse, but this was one marathon she'd run before, and the physical sensations, even at their worse, were bearable.

Despite the pain in her body, an almost philosophical serenity overcame her mind, a fasting high like the first time she was in hospital, and she remembered her past in a different light. She wasn't cursed, she didn't deserve all that had happened to her, she'd just had bad luck growing up, shit parents, whatever. But from that beginning, she'd made a life. She'd felt love from Lily that as a teenager she thought no-one would ever feel for her. *Be gentle with yourself,* she repeated, to pass the time. *Be grateful for what you had. Be proud that at the end you wanted to live.*

When that mantra failed to calm her, she stared at Spence, rotting on the floor six feet away. That was another positive, right? Him being dead. He could easily have had his way, emotionlessly going at her like a robot on Viagra, then strolled off to track the next target on his dating hit list, maybe even Lily, leaving Rachel to die here anyway. Plus the stink of his decomposing remains made it easier to not think about all the delicious food she'd love to eat, so there was that as well. In fact, when she really thought about it, her well of good fortune was fucking overflowing.

Looking at him there, so close, so, so close, something sparked in her chest. Trying to conserve energy, she hadn't moved in days, but now she tentatively lifted her leg. As expected, it came to a stop when the chain extended. She tipped her toes forward, and her heart beat suddenly faster.

She'd lost so much weight that there was more give in the manacle.

She shuffled down the bed and bent to get a closer look, her limbs in agony as she forced them into position. It wasn't much, but still, the skin of her ankle slid against the padding where before it had been tight.

Oh my god. The padding.

Why didn't she think!

Rachel grabbed at the faux fur – it was stitched into leather – but it wouldn't come away from the metal core.

The wine glass. She smashed it to the floor. She picked one of the shards and cut away the leather, revealing the dull iron core beneath.

She tried to pull the bare metal over her ankle, the edge scraping her skin, but although it was much looser now, she still couldn't quite bend her foot flat enough for it to come off. Was it enough to reach him? She got herself into position, breathing hard, muscles tensed, preparing herself to leap.

Three, two, one – *go!*

She propelled herself off the bed, arm stretched so hard it felt as though her shoulder might pop from the socket. She hit the floor with a thud. When she looked at where her hand landed, disappointment flooded through her so fast she burst into sobs.

He was still a couple of centimetres away.

No matter how hard she stretched, her fingertips were just short.

She pulled herself back onto the bed and picked up the shard of glass she'd used to cut away the padding. She didn't have to find much. A few centimetres…

She cut the arm off a jumper, tied it below her knee, tight enough for her calf to throb, then held the glass with a shred of fur.

Don't think. Just do it.

Rachel straightened her foot, pulled the restraint taut, then stabbed the glass into the top of the heel. She screamed as it tore into the thin flesh. Pain lit up her leg, going like an electric shock up her torso, to her brain. *Don't think.* She ripped at the skin, going all round her foot, blood slicking her hand, screaming with every new wound, her mind wild, her fingers sliced open, and the stain of blood on the mattress growing larger. She pulled at the manacle, twisting it this way and that, feeling the skin tear, gouging with the glass when it got stuck, her whole body shaking, sweat streaming into her eyes. Was that enough? *Was that enough?* She looked at the gory mess where her foot had been. Most of her heel was gone. Her ankle was wedged deep in the manacle. She couldn't move her foot, it felt dead. She dropped the glass and fell off the bed, crawling arm over arm to Spence, her breath sounding ragged and alien.

She didn't have to stretch far to reach him. A pinch of skin was enough to bring his arm close enough to grab. Rigor mortis had made his body heavy and unwieldy, but the euphoria that she'd done it, that she'd reached him, gave her the adrenaline shot she needed to pull him close enough to grab the trousers clenched in his other hand.

The key was still in the pocket.

Next time she flopped onto the floor, she was free of the manacles. The tourniquet was doing its job in keeping her alive, but blood still spilled from the wound, too much for her to lose, and she was barely out of the bedroom before her body shuddered, and all of a sudden her energy went to zero.

This couldn't be happening. Everything she'd done to stay alive, to get free – she had to at least get out the front door! She threw an arm, dragged herself into the kitchen, her leg a dead weight trailing behind. Every time she thought there was nothing left, she managed to fling her hand forward, pull herself a little closer. Her head was pounding and a cold sweat covered her skin. It was only when she got to the lounge that she realised – what if he'd locked the front door? Well, if that was it, then she was done. She was too spent to hunt for the keys.

She was whimpering already as she grabbed the handle,

expecting the door to stay fast to the frame, and was too shocked to react when it fell open and she collapsed on the concrete walkway. She'd done it. She was free! But she had nothing left, she couldn't move. Apartments lined the walkway, so all she had to do was wait for someone to come home, see her and call an ambulance.

By evening, that hope had evaporated. She'd been lying there all day, drifting in and out of consciousness, waiting for the moment when someone rushed over, checked that she was still alive. It was only as night fell, and Rachel shivered in the cold air, that she realised the truth. No-one was coming, because no-one lived here. In the whole time she'd been staying at the apartment, she'd never seen a shadow pass the curtains from the walkway. Spence probably owned all the apartments on the floor, or even in the block. *With a woman chained to the bed in each one!*

Soon it was too cold to stay outside. Somehow Rachel dragged herself back in and pulled the duvet that was thankfully still on the sofa, over herself. She lay curled by the door, keeping her breaths shallow, each one letting in a thin wisp of air that barely grazed her throat on its way to her lungs.

When she felt the need to pee and no urine came out, she knew it was nearly the end.

At least she wasn't going to die chained to that bed.

It was light, then it wasn't, and repeat. She chased the dreams, because when she was dreaming she was still alive. Events from her past, reimagined in bizarre ways; lucid delusions where she was walking around the apartment, looking for the way out, as real as being awake; Lily's birth, but without the pain, just being there for it again, and holding her when she came out. Rachel grabbed onto the tail end of that one and wouldn't let go, forcing her mind to imagine over and over the weight of her baby daughter in her arms.

With every dream, she worried that what would replace it was nothing. Soon that worry went as well, and she became just the sense of something, a feeling of resistance, like she was pulling with her mind. Not quite letting go.

Hold on... Just hold on – come on, hold on – and clear! No response. Recharge and let's go, and – clear! No response. Recharge one more time. Come on, come on, I know you're there. And – clear! Got a pulse. Start a line! I need an ABG, stat!

EPILOGUE

'If you don't eat your lunch,' Rachel said, leaning into Lily with a silly face. 'Then *I will*.'

Lily twisted her mouth, clearly deciding whether ownership of the toast was more important than not being hungry anymore.

Rachel snaked out a hand and in one move snatched the slice off Lily's plate, folded it in half, and shoved it in her mouth. 'Snooze you lose,' she spluttered between chews.

'Give me toast back!'

'Come here, little bird.' Rachel leaned towards her, mouth open.

'No, Mummy! Stop, Mummy!'

Konrad popped his head into the kitchen. 'This sounds suspiciously like fun, when you *could* be in here with me and your dad, putting up the decorations.'

'I'm going to have chocolates,' Lily declared, sliding from her chair and marching purposefully out.

Konrad gave Rachel a questioning but amused look, and in reply she shrugged.

'I'll have to bounce her to bed tonight,' she said, lifting a hand for him to help her. 'But it's a party.'

Konrad pulled her up with ridiculous care, pausing every other moment to check if she was okay, like she was a stop-motion animation, and it was getting worse as she became bigger and less mobile. Everyone told her she was so much larger than with Lily because she was expecting a boy, but Rachel knew the reason was much simpler than that: food. Perhaps unsurprisingly, she'd developed a pathological hatred of hunger. She still didn't like how the extra weight looked on her, especially at the rate she was currently inflating, but she loathed being hungry more.

'Give me a minute,' she said, knuckling the small of her back. He kissed her cheek, said to take her time.

She paused with her hand on the chair, and looked out the kitchen window. Somehow, London always seemed like a different city in the spring, with the bees lazily floating around the leafy bushes, the sunlight lifting the dull yellow of the bricks, the people going around without their winter coats, smiling and laughing like they were on holiday.

Even now, nearly a year and a half later, she moved slowly, always with a limp even after she got her body going, and accompanied, on good days as well as bad, with a low hum of pain. After being found, she'd spent months in and out of hospital. The physiotherapy had been gruelling – she'd severed a number of the tendons in her foot – but she knew what to expect, had done lots of the training herself, so tried to see the time as a chance to reflect before she somehow rejoined the real world. Her dad came to see her every day, and they talked at length about his past, his life. He told her for the first time about his own dad, also an alcoholic, and how he'd died in his arms, because back then there was no phone in the house to call an ambulance. Rachel cried about that for hours after he left.

Konrad came most days as well, first as a friend, but quickly as something more. When she was discharged the last time, he picked her up, they went back to hers, and, well, *this* happened. At her first scan, everyone declared it a miracle, although she preferred the term *fucking disaster.* Physically, she didn't know how she'd cope. She couldn't even pick Lily up anymore, those days were gone forever.

Knowing that her body was so destroyed that she couldn't even lift her own daughter made her so sad, tears appeared thinking about it, every time, until she reminded herself, *be gentle, be grateful, be proud*. Only words, but they always made a difference. So, she guessed, mentally she was probably doing better than could be hoped for, or than anyone expected when they found her.

It was her dad who discovered Spence's apartment. Along with Konrad, he went round every black cab rank in London, talking to the drivers, showing them pictures of her and Spence. One of the drivers they met at Euston said he might have picked them up, and allowed Mark to check his GPS history. He found they'd been dropped off at a parade of shops in Tottenham.

They went to the police, begging them to go door-to-door, but they refused. There were three hundred thousand people living in over seventy thousand properties in the same area. Besides, new evidence – romantic e-mails saved to her laptop, ferry bookings for two to France – suggested that she and Spence may have simply fled the country together.

If the police weren't going to search, they would. Her dad found her on the eighth day of looking. It turned out Rachel wasn't far wrong. Spence owned all the apartments on the top floor. Rowena's remains were found two doors down.

Rachel's dad came into the kitchen, wincing at the pain in his knee. Walking the pavement for twelve hours a day had ruined it. He was going to need an operation but kept putting it off, saying he wanted to be there to help with the baby. He took her hand and rubbed the back of it. 'We're nearly done in there. Why don't you head up and get yourself ready?'

Rachel leaned forward and gave him a hug. 'Thanks, Dad.'

She hadn't wanted this baby shower, or any of the other excuses for mass celebration that had been foisted on her since she'd got out of hospital; she hated being the centre of attention, and the inevitable questions about her recovery. But to be fair, they'd made the living room look nice. Paper chain bunting looped around the walls, and balloons of every colour were scattered over the floor. Mark had even dropped off a cute banner saying, "Hello World", which apparently was some kind of IT joke. Maybe it was. It was about as funny as the other IT jokes he'd told her.

Mark was the first to arrive, laden with presents for both her and Lily. 'Couldn't do one lady without the other,' he said, warmly squeezing her shoulders.

Rachel held a finger up for him to wait, taking her time to chew and swallow a mouthful of cupcake. 'Is that a come on?'

Mark backed away from her like he'd just realised she was infected. 'You're an idiot.'

'Where's Ella?'

He pretended to smooth his hair in a mirror. 'I didn't want her to cramp my *style*.'

'You need to have style for it to be cramped.'

'Uh-uh, uh-uh,' he said, nodding sarcastically. 'I'll have to remember that one. She's coming later – she loves to par-*tay*.'

Deciding to let that one go, Rachel nudged him in the ribs. '*Sooooo?*'

Ella wasn't the first of Mark's girlfriends. Since Qui disappeared from his life, not so coincidently on the same day the news of the kidnapping broke, he'd had quite the run, hopping from girl to girl like a geeky Lothario. But the way he was about this new one seemed different.

Mark shrugged. He broke into a shy but illicit smile. 'We did some coding together last night. It was *sensational*.'

'You clearly belong together. Maybe in some secure facility for the terminally sad.'

'How about we come by for a visit? You can show us around.' He plucked the rest of the cupcake from Rachel's hand. 'Anyway,' he said, taking a bite. 'More important... What about *you*? You know, the *question*?'

Rachel caught herself mid-eye roll. She'd thought about little else for days. It's not that she didn't want to marry Konrad, or that she couldn't see themselves together in twenty years. She kind of did, and she definitely could, but she was worried it'd be for the wrong reason, for the sake of the baby rather than because of her. Although a more calculating part of her mind told her just to say yes. What did it matter if it was rushed, if it was more for the baby, because wasn't that all she wanted, for her and Lily to be part of a family?

'For what it's worth,' Mark said. 'I think you should go for it.'

'I forgot. You're hardcore bros these days.'

Mark grinned. 'He's got me pounding my abs, working my protein shakes. Oh wait, I think that's the other way round.'

'You're funny. One day I'll be as funny as you.'

He dug his fingers into her ribs so she yelped and jumped back. 'You'll never be as funny as me.'

'Watch it,' she said, slapping his hand away. 'You'll make the baby come early.'

Konrad sauntered over, Lily dangling from his hand, her party hat skewed and eyes sparkling from sugar. He jerked a thumb at Mark. 'This guy bothering you?'

'Yeah, throw him out,' Rachel replied.

Lily swung from Konrad's arm, chanting, 'Throw him out! Throw him out!'

Mark looked hurt. 'Hey! I'm your daddy. You can't throw me out. Mummy, tell Lily she can't throw her daddy out.'

Before Rachel could answer, the doorbell rang. 'That'll be Becca.'

'She'd better have some fizz,' Mark said. 'If I've got to deal with you in this *funny* mood.'

'Sorry,' she replied, 'I think Becca's fizz free these days.' She patted him on the chest. 'I'll leave the door open for you.'

When Rachel got back, her dad was there with his phone

attached to his new toy, a selfie stick. 'Come on,' he said, opening his arm for her. 'Come in.'

She didn't bother holding back her groan, but moved into her dad's waiting arm anyway. Konrad came round the other side, lifting Lily higher so she'd be in the shot. As they smiled, waiting for the lens to focus, Rachel tried not to think about the people who might see this, people she didn't know, but who might know her, who might follow her, who might be waiting in the shadows to ruin her life again.

She tried not to, but she thought about them anyway.

Click.

ACKNOWLEDGMENTS

This book was hard to write. It deals with some dark issues, and I had to go to some dark places to get to the heart of them. There were many times when I thought I couldn't finish it, and even when it was finished, the last of many drafts complete, I still had my doubts as to whether I'd done Rachel and her story justice. This makes it all the more special to find a publisher like Bloodhound Books willing to take it on. So I want to thank them first of all for making this happen – to Fred, who listened to my stumbling pitch at Harrogate and told me to send it in (even though he probably only said that to be polite), Betsy for picking it out and taking a punt on an unpublished novelist, and all the rest of the design and editorial team for doing such a fantastic job on making *The Regret* the best book it could be.

Next, I'd like to thank my great friends/early readers/punishment gluttons who gave me such incredible feedback on the early drafts. Val, who read the original short story and suggested it might make a good novel; Jilly, who made me realise I had to rethink the main character's name; Jonny, for insisting I made the ending more gruesome; Tashy, for really warming to Dimitri's character; to my dear brother Adam, who told me what I didn't want to hear, and for being right about all of it.

Special mention to a few people who gave thoughtful, incisive opinions on the opening chapters at just the right times – Liz Barnsley, Kate Burke, and especially Marie Henderson, who also dragged me to Harrogate, where I pitched the book to Fred.

Most importantly, my family. My mum and dad, who worked hard to make me the person I am today, and provided all the chicken soup to make that happen. My hairy best friend Boddington, and my magical daughter Amelie, whose greatest trick is to bring me joy every moment of every day. Finally, and most important of all, my fabulous wife Delia. Thank you for reading pretty much everything I've ever written (and it's a lot!), no matter how confused, depraved, or downright terrible. You mean everything to me. I couldn't have done this without you.

ABOUT THE AUTHOR

When not writing, Dan works as a data security consultant, demonstrating to corporations that should know better just how easy it is for hackers to access their most sensitive information. As a writer, his short stories have been widely published both in print and online, and he has twice been shortlisted for the Bridport Prize. In 2013 he completed a Masters in Creative Writing at Brunel University. He lives in North London with his wife, daughter, and very, very hairy dog.

Come say hi on Twitter @danmalakin, or visit www.danmalakin.com to sign up for his newsletter and read some short stories.